To Give and To Take

To Give and To Take

Elizabeth Murphy

CANELO

First published in the United Kingdom in 1990 by Headline Book Publishing

This edition published in the United Kingdom in 2019 by

Canelo Digital Publishing Limited
57 Shepherds Lane
Beaconsfield, Bucks HP9 2DU
United Kingdom

A CIP catalogue record for this book is available from the British Library.

Print ISBN 978 1 78863 381 9
Ebook ISBN 978 1 78863 109 9

Look for more great books at www.canelo.co

Printed and bound in Great Britain by Clays Ltd, Elcograf S.p.A.

In proud and loving memory of my mother and father

Chapter One

September 1906.

The rich crimson folds of the skirt lay on the kitchen table, glowing like a jewel. Cathy Ward leaned over it folding it carefully with the braided hem uppermost.

'Teacher says the wool for this comes off the back of a sheep,' she said.

Her sister Mary stood looking into a mirror propped on the windowsill, drawing tendrils of curly hair forward to lie becomingly on her forehead. At fourteen years of age she gave every promise of becoming a beauty and the proud tilt of her head showed that she was well aware of the fact.

Her budding breasts and neat waist were outlined by a well-fitting dark dress, and her tiny feet were encased in shining button boots. Her skin was pale and clear with a scattering of freckles across a straight nose, and her curling red-gold hair hung almost to her waist, tied back with a black bow.

She glanced at the skirt. 'The sheep had better look out then,' she said with a toss of her head. 'Because I'm going to have lots of skirts like that when I'm older.'

'I hope it keeps fine for you,' her mother said drily, taking brown paper and string from the dresser drawer, and deftly wrapping the skirt.

'Never mind standing there admiring yourself, Mary,' she went on, as church bells broke the quiet of the Sunday morning, 'Get your hat and jacket. You too, Cathy. I want both of you back here at one o'clock for your dinner.'

'But, Mam, Mrs Malloy's going to High Mass at eleven o'clock today, so it'll be after half-past twelve when we get back to the house,' Cathy protested. 'It takes her so long to get home when she's been sitting down for an hour.'

'All right, I'll say half-past one then,' said Sally Ward, drawing her purse from her apron pocket. 'Here's the fare for the tram to Aigburth, Mary. You can walk back – and no dawdling. Remember, I want you back at half-past one.'

Mary looked sulky. 'Can't I stay if Aunt Emily asks me?'

'No, come home for your dinner, *straight* home, no hanging about talking to impudent lads.'

Mary tossed her head and walked into the lobby, followed by Cathy and her mother, just as their father came downstairs.

'Off already,' he said smiling, 'and here's me, only just getting up.'

'You need your lie in on a Sunday, the hours you work,' said Sally. 'Mary's taking the skirt I made for our Emily, and Cathy's going to help Mrs Mal along to Mass.'

As Lawrie Ward bent to kiss the girls, the likeness between him and ten-year-old Cathy was striking. Both had dark curly hair and brown eyes, and the same humorous quirk to the lips. But whereas Cathy's hair hung in a shining plait, Lawrie's, although still thick, was streaked with grey.

He turned to Mary. 'I'm almost afraid to kiss you, you're looking so beautiful this morning, Miss Ward,' he said. Both girls giggled, but Sally clicked her tongue and shook her head reprovingly. He winked at Sally and opened the front door.

'Ta ra then, girls,' he said cheerfully. 'Off you go and astound the population.' They walked away smiling, Mary carrying the skirt and Cathy a covered basket, but as soon as they were away from the house Mary burst out: 'Did you hear Mam? She hates anyone to praise me. She's always picking on me lately.'

'I suppose she's afraid you'll get a swelled head,' Cathy said with sisterly frankness.

'Small fear of that in *our* house. And making me come home for my dinner. What'll I say if Aunt Emily asks me to stay?'

'She won't, 'cos Uncle Albert's at home today. Anyway, it'll be better for you to come home. You get such a little bit to eat there.'

'Yes, but a maid brings it in,' Mary said dreamily, 'and all the glasses and dishes and things are so posh. I'd love to live in a house like that.'

'*I* wouldn't,' Cathy said. 'I like living in our house. I'd love their garden but I'd like to do it myself. I hate the crabby old gardener there.'

The late September day was bright and sunny, and the pavements were already thronged with people. Two young men who passed tipped their straw boaters to Mary and she turned away haughtily but with a pleased smile on her face.

'Good job Mam didn't see that,' Cathy giggled.

'She should have been in the shop on Friday,' Mary said. 'There was a man there waiting for his wife while she had a fitting, and he told Mr Carruthers that I was the prettiest girl he'd seen in Liverpool.'

'*Did* he? What did Mr Carruthers say?'

'He just bowed and smiled all smarmy at the man, but he turned round and gave me a dirty look and sent me off to the stockroom.'

'Why? Why was he annoyed?' asked Cathy.

'Because Miss Benson heard the man, and old Carry has a *tendresse* for her.'

'A what?'

'A *tendresse*. It's French. It means he's soft on her. I heard one of the milliners say it,' Mary said. Cathy gazed at her admiringly, feeling proud that her sister was so clever as well as beautiful.

At Shaw Street they parted, Mary walking away to catch the tram to Aigburth, and Cathy going down William Henry Street to Gell Street where Mrs Malloy's house was, and where the Ward family had lived as her next-door neighbours until Mary was four years old.

The front door of Mrs Malloy's house opened into the living room-kitchen, and when Cathy lifted the latch and stepped in Mrs Mal was tipping up the big black kettle that stood beside the fire, and pouring boiling water into a teapot.

'I seen ye coming round the corner, child, so I wet the tea for a cup before we go,' she said. Cathy put the basket on the table.

'Are you feeling better this morning, Mrs Mal?'

'I am, thank God. I've been moving about, getting the ould legs in working order,' Mrs Malloy said, putting the teapot on the hob, and taking the white cover from the basket.

'Ah now, isn't your mam kindness itself to me, girlie?' she went on, as she took out a jug of soup, a ham shank and a crusty loaf. She hobbled to the corner cupboard to put the food away while Cathy set out cups and saucers and poured out the tea.

'Our Mary's gone to take the skirt Mam made for Aunt Emily,' she said. 'D'you know what, Mrs Mal? A man told the floorwalker in Denby's that Mary was the prettiest girl he'd seen in Liverpool.'

'Did he now? Sure, she'll never get tired of that class of talk, but she's maybe too pretty for her own good,' said Mrs Malloy, draining her teacup and picking up her shawl. 'We'd best be off right away, child, to give us plenty of time to get a seat.'

They set off, Mrs Malloy hobbling along, supporting herself with a stick on one side and a firm grip on Cathy's arm on the other.

'You're growing tall, child,' she gasped. 'Or maybe it's me growing downward like the cow's tail.' Cathy was relieved when they reached the porch of Saint Francis Xavier's and they could pause while Mrs Malloy regained her breath and drew her shawl over her head. The church was crowded, but they found seats under the organ loft.

Cathy's love of beauty, nurtured by her parents but starved in the bleak classrooms and drab streets of Liverpool, was richly fed by the magnificence of the church. The elaborately carved altar was almost hidden by masses of flowers and ablaze with many candles.

On the stroke of eleven the door of the Sacristy opened and a priest robed in rich vestments moved to the altar, preceded by altar boys carrying a crucifix and candles, and followed by others, walking two by two, wearing red cassocks and stiffly starched white surplices.

Cathy sat entranced, listening to the glorious singing of the choir and watching the elaborate ritual of the Mass. Unusually for the Liverpool of 1906, riven by religious differences, her parents followed no formal religion but were broadminded enough to allow Cathy to attend Mass, to help their old friend and neighbour, Mrs Malloy.

When it was over Cathy and Mrs Mal waited for the crowds to disperse before moving, but one member of the congregation stayed to help them.

'I'll be grand when I get me legs goin',' Mrs Malloy gasped as they struggled along. 'I stiffen up, d'ye see, when I sit for long.'

'Wasn't it a beautiful sermon?' the woman said. 'It's a pity you can't get along in the evening, to see the new electric light in the church. The only thing is, it really shows up the dirt on the ceilings.'

'Ah well, sure there's drawbacks to everything,' said Mrs Malloy. 'I don't think I'll be seeing either the new lights or the dirt, the way I am now.'

The woman left them at the end of Gell Street, and when they reached Mrs Mal's house she sank thankfully into her chair.

'I think I've shot me bolt, child,' she gasped. 'I'll not manage that again.' Cathy brought her a cup of water.

'Mam says the parlour's ready for you whenever you want it, Mrs Mal,' she said. 'You could come and live with us now.'

'Aye, and thankful I am to know it, child. I was hoping I'd carry on here a bit longer, to give your mam a bit of a break after the years she was looking after your grandad in that self same parlour but I think I'm done, and the winter not on me yet.'

'But it was different with Grandad,' Cathy protested. 'Mam says you'll be company for her.'

'God bless her,' said Mrs Malloy, handing the cup back to Cathy. 'Sure this has knocked all the breath outa me. I'm not able for even me Mass any more.'

'Will you miss the sermons?' Cathy asked.

'Some of them. Father Nicholson now is a good preacher, but most of them are too clever for the likes of me. I mind one priest was here the year the river froze, '81 that'd be – Father Hopkins. He'd get up in the pulpit and as God's me judge, Cathy, I'd be as wise when he finished as when he started. A terrible squeaky voice on him too. He was standing in Langsdale Street one time and I said goodday and dropped me curtsey, and sure he never took his eyes off the gutter. He must 'a heard me for he took off his top hat and stood there bareheaded, staring at some ould stones. He took not a bit of notice of what went on around him, yet I heard he was reckoned to be very clever, and didn't he do his best anyhow in the service of God.'

Cathy little thought on that September morning of 1906, how often in later years her children and grandchildren would ask her to repeat the words of the old lady who knew the poet, Father Gerard Manley Hopkins, and only thought of him as a man 'who did his best in the service of God'.

–

Mary left the tram at Aigburth and walked to her uncle's mansion. It was set in extensive gardens near the river. She stopped at the gate to settle her hat more firmly and to wipe the dust from her boots before walking up the gravelled drive which curved round the front of the house. The maid who took her hat and jacket ushered her into the drawing room where her aunt and uncle were sitting.

Mary disliked the smell and feel of her uncle's moustache against her lips as he came forward and kissed her, but she gave no sign of it as she smiled and turned to kiss her aunt's thin cheek.

'How are you today, Aunt Emily?' she asked.

'Better, love, much better,' Emily replied. 'It's very warm today though, and a long walk for you I'm afraid.'

'I got the tram most of the way.' But Albert said heartily, 'Far enough though, far enough, even for your young legs.'

He poured a small glass of wine and water for Mary and she sat sipping it and nibbling a biscuit, wishing that the girls in Denby's could see her. She often talked about her rich uncle but she knew that not all the girls believed her. She had even heard one of the girls say that she was 'romancing again', when she talked of the box factory her uncle owned in Islington and his mansion at Aigburth.

She had put down the parcel beside her aunt, and Emily opened it and exclaimed in delight at the skirt.

'It's beautiful, Mary,' she said. 'Your mam's so clever with her needle. It's a pity you don't care for sewing, love.'

'I like clothes but I don't like making them,' Mary said, 'Cathy's more fond of sewing then I am.'

It was impossible for Mary to be in the company of any man, even a stout, elderly one like her Uncle Albert, and refrain from practising her feminine wiles on him. Now she smiled coquettishly at Albert from under lowered eyelids and he preened himself, stroking his bushy moustache and smirking self-consciously.

'Shall we have a turn round the garden?' he said. 'It's looking well just now.' Emily drew her silk shawl around her but he said quickly, 'No. It'll be too warm for you, Emily. You'd best put your feet up and have a little rest.'

She sighed, but lay back obediently on the sofa while Albert and Mary went out, his thick arm lying heavily on her shoulders. She admired the weedless beds and the clipped hedges, but she was even more impressed by the orchard where all the trees were heavy with fruit. Albert picked two pears from one of the trees and bestowed them on her with a flourish.

'Give one to your little sister,' he said benevolently. 'They're just ripe and really juicy.'

Later they went back to the house and Emily looked with concern at Mary's flushed face.

'You need a cool drink, love,' she said. 'Albert, should I ring for lemonade?'

'Just a glass of water please, Auntie,' Mary said quickly, and when the jug of water came Albert poured a glass of water for himself also and stood sipping it and jingling the keys in his pocket.

'Tell your mother, Mary' he said suddenly, 'that I'll set your Aunt Emily down at your house on Wednesday on my way to the works, and collect her on my way home.'

'That's if Wednesday suits your mam, love,' Emily said.

'Well, if it doesn't she can easy send a lad down with a message or walk down herself to the works. It's only ten minutes' walk from Egremont Street to my place,' Albert snapped.

'I'm sure it will be all right, Aunt Emily,' Mary said with a challenging look at her uncle. 'Mam will enjoy the day with you.' She left a little later and as he kissed her goodbye Albert pressed sixpence into her hand.

'Our little secret,' he whispered, and Mary smiled demurely.

She reached home before Cathy, and put the two pears down beside her mother.

'Uncle Albert sent these,' she said.

'Could he spare them?' Sally said acidly. Mary laughed.

'There were hundreds on the trees, and apples too, but he handed me these like they were the Crown Jewels.'

'Lay the table,' Sally said, seeming to regret speaking frankly to Mary about her elders, but the girl went on undeterred, 'He announced he'd bring Aunt Emily here on Wednesday for the day, but Aunt Emily said only if it suited you.'

'Of course it'll suit me. Does she look any better?' Sally said anxiously.

'She said she felt better,' Mary said, 'but she looks so thin and weak.'

'I'm glad she's coming here on Wednesday. The change will do her good.'

Lawrie put down his newspaper. 'A proper dinner will do her even more good,' he said, but Sally glanced at him warningly and walked into the back kitchen. He followed her.

'It's the truth, Sal, that's what she needs. I can't understand them, with the money they've got, living on the smell of an oily rag.'

'It's not our Emily's fault, it's his. He's so tight-fisted and she's not well enough to stand up for herself. I don't know how he keeps so fat, though.'

'No mystery there, love. He does himself well in some chop house at dinner time, but it's Emily that needs the building up with plenty of good food.'

'I'll see she gets it on Wednesday anyway,' Sally said with a sigh. 'My poor Emily. Nothing goes right for her.'

A few minutes later Cathy arrived home.

'How was Mrs Mal?' Sally asked.

'Her legs were bad and we had a job to get home,' Cathy said. 'I asked why she didn't come to live here like you want her to.'

'I wish she would,' Sally said. 'It worries me to death to think of her struggling along on her own there. Did you make sure she was all right before you left her?'

Cathy nodded. 'Yes Mam. I heated up the soup and cut some bread and ham, and made a pot of tea.'

'That's a good girl. What did she say when you said about coming here?'

'She said she wanted to wait a bit to give you a break after looking after Grandad until last winter, but she said she was done and she wouldn't get to Mass again.'

Sally and Lawrie looked at each other. 'I thought that was what was holding her back,' said Sally. 'Should we take a walk down to see her this evening, Lol?'

'Aye, I think the time's right, love,' he said. 'And we won't take no for an answer this time, seeing as that's the reason she's put us off before.'

'Yes, we'll get her settled in here before the winter,' Sally agreed.

Chapter Two

Mrs Malloy's move from Gell Street to the parlour of the Wards' house in Egremont Street was quickly accomplished, and the old lady declared that she had never known such comfort. She was unable to climb stairs so her bed stood against the wall behind the door, and her rocking chair and other treasured pieces of furniture filled the room. A bright fire, constantly replenished, burned in the grate and helped to ease her rheumatism. Although she spent much of her time in Sally's kitchen, her own room was always warm and ready for her return. She enjoyed entertaining the family or an old friend there.

Sally had arranged for the priests from Saint Francis Xavier's to visit the old lady, much to the disgust of the cantankerous widow, Mrs Kilgannon, who lived next door.

'Bad enough taking a pape into yer house,' she grumbled, 'without having *them* here as well. Yer'll bring bad luck on the street.' Sally ignored her and was repaid by Mrs Malloy's pleasure in still being in touch with her church.

Cathy was delighted to have Mrs Mal living with them. The old lady and the quiet little girl had always been good friends and as the months passed they grew ever closer. Cathy loved to hear tales of the days when her family and Mrs Malloy had been neighbours in Gell Street, and she spent many happy hours sitting on a stool beside the rocking chair, listening entranced to the old lady's reminiscences.

'Ye'll only remember your grandad as a sick man lying in this very parlour,' Mrs Malloy said one day, 'but when I knew him first he was a fine young man, and his wife, poor Julie, Lord ha' mercy on her, she was as blithe as a bird.'

'She died when Aunt Emily was a baby, didn't she?' Cathy prompted.

'Aye, and your mam only a girl of twelve, but she brought up Emily and her two young brothers. She was a grand little mother to all of them, but Emily was ever the core of her heart.'

'Mam told us how her two brothers died at the same time and were buried together,' Cathy said. 'It must have been awful for her.'

9

'Within hours of each other,' the old lady agreed. 'And them only lads of ten and fourteen. But your mam was more heartbroken about losing Emily at the same time. Taken away from her by them stuck-up relations from Ormesdale after she'd reared the child for five years very near.'

'Mam told us about that when the letter came about Aunt Emily getting married and coming to live in Aigburth. She said that's what she'd always wanted for Emily when she was a baby.'

'Ah, poor Emily,' Mrs Malloy sighed. 'Sure she never knew a happy day from when she left Gell Street, although her da did it all for the best.'

Cathy was amazed.

'But she's happy now, Mrs Mal,' she said. 'That great big house, and servants, and lovely clothes. Even their own carriage.'

'Indeed—' began Mrs Malloy, then she checked herself and said only, 'Strange how things work out, child, and not always the way we expect.'

'Mary would like to live in a house like Aunt Emily's, and be a lady,' Cathy said. 'She hates it when we go down Great Homer Street, but I love it.'

'So did I, girlie, especially on a Saturday night.'

'Yes, all the crowds,' Cathy said eagerly. 'And the jokes, and the men codding people while they sell the meat off cheap.'

'It's as good as many a turn on the Music Hall,' Mrs Malloy said. 'And I've many a time had a piece of meat for threepence would have cost me a shilling earlier on.'

'We get better meat if me and Mary do the shopping when Mam's got a lot of sewing,' Cathy said, 'because the men always joke with Mary and say things like, "This'll put a skin on yer like velvet" or "This'll make your eyes shine even brighter, girl." All the women laugh but Mary gets annoyed.'

'It's a wonder now that class of talk doesn't suit her,' said Mrs Malloy.

'She says she doesn't want common men talking to her like that,' Cathy explained.

'It's a pity about her. She'll eat the meat fast enough,' Mrs Malloy sniffed. 'Don't you get them notions now, Cathy.'

'I wouldn't get the chance,' Cathy said wistfully. 'They only shout to Mary because she's so beautiful.'

'Don't be putting yourself down now, child. You're a nice-looking girl yourself though maybe not so striking-looking as Mary, and not so bold neither. Handsome is as handsome does, as the ould woman said when she killed the cow.'

Cathy's favourite tale was of the first time her father and mother met. Mrs Malloy never seemed to tire of repeating it.

'Your dad had been a seaman,' she said, 'but he'd left the sea to work on the building, and him and Paddy Ryan – you remember Paddy, child? – came to lodge with me. I was seeing them out of the house the very first day to go for a pint, when your mam walked down the street.'

Mrs Malloy always paused dramatically at this point, then went on. 'I declare to God, child, they stood looking at each other as if they'd been struck by lightning.'

'And they got married soon after, didn't they?'

'As soon as your grandad would let them, but sure I soon talked him into it. I could always manage Matt, but I never put in me oar where it wasn't wanted, girlie.'

The tales were told and re-told almost word for word, but Cathy always enjoyed hearing them, and they made her parents and her Aunt Emily endlessly interesting to her. The days passed happily for Mrs Malloy, and Sally and Lawrie did all they could to make her comfortable and to ease the pain of her rheumatism.

One night Lawrie brought home a bottle of embrocation which had been given to him at a farmhouse where he had delivered some goods from the railway. Sally rubbed it vigorously into Mrs Malloy's legs, but within a short time she was as vigorously trying to rub it off again.

'Are you sure it wasn't the horses was rubbed with it, Lawrie?' the old lady gasped. 'Sure I feel as though me legs'll drop off. They're on fire.'

Other gifts he brought home were more welcome. Sometimes an ounce of snuff or a bag of cough candy, and once a bagful of goose feathers to make a soft pillow for her.

'Ye'll never be a penny above a beggar, lad,' the old lady scolded him, but her eyes were soft. Sally felt that she could speak freely to Mrs Malloy about any worries within the family, knowing that the wise old lady who loved all of them could always give her shrewd advice and comfort.

'Don't be always worrying now, Sally,' Mrs Mal said to her one day. 'Haven't you the best of husbands in steady work, and the two girls growing up strong and healthy, thanks be to God.'

'But Mary's so vain and flighty, Mrs Mal, and Cathy's in a dream world half the time, and takes things to heart so much. I'm afraid she'll get hurt, and Mary'll come to a bad end.'

'Don't be foolish, girl! There's no harm in Mary, only she's maybe too pretty for her own good, and Cathy'll grow out of the daydreaming.'

'I worry about Lawrie too, Mrs Mal,' Sally said. 'The hours are long at the goods yard and the pay's poor. Still, at least it's a steady job. The railway never sacks a man except for misconduct.'

'Then what are you worrying about? Isn't Lawrie a sober, well-behaved man and a grand worker? Sure, he cares more for them horses than he does for himself.'

'If he'd only keep away from these agitators! He's so easy-going as a rule, but when he starts about injustice and all getting together to make things better, he's a different man. I'm afraid he'll get a name as a troublemaker.'

'Doesn't he do right to try to help them as can't help themselves, Sally? Sure you're very comfortable now with Lawrie and Mary working and your own bit from the sewing, but you know well, girl, there's many in Liverpool live and die hungry. Poor widder women and their children and them that are too sick or too old to work – they're the ones the lad worries about. More credit to Lawrie that he doesn't sit back now he's all right himself.'

Sally was toasting bread at the fire. She stood up, red-faced, and not only with the heat of the fire.

'Do you think I'm selfish, talking like this, Mrs Mal?'

'Not at all, girl. You've had hard times and it's only natural that you'll worry. I know it's always in your mind about Lawrie losing his job that time for trying to stand up for that poor feller, but he's not one on his own now, girl.'

'If he'd only stick to just helping in the Boys' Club, mending the boots and going round with the soup wagon at night, but he wants to cure the world singlehanded.'

'Ah well, he was ever too soft hearted for his own good. Giving away his few pence to the first poor child he saw, and even his carry out, God bless him.'

'We've had many a row about that,' Sally said with a smile. 'It's a good thing I'm more hard-hearted or we'd have nothing left.'

'Aye, *very* hard-hearted,' Mrs Malloy said drily. 'That's why you cared for your poor da all the years he lay ill, and why you've brought me here now.'

Sally had buttered the toast, and now she put a plateful and a cup of tea down beside Mrs Malloy and sat down opposite to her.

'You know we all enjoy having you here. I don't know how I managed without you here to talk to.'

'Well, a trouble shared is a trouble halved, they say, but you've little enough to trouble you now, girl.'

'I know,' said Sally. 'Even Lawrie says that things should get better with the men who're in Parliament now.'

'And so they will, child, but these things don't happen by themselves. There have to be the likes of Lawrie who see the misery around them and speak up to get things done about it. Sure, the rich don't know how the poor live any more than we know about them.'

'He's always ready to speak up, all right,' Sally said grimly. 'He was made up when the Clearing House opened so the dockers could draw their wages in one place instead of tramping the length of the docks for half a day's pay here and half a day there, but he can't leave well alone. Now he's going on about the dockers having to stand in pens like cattle to be picked out for work.'

'Aye, it's a disgrace so it is,' Mrs Malloy said vaguely.

Sally poured another cup of tea for her. 'I'm sorry. I've tired you out going on about my worries,' she said penitently. 'No wonder you say I'm a born worrier.'

'You're as God made you and so is Lawrie,' the old lady said placidly. 'That's why you fit so well together.'

Although Mrs Malloy had dismissed her worry about Mary, Sally was still uneasy about her eldest daughter. Mary spent as little time as possible at home. She would do the household tasks she was given as rapidly as possible after she returned from work or on Sundays, then escape to spend her time with her numerous friends, many of whom were unknown to her mother.

'Why do you always go to other houses?' Sally said. 'I want you to bring your friends here, so I'll know who you're with.'

'But, Mam, we've got no parlour,' Mary said, opening her blue eyes wide. 'If I could use the parlour I'd stay home and take my friends in there, but you know you don't want people in the kitchen when you're sewing, and Dad wants a bit of quiet when he gets home from work.'

Sally could only sigh and warn her to be home early. Although Mary was fond of Mrs Malloy, she saw less of her than did the rest of the family, and was always careful not to try out what her mother called her 'airs and graces' under the old lady's ironic gaze.

From Cathy's point of view the only drawback to having Mrs Malloy living with them, was that now she was sometimes expected to accompany Mary on her visits to The Grange, the home of their aunt and uncle. She never felt at ease in the large over-furnished house, or in the presence of her Uncle Albert, a portly, red-faced man much older than her Aunt Emily, who was his second wife. He had a hearty manner which embarrassed Cathy, but fortunately he paid little attention to her as Mary seemed to be his favourite. Cathy usually stayed with her aunt while he took Mary around the garden or hothouses.

Cathy always watched admiringly while Mary sipped a glass of wine and water, sitting gracefully on a plush-covered chair, her back straight and her voice low as she talked to her aunt and uncle. She's a real lady, Cathy thought admiringly. She belongs in a house like this. She's not a bit shy or embarrassed like I am.

Although so young, Mary seemed to know instinctively how to charm. The combination of her beauty and the glances from her blue eyes – flirtatious and provocative for young men, demure and sidelong glances for their elders – seemed to enslave every man she met. Uncle Albert was completely under her spell. Cathy would watch in amazement as her uncle recklessly poured wine and water for Mary and his wife, and ordered more lemonade for the younger girl, although his meanness was a byword in the family.

'He'd skin a flea for its hide, so he would,' Mrs Malloy said, but he was a different man in the presence of Mary.

Mary's behaviour was closely watched and criticised by the neighbours, who were jealous of the way she outshone their own daughters. They told each other that she would come to a bad end, but none of them watched Mary as closely as their next-door neighbour, Mrs Kilgannon, and she was the only one who dared to speak to Sally about her.

She waited until Sally was scrubbing the step one morning and then came out and stood leaning on the railings which separated the two houses.

'I seen your Mary larkin' about with a gang of lads in Brunswick Road last night,' she began. 'And she's been seen with three different lads this week. It's no wonder she's gettin' herself a bad name.'

Before she could say any more, Mrs Malloy came hobbling down the lobby like an avenging angel.

'You dirty, foul-mouthed ould bitch!' she said. 'You're not fit to lick the boots of anyone in this house, and you've the impudence to lay your dirty tongue on them. I heard you yesterday – you and the creature from across the road.' She disregarded Mrs Kilgannon's squeals of protest and swept on.

'Mary's a good girl, and well you know it. It's a pity you can't say the same about your own ugly lumps of girls that had to trick lads into marrying them. And what about yourself and the ould feller you've got tucked away upstairs?'

Mrs Kilgannon's face was purple and she was gasping for breath, but Mrs Malloy turned away from her and said to Sally, 'Leave the step, girl, and come inside away from the creature. Sure ye can't touch pitch and not be defiled.'

She went back along the lobby and Sally picked up her bucket and followed, leaving Mrs Kilgannon clutching the railings and gasping like a stranded whale.

Mrs Malloy looked ruefully at Sally when they reached the kitchen.

'Me tongue ran away with me there, girl,' she said, 'but I was that mad! I heard her and the other one giving out about Mary yesterday outside the parlour winder, but by the time I got out they'd cleared off. I was going to tackle her the first chance I got, and when I heard her with you me blood just boiled.'

Sally's face was white and her hands trembled as she moved the kettle over the fire. 'I'll make a cup of tea,' she said quietly.

'I've upset you now, girl, and I wouldn't do that for the world,' Mrs Malloy said, but Sally shook her head.

'No, it wasn't you, Mrs Mal. I'm glad you tackled her, but it was just a bit of a shock to hear it right out about our Mary. Mind you, I guessed there'd be some talk about her.'

'And what if there is? It was a true word I said, girl. They're only jealous.'

'If only she'd be straight with me, though. I know she's bound to be getting interested in boys, and I wouldn't mind if I knew who they were, but she's so hardfaced. I *know* she's telling me lies about where she's been but she'll stand there and brazen it out.'

'Don't be worrying now, girl. She's pretty and the lads are bound to be eyeing her, but she's a good girl and she's been well reared. She'll come to no harm and will soon grow out of her skittish ways.'

Sally said no more, but she was not convinced. When Mary came home from work, she said firmly, 'You can stay in tonight, and in future I'm going to know where you are and who you're with. I'm not having people telling me you're carrying on in the street when you're supposed to be in Bella's or Janie's house. You'll be getting yourself a bad name.'

'It's not fair!' Mary said with a toss of her head. 'I've had a terrible day at work and I was looking forward to going to Janie's to help her to trim a hat. It's not my fault if people tell lies about me.'

Sally took her meal from the oven and banged it down on the table.

'It's a pity you ever moved from the china department in Denby's. Working with those girls in the dress department has gone to your head.'

'I thought you liked me working in the dress department,' Mary said sulkily, 'You said you were pleased when I got the chance to move.'

'I didn't know then that you were going to turn out so vain and flighty. For two pins I'd go and ask for you to be moved back.'

Mary thought it wiser to say nothing, but later when she joined Cathy in bed she whispered angrily, 'Did you hear Mam carrying on? Nothing but sermons, sermons, sermons in this house.'

'I think Mrs Killy was telling tales about you,' Cathy whispered in reply. 'Josie told me her mother said Mrs Killy came out when Mam was doing the step and started talking to her, then Mrs Mal came out and she gave Mrs Kilgannon an awful telling off.'

'About time somebody did,' Mary said. 'Mam just listens to people like that and believes them.'

Cathy giggled. 'Josie said after Mrs Malloy and Mam went in, Mrs Killy shouted across to her mam, "Did you hear what that dirty pape said? She said I was carrying on with old Sam just because he has me back bedroom." All the neighbours were laughing, Josie said.'

'Imagine it,' Mary whispered. 'Old Sam! Three hairs on his head and two on his chin.' They began to giggle uncontrollably, stuffing the sheet in their mouths to muffle the noise, but a little later Mary returned to her grievance.

'I'm sick of the tittle tattle round here,' she said. 'I can't wait to get away from it. I wish I could live at The Grange.'

Cathy was astonished. 'You mean – leave Mam and Dad, and live with Aunt Emily?'

'No. I mean a house like The Grange, in a posh neighbourhood. I just hate living round here. I'd do anything, *anything* to get away, Cath.'

'Perhaps they won't say anything else now in case Mrs Mal starts on them,' Cathy said, but there was no reply.

They lay in silence for a while before Mary said suddenly, 'The only way is to marry a rich man, and that's what I'll do as soon as I'm old enough.'

'Will you?' Cathy murmured sleepily. 'Don't go too far away though, will you?'

'You can come and stay with me,' Mary promised, before snuggling up to her and falling asleep.

Lawrie was on late duty. When he finally came home Sally poured out the tale to him. He shouted with laughter when he heard of Mrs Malloy's rout of Mrs Kilgannon, and Sally smiled with him. Then she said quietly, 'It's all right laughing, Lawrie, but it worries me to death to think of our Mary larking about with lads, making herself cheap, and filling the neighbours' mouths too.'

'Don't worry about them,' Lawrie said. 'If they're talking about us, they're leaving someone else alone. But if our Mary *is* getting interested in lads, you'd better have a talk to her, love. She's too innocent to know the dangers.'

'I hope you're right,' Sally said grimly. 'She's been interested in lads since she was twelve but maybe it's different now she's turned sixteen. I'll talk to her anyhow, but I think the same one could tell me more than I know myself!'

Mary had been alarmed by her mother's threat of having her moved from the dress department at Denby's. She enjoyed working among the beautiful clothes, especially as she was now sometimes told to model dresses so that customers could decide whether they wished for some alteration in a bodice or in the hang of a skirt. She enjoyed the admiring glances of the men who accompanied their wives or lady friends to the department, although she knew that she would never see these people outside the shop.

She raged to her friends about the injustice of rich girls wearing the beautiful clothes which she knew looked so much better on herself.

'She'll make it look like a sack,' she told Janie when they discussed a dress her friend had helped to make in the workroom and Mary had modelled. 'She's got a face like a pudding and a figure like a sack of spuds.'

'But she's got money,' Janie said shrewdly, 'that's why she's got that nice-looking feller tagging after her.'

'It's not fair,' Mary raged. 'When I think what I could do with those clothes or that money I could go mad! Why should some people have all the money and others nothing? Look at my mother slaving away, and my aunt just sitting in that posh house being waited on.'

'It's just chance,' Janie said with a sigh. 'We just happened to be born in this class and here we'll stay, I suppose.'

'*I* won't,' Mary declared. 'I'll get on. I'll marry a rich man, just you wait and see.'

Meanwhile her mother had to be placated, and Mary arranged for Janie to call for her one evening, and to talk to her mother about the girls who met in her house to talk and to play the piano and have a sing song.

'We like to walk out and get some fresh air after being in the shop all day, but it's too cold these nights, isn't it, Mary?' Janie said guilelessly.

Sally had an uneasy feeling that she was being fooled but she stifled her doubts, glad to think that the tales about Mary were untrue.

Cathy knew the truth: that Mary and Janie entertained young men in the parlour while Janie's father was out drinking and her mother working as a waitress, but she saw no harm in it, and in any case would never have betrayed Mary.

Mrs Kilgannon still peeped from behind her curtains when Emily visited her sister or people came for dressmaking fittings, and she still gossiped about Mary to other neighbours, but in the street she passed Sally with her head averted.

None of the other neighbours dared to carry tales, so Sally knew a period of peace and told herself that Mary had only been foolish and that her own lectures had convinced her and nipped the trouble in the bud.

Although Cathy had laughed about the incident with Mrs Kilgannon, the more she thought of it the more angry she became about the criticism. To her, Mary was perfect, and she was as indignant as Mrs Malloy at her sister's being besmirched by the neighbours' gossip.

Timid and shy though Cathy was, her anger was fierce when aroused, especially about anything concerning her family. She longed for a chance to defend Mary. Often she wove fantasies of approaching a group of gossiping neighbours and telling them that Mary was to be married to a rich and handsome young man who loved her because she was not only beautiful but good. She dreamt of Mrs Kilgannon being told that she must leave her house because she was not fit to live beside respectable neighbours like the Wards, and of their neighbour begging Cathy to intercede for her. Even to the little girl's lively imagination this seemed unlikely, and all that she was able to do in fact was to ignore Mrs Kilgannon when she called her to run a message for her.

She was not sure that her mother would approve of this, but she told Mrs Malloy who was in complete agreement with her.

'The cheek of the ould faggot, to be asking favours of anyone in this house!' she said. 'Let her see what we think of her.' And Cathy felt that she had struck a blow for her beloved sister.

Chapter Three

The winter of 1908–9 was a trying one for Mrs Malloy. In spite of blazing fires, and a hot water bottle in her bed, and Lawrie's careful plugging of draughty door and windows, the chill fingers of winter reached into the house and gripped the old lady.

It became impossible for her to hobble into Sally's kitchen or down the yard to the lavatory and to her great distress she was compelled to use the commode which Sally placed by her bed. It was in vain for Sally to assure her that she thought nothing of attending to it, that she had performed even more personal duties for her father when he was ill, and that the day would come when she herself would need to be cared for by her daughters.

The independent old lady was far more distressed by her bodily helplessness than by the intense pain she suffered in her twisted limbs.

'It's degrading, so it is, girl, for you and for me,' she wept, and Sally was unable to comfort her, but as with every situation time and repetition made it acceptable.

For a while Mrs Mal was still able to knit socks as she had always done, but when it became difficult for her to manage the four thin steel needles required, Lawrie managed to find a shop which sold bone needles. With these she could knit scarves for the family, but the day came when her fingers were too swollen and twisted even for that.

Cathy was distressed by her old friend's suffering, and spent many hours in the parlour, reading a newspaper to Mrs Mal or talking about happenings at school or among the neighbours.

They had a similar sense of humour and would laugh together when Mrs Malloy made a salty comment on the news or Cathy mimicked a teacher or one of the neighbours.

Lawrie occasionally took the family to the theatre when he had worked a Sunday and had extra in his pay packet, and Cathy would go through all the acts the following day to amuse Mrs Malloy. Sally went into the parlour one day and found Cathy prancing up and down singing 'Ta ra ra boom de ay' and giving high kicks.

'*Cathy*, you're showing your drawers,' she exclaimed, but when she realised that Mrs Malloy was awkwardly lifting the corner of her apron to wipe away tears of laughter she said no more.

Cathy had early learned to whistle, and soon she had an even more extensive repertoire than the errand boys who sang or whistled the latest tunes as they delivered orders on foot or by bicycle.

'Isn't she the living model of your mam, Lord ha' mercy on her?' Mrs Malloy said to Sally. 'Always whistling and singing about the house, poor Julie was. "A whistling woman, a crowing hen, would frighten the devil outa his den" your Da used to say to her, but sure it was only his fun. Poor Matt. He missed that sound about the house when God took her from him.'

'I remember Mam well,' Sally said, 'although I was only twelve when she died. Her lovely brown eyes and the way she was always laughing.'

'Your Emily used to put me in mind of her too,' Mrs Malloy said, 'but God knows she's different now.'

'She is,' Sally agreed sadly. 'So thin and pale and no life in her somehow. Anyone but Albert would have had a doctor to her or taken her for a holiday, but he's too mean.'

'Never mind, girl, she gets good food and plenty of it when she comes to you of a Wednesday. And she enjoys the day so much it must do her good.'

'Our Mary's very fond of Emily. She'll sit for hours talking to her, and she's always ready to go to The Grange,' said Sally. She laughed. 'I think she's trying to find out how to behave if she ever has a house like that.'

'Stranger things have happened,' said Mrs Malloy. 'Have you seen anything of the quare one next door?'

'Mrs Kilgannon?' Sally said. 'She was peeping from behind the curtains when Emily came on Wednesday, and she's always snooping when people come for fittings, but I think she's afraid to come out or say anything now in case you start on her.'

'Ah, the days are gone, child,' Mrs Malloy sighed, 'when I could get out to tackle the likes of her. Still, I've had a good innings. When this trouble first came on me I couldn't move a limb – d'you remember how Lawrie used to carry me in to see your poor da? And then it eased off for a while, thanks be to God.'

'Perhaps it will again,' Sally comforted her, 'when we get this winter over and the better weather comes.'

'Aye, maybe,' was Mrs Malloy's reply.

The priests from Saint Francis Xavier's called occasionally to see Mrs Malloy, and one day when Cathy came home from school and rushed into the parlour to see her old friend, she found a Sister of Charity sitting with her.

Cathy had often seen the nun going about the neighbourhood on her work for the sick poor, and she had been fascinated by the large rosary hanging from the waist of the nun's heavy skirt, and her stiffly starched white headdress.

The shape of the headdress and the stiff outward curving folds always made Cathy think of a swan being borne along, but she had never been close to a nun. Now she stood tongue-tied with shyness as Mrs Malloy beckoned her forward.

'This is Cathy who I was telling you about, Sister. Hasn't she been my treasure entirely these last months?'

The nun's wrinkled face broke into a smile.

'I've been hearing all about you, child. The help you've given Mrs Malloy to bear her affliction. God will reward you for your kindness.'

'She's put many a weary hour past for me, Sister. Sure the pain doesn't trouble me while I can have a laugh with Cathy,' Mrs Malloy said, taking the girl's hand. The nun rose to her feet.

'I'll go and see that poor man in Brewster Street now that you have company, Mrs Malloy,' she said. She patted Cathy's cheek and drew up the large crucifix on the end of the rosary, holding it while Mrs Malloy bent forward and kissed it.

'I'll pray that your pain may be eased,' the nun said gently, 'and for these good people who care for you.'

'Ah, Sister, don't I thank God for them every hour of the day. Me with neither chick nor child that could have finished up in the Workhouse if it wasn't for their goodness to me. Flesh and blood couldn't have done more for me, and nothing too much trouble.' Tears ran down her cheeks and Cathy suddenly found her voice.

'You've been good to us too, Mrs Mal,' she said shyly. 'Mam says you've helped her all her life.'

'I can see I leave you in good hands,' the nun said. 'Take care now. I'll tell Bridie Daly you were asking about her.'

She moved from the room and Cathy went with her to open the front door, and to say goodbye. When she went back to the parlour Mrs Malloy had recovered. A moment later her mother came in.

'I met Sister Martha in the street,' she said. 'Did you have a nice talk?'

'We did,' said Mrs Malloy. 'And she said not to forget now, Sally, if you need any help you've only to send a message to her.'

'She doesn't know how independent you are,' Sally said, smiling affectionately at the old lady. 'I haven't got enough to do for you, never mind needing help with nursing.'

She took a parcel of fish from her basket and gave it to Cathy.

'Put it in the back kitchen and we'll have the kettle on for a cup of tea,' she said, so Cathy had no opportunity to talk to Mrs Malloy about the conversation with the nun. She remembered every word that Mrs Mal had said, however, and it was a great comfort to her in time to come.

The priest called to see Mrs Malloy a few weeks later, and it was arranged that on Easter Saturday he would bring Holy Communion to her.

Sally set out a small altar on the bamboo occasional table, and as Mrs Malloy directed she met the priest at the door with a lighted candle. She led him into the parlour then went out, closing the door behind her.

A little later the priest came into the lobby where Sally hovered. Mrs Malloy had warned Sally that he would have other visits to make and that he would not speak while he carried the Host so she inclined her head and the priest bowed, then she opened the door for him without a word.

When she went into the parlour, Mrs Malloy looked up with a smile.

'Well now, that's a great relief to me, girl,' she said. 'I scraped me kettle and all.' Sally looked mystified and the old lady laughed.

'I made me Confession,' she explained. 'That was an old saying of me mother's, Lord rest her. I'm ready now for when God calls me.'

Sally often wondered later if Mrs Malloy had experienced a premonition of her death. As they usually did now, the family sat round the parlour fire after the evening meal, talking to Mrs Malloy for a while before leaving her to rest while they made preparations for the next day. When Sally went in with her bedtime cocoa she found the old lady apparently peacefully asleep in her rocking chair, her rosary beads in her hand, but it was her last long sleep.

Shocked and grieved though they were the family could only be thankful that her last years had been as happy as they could make them, and that her end was a merciful one.

Years before, the independent old lady had given Sally a cocoa tin which contained the money for her funeral. Her long-dead husband had been buried in Ford Cemetery in the grave which had been bought with the money she received in compensation after he was killed at work. Lawrie arranged that she too should be buried there, after a Requiem Mass at St Francis Xavier's.

Mary was not allowed time off for funerals so she went off to the shop on the morning of the funeral, secretly glad of the excuse to miss it.

Cathy, Sally, and Lawrie, the three who had loved the old lady the most, were the ones who followed her coffin to the church. They were amazed at the number of old people who were at the church to pay their last respects. The priest who had brought the Holy Communion to the house said the Mass, and he spoke with sincerity of Mrs Malloy's courage and goodness, but it was the words of her old friends who were clustered in the porch to speak to the family who gave them most comfort.

'She had the best of care with you, and she couldn't speak highly enough of all you done for her,' one old lady said. 'But the rheumaticks crucified her and she'd be glad to go, God help her. There'll be plenty waiting for her in Heaven.' Many others spoke in the same way and of their belief that Mrs Malloy had gone to the reward in Heaven of a good life on earth, and in the expectation of meeting those who had gone before. In their words, Cathy could recognise the same simple faith which had been Mrs Malloy's mainstay throughout her life.

It was a long drive to Ford Cemetery which lay in the country-side on the outskirts of Liverpool. Larks were singing above them as they stood at the graveside. Sally voiced the feeling they all had, that Mrs Malloy would rest in peace in this quiet place, close to the little Catholic chapel.

–

Sally found relief from her grief in hard physical work, and Mary was dismayed by the speed with which the parlour was transformed. Mrs Malloy's rocking chair and bed were very gratefully accepted by one of her old friends, who lived in great poverty in a bare and comfortless attic room, and other small items went as mementoes to other friends.

Sally chose fresh bright wallpaper for the walls, the curtains were washed and the floor polished, and she took some of the money she had saved in the handless teapot on the mantelpiece and bought a sofa and two armchairs covered in green plush from a nephew of old Solly who kept the pawnbroker's on the street corner.

'I don't know what all the rush is for,' Mary grumbled to Cathy.

'I think Mam is just taking her mind off Mrs Malloy,' Cathy surmised, but Mary was not convinced.

'She can't wait to have me under her eye all the time,' she said. 'I suppose I'll never get out now. She's even ordered a piano from Crane's, so she can hear us playing or singing and know exactly what we're doing.'

'I thought you'd like to have a nice parlour to bring people to,' Cathy said. 'And it's really posh. I'm sure it's much nicer than Janie's.'

'I know what it'll be like here,' Mary said, 'with Mam on guard duty all the time. We can have fun in Janie's – her mam and dad are always out so we can do what we like.'

'What do you do?' Cathy said innocently, and Mary hesitated.

'We play parlour games,' she said finally. She knew that Cathy would be shocked if she knew what followed the parlour games. The fumbling in the darkened room when the boys and girls paired off, the excitement of the boys' kisses and their hands exploring her body, and her sense of power when the boy was roused and she refused to go any further. They called her a tease and said she was mean not to allow them to go all the way, as they declared some of the other girls did, but there was always someone willing to pair off with her and hope that they would be the one to break down her resistance.

'But Mam would let you play parlour games here,' Cathy said. 'And she'd let you bring boys as well. I'm sure she knows you know boys, Mary. I don't suppose she'd let me join in though, even if you didn't mind,' she added wistfully.

'I'll just have to work something out,' Mary said vaguely. 'Goodnight, Cath.' She blew out the candle and they settled down to sleep.

Cathy was too full of grief for Mrs Malloy to be interested for long in Mary's problems. Every morning when she woke the thought of Mrs Mal's death came as a fresh shock to her, and during the day she was constantly reminded of it when for a moment she thought of telling her old friend something, and then realised that she would never see her again. Sometimes when her sorrow became unbearable she would weep bitterly but she felt that she received little sympathy.

Her mother, usually so understanding, had her own sorrow to bear, and she would tell Cathy that it was selfish to grieve for Mrs Malloy. 'Remember how much she suffered, Cathy,' she often said, 'and that her end was peaceful, when she felt herself that she was ready for it.' Sally talked as much to convince herself as her daughter but to Cathy she seemed hard and unfeeling.

If she waited until she was in bed to indulge in tears, Mary would say impatiently, 'Oh, stop crying, Cathy. You'll make your face all blotchy and your eyes will be all swollen tomorrow morning.' The only place where Cathy felt free to give herself up to her bitter grief was in the lavatory at the bottom of the yard, where she could lean against the whitewashed wall and weep without restraint.

Although it was like probing an aching tooth, she was unable to resist thinking of various happy times she had spent with the old lady, and one day recalled a time when she had been taught some simple card games by Mrs Mal. Her father had come into the room and said with a laugh, 'I didn't know you were a card sharp.'

'Ah, you don't know the half of me, lad,' Mrs Mal had chuckled. Now Cathy felt that she had not known the half of what Mrs Malloy had meant to her.

Gradually, with the resilience of youth, Cathy began to recover her cheerful spirit and to come to terms with her loss. She was unobtrusively helped by her father. He often brought her books from the secondhand bookstalls in St John's Lane, and took her with him when he went out on Sundays. They would walk to the Landing Stage sometimes to see the ships in the River Mersey, and her father would tell her tales of his seafaring days, or they would stop to listen to the soap box orators at the Pier Head. Cathy enjoyed listening to the heckling by the crowd, and the way the speakers answered with wit and humour, and she was proud when her father asked a question one day and the speaker replied carefully and seriously as one thinking man to another.

The greatest help and comfort that Cathy received from her father came from a conversation they had one Sunday when they were out walking. Cathy had been suddenly overcome with tears earlier in the morning and as they walked along Lawrie said gently, 'Don't grieve too much for Mrs Mal, love. She's finished with suffering now.'

'I know, Dad. I'm really crying for myself, because I miss her so much,' Cathy said truthfully.

'Aye, well, that's how it is when we lose someone. But y'know, love, although Mrs Mal put a brave face on it, the pain was getting worse and worse. Before long she'd have been completely helpless too, and you know how she'd have hated that, Cath. She was so independent.'

'I know she was, Dad. She liked doing for people, she told me so. She hated to put anyone out.'

'Yes, well, think of that when you get upset about her. I tell you what, Cath, if she saw you crying about her she'd be really annoyed with you. Just be glad we knew her, and we had her to tell us off for so long.'

Cathy laughed as her father had intended her to, and he began to talk of what she would do after she had left school.

The time was drawing near for Cathy to leave school but before she did so, something occurred which influenced her throughout her life.

She disliked her current teacher, Miss Mensor, who savagely punished the dirty and neglected girls in the class, but allowed clean, well-dressed girls to commit the same offences without reprimand.

'I hate Miss Mensor,' she told her father one night as she sat beside him while he ate his meal. 'She always picks on poor girls. She gave Lizzie Clark six of the cane for talking, yet Isabella Buckly was talking quite loud and she didn't tell her off even. Lizzie had a sore foot too.'

'I suppose Isabella is from Buckly's shop, and Lizzie is one of the poor girls,' her father said.

'Yes, she wears police clothes, and she told me she waits outside Tate and Lyle's for the men coming off shift in case they have any butties left.'

She saw her parents glance at each other and remembered that Mrs Malloy had told her that her father used to give his carry out away to hungry children when he was nearly starving himself.

But her mother said reprovingly, 'You shouldn't criticise your teachers, Cathy. Remember they're older than you, and that they're set in authority over you.'

Cathy scowled. All very well, she thought, but what about poor Lizzie Clark, with her tangled hair and dirty face, hobbling back to her seat at the back of the class with tears in her eyes and her hands tucked beneath her arms to relieve the pain?

The following day at playtime she gave Lizzie half of the bread and jam she took to school, and Lizzie showed her her foot which was swollen and bleeding where it was rubbed by her heavy clogs, unprotected by stockings. Cathy's friend Ellen pulled at her arm.

'Come away from her,' she urged. 'She's walking alive with bugs and fleas and yer mam'll kill you if you catch sumpn off her.' She spoke loudly and Cathy saw Lizzie cringe. She flung Ellen's arm away.

'Clear off, and mind your own business!' she said furiously. Like many normally placid people her anger when aroused was fierce. Ellen said placatingly, 'I didn't mean no harm. You're my friend, aren't you?'

'Yes, but I'll talk to who I like,' Cathy said. She recognised the olive branch, but she was still shaken by conflicting emotions: pity for Lizzie, anger at the injustice of her plight and the cruelty shown

26

to her, and a vague feeling of baffled rage that she was helpless to change things.

She usually walked home with Ellen who lived a few doors away in Egremont Street, but at four o'clock she asked Lizzie to come home with her and let her mother bandage the foot.

Ellen flounced off in a huff. By the time the two girls reached the Wards' house, Cathy supporting Lizzie who found it difficult to walk, her mother had been forewarned by Ellen.

'This is Lizzie Clark, Mam,' Cathy said breathlessly. Sally showed no surprise at the sight of the dirty, frightened child as she helped them into the back kitchen.

'Sit down, Lizzie' she said, moving a kitchen chair forward. She drew in her breath when she took off the little girl's clog and saw the bleeding flesh.

'It must be very sore, love,' she said gently. Lizzie nodded dumbly, staring wide-eyed round the neat back kitchen, at the pans and dishes arranged on shelves edged with fancy paper, the shining tap above the sink, and the gas ring on a cupboard.

'Put that bowl on the floor, Cathy, and pour some cold water in it,' Sally ordered. She went into the kitchen for the black kettle which purred beside the fire, then added hot water and a handful of borax to the bowl.

'Put your foot in that water and let it soak, Lizzie. And Cathy, put the small kettle on the gas ring and make us a cup of tea.'

She washed her hands and brought out the box in which she kept strips of old sheeting for bandages, jars of ointment, cloves for toothache and various other remedies. Cathy made the tea and Sally cut thick slices of bread and spread them with dripping, then she washed Lizzie's face and hands with a flannel.

'Now, love, drink this tea and eat the dripping butties while your foot's soaking,' she said, arranging a mug of tea and a plateful of bread on the scrubbed board of the mangle beside Lizzie. 'I'll be back in a minute but I want Cathy to do a job for me.' She drew Cathy into the lobby, leaving Lizzie to gulp down the tea and wolf down the bread in privacy.

'There's a pair of old boots on the bottom shelf of my bedroom cupboard,' she said. 'They'll be a bit big for Lizzie but there'll be room for the bandages. Run up and get them.'

She went back to Lizzie. 'How long has your foot been like this, love?'

'I dunno. It just got worser and worser,' Lizzie said, looking up at her trustfully. Sally gently dabbed the foot dry, alarmed to see how much more inflamed the flesh looked without the covering of dirt, then she spread it with ointment and wrapped the strips of sheeting around it.

Cathy had come back with the boots and Sally opened the laces of one of them as far as they would go, and eased the boot over the bandaged foot.

'Tell me if I'm hurting you, love,' she said, but Lizzie shook her head. Sally loosely laced up the boot, then took a pair of knitted socks from the dresser drawer.

'These socks shrunk in the wash and they're too small for Cathy's dad now,' she said, drawing one of them on to Lizzie's good foot and putting the boot on over it. 'You can take the other one to change, because the boot'll be too big otherwise.'

'Yer mean – keep the boots an' all when I go 'ome?' Lizzie said eagerly.

'Yes, love. Someone gave us a pair of boots once when we needed them and they made all the difference to us,' said Sally.

Lizzie still looked doubtful and Sally smiled at her.

'Some day, love, you'll give someone a pair of boots when they need them. That's how the world goes round.' She washed her hands again and Lizzie watched her sadly.

'Yer 'ave ter wash yer 'ands after yer've touched me,' she said, but Sally shook her head.

'No. I always wash my hands before I touch food. My mother was taught to do it when she was in good service, so she taught me and I've taught my girls to do the same.'

'Like with the boots. Goin' round and round,' Lizzie said.

'Like with the boots,' Sally agreed with a smile. She cut another slice of bread and dripping and poured more tea for the two girls, then when they had finished eating she told Cathy to help Lizzie part of her way home, then come straight back.

'Come again after school, Lizzie,' she said. 'I'll do your foot each day until it's better.'

Soon after the two girls left the house, Cathy realised that Lizzie was crying.

'Is your foot hurting?' she asked, but Lizzie shook her head, sniffing loudly.

'I wish I lived in your 'ouse,' she gulped. 'Yer mam's luvly.' Cathy was silent, uncertain what to say, and when they had gone half way down William Henry Street, Lizzie pulled her arm away from Cathy's.

'Go back,' she said. 'I'm orlright now.'

'All right. See you tomorrow,' Cathy said, turning away immediately and running back home. A zinc bath stood on the rag rug
before the fire, filled with steaming water.

'Give me your clothes and get in the bath,' her mother said
briskly.

'But why, Mam? It isn't Saturday,' Cathy protested.

'Because I tell you to,' Sally said. 'There's a piece of carbolic soap
there. Give yourself a good scrub.' She took Cathy's clothes into the
backyard and hung them over the washing line, then went back to
Cathy and vigorously rubbed sassafrass soap into her hair.

'Not a word of this at school,' she said.

'I wouldn't, Mam,' Cathy said indignantly. 'I came back right
away when Lizzie told me to. I knew she didn't want me to see
where she lived.'

'Poor child,' her mother said.

'She said she wished she lived here. She thinks I'm lucky,' Cathy
said.

'Mm. Well, remember that the next time you grumble about
going a message,' Sally said.

Mary's right, Cathy thought, there's always a lecture. But she felt
ashamed when she thought of her mother's kindness to Lizzie. Her
mother might have a sharp tongue, but she always behaved with
tactful kindness to anyone in trouble.

Lizzie came again the following night to have her foot dressed
and to eat a portion of rabbit pie, with slices of bread and dripping
to carry home, but the next morning when Cathy approached her
in the playground, she thrust her away.

'Bugger off,' she snarled. 'Go on. I don't want nothing to do with
yer.'

'But why—' Cathy began, but Lizzie lunged at her. 'Just bugger
off, that's all,' she said. She was barefoot and the bandages on her
left foot were wet and muddy, but she hobbled away.

After playtime Cathy went back to the classroom trembling with
shock. Her hand shook as she tried to write to dictation so that
she was one of those who received the cane for careless work, but
even the pain in her hand could not distract her from her pain and
bewilderment at Lizzie's rejection of her.

When she went home at dinner time a woman had called with
an order for mourning clothes, so Cathy was unable to talk to her
mother about Lizzie, except to say that she would not be coming
to have her foot dressed.

Sally only nodded abstractedly. Cathy went back to school determined to see Lizzie and find out how she had offended her, but as

soon as the register had been called, Miss Mensor announced that the schools nurse had arrived. The girls went out to the nurse a row at a time, starting with the back row. As Lizzie limped out, Cathy could see that she looked ill, and the bandages on her foot were wet and even more dirty.

When it was Cathy's turn she went into the staffroom which the nurse was using and lined up with four other girls to wait for the nurse to part their hair with two spatulas, then measure their height and examine their eyes and ears.

Ellen, who was next to Cathy, whispered triumphantly, 'Look at Lizzie Clark. She's with the lousy ones.'

Cathy peeped round at a cowed-looking group, many of them barefoot, who were huddled in the corner of the room. Lizzie was among them, standing with her head bent and her tangled hair hiding her face.

'She'll have all her hair cut off,' Ellen whispered as they were marched back to the classroom by the monitors. 'You see, she'll be baldy tomorrow.'

'She'll still look better than you,' Cathy flashed back.

'I'll never speak to you no more, Cathy Ward,' Ellen said, and afterwards avoided her.

Cathy longed for four o'clock when she could confide in her mother, but when she reached home Sally was in the parlour measuring women for mourning clothes, and she only looked out and told Cathy to peel the potatoes. For the rest of the evening she was too busy to talk, and when Cathy tried to speak to Mary about Lizzie, Mary snapped, 'I just hope you haven't brought any vermin here. I'm fed up. I suppose Mam will leave the blouse she's making for me to do this mourning order.'

Cathy found it impossible to stop thinking about Lizzie, and when she was absent from school the next day, worried even more about her. No one seemed to know anything about her, and Cathy was afraid to ask Miss Mensor.

Her mother was out at dinner time and again when Cathy reached home after school, but her father was asleep on the sofa after being on early shift.

He woke and sat up, and patted the sofa beside him.

'Come and sit down and tell me what you've been doing today, love,' he said, not appearing to notice Cathy's woebegone expression. She sat down beside him, and he said casually, 'How's your friend with the sore foot?'

Cathy burst into tears, then in a torrent of words told him about the scene in the playground, the visit of the nurse, and Lizzie's absence from school. He listened quietly, then drew her close to him.

'Now don't upset yourself any more,' he said. 'The nurse will have sent Lizzie to the Infirmary when she saw the state of her foot.'

'But why did Lizzie turn on me like that?' Cathy asked.

'Because she didn't want to tell you that her boots had been pawned,' he said calmly. Cathy's eyes widened.

'Pawned!' she exclaimed.

'Of course. That's why the police give out special clogs and clothes made from old police uniforms, so pawnbrokers won't take them,' he said.

'I'm thick,' Cathy said. 'I never thought of that, Dad. I thought it was something I'd done.' She was comforted, realising that she was not to blame for Lizzie's outburst, but after a moment she said quietly, 'Poor Lizzie. She was made up with the boots, and then she was ashamed to tell me as well as losing them. It's not fair, is it, Dad?'

'No, love, life's not fair to girls like Lizzie.'

'I mean, Miss Mensor picks on the dirty girls but it's not their fault. Lizzie lives in one of those horrible courts near Greaty, and Ellen said her mam and dad are always drunk – I don't know how *she* knows – but it's not Lizzie's fault, and it's not our fault that we live in a nice house.' She stopped, realising that her words were becoming muddled, but her father seemed to understand.

'Aye, it's what clever men call "an accident of birth", Cath, although they're talking about palaces rather than houses like this. But people in those courts should have the chance to have a decent house and live respectable lives. They haven't got a chance the way things are, and they can't help themselves.'

'But who could, then?' Cathy asked.

'I don't know, love,' he said with a sigh. 'I had high hopes of Lloyd George but I have me doubts now. If we could only get more working men into Parliament, that'd be the answer. They'd know what was needed and get it done. Clear those courts and build decent houses. Give men the chance to earn enough to keep their families. Look after the old people and the sick and widows with little children.'

Cathy's eyes glowed. 'That's what that man at the Pier Head was saying, wasn't it, Dad?'

'Aye, and you heard the way he was heckled. Some people think poverty's a sin, you see, Cath, but folks can't help what they're born into, and if they never see anything different, how can they change?

You can't blame them for boozing either when you think of the lives they live. Most people would lift themselves if they got the chance.'

He took out his pipe and said ruefully, 'I'm on my hobby horse again, as your mam would say, but listen, chick, I'm glad you brought Lizzie here. I hope you'll always keep a feeling heart, love, and try to help anyone in trouble.'

'Like you do, Dad.'

'I've tried, love, but it's never made much difference. Still, I often think of what one of them fellows at the Pier Head said: that all the little bits of kindness we were able to do were like drops of water that together would form a mighty river to sweep away injustice. I think of that when I feel disheartened.'

He turned the talk to other topics, but Cathy always remembered his words about poverty and injustice. They sank into her mind and influenced her throughout her life.

Chapter Four

Mary still went to visit her aunt and uncle in Aigburth every Sunday, and after Mrs Malloy's death Sally felt that it would distract Cathy's mind from her loss if she accompanied Mary more often.

Cathy would have preferred to stay at home, or go out with her friends, but she was unwilling to hurt her mother's feelings by telling her how much she disliked visiting The Grange, even to see Aunt Emily. She wished that she could be like Mary who always seemed at home there and loved the luxury of the house and being waited on by a maid.

Aunt Emily seemed ever more frail as time went on, and Cathy usually stayed with her as she rested on a sofa by an open window, while Mary walked round the extensive gardens with her uncle.

One very hot Sunday in the late summer of 1909, Cathy was sitting with her aunt while Mary and her Uncle Albert strolled round the garden.

'Those roses smell lovely, don't they, Aunt Emily?' Cathy said, sniffing rapturously at the scent of the roses which grew beneath the window.

'Yes, the heat brings out the fragrance,' Emily said. 'That's only a small bed though, Cath. There's a lot more further down the garden. Go and have a walk round, pet, and I'll close my eyes for a few minutes.'

Cathy knew that old Simmonds, the gardener, was off on a Sunday and for a while she enjoyed wandering round the garden while he was safely out of the way. She strolled round the rose garden, and then through the orchard where the fruit was beginning to form on the branches, then to a small formal garden, enclosed by high hedges.

She stopped, frozen in shock. Albert and Mary sat on a seat by the hedge. Mary's dress had been pulled down from her shoulders and Albert's arm was around her, with his left hand cupping her breast. His other hand was beneath Mary's skirt, which had been pulled up over her knees. Cathy's horrified eyes darted to Mary's face, expecting to see her opening her mouth to scream, but instead she was smiling up into Albert's red and sweating face, and leaning close to him.

They were unaware of Cathy approaching, her steps silent on the grass, and she turned and fled to the far end of the orchard, whimpering with shock and horror. She stayed there, unaware of the passage of time, until the new maid, Myfanwy, came to look for her.

'What is it, *cariad*?' the girl said gently, as she looked at Cathy crouching by the tree, white-faced and trembling. 'Did a bee sting you?' Cathy shook her head. 'Is it your monthly's started,' Myfanwy whispered, but when Cathy only looked at her dumbly the girl drew her to her feet and took her arm.

'Come now. Your sister is waiting for you,' she said gently, leading Cathy back to the house.

Albert and Mary had returned to the house and he was fussing about Mary's gloves which had been mislaid. In the confusion Cathy managed to kiss her aunt then escape on to the path to wait for Mary, without going near him. She and Mary walked home without speaking. Mary seemed unaware of her sister's silence as she walked along, humming to herself and glancing flirtatiously at any young man who passed.

When they reached home Mary rattled away to her mother about the new maid, and did full justice to the meal that was ready for them, but Cathy could only pick at her food although she drank several cups of tea. She told her mother that she had a headache and lay down on the sofa holding up a book to hide her face, while Mary disappeared upstairs to get ready to go out.

As soon as Mary had gone Cathy told her mother that she was tired and would go to bed. She felt that she must be alone to face the blow that had fallen on her. Her mother looked searchingly at her.

'Are you all right, love?' she asked, feeling Cathy's forehead then taking her hand. 'Why, your hand's freezing and yet your forehead's so hot! You'd better have a Dr Grey's powder.'

Cathy obediently swallowed the powder in a spoonful of jam and went up to bed. A little later her mother came upstairs and tucked the bedclothes around her, then bent to kiss her goodnight. Cathy flung her arms around her mother's neck.

'What is it, love?' she said, smoothing the child's hair back from her forehead but Cathy said hastily, 'Nothing, Mam. I just feel shivery, but I'll be all right now I'm in bed.'

'You might have caught a summer cold or eaten something that's disagreed with you,' her mother said. 'Try to sleep now, pet, and you'll feel better in the morning.'

She went away and Cathy lay curled up, staring at the wall. Better in the morning? she thought. I'll *never* feel better. Hot tears ran down her face and wet the pillow as the scene in the garden passed through her mind again and again.

That hand, that hairy hand, so roughly squeezing Mary's breast and her not minding, even seeming to like it. And his other hand... Cathy shivered uncontrollably. I'll never get over the shock, she thought, never. I'll never go there again, but what excuse can I make? She wept even more bitterly.

She was still awake hours later when Mary came up to bed, carrying a candle in a tin holder. Cathy kept her eyes firmly shut until a strange sound made her open them. Mary, wearing her nightdress, was kneeling before the fireplace which was never used and taking out a brick from the back of the grate. She put her hand in the cavity and Cathy heard the chink of money. She closed her eyes again and a moment later Mary blew out the candle and climbed into bed. Cathy drew as far away from her as she could.

The following morning Mary had gone to work when Cathy got up for school and it was easier for her to behave normally. Her mother looked at her closely.

'I don't know whether you'd better go to school this morning,' she said. 'You look like a whitewashed ghost.'

'I'm all right, Mam, honest,' Cathy insisted, and went to school, glad to escape from her mother's sharp eyes.

During the following days the episode in the garden was never far from Cathy's mind. It was her last thought before she fell asleep and the first when she woke in the morning. At times the burden of her knowledge seemed too much for her to bear and she felt that she must tell *somebody* – but who? Mary herself? But Cathy shrank from putting what she had seen into words.

Not her mother or her father. She cared too much for them to distress them so much to gain relief herself. Not Josie or any of her other friends. Loyalty to Mary and distrust of her friends' discretion kept her silent and she longed as never before for Mrs Malloy's comfort and advice. She too had loved Mary and she might have been able to make some sense of that dreadful scene.

Sometimes the business in the garden seemed so unbelievable that Cathy felt that she must have dreamt it, then she would remember again Uncle Albert's hand on Mary's breast and the expression on both their faces, and she would be overwhelmed by shock and revulsion made all the more severe because of the love and admiration she had always felt for her sister.

'You look very peaky. You're not still brooding about Mrs Mal, are you, love?' her mother asked anxiously. 'Try to remember, Cath, how peaceful her end was, and how much pain she's been spared.'

'I know, Mam,' Cathy said, but she felt her eyes filling with tears and took refuge in the outside lavatory to weep in private. She felt ashamed that her mother was being deceived but thankful that she was unaware of the real reason for her distress.

She dreaded Sunday and wondered how she could contrive to avoid going to Aigburth, but on the following weekend rain fell so continuously that there was no question of the girls visiting their aunt and uncle.

The next Wednesday Emily was brought to see Sally for the first time for several weeks. Sally was shocked by the change in her sister. She had become noticeably thinner, and could only sit languidly in her chair, smiling at Sally but saying little.

Sally pressed her to eat, but Emily seemed too tired to make the effort. Cathy felt nervous and self-conscious before her aunt, feeling the burden of her knowledge, but Mary seemed quite unconcerned when she arrived home and saw her aunt. When Albert arrived to take Emily home Mary stayed in the kitchen, but Cathy fled into the backyard, only returning when the carriage had driven away.

Later that evening when they were in bed, Mary said contemptuously, 'I wish Mam wouldn't *fuss* so much. It gets on my nerves. All those questions about how often Aunt Emily coughed when I was at their house – as though I was keeping a log book on it!'

'Mam's worried about her,' Cathy said quietly.

'She's worried about *everything*. It drives me mad. A stupid woman in Magnolia Street turns the gas on and doesn't light it so we have to manage with candles while there's a perfectly good gas bracket in the bedroom. You were ill when you were a child so you have to be wrapped up like an Egyptian mummy every winter, and *I* can't move a step without a hundred questions.'

And that's all that really worries you, Cathy thought cynically. She turned over and pretended to go to sleep. She wondered that Mary never noticed that she was avoiding her, or that she was never awake at night to hear the stories of her conquests, but Mary seemed oblivious to the change in Cathy's attitude.

A few days later Mary brought home a velvet shoulder cape which she said she had bought from a girl at work for sixpence.

'*Sixpence*,' her mother said sharply. 'It's like new. You've got generous friends.' She fingered the cape then looked searchingly at Mary. 'Like the material you got so cheaply in the market. I was all round the market and I didn't see anything like that at the price.'

'I was just lucky, Mam,' Mary said, opening her blue eyes wide. 'And lucky that you could make it up so nice for me.'

'Aye, lucky,' her mother said. 'You just watch your step, milady. If I find any of these lads have bought clothes for you there'll be trouble, I'm warning you.'

'Oh, Mam, I don't know how you can think such things,' Mary said, flouncing away with an outraged expression on her face.

Cathy watched and listened silently. A short time earlier her sympathy would have all been with Mary, and she would have been indignant that her sister was falsely accused but now she looked at Mary with different eyes. Had the cape been bought with money from the fireplace? she wondered. With part of her mind she felt ashamed that she suspected Mary, yet she was unable to forget the sight of her kneeling before her secret cache to hide money after the incident with Uncle Albert.

It was a confused and unhappy time for Cathy and sometimes her longing for her confidante, Mrs Malloy, was like a physical pain. She avoided her friends, feeling too miserable to be bothered to talk to them, and stayed in at night.

Sally's fears for Emily were proved correct when a message came for her that her sister had coughed up blood. She hastened to The Grange immediately.

'Even Albert is worried now,' she reported when she came home. 'The doctor's arranging for Emily to go to Scarborough with a nurse/companion for a month, and I told him that she needs building up with special invalid food. That's half the trouble, that she doesn't eat enough, and I told Albert so, straight out.'

'Aye, well, now he's opened his purse strings she'll get what she needs,' Lawrie said. 'Don't worry too much, love.'

'She looks so ill though,' Sally said, twisting her hands nervously.

'She'll be better after a little break, love,' Lawrie comforted her. 'The air in Scarborough is very bracing, and the nurse will see she gets all she needs.'

Cathy felt guiltily relieved at the news because it solved her problem about visiting The Grange, but Mary said artlessly, 'Uncle Albert will be very lonely, won't he? There on his own.'

'Don't worry about Albert,' her mother said grimly. 'He can look out for himself, the same feller.'

'He's not on his own anyway,' Cathy said. 'What about Myfanwy and the cook and Mr Simmonds?'

'Servants,' Mary said superciliously. 'Really, Cathy, you're such a *child*.'

'No, I'm not. I'm leaving school soon,' she flashed, but her mother rapped on the table.

'That'll do! I've got enough on my mind without you two spitting at each other like a pair of cats.'

After that Cathy avoided Mary even more, and it was made easier by the fact that she was rarely at home in the evenings. Sally was less vigilant than usual, partly because she was so worried about Emily and partly because she had two large mourning orders in quick succession. Mary took full advantage of the situation, with different young men calling for her nearly every night. Her usual routine was to have a hurried meal after she returned from work then to spend all her time in the bedroom, preparing to dazzle the latest conquest, and only appear when the young man called.

She would then bring him in and introduce him to her mother saying airily, 'We're just going for a walk — a breath of fresh air.' And the young man would be hustled out. By the time they reappeared Cathy was usually in bed, so she saw little of Mary. If their mother had been less worried and harassed she might have noticed that Cathy was avoiding her sister, and that she was miserable, but it was Lawrie who realised the state of things first. One night he brought Cathy some books and a bag of stickjaw toffee.

'Are you feeling a bit lonely, love?' he said gently. 'Missing Mary now she's out every night? Your turn will come soon, y'know, and our Mary will soon be outshone when you start on the lads.' He tweaked her hair playfully and Cathy blushed. He thinks I'm envying her, she thought in dismay.

'I just don't feel like going out, Dad,' she said. 'It's not that I'm missing Mary. She's always gone out a lot.'

'Yes, but you don't seem to be the good mates you used to be,' he said. 'That four years' difference, Cath. It didn't matter when you were both at school. Now she's a young lady and you're still a schoolgirl. But it'll change again soon. You'll both be young ladies and you'll have a lot to talk about again.'

Cathy was thunderstruck. Fancy Dad noticing how things are with us, yet Mary seems to think we're just the same and even Mam hasn't noticed anything wrong. She forced a smile.

'It's not that, Dad,' she said. 'It's just that Ellen and Josie have had to do jobs for their mams, and I felt like staying in anyway.' Her father nodded and picked up the books.

'I think you'll enjoy these, Cath. *Bleak House* by Mr Dickens and *East Lynne* by Mrs Henry Wood. You can never be lonely while you've got a book, I say. There's another world between them covers.'

Cathy felt a rush of affection for her father. She flung her arms around his neck and kissed him. He hugged her.

'Don't grow up *too* soon, will you, chicken?' he said, smiling. Nothing more was said, but afterwards Cathy made an effort to go out more and to appear more cheerful, although even to convince her father she found it impossible to warm towards Mary. Her friend Josie who lived across the road had been given a pair of roller skates by her sailor brother, and one evening Cathy and she were at Rupert Hill, taking turns to wear the skates or to be the one who ran along pulling the skater, when Mary suddenly appeared with a young man. She ignored the girls, turning her head towards the man who walked along with his arm around her waist.

Josie propped herself against the wall and stared after them.

'Gosh, Cath, I'll bet she didn't take *him* for your Mam to look at,' she said. 'He's real flashy, isn't he?' Cathy said nothing although she had to agree with Josie. The man *was* flashy. He wore a loudly checked suit and a low-crowned brown bowler hat with a curling brim. He flourished a cane in one hand while he gripped Mary round the waist with the other.

Cathy knew that Mary was supposed to be taking the ferry across the Mersey to Wallasey with Bella and Janie, but while she hesitated about saying this, Josie said critically, 'May Beddoes says *she* wouldn't take fellows home to be looked over the way your Mary does. She says your mam's making a laughing stock of your Mary *and* the lads.'

Cathy's anger flared immediately. 'Oh, does she?' she said. 'Well, you can tell her from me that chance would be a fine thing. She couldn't get the lads to go out with her, never mind get them to go to see her mam!'

'I suppose they're all jealous really,' Josie said soothingly, 'Your Mary's so pretty and she looks a real lady, doesn't she? I suppose your mam's bound to worry over her.'

'Mam says decent lads will respect Mary more because her parents watch over her,' Cathy said.

'I wonder will your mam make you take lads home when you start courting, Cath,' Josie said, but Cathy laughed.

'I'll have the same trouble as May Beddoes,' she said cheerfully. 'Chance'll be a fine thing.'

The time had come for her to leave school and although she looked forward to leaving the unpleasant Miss Mensor, she dreaded going among strangers to work.

'Would you like to go in the tailoring?' her mother asked her one day shortly before she left school. 'I've heard there's a job as messenger girl in Finestone's in Crown Street. You'd go on to be trained as a tailoress and you'd always have a trade in your fingers, love.'

'Oh, yes, I'd love it, Mam,' Cathy said eagerly. 'But will you come with me to ask for it?'

'Of course. It'd be a good berth if you could get it. The girls there are nice refined sorts and they're nearly all related. Once a girl gets a job there she speaks for her younger sisters or her cousins when they're old enough. I only heard of the job through my sewing.'

Mr Finestone proved to be a benign old man with a flowing white beard. He wore a black skull cap.

'You vill be a messenger girl, little von,' he said to Cathy. 'To you I vill pay three and sixpence a week and you vill be a goot girl and work hard, hein?'

Cathy nodded and her mother said sharply, 'Don't nod. Speak up, Catherine.'

The old man smiled. 'You are nervous, little von,' he said. 'But all vill be vell.'

He outlined Cathy's duties and she was glad that her mother was there to take in his words. She was overwhelmed by shyness and by the noise of the machines and the curious glances from the young men who sat cross-legged on benches, sewing rapidly.

When she started work the following Monday it was not the ordeal she expected. The girls were a pleasant harmonious group and they were all kind and helpful towards the shy little newcomer. The present messenger girl, Ada, took Cathy with her to deliver a suit to a doctor's house in Myrtle Street, then farther afield to deliver suits to two large houses near Princes Park.

'I'm just showing you the ropes,' Ada explained. 'I'll be going on the machines next week and you'll be doing this by yourself.'

'But what if I can't find the houses?' Cathy said in dismay. Ada reassured her.

'Don't worry. You'll see lots of other messenger girls when you're out and they'll tell you,' she said.

Cathy found that Ada was right, and made many friends among the girls who worked for other firms. They often exchanged details about their jobs, and frequently a girl left one firm and went to another that paid a little more, but Cathy was never tempted to leave Finestones. She was happy there from the first, and gradually she forgot her woes and resumed her cheerful, carefree outlook on life. She never forgot Mrs Malloy but she remembered only the happy times they had spent together.

Her mother was happier too. The bracing air of Scarborough and the careful nursing she received made such an improvement in Emily's health that it was decided that she would stay there until Christmas. Sally hoped that she would then return home fully restored to health.

As the winter drew on Mary was forced to spend more time indoors so that she entertained her admirers in the parlour, and Sally began to worry afresh about the number of different young men who appeared.

'I can't keep up with her,' she complained to Lawrie. 'I no sooner decide that I like a fellow than he's cast off and a different one appears. The only steady one is Sam Glover, and I'm ashamed of the way she treats him sometimes.'

'Never mind, love, there's safety in numbers,' Lawrie laughed.

'But you know what they are round here – God knows what they're saying about her,' Sally said anxiously. She looked so concerned as she stood rubbing her hand over the back of the chair that Lawrie stood up and put his arm around her.

'Now stop worrying, Sal,' he said. 'They're all respectable lads. You'll see, our Mary will soon pick one out and settle with him. She's just looking them over.'

'I hope you're right,' Sally said doubtfully.

'She just hasn't met the right one yet,' Lawrie said. 'It doesn't hit everyone like it hit us, you know, love. Like a flash of lightning.' The lines of worry on Sally's face became smooth as she smiled reminiscently.

'Aye, we knew from the first minute, didn't we?' she said. 'I hope it happens like that for Cathy. Our Mary will never break her heart over anyone, but you know what Cathy's like. I don't want her to get hurt.'

Lawrie gave a gusty sigh. 'Now, Sally love, I know you have to have *something* to worry about, but don't you think it's a bit soon to start about Cathy? And there's nothing to worry about where Mary's concerned either. Just be glad we've got two daughters ye can to be proud of.'

Sally shrugged and smiled.

'Mrs Mal was right,' she said. 'We make a good pair. One worrying too much and the other one not worrying at all. We balance each other out.'

Chapter Five

One of the friends that Cathy made from among the messenger girls was Rosie Johnson who worked for a milliner. Her mother was a Liverpool girl who had married a weaver and gone to live in Bolton, and after his death she returned to the haven of her family in Liverpool with Rosie and five younger children.

'I've got another sister,' Rosie told Cathy. 'Oor Clara. She's workin' in t'mill and she din't want to coom here. She's took up wi' Mrs Cooper and the Suffragists, y'see.'

'What are they?' asked Cathy.

'They want wimmin' to vote same as men. Oor Clara's teacher Miss Collinge telt them aboot it. It's a wonder as you knows nowt aboot it. Seliner Cooper were here in 1907 and Eleanor Rathbone from Liverpool were workin' wi' her, speakin' and gooin' round t'houses wi' leaflets.'

'I've heard of Miss Rathbone,' Cathy said 'My dad says she's a good woman. All the Rathbones do good.'

'Folk round here'll have to stir theirselves a bit more, oor Clara says. They're allus having meetin's in Bolton. Us'll have to stand together to get votes for wimmin.'

Rosie worked for a milliner and she could scarcely see over the huge boxes she carried. Suddenly the sight of her earnest face peeping round the boxes as she declaimed about women's suffrage was too much for Cathy and she leaned against the wall, laughing helplessly. Rosie was offended.

'What's up wi' yer? Got a feather in yer bloomers?' she said, trying to hurry away. Cathy caught her up.

'I'm sorry, Rosie, I shouldn't have laughed,' she said. 'It was just the idea of us holding a meeting laden down like this.'

Rosie was partly mollified but she said severely, 'It's nowt ter laugh at. Oor Clara lost her job along of gooin' ter meetings. She's a good worker though and her soon got on at another mill.' After that day Cathy often had discussions with Rosie when they met, and one night she mentioned them at home.

'Do *you* think women should vote, Dad?' she asked her father.

'Sometime, love,' he said. 'But there's more important things to be seen to first. Things are a bit better but there's still people dying of starvation, and thousands dying of consumption for want of better houses and food.'

'Now don't be filling her head with that, Lawrie,' her mother said, banging the iron down on the stand. 'Things are a lot better. You're just too impatient. Look at old Mr Tanner.'

He lived at the other end of the street. Since his wife had died and he had become too infirm to work he had been grudgingly given a home by his son and his shrewish wife. He had been constantly told that he was a burden and driven out from 'under her feet' by his daughter-in-law, and sometimes on cold days he had taken refuge in Sally's kitchen, often to be given a meal by her and have tobacco money slipped to him by Lawrie.

Now he proudly trotted down to the post office each week clutching his blue book, to draw his five shillings pension. 'God Bless Lloyd George,' he often said. 'I'm independent now. I keep a few coppers for me 'baccy and give her the rest and by gow she sings a different tune now.' Cathy thought that it was wonderful that five shillings, only a little more than she earned, could make all the difference between happiness and misery for the old man.

Cathy said eagerly, 'Rosie used to go to meetings with her sister sometimes. Miss Collinge and Mrs Cooper used to stand on a cart to speak and all the women had banners. Sometimes the men shouted things but Mrs Cooper always had an answer for them, Rosie said.'

'Now don't you get mixed up in that sort of thing, Cathy,' her mother said. 'That's no way for a woman to behave. Look round and see what wants doing, and do what's next to your hand. That's the right way for women to do things, not going about making a spectacle of themselves.'

Cathy said nothing. She was not convinced by her mother's argument although she had to admit that Sally practised what she preached. She thought of her mother's kindness to Lizzie Clark, and to old Mr Tanner, and the number of times she sat up with a sick child, or washed and cooked for a family where the mother was ill.

But that was all right for an old woman like her mother, she told herself. Her own generation should be fighting to make life better for everyone. Sally, who was not yet forty years old, would have been amazed and indignant if she'd known what was passing through her younger daughter's mind.

Cathy sometimes went to meetings with Rosie, but she was enjoying herself too much to have time for more serious matters. Josie and Ellen were now working in the matchworks, as the Bryant and May factory was known, and they had heard of a working girls' club which had been opened by the two sisters of a local clergyman. The girls learned various handicrafts and could play ping-pong, and every Saturday night a concert was given by the friends of the Misses Whitty.

Cathy was allowed to keep sixpence spending money from her wage of three and six, so in addition to the girls' club she could afford to go to the Roller Rink once a week. Sometimes she spent the evening in the Mellors' house opposite, among Josie's large and cheerful family, playing the piano and singing or playing noisy guessing games.

Mary sometimes complained to Cathy about the noise from Josie's house when she was entertaining one of her admirers, but Cathy's parents encouraged her to enjoy herself as much as possible, relieved to see that she had recovered her spirits.

'Our Cathy's her old self again,' Lawrie said to his wife one night. 'I got quite worried about her earlier in the year.'

'Yes, she took Mrs Mal's death to heart so much,' Sally said. 'Thank God she seems to have got over it a bit.' It was well for their peace of mind that they knew nothing about the real reason for Cathy's misery earlier in the year.

One of Sally's greatest worries had now been removed. Emily had stayed in Scarborough throughout the winter, and had returned home much improved in health in the spring of 1910.

With restored health and confidence, Emily was able to insist on changes at The Grange. Albert, shaken by the doctor's warnings and Emily's long absence from home, willingly agreed.

She took over the running of the house, so that the meals improved in quantity and variety, and they began to entertain in a modest way. Albert took a pew in the fashionable church of St Bonaventure and they attended church every Sunday and took part afterwards in the Church Parade along Princes Boulevard.

Emily still visited Sally on one day a week but on Sundays she entertained friends to afternoon tea. Mary was invited but she told Cathy that she found the church ladies very dull.

'Even Aunt Emily is different while those old "fades" are there,' she said. 'I had to sit there like a dummy listening to them prosing on and on and on. I'll make some excuse next time.'

Cathy was relieved to hear it. She knew there would be no wandering into the garden with Uncle Albert under the eagle eyes of the ladies, but she felt uneasy when Mary was near him.

By now the incident in the garden had faded enough in her memory for her to convince herself that Mary had been quite innocent and that their uncle had taken advantage of her. Gradually her old love and admiration for Mary had returned.

They had slipped back into the habit of exchanging confidences when they were in bed, and Mary told Cathy of the young men who told her that they loved her. But, she declared, she had no intention of marrying any of them.

'I like Hugh Desmond,' she said one night. 'His manners are beautiful and he's so handsome, but he's only a checker in a fruit warehouse.'

'But it's a *job*,' Cathy said. 'And if you really like him…' Mary shook her head. 'No, I'm not throwing myself away,' she said firmly. 'I'm not going to spend my life round here.' She sighed. 'It's so hard to meet anyone different, Cath. Sam Glover's going to be made a partner in his uncle's business when he's twenty-five, but he's so *gawky*. Anyway, I want to marry a real gentleman.'

She was sitting on the side of the bed brushing her hair, and Cathy thought that she had never looked more beautiful. The candle burning beside her cast shadows from her long eyelashes on to her cheeks and put stars in her eyes, and her curling red-gold hair crackled with life as she drew the brush through it.

'You could marry anyone. You're so pretty, Mary,' Cathy exclaimed impulsively. Her sister looked gratified for a moment then she pouted.

'How am I ever going to meet anyone?' she demanded. 'The men who come to Denby's are rich but they're always with their wives or the girls they are going to marry. I never see people like that outside work.' She flung down the hairbrush violently.

'Honestly, Cathy, I'd do anything, *anything* to get away from here.'

Cathy was silent, and suddenly shivered. 'I'm sure you'll meet someone, someday,' she whispered, plucking nervously at the sheet, and with a sudden change of mood Mary laughed and blew out the candle.

'Yes, riding up Low Hill on a white horse,' she said.

Cathy often thought that Mary was like a juggler in the skill with which she kept so many young men happy without committing herself to any of them. Even Sam Glover, whom she treated with a lack of consideration that brought protests from her mother, could always be charmed back if he showed signs of being driven too far.

One spring evening Cathy stood at the parlour window, pretending to adjust the satin ribbons which tied back the lace curtains while she peered down the street. She was hoping to see Mary approaching, yet feared that she might walk up to the house with another young man before she could be warned that Sam was inside.

He sat stiffly on a chair behind Cathy, glowering at the floor. A box of chocolates lay on his bony knees and his bowler hat was placed neatly beside him.

'A red sky, Sam,' Cathy said, smiling at him. 'It should be a good day tomorrow.' But there was no answering smile.

'Aye,' he said glumly, easing his scrawny neck inside his stiff high collar. He *is* a stick, Cathy thought. Mary's worth better than him. But nevertheless her soft heart was touched by his evident misery.

When she saw through the window that Mary was turning into the street, accompanied by a young man, she slipped out to intercept her. She grimaced at Mary and said quietly, 'There's someone in the parlour.'

Mary turned to smile graciously at the young man and hold out her hand. 'Thank you for seeing me home, Arthur.'

'But—but I thought I was coming to the house,' he stuttered.

She sighed and looked downcast. 'I'm afraid not. Mother's friends have called and are using the parlour, Cathy says.'

'But when can I see you? Can I wait outside the shop tomorrow night?' he said. Mary smiled and withdrew her hand from his clasp. 'Very well. Tomorrow then, dear,' she said, and glided away towards the house.

Cathy had been so lost in admiration at her sister's performance that Mary had almost reached the door before she remembered the rest of what she had to say. She hurried after her sister. 'Sam Glover's in the parlour,' she gasped. 'He's been there nearly an hour.'

'Drat,' Mary snapped, swiftly discarding her elegant air. 'I forgot all about him. I thought you meant Mam was on the warpath.'

'I think she is,' Cathy admitted, 'and Sam seems mad too.'

Mary tossed her head. 'I'm not worried about *him*,' she said scornfully. 'But I suppose I'll get a lecture a mile long from Mam.'

'She might be all right,' Cathy said. 'Dad went in just as I came out to warn you.'

When they went into the house they could hear their father's voice coming from the parlour. Mary swept in and kissed him.

'Hello, Dad,' she said, then she turned to Sam Glover, widening her eyes.

'*Sam!*' she said. 'But it's only Tuesday. I thought you were coming on Wednesday.'

His grim expression relaxed into a foolish smile.

'You said Tuesday, Mary, I'm sure you did,' he said.

'*Did* I? Oh dear, and I've been sitting in Murry's nearly dead with ennui, listening to Sadie going on and on, and you've been here all the time? You could have rescued me.'

She gave him a dazzling smile and her father moved unnoticed to the door. He almost collided with Cathy and they went into the kitchen together, trying to stifle their laughter. Sally looked up suspiciously as she lifted Lawrie's dinner from the oven.

'What's going on?' she demanded.

'She should be on the stage,' Lawrie chuckled. 'Mrs Siddons is nothing to her. Pretending she expected him tomorrow and the young fool believing her.'

'Well, she might talk him round, but she'll get the length of my tongue when he's gone,' Sally said. 'I'd go and sort her out now but I don't want to make a fool of that poor lad.'

Lawrie suddenly threw back his head and laughed aloud.

'The style of her,' he said. 'Saying she was half dead with ennui in Murry's. He didn't know what she was talking about.'

'It's all very well to laugh, Lawrie,' Sally said, 'but she's going too far with these airs and graces. "Jumping out of her latitude" as Da would say. It's those snobbish girls in Denby's teaching her these fancy words.'

'Ah, there's no harm in her,' Lawrie said, still laughing, 'I'll bet she's got him apologizing now for coming the wrong night.'

'Poor Sam,' Sally sighed, but then she caught Lawrie's eye and laughed. 'She'd think more of him if he gave her a clout' she added, and when Mary came a few minutes later to take a pack of cards from the dresser, she smiled at her fondly and promised to take supper into the parlour later.

Cathy agreed with her mother and had even urged Sam to stand up for himself more when she saw how meekly he endured snubs and offhand treatment.

'Mary likes strong men, Sam,' she had told him. 'Why don't you tell her you won't stand for it?'

'I daren't, Cath,' he said mournfully. 'She might make it an excuse to turn me off altogether.' Cathy looked at him drooping beside the door and felt that she could shake him, but she also felt that Mary was worthy of someone who was more of a man.

Mary seemed to grow ever more beautiful. She pressed powder leaves on her face and darkened her eyelashes with Vaseline but her beauty needed no adornment. She always dressed carefully to emphasise her fashionably tiny waist and large bust, and she walked as she had seen stylish ladies walk with her back straight and her head flung back.

Those who admired her beauty and her dainty refined air would have been surprised to learn that there was another side to Mary, a coarser side which enjoyed risqué stories and leading young men on to take liberties which she eventually indignantly repulsed but not until she had enjoyed all she could and stay safe.

The girls in the dress department at Denby's felt that they were superior to the girls in the workroom so there was little contact between them, but Mary usually spent some part of her brief break with the workroom girls.

Her excuse was that she was friendly with Janey Power from the workroom, but the real reason was that there was a group there who exchanged salacious stories about scandals in Society, and told dirty jokes, and Mary enjoyed listening to them.

Nevertheless, she was careful to preserve her reputation with the young men who admired her, and even those who thought she had been leading them on decided that she was too innocent to realise what she was doing and apologised abjectly when she became indignant. Mary would have willingly lost her virginity to ensure marriage with a rich and presentable man, but she was determined not to lose it for anything less.

Sally would have been horrified if she had realised how cynical her daughter had become about men, but Mary was intelligent as well as beautiful, and she had soon recognised the hypocrisy among the wealthy customers of Denby's. She knew that most of the men would have been willing to use her as a mistress if they could have done so without risk of offending their rich families or the wealthy girls they hoped to marry, but none of them would be prepared to offer marriage to her, no matter how much they admired her.

Sometimes when she compared the integrity of her parents, and their love and respect for each other with the people she saw at work, she felt doubtful about her wish to leave the life she had been born into and to become a 'lady' with a wealthy husband. But she soon stifled her doubts and cast about for ways of moving into a higher social class.

At night when they were in bed she often raged to Cathy about the lack of opportunities for meeting gentlemen.

'We don't even attend church,' she said, 'that's one place where you can meet men from a different class.' So Cathy was not surprised when a few weeks later Mary suggested that she should ask Aunt Emily if she could accompany her to church.

'I don't know, Mary,' her father said. 'We've always tried to live by Christian principles, but I haven't got much time for organised religion, you know. It divides people and stops working men getting together and demanding a better life for their families. Look at the riots in Liverpool last year. That Catholic archbishop – what's his name? Whiteside – insisting on carrying on with processions, and that other rabble rouser George Wise stirring up the Orangemen to attack them. It's all a far cry from what religion's supposed to be about.'

Mary was standing behind his chair, a long-suffering expression on her face. She said swiftly, 'There's nothing like that in Aunt Emily's church, Dad. They're all respectable people. All the girls at work go to church and they think I'm a heathen.'

Lawrie smiled.

'We can't have that, can we? Go ahead and ask Aunt Emily then, love.'

Later in bed Mary confided her plan to Cathy. 'It's my one chance of meeting someone different,' she said. 'And if I go with Aunt Emily and Uncle Albert, they'll accept me. But did you ever hear anything like that sermon from Dad. Going on and on about religion, as if that's got anything to do with it.'

Aunt Emily willingly agreed to take Mary to church with her, and the following Sunday she created a stir when she walked demurely down the aisle after her aunt, wearing a cream costume and a large hat trimmed with roses. After the service the vicar stood at the door, shaking hands with the congregation, and Mary was introduced to him. She continued to attend the church, and a few weeks later the vicar introduced her to a girl of her own age, Isabel Willard, who lived near to the church with her widowed mother.

Isabel's father had been a wholesale grocer, and her mother was the daughter of a solicitor. Although they were comparatively wealthy, the Willards lived quiet lives. Isabel spent her time gardening, changing her mother's library books and making items for the church bazaars. Mary, quiet and ladylike in appearance, seemed a suitable friend for Isabel and Mrs Willard encouraged the friendship.

Mary felt that it was a pity that the Willards had no young male relatives whom she could charm, but Isabel and her mother had a wide circle of friends and acquaintances among the church congregation, all belonging to the wealthy middle class. Mary was gradually introduced to most of these people and felt sure that soon she would meet a young man of the type she hoped to marry.

Chapter Six

Mary still spent some evenings with various young men but most of her precious free time was now spent with Isabel Willard, so the faithful Sam was finally discarded. He still hung about Egremont Street hoping for a glimpse of Mary, and several times he waylaid Cathy on her way home from work to ask her to intercede for him.

Fellow feeling made Cathy even more sympathetic towards him at this time, because she was suffering all the pangs of first love for Josie Mellor's brother Frank.

Josie was the youngest in a family of two girls and six sons. Her sister was married, but her unmarried brothers were either dockers or merchant seamen, except for Frank, six years older than Josie, who was in the Royal Navy.

Cathy had been looking out of the parlour window one day and had seen Frank swaggering up the street with his rolling seaman's gait, wearing bell bottom trousers, his cap set at a jaunty angle on his crisp fair curls. She thought he was the most romantic figure she had ever seen, and it was an effort for her to wait for a decent interval before, with beating heart, she had gone over, ostensibly to call for Josie.

Her friend had opened the door and pulled her inside the house.

'Our Frank's home,' she said breathlessly. 'He's been away for two years and he's telling us all about China and everything.' They went into the kitchen where Frank sprawled in a chair, watched adoringly by his mother. Other relations filled the room and Cathy and Josie slipped in quietly and stood by the kitchen dresser.

Frank looked round the cluttered kitchen, at the piles of magazines, shirts waiting for mending, socks for darning, and other miscellaneous objects which lay in untidy heaps on the dresser and side tables.

'Nothing's changed, Ma,' he said, then bent and whispered in her ear. She struck him playfully.

'Go way with yer!' she cried, wheezing with laughter. Cathy was too far away to hear the remark but she guessed what it was. Mrs Mellor started every day with her bulk confined in strong corsets but before long her craving for comfort won the day, and she retired to the lavatory in the yard to remove them. They were then hidden under one of the piles of clutter, until someone pulled out a magazine or a docker's hook and the corsets were exposed to view. 'Josie, hide me stays,' was a frequent cry from Mrs Mellor, and Cathy often wondered why they were not simply taken upstairs.

Now she realised that vast pink laces were dangling down the front of the dresser from the corsets which were only partly concealed by magazines. Quickly she bundled them up and thrust them back beneath the pile. As she turned back to the room she caught Frank's eye and he flung back his head and laughed, his teeth flashing white against his tanned face. Cathy felt as though her heart fluttered as she looked at him.

'You haven't changed either, Ma.' Frank said. 'But our Josie's grown up, and who's this?'

'Cathy Ward from over the road,' Josie said, and Frank stood up and came over to them, bending his knees to look into Cathy's face.

'Cathy Ward,' he said. 'Who'd have thought it? That skinny little girl growing into a beauty like this.' Cathy smiled at him in delight and he added softly, 'Dimples an' all.'

'You should see their Mary,' Josie said, but Mrs Mellor, usually so lethargic, said swiftly and sharply, 'Never mind Mary. It's Cathy 'e's talking about.' Before anyone else could speak she went on, 'You'll have to go and see *our* Mary, Frank. She'll be confined in a few days and she's not a bit well.'

His face darkened. 'She's still with that swine then?' he said, but one of his aunts brought him a glass of ale.

'Here, get that down yer, lad,' she said. 'You don't want to be worrying about nothing your first day home.' There was a noise in the lobby and several of his brothers erupted into the room to shake Frank's hand and thump his back. There was scarcely room to move in the kitchen and when the women began to discuss preparations for a meal, Cathy slipped away, but not before she had feasted her eyes on Frank for a final few minutes.

Later in the day Josie came over to tell Cathy that a party had been arranged for the evening and she was invited.

'Can I go, Mam?' Cathy said eagerly, her eyes shining. Her mother nodded. 'Yes, as long as you're not too late home,' she said.

'It's only across the road and it's Sunday tomorrow,' Cathy said.

Josie had sped away and Mary said angrily, 'Anything's an excuse for a party with that family. I'm going out with Hugh tonight and I suppose when we come back we'll be deafened with the noise from over there. Shouting and singing and playing the piano and that melodeon. He'll think I live in a slum.'

'It's a pity about him, and you too,' Cathy flashed. 'Mellors are as good as he is, any day.'

'Don't be so hardfaced. You should be trying to raise yourself, not mixing with people like them, roughnecks with no consideration for their neighbours.'

'They can do what they like in their own home,' Cathy began, but her mother banged on the table. 'That's enough! I don't want to hear another word. You've both got jobs to do before either of you stir out of this house. Mary, you clear the table and wash the dishes, and you, Cathy, take the basting threads out of that skirt and tack the side of that blouse, then dry the dishes.' She followed Mary into the scullery and said in a low voice, 'And don't let me hear you speak about the neighbours like that again. You're getting too big for your boots, milady.'

Mary had prepared for the evening and gone off to the theatre escorted by Hugh Desmond before Cathy went upstairs to wash and change for the party. When she was dressed she took one of Mary's powder leaves from their hiding place and pressed it on her face as she had seen Mary do. It seemed to make little difference to her skin, but Vaseline stroked on her eyelashes and eyebrows did seem to make them shine.

There were no men in the Mellors' when she went across but the kitchen was full of women, neighbours and the girlfriends of the Mellor sons. Josie called Cathy into the scullery.

'Come and help me with the sandwiches,' she said. 'The "do" doesn't really start until the fellers come back from the pub.'

'Has Frank gone to the pub?' asked Cathy.

'Yes, he went to our Mary's with me ma,' Josie said, 'then he followed the others down to Gregson's Well. He brought me ma back first.'

'He's a good son, isn't he?' Cathy said eagerly. Josie laughed. 'Yes, me ma's made up with him. He brought her that shawl.' Cathy peeped into the kitchen to where Mrs Mellor sat, proudly draped in a brightly coloured shawl. The girl felt reassured by this proof of Frank's good nature.

'Fancy him saying that about you, Cath,' Josie went on. 'He seemed to take a proper shine to you, didn't he?' Cathy felt like dancing a jig on the scullery floor. To hear Josie's words and to know that soon Frank would return and she would be in his company for hours made her feel wildly excited, and she cut and buttered the bread at such a speed that Josie protested. 'Hold on. We're not feeding the five thousand, y'know.'

It was about an hour and a half later that the vanguard of the male guests arrived carrying bottles and jugs of ale and closely followed by others similarly laden. The house seemed to come alive, but for Cathy the party really began when Frank and two of his brothers came through to the scullery.

'Sandwiches!' he exclaimed. 'God, I'm starving. You've saved my life.' He hugged Cathy with one arm while with the other he reached for some sandwiches, and her eyes shone with delight.

All the younger people moved into the parlour, leaving older neighbours sitting round the kitchen fire with Mrs Mellor, and the man with the melodeon played some sprightly music. A glass of ale was thrust into Cathy's hand and she sipped it, but the bitter taste made her screw up her mouth and at the first opportunity she slipped the glass among others on the top of the piano. Her eyes rarely left Frank. When the melodeon player paused for a rest and someone began to play the piano, she found herself standing by Frank with his arm around her shoulders.

He hugged her tightly, and when the piano player struck up 'Drink to me only with thine eyes' Frank bent to look into Cathy's face as he sang, then kissed her cheek as the song finished. She blushed as everyone laughed and there was more laughter when one of the brothers sang a song about Cupid's Dart and added, 'Like the one Cathy's fired at our Frank.' It was all exciting and wonderful and Cathy felt that she loved everyone there. It seemed no time at all before Mr Mellor drew her out into the lobby.

'It's twelve o'clock, girl,' he said. 'I promised your da I'd bring you home by twelve.'

'Twelve o'clock,' Cathy said in amazement. 'I thought it was about nine.'

'No, it's twelve o'clock,' he repeated. He was a quiet man, a cooper by trade, and Cathy always felt at home with him so she said resentfully, 'What's Frank going to think, seeing me having to go home like a child?'

'Our Frank and every man John of them won't know who's there and who isn't before long. That's 100 per cent proof rum our Frankie brought home. No, girl, you've seen the best of it and your da's right to fetch you home. I'm sending our Josie to bed when I get back.'

He accompanied her over the road and her father opened the door. 'Thanks, Billy,' he said, then to Cathy, 'Had a good time, love?'

'Oh yes, Dad,' she said fervently.

'That's good,' he said leading the way into the kitchen. 'Your mam and Mary are in bed. Do you want a cup of cocoa?'

'No thanks,' Cathy said quickly. It seemed like sacrilege to think of anything as mundane as cocoa on this enchanted evening, and she floated upstairs to bed as though on wings.

On Sunday morning Cathy volunteered to dust the parlour so that she could watch the Mellors' house for any sign of Frank, but no one emerged. Billy's girlfriend, then a little later Johnny's girlfriend and another girl went into the house, and Cathy was just debating whether she dared go over when Josie ran across the street. Cathy flew to meet her.

'Can me mam have a bit of your dad's mint?' Josie asked. 'She got a leg of lamb for the dinner and forgot the mint.'

'I'll ask him to cut some then I'll bring it over,' Cathy said eagerly. 'It was good last night, wasn't it?'

'Yes, but it got a bit rough later on after you'd gone. And the state of the parlour this morning! They've all got bad heads today.'

'Your Frank as well?' Cathy said doubtfully.

'Yes, but mind you he helped me to clear up the parlour. I'd better get back,' Josie said.

'I'll bring the mint over in a minute,' Cathy promised, and went in humming happily to ask her father for the mint. Lawrie had taken up a few flags in the backyard and put down soil where he grew herbs and a few flowers and was delighted to cut the mint for Mrs Mellor. Cathy dashed across the street with it but was disappointed to find only women in the house. She could only surmise that she had missed seeing Frank go out while she was in the yard.

'Where are the fellers?' she whispered to Josie.

'They've gone for a hair of the dog,' her friend said and when Cathy looked blankly at her she explained: 'They've gone to have another drink to cure their bad heads. A hair of the dog that bit them, they call it.'

Cathy went home for her dinner, but later in the afternoon when she thought that Frank would have returned and had his dinner, she went to the Mellors' house again. Frank greeted her cheerfully but made no attempt to single her out. Cathy had to be content merely with gazing at him and listening to the sound of his voice.

The conversation was general so she was surprised when Bella, Johnny's girlfriend, suddenly said sharply, 'It's a wonder your Mary hasn't come over here, Cathy.'

'Why? Our Mary doesn't come here. I mean, I come to see Josie but there's no one here Mary's age,' Cathy said, bewildered.

'I know but I thought she might have come today, like,' Bella sniggered, and Cathy suddenly realised that she was being spiteful. She threw back her head and looked angrily at the girl. 'Mary has gone to tea with her friend, Isabel Willard, in Aigburth,' she said coldly.

'Oh Jeez, Isabel! That's my name – Isabella,' Bella cackled. 'Youse'll all have to call me Isabel from now on.'

Cathy's face flamed and she was about to make an angry retort when Frank created a diversion, 'Are your mam and dad in, Cathy?' he asked. 'I'd like to see them before I go back.'

She nodded, and he stood up and took her arm. 'Won't be long, Ma,' he said, shepherding Cathy before him down the lobby. He gave her a swift kiss before they stepped into the street, but Cathy was too agitated to appreciate it. 'Don't take any notice of Bella,' he said. 'I think she lives on green apples.'

'They're just jealous of Mary because she's pretty,' Cathy burst out. 'And because she looks like a lady.' Frank squeezed her arm.

'I'll bet you have plenty of that to put up with too,' he said, so Cathy went into her house smiling. Frank was warmly welcomed by her mother and father, and Cathy sat entranced, listening to him talking about his visits to foreign ports, and discussing events in Liverpool with her father, until he glanced at the clock and jumped to his feet.

'I'd better get back,' he said. 'I'll be on long leave in a couple of weeks so I'll see you then.'

Cathy would have gone back with him to the Mellors' but her mother signed to her to stay. Frank shook hands with her parents then bent and kissed Cathy's cheek.

'I can't get over it,' he said to her father, 'her and Josie were kids when I went away and here they are, grown-up young ladies.'

'Yes, she's a working woman now, aren't you, Cath?' her father laughed. 'Keeping the house.' Cathy raged inwardly at his bantering tone. As though I'm a child, she thought. But she managed to smile at Frank, and he waved cheerfully before crossing the street.

'I gave you the wire not to go with him,' Sally said, 'because his mam and dad will want him to themselves seeing he's got to go at eight o'clock. Hardly worth coming home for such a short time, but I suppose his mam will think it was long enough to see him at least.' And it was long enough for me to fall in love, Cathy thought, hugging the thought of Frank to her.

Later, when he was leaving, the crowd around him almost filling the pavement, Cathy went out and stood at the gate to watch.

As Frank extricated himself from the hugs and kisses of his relations, he looked over and saw her.

'Ta ra, Cathy,' he shouted, and blew her a kiss before moving off escorted by his brothers. Josie joined Cathy at the gate.

'Are you coming out?' she asked. 'There'll be nothing but whingeing in our house, or else a row. Me ma kept saying our Frank was the best of the bunch, and the others were getting narked. Bella had a face on her like a wet Monday.'

'That's nothing new,' Cathy replied. 'Even Frank said she lived on green apples, and the cheek of her making out our Mary would go to your house because Frank was home! She doesn't need to chase after a feller like Bella chases Johnny. I was going to tell her that when Frank said he wanted to see my mam and dad.'

'I know,' Josie giggled. 'Me ma said to Bella when you went out, "Frank saved you from a mouthful there, girl. Cathy'd scratch anyone's eyes out for calling their Mary."'

'What harm has Mary ever done to her anyhow?' Cathy demanded. But she was too anxious to talk about Frank to spend any more time discussing Bella.

Cathy said nothing at home about Bella's remarks, although she often thought of them when Mary talked about Isabel Willard. The family were having a meal one evening and Mary was talking about Isabel when Sally suddenly said that she must bring her home to tea. Mary was dismayed.

'Why, Mam, there's no need,' she said.

'Yes, there is,' Sally said firmly. 'You've been there so often that you must return it.'

'But I go there because it's near the church,' Mary said. 'I'll ask Aunt Emily to invite her if you like.'

'*This* is your home, Mary,' her mother said. 'I'll write to Mrs Willard and ask if Isabel can come to tea next Sunday.' Mary flung herself back in her chair, pouting.

'I'm always welcome there. There's no need to return it,' she said. 'And Isabel might feel out of place here.'

'Are you ashamed of your home, Mary?' her mother demanded.

'Of course not,' the girl muttered. 'I don't know why you want to ask her, that's all.'

'Because I want to know who you're with, for one thing. I'm sure they're very nice people, but they could be white slavers for all I've seen. Anyway this will put things on a proper footing.' Mary still looked sulky but after the meal her mother calmly took out a pen and a bottle of ink and wrote to Mrs Willard.

A few days later a reply came accepting the invitation. Mary surveyed the parlour and kitchen critically, trying to see them as they would appear to Isabel. She then turned her attention to her parents and Cathy.

'Father will wear a stiff collar and tie, won't he, Mother?' she said. 'What will you wear?'

'Don't worry, Mary, we won't disgrace you,' her mother said quietly. 'If Isabel is the nice girl you say she is, she'll appreciate that you've got a good respectable home, and things will be on an honest footing between you.'

'I haven't told any lies,' Mary flared, but later she confided to Cathy that she was worried about the visit.

'I didn't say anything that wasn't true,' she said, 'but Isabel might expect us to be a better class than we are.'

'Mam and Dad are as good as anybody,' Cathy said indignantly.

'I know,' Mary said impatiently. 'And why do you keep saying Mam and Dad? Why can't you say Mother and Father?'

'Why should I? We said Mama and Dada when we were little, and now we say Mam and Dad. What's wrong with that?'

'It's not elegant,' Mary said. 'You should be trying to better yourself too.' But Cathy only laughed.

The following night, when Lawrie was alone with Mary, he said jokingly, 'I believe I'm under instructions to wear a stiff collar on Sunday for your fashionable visitor.' Mary smiled. 'Will you, Dad?' she said coaxingly. 'I want Isabel to get a good impression. She's so elegant.'

'Aye, but be careful,' he said, nodding towards the back kitchen where Sally was working. 'Don't hurt your mam's feelings, making out the house isn't posh enough.'

Mary blushed. Under the veneer of a fashionable young lady, there was still a loving daughter, and now she slipped her arm around her father's neck.

'Oh, Dad, don't think I'm not proud of both of you, and I do appreciate my home, but I want to make nice friends and I want to get on.'

'No harm in that, love, and it's what me and your mam want for you too, as long as you don't get too ambitious. Don't feel you'll do *anything* to get on, Mary. Keep your principles.'

She turned away quickly and opened the dresser drawer, pretending to search for something, keeping her face averted from her father.

The two girls willingly worked hard to help their mother make the house look its best for Sunday, and Sally spent hours baking cakes and preparing the food for tea.

On Sunday they were all dressed in their best, and Mary's worries vanished when the preparations were complete. Sally wore a dark blue dress with a small embroidered apron over the full skirt, and a cameo brooch at her throat. Mary thought her father looked distinguished in his suit with braided lapels and a wing collar and full silk tie. Cathy wore a brown dress with a lace collar, and a brown petersham ribbon tied back her curls. Mary felt proud of all the family and satisfied with her own navy blue costume and large hat trimmed with marguerites. She met Isabel at the tram stop and they walked up the hill to Egremont Street, with Mary hoping that most of her neighbours were indoors.

Isabel was a tall thin girl, with dark eyes and a pale face. She was a complete contrast to pretty, vivacious Mary, but her air of quiet dignity was very attractive and Sally and Lawrie liked her immediately. She was evidently shy so Cathy soon conquered her own shyness in helping to put Isabel at ease.

A fire had been lit in the parlour, and they sat there chatting before going into the kitchen for their tea. When they went into the kitchen Lawrie drew Isabel over to the fireplace to see a wounded bird he was tending. It lay in a box beside the grate with its injured wing in a splint.

'Oh, poor thing,' Isabel exclaimed. 'Will it live?'

'It'll be as right as ninepence in a few days,' Lawrie said cheerfully. 'It's not the first I've fixed up, but I've got to keep it in here away from cats.' The bird was a safe topic for the first few moments when they sat down at the table, and helped Isabel to overcome her nervousness.

The table looked a picture, covered with a stiffly starched damask cloth and adorned with trailing ivy leaves. There was a baked ham stuck with cloves, and small glass dishes of Sally's pickles and chutneys. A glass picked up at the market for a few pence held celery, and there was trifle in a cut-glass dish given to Mrs Malloy by her employer and passed on to Sally. She had made damson tarts, sponge cakes and madelines, and a large fruit cake, but Isabel seemed to enjoy most the crusty bread and butter.

'This bread is delicious, Mrs Ward,' she said. 'Such a lovely nutty flavour.' Sally was pleased although she looked ruefully at all her more elaborate baking. She told Isabel of her efforts to make bread after her mother died, when she omitted to put the dough to rise, so that it rose in the oven and filled it, even running out and down the grate, and how she had fled in panic to Mrs Malloy who lived next door. This led to talk of Mrs Mal and Isabel endeared herself to Cathy by saying gently, 'She seems to have been a unique character, and Mary has told me how kind you all were to her.' Fortunately Cathy was unaware of Mary's portrayal of Mrs Malloy as a poor woman graciously befriended by the Ward family.

When it was time for church Lawrie walked down to the tram with Isabel and Mary, and when he returned home Cathy and her mother had cleared away the feast.

'That's a nice girl,' he said. 'I'm pleased to see our Mary with a friend like that.'

'She is,' Sally agreed. 'A nice ladylike girl. Fancy her liking my bread best, and the time and money I spent on the other stuff.'

'It won't go to waste, I can promise you, girl,' Lawrie laughed. Mary was delighted with the success of the visit, and she admitted to her mother it had been wise to arrange it.

'Isabel told me her mother was very pleased about the invitation, because she didn't know whether she should let Isabel become so friendly with me when she knew nothing about my background except that I was related to Aunt Emily and Uncle Albert. Isabel said her mother worries because she's a widow and has to make all the decisions.'

Sally was pleased to receive a letter of thanks from Isabel, and proud that Mary was accepted by such superior people. It was with some difficulty she refrained from saying, 'I told you so' to her daughter.

Chapter Seven

Cathy eagerly watched the post for a few days hoping for a letter from Frank, but none arrived. She tried to pick up crumbs of information from the Mellors, but the excitement of Frank's leave had been quickly forgotten in their concern for Josie's older sister, Mary, and the baby she expected.

Cathy came home from work one evening to find that her mother had gone with Mrs Mellor to help with her daughter, who had started in labour. She had not returned when Cathy went to bed, but the next morning when she came downstairs she found the fire burning brightly, and her mother cooking breakfast. Sally was pale but otherwise showed no sign of having been up all night.

'Is the baby born, Mam?' Cathy asked.

'No,' her mother said briefly. 'I'm going back there, but I'll put a hotpot in the oven first.'

As soon as Cathy entered the house that evening, she heard the sound of loud sobbing. She saw Mrs Mellor sitting by the kitchen fire with Sally beside her, holding her hand.

Mrs Mellor was wailing, 'Oh, me poor girl, me poor girl,' and Cathy retreated into the parlour, wondering what had happened to Mary Mellor. She was uncertain what to do. It seemed heartless to think of food, yet the savoury smell of hotpot filled the house and Cathy realised that she was ferociously hungry. Also, she needed to visit the lavatory. It would mean going through the kitchen but finally she could wait no longer. She crept through the room. Her mother looked up and Cathy indicated in dumb show where she was going.

When she returned to the scullery and was washing her hands, her mother Came in with the dish of hotpot and served a plateful for Cathy.

'Eat this out here,' she whispered. 'Mrs Mellor's upset.'

Cathy could see Josie's mother through the open doorway, sipping a cup of tea, her face blotched and swollen with crying. She whispered to her mother, 'Is Mary—?' but Sally shook her head.

'Mary's all right,' she said quietly, 'but the baby was born dead,' She went back into the kitchen, closing the door behind her, but as Cathy ate the hotpot she could hear Mrs Mellor's voice raised in anger.

'Not an inch of her poor body not covered in bruises, and yet not a mark on her face, the crafty swine! God stiffen that magistrate that made her go back to him,' she cried. 'It was him killed that baby. The mark of his hobnails was on her stummick.'

Cathy heard her mother say soothingly, 'I know, I know, she'll have to leave him. I know you'd keep her if she came home.'

'How can she?' Mrs Mellor sobbed. 'Look what happened last year when she come home. The sod got the law on her – said she was took away by us and he missed her an' all that, and that friggin' magistrate put that paper on her, jug something.'

'Restitution of conjugal rights,' Sally said. 'But surely now she can go back to the court and tell them what happened?'

'It's no use,' Mrs Mellor wailed. 'He's got that parson feller on his side that visited him in jail. We wouldn't know where to start.'

Cathy remembered the scenes over a year earlier when Mary Mellor had left her husband and come home to her family. The husband, Charlie Jenkins, had arrived at the Mellors' after drinking all evening, and tried to kick in the front door then broken the windows. The sound of breaking glass had brought Stoney White, the policeman on the beat, and Charlie had been arrested and jailed for four months. Cathy recalled being told by Josie that other prisoners had told him how to get his own back on Mary, and he had asked for a prison visitor and told him a pathetic tale. Josie had told Cathy how angry and helpless the family had felt when the prison visitor had gone to court with Charlie to speak for him and Mary had been forced to return to her brutal husband.

Now she could hear Mrs Mellor's voice raised again.

'I'm not going to let our Josie get married,' she was saying. 'She can live "tally". Once a feller pays seven and six for the marriage lines he owns a girl, body and soul. He can do what he friggin' likes with her and no one can do nothing.'

Cathy opened the door into the kitchen and peeped in. Mrs Mellor was sitting, rocking back and forth with her hands over her face, and Sally was pouring out tea. She pushed a fresh cup towards Mrs Mellor and gestured to Cathy to come into the kitchen and take some for herself.

Mrs Mellor looked up and noticed Cathy. She lifted her apron and wiped her face.

'You've got your family coming in from work,' she said. 'I'll get back home.'

'Will you be all right?' Sally asked. 'Try not to upset yourself. We'll think of something.'

Mrs Mellor lumbered to her feet and went home. Sally sank down into the chair she had vacated and sat looking into the fire, her hand covering her mouth. Presently tears began to slide down her face. Cathy went to her and put her arm around her shoulders.

'What's the matter, Mam? Is Mary going to die?' she asked, but Sally shook her head.

'No, but that poor girl! She kept it all to herself so her mam wouldn't be upset. She had such a bad time, too, because the poor baby was already dead.' Cathy realised how upset her mother was by the way she spoke so freely to her when usually she was so reticent with her daughters on the subject of childbirth. She hugged her mother, wondering how to console her.

A few minutes later she was relieved to hear her father's step in the lobby. He stopped in alarm at the sight of Cathy with her arm around Sally's shoulders, and his face paled.

'Mary?' he said hoarsely, but Sally said quickly: 'Oh no, thank God. Trouble at Mellors'.' She told him the sad tale, adding in a low voice, 'I kept thinking, it could have been our Mary or Cathy.'

'Put that out of your head, love,' he said, and Sally got up and took out the hotpot again from the oven.

Lawrie was silent but seemed to be thinking deeply as he ate his meal. Finally he asked Sally if a doctor had been called to Mary.

'Yes, but he was in a hurry,' Sally said. 'He looked at the baby and told Mrs Mellor she could arrange to have it buried, and he told us to give Mary some black medicine and put the foot of the bed up on bricks.'

'Did he see the bruises?' Lawrie asked. Sally shook her head. 'He was in a hurry,' she repeated, 'and I think Mary was ashamed, poor girl.'

'Listen, Sal, it's important that he should see the bruises,' Lawrie said. 'Tell him the circumstances and ask if he'll testify. If the Mellors could get hold of that parson who spoke for Charlie Jenkins, and tell him the doctor would give evidence, I'm sure that order could be cancelled and Mary could get a legal separation from that swine.'

Sally cheered up immediately. 'I'll tell them when I go over,' she said. 'It'll do Mary the world of good to hear that. I'm going back there with Mrs Mellor as soon as she's seen to the family, and we'll probably stay the night, Lol.'

'Will you be all right? What if Charlie cuts up rough?'

Sally said grimly, 'Don't worry. We'll be ready for him. He's been missing all day and is probably legless with drink now. Mary's terrified of him coming home; that's why we're going to stay with her. Me and Sophie Mellor will be able for him, don't worry. I'll tell him the coppers are looking for him.'

'I think I'd better come with you,' Lawrie said, but Sally firmly vetoed the idea.

The kitchen of the Mellors' house was full of people when she went across, and she felt proud to tell them of Lawrie's idea. The sons looked at each other and agreed that it was a good idea, but without much enthusiasm, and even Mrs Mellor only said vaguely, 'Mr Ward's got a good head on him.'

They found Mary asleep and the neighbour who was sitting with her said that she had been since taking the doctor's medicine. 'Prob'ly some kind of knock-out drops,' she said.

'Has *he* been home?' Sally asked, but the neighbour said that nobody had seen Charlie Jenkins. Mary slept on, and Sally and Mrs Mellor dozed or chatted beside her as the long night passed. Dawn was breaking when there was a loud knock on the door. Mary woke instantly, but Sally said quickly, 'It's all right, love. Your mam and I will see to it.'

She went downstairs, closely followed by Mrs Mellor. It was not Charlie on the step but a policeman.

'Name of Jenkins?' he said.

'Mrs Jenkins is in bed,' Sally said quickly. 'She had a stillborn baby yesterday. This is her mother.'

'I'm sorry, missis,' the policeman said to Mrs Mellor. 'I've got more bad news for you. Charles Jenkins has had an accident. He's in the Infirmary.'

'An accident,' Mrs Mellor quavered. 'What kind of an accident?'

'He was found laying in the road in Shaw Street and it looks as if a wagon wheel went over him. He was very drunk, missis, but maybe he was drowning his sorrows like.'

'Is he badly hurt?' Sally asked, and the man shrugged.

'He won't work for a while,' he said. 'His ribs is broke and the wheel must 'a gone over the top of his legs, like, his private parts. He's very badly bruised but no broken limbs, and his face is in a mess. He might've been trod on by a horse's hoof – he could'a been laying there for a while, y'see.'

'Did he have his wages on him?' Mrs Mellor asked.

'Not a ha'penny,' the policeman said sympathetically. 'Always the way, Ma. Troubles never come singly.'

Mary could be heard calling weakly and her mother went back upstairs. After telling Sally the hospital visiting hours, the policeman left.

Sally was surprised to see Mary and her mother smiling when she returned to the bedroom.

'How do you feel, love?' she asked Mary.

'Much better after what me mam's told me.'

'It'll solve your problem for a while, love,' Sally said. 'But I think you should have the doctor again. Did your mam tell you what Lawrie said about a legal separation?'

'Doesn't matter now,' Mrs Mellor said. 'God helps them that helps themselves. Our lads have learned him.'

'You mean – it wasn't a wagon wheel?' Sally gasped.

'More like a steam roller,' Mrs Mellor laughed. 'I told the lads what had been going on, and they went looking for him. Me heart stopped when I seen the policeman, but then he said about the wagon wheel and the horse stepping on him.' She sat down on the bed, her huge stomach shaking as she wheezed and gasped with laughter. 'I could hardly keep me face straight when he said about his – private parts, but I asked about his wages in case they had second thoughts.'

'That was crafty, Mam,' Mary said admiringly. 'If they change their minds about the wheel they'll think he got knocked about and robbed.'

'Aye, well, it's a pity they didn't fix him the last time,' Mrs Mellor said. 'But this'll cure him anyroad.'

Sally sat in silent amazement. To think that Mrs Mellor had kept that to herself all evening and then thought so quickly when confronted by the policeman. She stood up and said quietly, 'I'll get back home then, as long as you're all right now.'

'Thanks for what you've done. You're a good neighbour,' Mrs Mellor said gratefully.

Cathy had tried to tell Mary about Mary Mellor when they were in the bedroom, but Mary had covered her ears and refused to listen.

'Don't tell me, don't tell me,' she said. 'I don't want to know.' Cathy told her about Mrs Mellor's remark that she would make Josie live 'tally' rather than marry, and Mary laughed scornfully. 'Yes, and if she did live "tally" her mother'd be the first to make a song and dance about it. I don't know why you bother with them, Cathy, people like that.'

Cathy said nothing, but she wondered what Mary would say if she found herself related to the Mellors through her sister's marriage to Frank. Not that it seemed very likely, Cathy admitted to herself ruefully. She had been with Josie to see a melodrama at the Star Theatre and they had decided that the leading man looked like Frank. Josie had written to tell him so, and he had sent her a postcard, promising to take her and 'her friend Cathy' to the Star when he came on leave. Evidently that was how Frank thought of her, Cathy reflected sadly, simply as Josie's friend, in spite of his remarks about her beauty.

Mrs Mellor asked Sally to enquire at the Infirmary about Charlie Jenkins.

'I don't give a bugger what's happening to him,' she said. 'But I just want to make sure they still think he was run over by a wagon. You look so respectable, you see, Sally.'

Sally was unwilling to become involved but she could think of no excuse to refuse, so she went to the Infirmary on the next visiting day. The Ward Sister told her that Jenkins was a troublesome patient.

'What exactly is wrong, please?' Sally asked meekly.

'Extensive bruising, cracked ribs and possibly some damage to his kidneys,' the Sister said. 'Also his jawbone has been fractured and some teeth are missing, but it is entirely his own fault.'

'In what way, Sister?' Sally asked.

'He was found lying helplessly drunk in the roadway where heavy wagons passed on the way to the docks,' the Sister said severely. 'He's foul-mouthed to my nurses and impertinent to me, and I won't keep him on my ward unless he behaves himself. Are you Mrs Jenkins?'

'No, indeed I'm not,' Sally exclaimed. 'I'm just a neighbour. Mrs Jenkins had a stillborn baby yesterday and she asked me to enquire.'

'Really, these women,' the Sister said in disgust. 'Still concerned about a man like that.'

For form's sake Sally went to the bedside, but when she saw Charlie Jenkins' battered face she could understand why the police thought he had been stepped on by a horse. He opened his eyes and snarled 'Sod off' through puffed lips, so she left feeling that the Mellors' rough justice was justified.

The next day the Mellors hired a carriage to drive to the ceme-tery. Sally sat with the tiny coffin on her knee, facing one of the Mellor sons who was not working and Lawrie who was on late shift. There was much sympathy for the Mellors among the neighbours and groups of them gathered to watch the carriage pass. Among them Sally could see Mrs Kilgannon's scarecrow figure, wearing her usual sacking apron and a man's cap pinned crookedly on her untidy grey hair.

Mrs Kilgannon had failed mentally and physically since her lodger's death some months earlier, and there was now an uneasy truce between her and the Ward family. Sally lit her fire and made her meals on the days when her daughter Nellie was unable to visit her, but her dislike for the malevolent old woman made it an unpleasant duty and she longed for the day when Nelly could persuade her mother to live with her.

As it was Saturday Cathy was home from work at four o'clock and her mother told her about the funeral.

'Didn't you feel awful though, Mam, with the coffin on your knee?' she asked with a shudder.

Sally shrugged. 'It had to be done, and it was the Mellors' way of showing appreciation to me,' she said. But her calmness deserted her when Mary arrived home a few hours later in a furious temper.

'D'you know what that creature next door is saying?' she yelled, pounding her fists on the back of the chair. 'That woman in the end house told me that Killy was telling everyone that *I'd* had a stillborn baby and it was buried in the same coffin as the Mellor baby. There was a gang of them sniggering there, pretending to laugh it off and eyeing me up and down.' She burst into angry tears. 'I'm getting away from here. I don't care where or how or anything!'

Cathy and Sally tried to console her, then Sally stormed out of the house and into Kilgannon's. Through the wall they could hear her voice raised in anger and loud cries from Mrs Kilgannon, then Nellie's voice.

Sally came rushing back into the house. 'I'll swing for that woman,' she cried. 'Nellie says it's old age, but she's always been a bitch.'

Mary had become calmer, and said scornfully, 'I don't know why we upset ourselves about them. They're all the same round here, the scum of the earth.'

'That's not true, Mary,' her mother said quickly. 'We've got some good neighbours in this street, but I've always detested that one next door.' Mary tossed her head. 'I'd better get my tea and get ready,' she said. 'Hugh will be here soon. We're going to the Empire.'

Nothing more was said about Mrs Kilgannon but after Mary had left with her escort Sally stopped Cathy as she was preparing to go out.

'Has our Mary said anything to you about leaving here?' she said. 'Do you know what she meant about getting away?'

'No, only that she wants to marry a rich man,' Cathy said.

'Oh, that,' Sally snorted. 'That's empty talk, but she hasn't said anything about going into service or getting a job on the liners or anything?'

'No, she just gets fed up with the jangling about her,' Cathy said.

Her mother sighed. 'I never know where I am with her,' she said. 'I thought she'd be more settled after getting pally with Isabel Willard, but it seems to have made her worse.'

'I wouldn't worry, Mam,' Cathy said, wondering how her mother could imagine Mary going into service. Mary saw herself as a mistress, not a maid, Cathy knew.

Her mother sighed. 'I'm all on edge,' she admitted. 'I'll be glad to get to bed and put this day behind me.' But there was no peace for Sally even then. They were all peacefully asleep when they were awakened by a commotion in the street, and stones being thrown against the window.

Cathy could hear the window being raised in her parents' bedroom, and then the voice of one of the neighbours.

'Mrs Ward, Mrs Ward! Mrs Killy's gone off her head. She's runnin' round, naked as the day she was born, and she won't let no one near 'er.'

Cathy peeped out of her bedroom door and saw her mother running downstairs in her nightdress and her father following, fastening his trousers. The next moment they were along the lobby, her mother with a coat over her nightdress and an old shawl over her arm. Cathy put her coat and shoes on and looked out of the door. The street was bright with moonlight and groups of people were out, looking down towards Plumpton Street. A few moments later her mother and father appeared with Mrs Kilgannon between them, wrapped in the shawl below her armpits, but waving her arms about and singing incoherently.

They went into Mrs Kilgannon's house, but Sally paused on the way in and said quietly, 'Cathy, make a cup of tea. I'll get her dressed, Lawrie, while you get Nellie.'

'Will you be all right?' he asked.

'Yes. Come on now, Mrs Killy. Get nice and warm.'

Lawrie sped off and Cathy turned back to the house. Mary was crouching on the stairs. 'What's going on?' she asked.

'Mrs Killy's been running round without her clothes. Dad's gone for Nellie and Mam's getting her dressed,' Cathy said. She giggled. 'Mrs Bennet said she was as "naked as the day she was born". Mam took the shawl out for her.'

'I'd have let her freeze,' Mary said, turning and going back to bed.

It was a relief to all of them when Nellie took her mother to live with her, refusing to listen further to her objections.

Chapter Eight

Mary still went to Aigburth on Sundays and attended church with her aunt and uncle, but more and more often during the winter of 1910–11 Aunt Emily was too ill to leave the house even to attend church. Mary joined Isabel and her mother in their pew on these occasions, but there was a growing coldness between her and the Willards. Many small things contributed to it. Isabel and her mother had always been in charge of the fancy goods stall at the Christmas Bazaar, and this year Mary was invited to help with it. She had asked her mother to make some items for her, and Sally had readily and skilfully made numerous handkerchief sachets, lavender bags, egg and tea cosies, kettle holders, and beautifully embroidered collar and cuff sets from oddments of material left from her dressmaking. Mary let it be thought that they were her own work and although Isabel suspected that they had been made by Mary's mother, she felt that she could not make an outright accusation of deceit.

On the day of the Bazaar Isabel's crocheted hair tidies and doilies were ignored while Mary's contributions were highly praised, and the Willards had the mortification of knowing that the success of their stall was largely due to the fact that Mary's pretty smiling face and bell-like laugh attracted the customers, especially free-spending young men.

Then one of the ladies of the parish started holding what she called monthly soirées. Mary, who was invited as Isabel's friend, was the centre of attention while Isabel was ignored. Mrs Willard resented this even more than Isabel, and she let it be known discreetly that Mary Ward, although she had done a great deal to improve herself, was only the poor relation of the affluent Albert Deakin.

Invitations to visit the Willards or to attend events at the church became fewer, and as Aunt Emily's illness meant that she was confined to the house, Mary had little opportunity to move into the Aigburth society in which she had placed such hope.

Sam Glover seized the chance to ask her out again, and about once a week she went with him to the theatre or a concert. Mary's moods swung between ill temper and moroseness at her disappointment, and fits of optimism when she was sure she could soon charm her way back into the inner circle at St Bonaventure's. Sam would bear with any mood just to be with her.

Cathy was pleased to see him so happy, but her own affair was not going so well. Frank's leave had been postponed and, egged on by Josie, Cathy wrote to him telling him how disappointed his family and friends were at the delay in seeing him. The only response was a picture postcard with a brief message scrawled on the back. 'Thanks for the letter. Hope to be home in March. Best wishes, Frank.'

Not even 'love', Cathy thought dolefully. Evidently Frank still thought of her just as Josie's friend, although she had thought so often about him, recalling his words at the piano, and his kisses, including the one he had blown her before leaving, until she had convinced herself that theirs was a love affair like those she read of in the novelettes she now devoured. Still, perhaps he was wise not to put 'love' on a postcard she thought when Mary picked up the card and said, 'Who's this Frank?'

'Frank Mellor,' Cathy said, blushing. 'Me and Josie wrote to him, because he was away from home.'

'Terrible handwriting,' Mary said, tossing the card down again. Cathy was glad that she had said nothing to Mary about her feelings for Frank, and she consoled herself for the brief reply by dreaming of how different it would be when she met him face to face again, with a whole fortnight in which to get to know each other.

Cathy was becoming disenchanted with the girls' club, run by the Misses Whitty. She had inherited too much of her father's independent spirit to relish being treated as an object of charity, and patronised by the Misses Whitty and their rich friends. She soon realised that they lumped every one of the working classes under the blanket description of 'The Poor'. Cathy from her orderly home, and Rosie who lived in a dark and dilapidated court whose inhabitants yet struggled to maintain respectability, and the denizens of the filthy courts where hope had been abandoned and people lived like animals, were equally despised and regarded as a 'mission' by the superior ladies. Not that they had any contact with girls from surroundings like Lizzie Clark's. She would have received short shrift if she had appeared at the club, Cathy knew, and she listened cynically to the ladies' 'uplifting talks' and wished that she could take them to the scenes of real poverty and destitution.

Josie had none of Cathy's doubts about the club, but in spite of her sister's experience and advice to have nothing to do with men, she was now walking out with a lad who worked at the matchworks.

Ellen's father had obtained work in St Helen's in Lancashire so the family had moved there, and Cathy found herself without a companion to accompany her to the club, so with few regrets she stopped going there.

She still attended meetings with Rosie and argued with the girls at Finestone's about women's suffrage. The refined girls thought that it was not nice or ladylike to march with banners or to heckle speakers at meetings, and they were horrified by reports of Christabel Pankhurst and Annie Kenny disrupting meetings and breaking windows, then being sent to jail.

'You should be horrified by women having to put up with forced feeding just because they want the vote,' Cathy told them. 'They're doing it for you, you know. If women could vote they could stop sweated labour and all the other things men don't care about because it's not them who suffer.'

'Why don't they just ask?' one of the girls said. 'Instead of damaging property.'

Cathy was almost speechless with indignation. 'Just ask?' she spluttered. 'Mrs Fawcett and other women have been asking politely for over forty years, and what's happened? They've been ignored – but women who damage property won't be ignored.'

'What about that woman from Preston, Mrs Rigby, who made a scene when Winston Churchill spoke at Crosby? She was a lady, a doctor's wife too, and she broke a window in the police station in Church Road. That's only a couple of miles away so I hope it's not going to start here,' another girl said. 'She was sent to jail, and quite right too!'

'Was it quite right for her to be forcibly fed?' demanded Cathy. 'It's a disgrace to a civilized country, my father says.'

'*My* father says they're all wealthy idle women with not enough to do, trying to attract attention to themselves because they're bored.'

'That's not true,' Cathy said hotly. 'What about people like Rosie's sister and the women she works with in the mills? They can't risk going to jail because their families need them, and very often they're working and they need their wages too, but they still march and do all they can for the cause.'

'The cause!' one girl exclaimed scornfully.

'Yes, the cause,' Cathy said. 'It is a cause. Just think of the good women could do if they had the vote. And anyway, why shouldn't we vote? The laws passed in Parliament affect us just as much as men, if not more. It's not much to ask for, yet women get knocked about and badly treated in prison just for trying.' She looked round the hostile faces despairingly, wondering if such women were worth fighting for, but suddenly she received support from an unexpected quarter. One of the tailors who sat cross-legged on a bench sewing, said mildly, 'That's true that. I seen it when I was working in London. A big crowd of women marchin' in Hyde Park one mornin' – a terrible mornin' too, sleet and that – about half past six. And I seen them another time, a deputation going to the 'ouses of Parliament, peaceful-like, but the coppers didn't half knock them about.'

Cathy smiled at him gratefully. 'Would *you* give women the vote, Sammy?' she asked.

'I suppose so,' he said doubtfully, 'but it wouldn't make no difference with a lot of them. They'd vote the way their husbands told them to.'

The forewoman banged on a machine to remind them that the break was over, and they returned to their machines. Cathy pondered on Sammy's last remark, ruefully conceding that he was probably right.

The following morning she went over to Sammy at the break, carrying a spice cake from her lunch box. She wanted to learn more about the incidents he had witnessed so that she could repeat them at the next meeting as an eye witness account, but Sammy could add little to what he had said the day before. He could only tell her that the march in Hyde Park had taken place about February 1907, and that there had been 'thousands and thousands' of women there carrying banners and wearing sashes. About the other incident he could tell her even less, only that the police had charged very suddenly, and he had seen a police sergeant 'grabbing a woman's chest, like'.

At least, Cathy told herself, there were some men who could see the justice of their demand for the vote, even though very often women were opposed to them.

All this was forgotten when Josie told Cathy that Frank was due home on Friday for fourteen days' leave. She took out the postcard that his hands had touched and the message, even though unsatisfactory, that he had written, and tried to conjure up a picture of him in her mind. To her dismay she could scarcely remember what he looked like except that his eyes were blue and his hair fair, but she would soon see him in the flesh, she consoled herself.

Mary had given Cathy a dress which she had outgrown, but there was another dress of Mary's that Cathy coveted. She wondered if she could borrow it on Friday night without Mary's knowledge. It was a favourite dress of her sister's worn only for special occasions.

Recently there had been less opportunity for Mary to wear it since the invitations to events in Aigburth had dwindled.

It was of brown watered silk, with an underblouse of flowered chiffon showing below the three-quarter sleeves and the neck, and with three large buttons gracefully gathering the full skirt at one side. Cathy had tried it on and discovered that it fitted her and made her look older and more sophisticated. She wondered if she dared to wear it on Friday night. Josie knew that it was her sister's dress, but she would say nothing, and Mary was to go with their mother to visit Aunt Emily on Friday evening.

Sally was becoming more and more concerned about Emily. She had been too ill to visit Egremont Street for several months, although when she wrote she was always cheerful and said she was expecting soon to be better. Sally hated visiting the house at Aigburth, especially when Emily's fashionable friends were there.

'They make me feel like an intruder.' she told Lawrie. 'I can never get a word with Emily while they're tittle tattling on.'

'Emily doesn't think you're an intruder, love,' he said. 'And that's all that matters. She'd be upset if she didn't see you.' As usual she was comforted by his words, but she decided to visit Emily when Mary could come with her and talk to any other visitors, leaving herself and Emily free to talk to each other.

Cathy washed her hair on Thursday, and on Friday rushed home from work to have as much time as possible for her preparations. When she went up to the bedroom she was dismayed to see the brown dress laid out on the bed, and Mary wearing only her under-skirt and bust bodice.

'I'll have to get washed first,' she said. 'Mam's already dressed to go.'

Cathy retreated downstairs, feeling frustrated, and scarcely listening as her mother talked about Emily. Mary came downstairs a little later wearing the dress and, Cathy had to admit, looking stunningly beautiful in it.

'That dress is too fancy, Mary, to visit someone who's sick,' her mother said. 'It's not suitable.'

Mary opened her eyes wide. 'But, Mam, Aunt Emily loved this dress. You don't have to wear frumpy clothes just because people are ill. It only makes them feel worse.'

'There's a difference between being nicely dressed and being overdressed,' Sally. 'But never mind, you might as well keep it on or we'll be here all night.' She went into the back kitchen, and Mary whispered to Cathy, 'You never know who you'll meet there.'

After they had gone Cathy went upstairs and took out her best skirt, and a white blouse which her mother had made. It had eyelet holes around the neck, through which Cathy threaded narrow velvet ribbon. When she was dressed she had to admit that she was more suitably dressed than she would have been in Mary's dress. If her mother had thought Mary overdressed in it for Aigburth, what would the Mellors have thought if she had appeared in it, especially as they knew it was not her own?

A commotion in the street drew her to her mother's bedroom window. She looked out and saw Frank walking down the street, with his two brothers beside him, one of them carrying his sea bag. Cathy could only catch a glimpse of Frank before he disappeared into the Mellors' house.

Cathy stayed at the window, watching. People seemed to be pouring into the house, and she wondered whether she should go over to the house or wait for Josie to call for her. Her problem was solved when her friend came out and stood on the pavement, talking to some of the numerous Mellor relatives who had just arrived. Cathy ran downstairs and joined them.

After a few minutes she went into the house with Josie, but it was impossible to reach Frank, surrounded as he was by well wishers. She had still been unable to speak to him when there was a sudden surge out on to the pavement. The March day had been like a foretaste of summer, except for a blustering wind, but the wind had now dropped and the evening was mild and pleasant.

Glasses of ale had appeared in nearly everyone's hand, and the melodeon player arrived and began to play, starting with 'The Blue Danube' waltz. Suddenly Frank caught sight of Cathy and greeted her boisterously, then drew her to a clear space on the pavement and started to dance with her. At first Cathy was delighted, smiling blissfully at him, but soon she realised that he was already half drunk. She was repelled by the smell of drink and sweat that flowed from him, and by the way he squeezed her waist and sagged drunkenly against her.

There was a scream of 'Frankie' and his mother's sister, who lived in the next street, waddled towards him, her arms outspread.

'Auntie Josie,' he shouted, abandoning Cathy, and allowing himself to be hugged and kissed by his aunt, and then by various female relatives who accompanied her.

Cathy was pushed aside and stood watching as the hugging and kissing continued. The relatives were joined by girls living in the street who seized the opportunity to throw their arms round Frank's neck and kiss him soundly.

He seemed to have forgotten Cathy and to be returning the kisses with enthusiasm. The Bennet twins were clutching him and he had an arm round each of them and was shouting, 'Let them all come,' amid laughter from the older women. A man near Cathy shouted, 'Look at 'im. Lappin' it up. I'll bet you've got a girl in every port, Frankie.'

'What do you think?' he laughed.

Cathy moved further back into the crowd, near to tears, but Josie appeared beside her and whispered, 'Our Frank's half seas over. He was at the rum before he got home and everyone's been drinking with him ever since.'

Cathy gave a sigh of relief. Of course, that was why he seemed so different. It would be better tomorrow when he was sober.

The melodeon player decided to have a break, but another man produced a comb and paper and began to play and the dancing continued. Mrs Mellor grabbed Josie's arm.

'Where've you been?' she said, pulling out her purse. 'Go down to Fitzpatrick's and get some spareribs and potted herrings for our Frank. He never got nothing to eat before they were all in on top of us. Come in the back way. I'm not feeding all this lot.'

Cathy went with Josie to the cooked meat shop which was open until twelve o'clock at night, then they went into the Mellors' house by the back door.

Frank was sitting on a chair in the back kitchen, smiling foolishly, with his mother standing beside him and the door to the kitchen firmly closed.

'Here, get these down yer, lad,' Mrs Mellor said. 'Yer stummick must think yer throat's cut.'

Frank ate the spareribs hungrily but refused the herrings, while Cathy made tea and Josie cut bread and buttered it. Mrs Mellor was now sitting on an upturned dolly tub and she urged Frank to drink a mug of tea and eat some bread and butter. Cathy handed the mug of tea to Frank and he took hold of her fingers.

'Cathy Ward – li'l beauty,' he mumbled. She smiled uncertainly but Mrs Mellor laughed and shook like a jelly.

'The state of 'im,' she wheezed fondly. The next moment the kitchen door was pushed open and Billy, another of her sons, looked in.

'Wharra yer doin' to 'im?' he demanded when he saw the mug of tea in Frank's hand.

'I don't want 'im passin' out on me,' Mrs Mellor defended herself. "E's 'ad nothin' to eat.'

"E doesn't want to get too sober to enjoy 'imself,' Billy said indignantly. Mrs Mellor waved him away.

'Don't you tell me what to do, you,' she said. 'Gerrout, and shut that door.' As Billy retreated, Cathy looked at Frank, chewing a sparerib with his eyes closed then slurping the tea. Finally he rose to his feet and sluiced water over his head and face, then dried himself on the roller towel, emerging to grin at his mother.

'There y'are, Mam,' he said. 'Sober as a judge.'

'Aye, and there's some bloody drunken judges,' his mother laughed, lumbering to her feet and following him down the lobby. Josie had already disappeared to join her boyfriend and Cathy walked behind Mrs Mellor, realising with dismay that she now felt only revulsion towards Frank.

Am I fickle? she wondered, but her commonsense told her that it was simply that Frank was quite different in reality to the picture that she had built of him in her mind.

As soon as he stepped out of the door he was seized by Maud Bennet. 'Come on, Frankie,' she screamed. 'A set of Lancers.' He was allowing himself to be pulled into the crowd when suddenly he stopped dead.

The lamplighter had been along earlier and in addition the moon had risen, so that Mary and her mother walked down the lit street as though on to a stage. Frank stood gaping at them until Sally came up and held out her hand to him.

'Welcome home, Frank,' she said quietly. He shook her hand, still staring at Mary who stood gracefully erect, her head thrown back, glancing disdainfully at the dishevelled crowd before holding out the tips of her fingers to Frank.

'Oh yes, welcome home,' she murmured in a bored voice. She looked as neat as when she had left the house hours ago, in the pretty dress with a short jacket over it and a large hat pinned to her shining hair. Frank seemed unable to speak or to take his eyes from her.

Her mother had gone over to Mrs Mellor. 'You don't mind if we don't stay, Sophie?' she said. 'Our Emily—' She brushed her hand over her eyes and Mary took her arm.

'Oh God, isn't she no better?' Mrs Mellor said, patting Sally's arm. 'Never mind, girl.'

Cathy moved towards her mother but Mary said quickly, 'You stay at the party, Cath, I'll look after Mother.' While Cathy stood still, uncertain what to do, Mary drew their mother across the street.

'"My mother",' Maud mimicked in a falsetto voice, when they had gone. 'She gives me a pain, that one, with the airs and graces of her.'

'Leave our Mary alone,' Cathy said furiously. 'You're only jealous, all of you, because she looks like a lady.'

'Yes, shut yer gob,' Frank said roughly to Maud, then turned back into the house. Mrs Mellor shot a venomous glance after Mary, then waddled into the house after him. Cathy slipped away to her own home. As she crossed the road she could hear Mrs Mellor's sister saying loudly, 'Our Sophie'll go mad if he gets mixed up with that one. She's nothing but trouble.'

Cathy debated with herself whether to go back and challenge the woman, but she knew she would be heavily outnumbered if she tried to defend Mary, and she felt that her sister would prefer her to treat such gossip with contempt.

When she went into the house her mother was sitting in a chair by the fire, staring sadly at the flames, and Mary was in the scullery making tea. Cathy went out to her.

'Aunt Emily had a haemorrhage while we were there,' Mary whispered. 'I was terrified but Mam was quite calm. The doctor came, and Aunt Emily's going in a private sanatorium tomorrow.'

They went in to their mother with the tea, and she tried to drink it, holding the cup in both hands because she was trembling so much, but after a little while she put it down.

'I'm sorry, love,' she said to Mary. 'I just can't manage it.'

'That's all right, Mam,' Mary said gently, and the two girls sat with Sally, holding her hands, trying to give her wordless comfort by their presence. The noise from the Mellors' party jarred on the girls, but their mother seemed oblivious to it, wrapped in her own sad thoughts.

They were all thankful to hear Lawrie walking down the lobby. Mary prepared to slip out to warn him, but it was plain that he had already heard the news. He came in and took Sally in his arms. Cathy and Mary murmured goodnight and slipped away to bed.

'Mam'll be all right now, won't she?' Cathy said, and Mary nodded without speaking. She was sitting on the side of the bed, staring down at the floor.

'Was it very bad, Mary?'

She nodded. 'It was terrible,' she said. 'One minute we were just sitting by the bed talking and the next minute the blood just gushed out of Aunt Emily's mouth – no warning. Mam was wonderful. I tell you, Cath, if I'd been there on my own I'd have rushed out screaming, but Mam just stood up and wiped Aunt Emily's mouth then folded the bedclothes back so she couldn't see the blood. She told me to get Dora but just quietly, no fuss, and she said to Aunt Emily, "You're all right, love. Better up, as Mrs Mal would say." I can't get over her.'

'I know,' Cathy said. 'I suppose that's why everyone round here relies on her when they're in trouble.' Mary was still sitting listlessly on the side of the bed, and Cathy slipped her arm around her sister's neck.

'It's a good thing you were with Mam,' she said. 'Although it must have been a shock to you, too.'

'I didn't do much to help,' Mary said, but Cathy hugged her.

'Just being there with her,' she said, 'and being with her to walk home, must have made all the difference.'

When they were in bed Mary as usual fell asleep immediately, but Cathy lay for a while, thinking. She studied Mary's sleeping face on the pillow beside her, in the moonlight which streamed through the window. She *is* beautiful, she thought. No wonder Frank was stunned by her.

She thought of Mary's cool elegance compared to the perspiration and untidiness of the other girls, and her disinterested glance at Frank in contrast to their clutching hands and ready lips. She thought too of the malice and envy Mary aroused in the partygoers and felt indignant on her sister's behalf, especially when she remembered Mary's loving care of their mother.

She's beautiful in character as well, Cathy thought. None of them are fit to black her boots.

She fell asleep eventually, with her heart once again full of love and admiration for her sister.

Cathy's infatuation with Frank Mellor faded as quickly as it had arisen when she saw him reeling home on every day of his leave. He had tried to persuade Mary to be 'his girl' but she had rejected him contemptuously. Cathy was glad that her sister knew nothing of her brief infatuation with him when Mary spoke scornfully of Frank.

Chapter Nine

When Cathy went downstairs on the day following the party and the visit by her mother and Mary to Aigburth she found Sally, pale and red-eyed, damping down the fire with slack.

'I'm going to Aigburth,' she said. 'I want to see your Aunt Emily before she goes to that sanatorium in Yorkshire.'

'She got better when she went away before, Mam,' Cathy said consolingly.

'Aye, but not for long.' Her mother sighed. Her eyes filled with tears but she brushed them away and said more cheerfully, 'Still, this might do her more good. It's a proper hospital where they sleep in the open air. Emily believes it will cure her.'

Fortunately their new neighbour was due to arrive that morning to clean the house next door, so when Sally returned from Aigburth she went in to help which took her mind off her own troubles.

When Mrs Kilgannon went to live with her daughter, Lawrie told a workmate, Jimmie Burns, that the house was vacant and he dashed off to secure the tenancy.

'Me missis has always hankered to live in Egremont Street,' he told Lawrie. 'We're too cramped where we are, and now we've got two working we can afford the extra rent.'

Sally was delighted to have Peggy Burns as her neighbour instead of the cantankerous Mrs Kilgannon, and she willingly helped to make the house clean and ready for the family. She told Peggy about the help she had received from Susan Kilgannon when she moved into her own house, and how hard Susan had worked in her own home.

'Mrs Kilgannon never lifted a finger in the house. Susan did everything while she was a schoolchild, and then when she went into service she cleaned through the house on her day off. Proper little drudge, she was, and got no thanks for it.'

'Mrs Kilgannon sounds like a real faggot,' Peggy observed.

'She was,' Sally agreed, 'and a troublemaker. Mind you, she saved my life once when I started a miscarriage and she found me and got help. I had a bad time and lost the baby, a little lad too. I never had any more.'

'Strange, isn't it?' Peggy said with a sigh. 'Jimmie only has to hang his trousers on the bedrail and I'm off again. Mind you, I wouldn't want to be without any of the seven of them now they're here, but it's a struggle to keep them on railway money.'

'Yes, but you've got two working now,' Sally consoled her. 'Even if they don't earn much they're bringing in instead of taking out, aren't they?'

'That's true,' Peggy agreed. 'We've had some hard times but I think they're behind us now.'

'So did we, and only a few years ago too,' Sally said. 'Lawrie lost his job, and there wasn't another to be had. My old da lived with us – he was bedridden so I couldn't sew, and Lawrie walked the boots off his feet trying to find odd jobs to keep us. When I think of it now... still, the tide turned for us, as Lawrie said.'

The two women smiled. They had liked each other on sight, and the friendship that began as they cleaned the grimy house lasted until the end of their lives.

Cathy had made a new friend too. She had become impatient with Rosie's extreme views, especially her dislike of men, which many of the women at the meetings shared.

'I believe women should have the vote but I don't see why we have to hate men,' Cathy argued. 'Some men are helping us.' But Rosie did not agree.

Cathy still went to meetings with her but they had little else in common. She felt that Rosie was too earnest, and knew that she believed that Cathy was too lighthearted, but one night she met a kindred spirit at the meeting. Norah Benson had been born on the same day as Cathy, and they shared the same capacity for enjoying life, and the same sense of humour.

As the winter passed and the spring of 1911 drew on, there was a growing sense of unrest both locally and nationally. Cathy and Norah were enjoying themselves too much to be aware of it. They were still at the stage of discovering how many ideas and interests they had in common, and were completely happy to spend their time strolling along the Landing Stage, watching the shipping in the river and eyeing other young people who were promenading like themselves. They flirted harmlessly with some of the promenading young men, or foreign seamen from ships in port, but it was all in fun. Their only complaint at this time was that their sides ached with laughing.

Soon they acquired bicycles, paying them off at a shilling a week, and joined a cycling club, the Mersey Wheelers, composed of boys and girls of about their own age. They rode to a different place in the surrounding countryside every fine Sunday.

None of the group was ready to settle to serious courtship although there was a certain amount of flirting. When they rode along country lanes singing songs from 'The Merry Widow' or 'The Arcadians', Cathy often received soulful glances from young men as they sang, but although her response was to smile and blush she knew it meant little. It was all part of the sunny day and their youth and sense of freedom.

As the hot summer days lengthened, the feeling of unrest in the city became more intense. Often Cathy heard arguments between her parents. Her mother's view was that things were gradually improving and she was anxious that Lawrie should not be involved in any pressure for reform.

'You've said yourself that things are getting better,' she said. 'Old Mr Tanner with the pension, and then this ninepence for fourpence.'

'What's that, Mam?' Cathy asked.

'It's insurance for workmen,' her father said. 'A man pays fourpence a week, the boss threepence and the State twopence so the man gets the worth of ninepence for fourpence, they reckon.'

'A man gets ten shillings a week if he's off work sick, and goes to the doctor for nothing,' her mother added. 'And anyone with consumption can go to a sanatorium. Just think what that would mean to our Emily if she didn't have Albert's money behind her.'

'We haven't got it yet,' Lawrie growled. 'They'll fight Lloyd George every step of the way on this, you see.'

'Well, I think you should keep out of it anyway,' Sally said stubbornly. 'It's got nothing to do with you. If the seamen or the miners want to strike, let them do their own fighting.'

'You don't understand, Sally. It's only by sticking together we'll ever get anything done. I can't renege on me mates.'

'They'd renege on you quick enough! You're just too soft,' she retorted.

Cathy listened quietly, her views changing with every argument. I'd never make a revolutionary, she thought ruefully. I change my mind too often!

She felt that she often changed her mind about Mary, too. Sometimes she was disgusted by her sister's behaviour yet at other times, especially if Mary was criticised by anyone else, all Cathy's love for her welled up again. Several incidents disturbed Cathy at this time.

One concerned a woman in her thirties, Bertha Johnson, who lived with her widowed invalid mother in one room further down Egremont Street. Bertha had been walking out with her young man, George, for nearly ten years but as he like herself was the only support of a widowed mother, marriage was not possible until their circumstances changed. They seemed quite happy to wait, taking walks together arm in arm, with an occasional ride on the ferry or a rare visit to the theatre as a treat.

They had been as familiar a sight to Mary as to others in the street but she had only passed them with a nod and a smile until one fateful evening she met them walking up from the ferry, and walked home with them.

Mary was in a furious temper. She was returning from a visit to the Willards, where she had been snubbed by Isabel's mother who had made it clear that Mary would not be welcome in future. Also, she had quarrelled with Hugh Desmond the previous evening when he had told her that he was sick of her playing fast and loose with him, and had just seen him walking along arm in arm with another girl.

She was in the mood for mischief and consequently ignored Bertha while deliberately setting out to charm George. Amazed and bewildered, but highly flattered, he had responded and Bertha had made the mistake of flouncing away in a huff. George might have gone after her if Mary had not slipped her hand through his arm and smiled up into his face. They turned down another street and by the time Mary returned home, an hour later, George was added to the list of her willing victims.

She went out with him several times but always met him well away from her home, so it was a complete shock to Sally when Bertha arrived to see her, tearful and accusing. Cathy was at home, helping her mother with a rush sewing order, and when Bertha had gone she was unable to escape in time to warn Mary. Her mother went into the attack at once.

'If you cared for George it would be bad enough to take him from Bertha, but it's only been done to satisfy your stupid vanity,' she raged while Mary leaned against the dresser with an air of long suffering.

'Can I help it if he's fed up with Bertha?' she said. 'Does she want to keep him in a glass case and stop him from speaking to anyone?'

'You must have encouraged him,' Sally insisted. 'I'm disgusted with you.'

Cathy felt disgusted too, especially when Mary followed her up to bed and told her more about the quarrel with the Willards.

'This man took a little notice of Isabel and, honestly, you'd have thought it was the world's greatest love story,' she told Cathy. 'I only smiled at him to be sociable but he wouldn't leave my side, and the Willards were furious. I told him he was breaking Isabel's heart but it made no difference.'

'I hope Isabel didn't know you said that,' Cathy said. 'It would hurt her pride.'

'For heaven's sake, *I* didn't want him. He wanted to be a missionary. Can you see me as a missionary's wife?'

'No, but I could Isabel,' Cathy said. 'I hope they got back together.'

'He went off somewhere, the Gold Coast I think,' Mary said carelessly. 'Such a fuss over nothing. Mrs Willard was ridiculous, quite hysterical.'

Cathy said no more, but felt she detested Mary sometimes. She was reminded of an incident she had seen in the park. A bird had alighted too close to a cat which seemed to be sleeping, but the cat's paw shot out and the little bird was dead in a moment. It was with the same careless cruelty, she felt, that Mary had destroyed the hopes of Isabel and Bertha, and she burned with indignation towards her sister.

Yet the following night when she was due to go to the Hippodrome with girls from work, Mary lent her a dress and curled her hair in a new style, then touched up her eyelashes and eyebrows with Vaseline.

'You look a stunner, Cath,' she said, hugging her sister, and Cathy felt a surge of the old affection between them. Perhaps the men were to blame, she thought. Mary couldn't help being beautiful, but they shouldn't be so weak.

To her mother Mary explained away the fact that she no longer visited the Willards by saying that Isabel had a new friend whom Mrs Willard preferred to Mary, so she was not now made welcome there.

'I don't go where I'm not wanted,' she said, with a toss of her head.

'Quite right too,' her mother said indignantly. 'Perhaps they're the sort of people who keep changing their friends. Never mind, love. You've got other friends and your own family so don't worry about them.'

Sally told Peggy Burns about it the following day. Although she felt that she could not speak as freely to Peggy as she had done to Mrs Malloy, she found Peggy a willing and sympathetic listener and their views were always in accord. They were both busy women,

Peggy Burns with her family of seven children between the ages of one and sixteen years, and Sally with her sewing in addition to her household duties, but they often managed to have a cup of tea together in the lull after the midday meal.

Peggy was as indignant as Sally at the Willards' treatment of Mary. 'They're just snobs, those sort of people,' she said. 'Mary's better off with her own sort. She's got plenty of friends.'

'Too many, I sometimes think,' Sally said with a sigh.

Peggy had brought her three-year-old son and her baby into the Wards' house and Sally gestured to the child, sitting quietly on the rag rug playing with his wood blocks.

'I think this is the best time, Peggy,' she said. 'While they're so young – before the worries start.'

Peggy agreed, a little doubtfully. 'He's a good child,' she confirmed. 'Different from our Michael.'

'Funny how different children can be,' Sally said. 'Born of the same parents and brought up the same way, you'd think they'd all be the same as one another, but my two are as different as chalk and cheese.'

'I know. Our Michael was never out of mischief right up to starting school,' Peggy said. 'But Ben's never been any trouble. Mind you, every one of my seven is different from the other. It makes me mad when I hear people say, when a woman loses a child, "It's not so bad for her. She's got a big family anyway".'

'Yes, as though they're not all as dear to you in different ways,' Sally agreed. 'They've all got good points and bad. Our Mary was a right handful when she was little. The tantrums, and screaming at the top of her voice for her own way, and yet in some ways she was easier to handle than Cathy.'

'I'm surprised to hear that,' Peggy said. 'Your Cathy always seems so pleasant and cheerful. Very like Lawrie.'

'Yes, but as stubborn as a mule,' Sally said. 'I could give Mary a smack and she'd do as she was told, but Cathy – if she made up her mind not to do something, you might coax her to do it, but you could smack her or shout at her until you were blue in the face and she wouldn't budge.'

'At least your girls don't quarrel,' Peggy said. 'Our Jimmie and Mabel fight like cat and dog. They can't see each other without falling out.'

'I don't know. Our girls were always good friends, but they don't seem the same lately,' Sally replied doubtfully. 'Still, I suppose they all have these spells. We're lucky we've got nothing more to worry about than a few quarrels, aren't we?'

'We are indeed,' Peggy agreed, smiling.

The long sunny days continued and as Cathy walked home from work she saw groups gathering everywhere, and the air of unrest intensified. There were reports of strikes in Hull and Salford and trouble in Parliament about Irish Home Rule. Even the pictures and the accounts in the *Echo* of the Coronation of King George V annoyed some people, because they emphasised the gulf between rich and poor.

To Cathy it all seemed remote from her own life, and far less important than the fact that her mother had made her a new dress, and that the cycling club were planning to ride to West Derby, until the day her father came home and announced that he was on strike.

Her mother sank down on a chair as though she had been struck.

'Now don't worry, Sal,' her father said. 'It's not just one or two of us this time.'

'But I heard they'd brought the troops out in Hull,' her mother said faintly. 'Oh, Lawrie, there'll be bloodshed before it's finished. The masters won't let you get away with it.'

'Yes, they will. They'll have to,' he declared. 'Everybody's in this together – railwaymen, carters, seamen, tramwaymen. We've got right on our side, and they know it.'

Jimmie Burns was also on strike, and Sally and Peggy were equally worried about the outcome, although Peggy was more sympathetic to the strikers than Sally.

'They're not asking for the moon,' she argued. 'The seamen are only asking for another ten bob a month to make the wages five pounds a month, and the railwaymen for the hours down to fifty-four a week and twenty-four shillings pay.'

'But no good will come of it,' Sally said. 'It's like a quarrel between drunken men. One word leads to another and murder's the result. If they'd only be patient, I'm sure things would come right in the end.'

'Patience hasn't got them very far,' Peggy said. 'I don't know why you're so bitter against them, Sal.'

'I suppose it's because of what happened soon after we were married,' she said. 'Lawrie left the sea and worked in a grain ware-house, and it was a terrible place, I know. The fellers were treated worse than dogs and they tried to have a union. Lawrie and another man were made stewards and they both got the sack. It didn't half give me a fright, Peggy, and I'm always worried about it happening again. Lawrie says he's not so hot-headed now, but he's kidding himself.'

'I wouldn't say that,' her friend demurred. 'Warm-hearted I'd say, more than hot-headed. Jimmie says they think the world of him in the yard.'

'Oh, I wouldn't have him any different,' Sally said hastily. 'And we're better off than most people now with my sewing.'

'I'll be glad of our Mabel's money and young Robbie's if this drags on,' Peggy said. 'Only it's come at a bad time for us just after moving. If I have to miss the rent, the landlord doesn't know us.'

'Mr Jones is very good,' Sally consoled her. 'He knows who he can trust and who he can't.'

A strikers' rally was organised for Sunday August 13th at the St George's Plateau in Lime Street. By this time all the transport workers were on strike, and police and troops had been moved in in numbers.

Sally tried to persuade Lawrie not to go to the meeting but he insisted.

'Tom Mann's going to speak, Sal, and Havelock Wilson. It's all going to be very orderly, I promise. Tom Mann has insisted that there'll be no religious or political arguments between the men until the strike's over.'

'How can he stop them? You know what they're like in Liverpool over religion,' said Sally.

'He's chairman and his word goes,' Lawrie said stubbornly.

Sunday was a hot sunny day, and Mary decided to walk up to see a married friend, living in Baker Street, who had given birth to twin boys a few days earlier. The cycling club outing had been cancelled so Cathy went with her.

'Keep away from that meeting,' their mother warned them, but soon after they left the house they saw men marching along, led by bands and banners. Mother and babies were asleep when Mary and Cathy reached Baker Street so they stayed only a few minutes. As they walked home they saw numerous people hastening towards Lime Street, families and groups of young people. Everyone seemed to be in a holiday mood.

'It's too nice to go home,' Mary said. Cathy agreed, so they followed the crowds to where people were massed in Lime Street before Saint George's Plateau. It was impossible to hear the speakers, who were like dots in the distance from where the girls stood at the bottom of London Road, but they were more interested in the people around them.

Mary was exchanging glances with two young men who were fanning themselves with their straw boaters when there was a sudden surge of movement among the crowd further along.

Mounted police appeared and Mary grabbed Cathy's arm.

'Quick, quick!' she said breathlessly, and as the crowd began to stream away in panic the two girls picked up their skirts and began to run up London Road. More mounted police began to ride down the side streets towards them and Mary pushed Cathy into a shop doorway.

'We'll stay here until it's all over,' she gasped. They huddled in the doorway, watching in terror as people ran past screaming and the police horses galloped among them, whinnying and tossing their heads.

Suddenly a policeman pulled his horse round and rode towards the doorway in which the girls cowered. In future years Cathy always remembered that Mary thrust her back and stepped in front of her to protect her as the horse reared up above them.

They jerked back. As Cathy's head struck the door behind them, her last sight was of the horse's head high above, saliva dripping from its teeth, and the policeman's laughing face. She slid to the ground unconscious.

The policeman wheeled his horse round and galloped away, and Mary tried to lift her sister, screaming wildly, 'Cathy, Cathy!' Her eyes remained closed and Mary ran out of the doorway, calling for the people running past to help her. She was ignored until a door on the opposite side of the road, beside a jeweller's shop window, was opened and a young man sped across the road.

'I saw what happened,' he said breathlessly. 'I'll take her into our house.'

He lifted the girl effortlessly and carried her over the road, and Mary picked up Cathy's hat and followed him, through the door and up the stairs to the rooms over the shop.

Cathy was vaguely aware of being lifted and carried along then she opened her eyes to find herself lying on a sofa with a folded towel under her head, and Mary and a young man bending over her.

'Cathy, Cathy,' Mary was saying, rubbing distractedly at her hands. But when Cathy opened her eyes the anxious expression faded from Mary's face and she bestowed a dazzling smile on the young man. He bent over Cathy and spoke reassuringly.

'You're quite safe now. Your head has been cut but I'll bandage it and you'll soon feel better.'

What a nice face he has, Cathy thought dreamily, looking at his grey eyes and even teeth, and his untidy dark hair. Not exactly handsome but nice. She suddenly realised that she was staring at him, and looked down shyly, feeling her face grow warm.

A tiny woman was hovering nearby, twittering, 'Oh dear, oh dear.' Now she said suddenly, 'Gregory dear, my heart! I feel quite faint.'

The young man quickly took her arm and guided her to a chair, then placed a footstool for her feet.

'Lie back and close your eyes for a moment, Mother,' he said. 'Here are your salts.' To Mary, he explained quietly that his mother was delicate. She went to offer her hand in greeting.

'I'm so sorry to trouble you,' she said sweetly, 'but so grateful for your help. I'm Mary Ward and this is my sister, Catherine.'

The tiny lady had been lying back in her chair, holding the bottle of smelling salts, but she sat up and took Mary's hand.

'How do you do?' she said, 'I'm Mrs Redmond. My son, Gregory. Sit down, my dear.' The young man smiled and nodded at Mary, then bent over Cathy again.

'I'll have to cut a little of your hair away,' he said gently, 'but it won't show.' She nodded, too overcome with shyness to speak as he gently bathed and bandaged the cut on her head. She felt very strange. She could hear Mary talking about Uncle Albert's box factory in Islington, and his mansion in Aigburth, and vaguely realised that she was implying that they had been returning from a visit there, but the voices and the unfamiliar room all seemed remote and insubstantial. Yet she was acutely aware of Gregory's nearness and the touch of his hands on her head. When he had finished, he put a cushion behind her and urged her to rest.

'I'll make tea, Mother,' he said, carrying out the bowl of water he had used and the box of bandages, marked with a red cross. It seemed only moments to Cathy before he returned and handed her a cup of tea.

'I've put plenty of sugar in it,' he said, smiling. 'That's the best treatment for shock. Much better than brandy.'

'Nicer too,' Cathy whispered shyly, wondering whether she felt dizzy because of the injury to her head or because he was smiling at her.

When they had finished the tea, Mary rose to her feet. 'You're all right now, Cathy, aren't you?' she said.

Cathy hastily agreed and stood up, surprised to feel her legs trembling. Mary smiled at Mrs Redmond and her son.

'Thank you so much for your help and hospitality,' she said. 'We were so *terrified* in that crowd – I don't know what would have happened to us without your help. We're most grateful.'

'I'll walk along with you, if I may,' Gregory said. 'There are no cabs available, and there may still be people about.' He looked at Cathy and added, 'You may feel a little shaky still.'

'You're very kind,' Mary purred, obviously seeing this as a ploy on his part to prolong his time with her. When they had walked down the stairs, Gregory offered his arm to Cathy saying, 'I'm sure you must feel quite weak.'

'I do,' she said truthfully, grateful of the support of his arm as they walked up the road, now clear of people. She had expected Mary to take her other arm, but Mary had slipped her hand through Gregory's left, so that he walked between them.

Cathy walked in silence, and now that the emergency was over Gregory seemed to be as stricken with shyness as she was, but Mary chatted easily. She extracted information from the young man that she had been too discreet to try to obtain from his mother. He was a member of the Red Cross, he told her. He had hoped to become a doctor but after his father's death four years earlier he had left school to help in the family business, the jewellery shop. He was an only son.

Cathy listened in amazement as Mary drew these details from someone who was obviously unused to talking about himself. How does she do it? she wondered. It must be a natural gift. When they reached the end of Egremont Street, Mary stopped and held out her hand.

'You've been very kind and I'm most grateful,' she said, 'but I won't ask you to come right to the house, this time. My mother might become hysterical when she sees Cathy's bandage so I'd rather deal with it alone.'

He stepped back and raised his hat then took Mary's outstretched hand.

'It was a pleasure,' he said. 'I'm glad I was able to help.' Then he held out his hand to Cathy.

'Thank you very much,' she said shyly. 'I hope your mother will be all right.'

'Thank you,' he said, still holding her hand and smiling at her. 'She's rather – nervous, and she doesn't like the sight of blood, but she'll be all right.'

They stood, still holding hands and smiling at each other, until Mary put her arm around Cathy's shoulders and said, 'Come along, Catherine. You must rest.' As they walked away from Gregory she said quietly, 'Mam'll probably raise the roof and I didn't want him to hear *that*. So it's their own business... I thought that house was very well furnished.'

Cathy was silent. She could think only of Gregory's face as he smiled at her, and the pressure of his hand.

As they drew near their own front door, she said curiously, 'Why did you say we'd been to Aigburth?'

'Just to let her know we had posh relations too,' Mary said. 'But that was another reason I didn't want him to meet Mam, in case she said something about Baker Street. Don't you say anything, just leave the talking to me.'

Chapter Ten

Mary walked down the lobby ahead of Cathy and into the kitchen where their mother was standing by the dresser. She whirled around but before she could speak, Mary said quickly, 'Oh, Mam, we got caught up in the crowds and Cathy cut her head but she's all right. Someone bandaged it.'

Cathy followed Mary into the kitchen. Sally drew in her breath in shock. 'Good God, I knew it! I knew there'd be trouble.'

'I'm all right, honest,' Cathy said, but her mother whipped off the hat which Mary had carefully arranged to cover the bandage. 'How did this happen?' she demanded. 'I told you to stay well away from that meeting.'

'We got swept along, Mam,' Mary said, all wide-eyed innocence. 'Beattie and the babies were asleep, and when we got to near Low Hill the crowds just swept us along. There were *thousands* going, and—'

'Did you see your dad?' her mother interrupted. 'There's all sorts of tales going round about people being trampled to death or shot. I've been worried to death with the three of you out and not knowing where any of you were.'

'We didn't see him but we were right at the edge of the crowd,' Mary said, 'and we got away as soon as we could.'

'He'll be in the thick of it, you may depend,' Sally said, pressing her knuckles against her teeth. 'I wish to God he'd come home.' But when Lawrie appeared a few moments later, she screamed at him, 'Look at the state of you! I knew there'd be trouble. A fine peaceful procession, I must say.' He was dusty and dishevelled and there was a smear of blood on his cheek.

'It all went wrong,' he said wearily. 'I'm sorry if you've been worried, girl.' Sally had sat down and he put his hand on her shoulder, but she jerked away from him.

'Worried?' she said. 'I've been nearly frantic here with the girls out as well and the tales I've heard. And now look at the state of you, and Cathy injured as well.' Lawrie seemed to notice the girls for the first time, and to see the bandage on Cathy's head.

'Great Scott, what happened?' he exclaimed, and Sally said sharply, 'Yes, what did happen, that's what I want to know? How did you two get mixed up in the riot.'

'There was no riot!' Lawrie exclaimed. 'It should've been a peaceful meeting but they've brought in so many police and troops that they had to have some trouble to justify all the money they've spent. It was a put-up job.'

'And where were you? In the middle of it all, I suppose.'

'I was near the platform,' Lawrie said. 'It was a great turn-out, Sal. All marching behind their banners and all united just like Tom Mann wanted. No splits on grounds of politics or religion – just working men, all standing together.' His face was flushed and his eyes shone as he spoke, but then his shoulders slumped. 'Then it all started,' he said, 'right at the back of the crowd. Suddenly police were everywhere, and men running—'

'Mrs Bennet said her lad was in Great Nelson Street and that was where it started. She said people were being trampled to death.'

'She would,' Lawrie said in disgust. 'Anything for sensation. No wonder you were worried, but it was only some small thing. It was just that the meeting broke up and there were so many there.'

'She said people in the Midland Hotel were throwing bread rolls at the crowd, and someone else said it was nothing to do with the Midland – it was lads larking about. They all said there was a lot of trouble,' Sally went on.

'There was nothing like that, Sal,' Lawrie said. 'And we're all here safe and sound, except – what happened to your head, Cathy?'

Mary launched into a carefully edited account of the accident, but Cathy sat in silence, still feeling as though it was all a dream.

'That sounds a cock and bull story to me, Mary,' her mother said wearily. 'But never mind. Help me with the meal.'

Lawrie came in from the back kitchen, washed and tidied, and they sat down in uneasy silence. When he glanced up at the clock as they finished the meal, Sally said, swiftly, 'I hope you're not thinking of going out again tonight.'

'I just want to find out what's happening,' he said.

She banged the teapot down and screamed at him: 'Lawrie, I'm warning you. You go out again and my nerves won't stand it. I was nearly out of my mind this afternoon, and I can't take any more.'

She burst into angry tears and the girls looked at each other in horror. Mam, always so calm and capable, always the one to offer strength and comfort, to behave like this.

'I've never seen her this way before,' Mary whispered as their father went to hold Sally in his arms.

'All right, all right, love,' he soothed her. 'I won't go out again. I didn't realise you were so upset.'

'What do you expect? I'm not made of stone,' she wept.

In later years when Cathy thought of the strike this scene always came to her mind. Never before had she seen her mother, usually so strong and reserved, break down like this. For the first time they all realised how much the tension in the city and in the house had affected her. Even Mary who might otherwise have gone out to enjoy the excitement, stayed home to help comfort Sally.

She made fresh tea and Sally was installed in the Windsor chair with Lawrie crouching beside her, talking soothingly to her. Cathy wanted to help but her limbs felt heavy, and she felt hot and cold in turn. Mary cleared the table and washed the dishes, but Cathy still sat in the chair, unable to stand up.

Mary must have realised that something was wrong. She bent over her and whispered, 'Come in the parlour.'

'I can't stand up,' Cathy whispered back. 'You'll have to help me.' Fortunately they were out of their mother's line of vision, and Mary pulled Cathy to her feet and helped her into the parlour.

'What's wrong with your legs?' she demanded. 'It was only your head that was hurt, wasn't it?'

'Yes, but I feel queer. Oh, Mary, I think everyone's gone mad! Even Mam going on like that.' Mary went out and came back with a drink of water for her.

'You look a bit better now,' she said as Cathy sipped it. 'Are your legs still shaky?'

Cathy rubbed her hand over her face. 'Yes, I think so,' she said doubtfully, but suddenly there was a knock on the door and she was gripped by terror.

It might be the police come to arrest Dad, she thought.

Mary walked calmly into the lobby. 'I'm going,' she called.

The next moment Cathy heard Jimmie Burn's voice, then Mary came back into the parlour.

'He's come with all the news, so Dad needn't go out again,' she said, then looked sharply at Cathy. 'Are you all right?'

'I feel funny,' Cathy said slowly. She knew that she was slurring the words but she could do nothing about it.

Mary dashed into the kitchen. 'Mam, there's something wrong with Cathy,' she screamed.

The next moment Sally and the two men were in the parlour. The bandage was unwound and the cut examined, but Sally said decidedly, 'It's not the cut. That's been properly dressed. It must be the knock on her head.'

'Not much use looking for a doctor,' Jimmie Burns said. 'They've all got their hands full. There's plenty with broken heads after today.'

Lawrie signalled to him to say no more, in case it upset Sally, and Cathy was carried upstairs and put to bed. She still felt dazed but was thankful to find herself in bed, with her mother plumping up pillows behind her and Mary bringing a hot water bottle for her feet.

'I'm hot, Mam,' she managed to say.

'Your feet are cold,' her mother said briskly. 'Now I've put you half sitting up, Cath. Don't slide down. You shouldn't lie flat with a cut on your head like that. Just rest now, love.' She jerked her head at Mary and they went downstairs.

For a while Cathy lay in a state between waking and sleeping, tormented by frightening dreams, but eventually she slipped into a sound sleep.

She woke at intervals, reassured to hear Mary breathing quietly beside her, but when morning came it was clear that she was not fit for work and a message was sent to Mr Finestone. In spite of her discomfort, thoughts of Gregory were continually in her mind. She lay picturing his face as he bent over her, and his gentleness as he bandaged her head, and wondered if she would ever see him again.

Her mother believed that it was as much the fright she had received as the injury to her head that had affected Cathy, and she told Mary and Lawrie that she was to be told nothing of the events in the city. On Wednesday evening, however, Rosie came to see Cathy and told her that two men had been shot in Vauxhall Road the previous night.

'There's nowt but fighting everywheer,' Rosie said with gusto. 'Not just i' Liverpool either. Troops is in Salford and Hull and I don't know wheer. It's Civil War, is this.'

Sally came upstairs in time to hear the last words and hustled Rosie downstairs for a cup of tea. As soon as she had gone, Sally went up to her daughter.

'I hope you didn't take any notice of Rosie's tales,' she said. 'Some people will make a drama out of nothing.'

'I'm not interested anyway,' Cathy said. She had been told by Mary that her mother thought she had been frightened by events, but felt unable to reveal that the real fright had been when her mother broke down. Cathy had been totally unprepared. It had felt as if the solid ground was opening beneath her feet.

'I'm glad to hear it,' her mother now said briskly. 'I'll have another look at that cut.' She took off the bandage and examined the wound.

'It's healing nicely,' she said, then hesitated. 'Tell me the truth now, Cathy,' she said finally. 'Did you hit your head on the door or was that from a policeman's truncheon?'

'Mam!' Cathy exclaimed. 'I can show you the door. Right opposite the jeweller's shop.'

'I thought it might be one of Mary's fairy tales and I knew you'd back her up,' Sally said. 'But I believe you. It seems such a bad cut, though.'

'I jumped back and Mary pushed me behind her at the same time,' Cathy explained. 'That's why I hit my head so hard. Mary tried to save me,' she added proudly, but Sally was unimpressed.

'There'd have been no need if you'd kept away like I warned you,' she said. 'It was lucky those people were good enough to take you in and look after you. I've written to thank Mrs Redmond and her son.'

A deep blush spread over Cathy's face at the mention of Gregory, but her mother had moved away to close the window so it passed unnoticed.

'Can I get up tomorrow?' Cathy asked. 'I feel much better.'

'Yes, but you'd better have Friday off. Your dad goes back on Tuesday.'

'Is the strike over then?' Cathy asked.

'Yes, and I don't want to hear another thing about it,' her mother said firmly.

Cathy lay back letting her mind dwell on thoughts of Gregory: his grey eyes, and the way his dark hair fell over his forehead, and his deep pleasant voice when he spoke to her. She would have been happy to know how often Gregory thought of her in the days following the accident.

When he left the girls at the end of Egremont Street he walked back to the flat, thinking of Cathy's brown eyes and the way the dimples appeared in her cheeks when she smiled.

I'll have to see her again, he thought, but he realised that he had learned nothing about the girls except that they lived in Egremont Street. Although Mary had carefully made references to the fact that she worked in Denby's when she was talking to his mother, Gregory had been too engrossed in Cathy to pay any attention to the conversation.

When he reached home he ran up the stairs two at a time, whistling. As he went into the living room, his mother held her hand to her head.

'Gregory, less noise, please,' she said fretfully. 'My poor head! And you've been such a long time.'

'Not really, Mother,' he said. 'I only took the girls to the end of the street where they live.'

She moaned faintly. 'I feel quite dreadful. All that noise and commotion, and then that girl brought in here covered in blood. Sometimes you have no consideration for my feelings, Gregory.'

'I'm sorry, Mother,' he said stiffly. 'I don't know what else I could have done under the circumstances. Catherine—' his voice grew softer as he spoke her name – 'had quite a bad injury to her head.'

'I can't understand young girls being among a crowd of rough men,' Mrs Redmond said. 'Surely they could have found another way home if they'd wanted to.'

'They were caught up in the crowd,' Gregory said. His tone was sharp and his mother peeped at him suspiciously, then closed her eyes and said no more.

Waking or sleeping, his mind was filled with thoughts of Cathy and his longing to see her again grew unbearable. He hung about Egremont Street hoping to meet her, but without success. One day he was accosted by a red-haired child who was chalking out hopscotch squares on the pavement.

'Are you a copper?' she asked. 'I seen you here last night and the night before.'

'Er – no,' he said. 'No. Er – do you know if Catherine Ward lives here?'

'Cathy. She lives next door to us. She got hurt by a copper's horse, me mam said. She's in bed.'

'In bed,' he echoed in dismay. 'She's ill then. Can you show me the house?'

The red-haired child left her game and led the way to the Wards' house, volunteering the information that she was Sarah Burns and that she liked Cathy but Mary was too stuck up. Gregory was too worried to pay much attention. He gave Sarah a penny and she went off gleefully while Greg knocked at the door. Normally he would have found it difficult to knock and introduce himself to strangers but the thought of Catherine lying ill drove everything else from his mind.

Sally opened the door and he said quickly, 'Er – Mrs Ward? I'm Gregory Redmond. I called to enquire – I dressed Catherine's head on Sunday.'

Sally smiled at the agitated young man.

'Mr Redmond,' she said. 'Come in. I'm glad to be able to thank you in person.'

'Catherine – I was told she was ill in bed?' he said anxiously.

'She's up today,' Sally said, leading the way down the lobby to the kitchen where Cathy was sitting reading.

She jumped to her feet and Gregory said quickly, 'Oh, please don't get up! I didn't want to disturb you – I just wondered…' He stopped, and he and Cathy stood smiling at each other until Sally pushed a chair forward.

'Sit down, Mr Redmond,' she said. 'It was very kind of you and your mother to help my daughters. You did a good job on that cut but the knock on her head made Cathy dizzy for a few days.'

'But you feel better now?' Gregory said to Cathy, and she smiled shyly and murmured, 'Yes, thank you.'

Gregory looked embarrassed and Sally asked if he would like a cup of tea or a glass of lemonade.

'Lemonade, please,' he said, and Cathy jumped to her feet again. 'I'll get it.'

She went into the back kitchen where a jug of homemade lemonade stood on the cold slab, covered with bead-weighted muslin to keep out flies. She felt that she wanted to dance and sing, but the few moments while she poured out the lemonade gave her time to compose herself before she returned to the kitchen. As she handed the glass to Gregory their fingers touched and a tingle seemed to run through her body.

She sat down further away from Greg so that she could study his face unobserved as he answered her mother's questions about the Red Cross. A few moments later her father came down the lobby, whistling.

Sally introduced him to Greg, and Lawrie said cheerfully, 'So you're the Good Samaritan who didn't pass by! You did a good job on that cut on Cathy's head.' He shook hands with Greg and sat down. 'I've just been to look at the horses in the Yard,' he explained. 'The men aren't back yet but we've been keeping an eye on the animals. You wouldn't believe the water they get through in this weather.' He turned to Cathy. 'I met that lad who runs the cycling club and he was asking about you. I didn't know who he was until he said something about the Mersey Wheelers.'

'Is that the name of the club?' Greg asked.

'Yes. It's run from the Albany Boys' Club, but our Cathy being a Suffragette, thinks girls should be in it too.' Lawrie laughed.

'It's not that, Dad,' Cathy protested. 'Sydney said he'd allow the boys' sisters to join, and Norah's brother got us in.'

'Well, Sydney wanted to know if you'd be all right for next Sunday and I said you might be.'

'Next Sunday! Indeed you won't, Cathy. You can't take any chances after a knock on the head like that!' Sally exclaimed.

'I feel all right now, Mam. There's only a few more runs this year and I don't want to let Norah down.'

'We'll have to see,' her mother said firmly.

Greg had noticed that one place had been laid at the end of the table, evidently for Lawrie's meal, and he rose hurriedly to his feet and said that he must go.

'Thanks for looking after the girls that day,' Lawrie said. 'Pity our Mary's out. She'd have liked to see you again to thank you herself.'

'It was nothing,' Greg said. 'But I'm sorry to have missed her.'

'Well, I'm glad to have met you,' Lawrie said heartily. 'Call in any time you're passing. Mary might be in the next time.'

Sally shook hands also but without repeating Lawrie's invitation, and Greg held out his hand to Cathy. She shook hands quickly, blushing and looking away, conscious of her parents' presence. Lawrie saw Greg to the front door then came back, rubbing his hands together and saying cheerfully, 'A nice lad that. Good manners.'

Sally shook her head at him. 'Honestly, Lawrie, you never stop to think. Talking about Mary missing him, and asking him to call in any time. He'll think we're trying to get her off our hands.'

'Rubbish, Sal,' he said with a hearty laugh. 'The lad wouldn't make anything out of what I said unless he was a bighead, and I don't think he is. You worry too much.'

'And you say the first thing that comes into your head,' she retorted.

Lawrie laughed again. 'All the same I bet our Mary'll be mad she missed him,' he said. 'A nice-looking young fellow like that.'

Cathy listened in dismay. She felt sure that there was something between herself and Greg. Something in the way he had looked at her and gripped her hand, and some deep feeling within herself which responded to him. Something quite different to the shallow fleeting attraction she had felt for Frank Mellor. But when she thought of Mary her heart sank. How easily she had charmed Frank. And Cathy wondered – had Greg really come to enquire about her, as he had said and she had believed to be true, or had he been hoping to see Mary, as her parents seemed to think?

Her mother had insisted on Cathy's going to bed early, but she was still awake when Mary came up to bed.

'Hello, Cath,' she said carelessly. 'Are you all right?'

'Yes, thanks.'

Mary sat down before the mirror and began to take the pins from her hair.

'I believe we had a visitor,' she said, picking up her hairbrush.

'Yes, Greg Redmond,' Cathy said eagerly. 'He was sorry he missed you.'

'So Dad said,' Mary replied. 'Still it won't do any harm for him to realise that I'm not available any time he cares to call in.' She leaned forward and examined her face in the mirror, smiling complacently, and Cathy watched her with consternation and anger. Why did I say that about Greg missing her? she thought. It was just something to say but she's already sure that every man she meets will fall in love with her.

She turned away and closed her eyes, willing herself to remember everything that Greg had said or done. He *does* like me, she told herself fiercely, I know he does. Nevertheless, much of her pleasure in his visit had gone and it was a long time before she could fall asleep.

Chapter Eleven

Greg's thoughts were in turmoil when he left the Wards' house, wondering whether his impulsive visit had been a mistake. Cathy had seemed pleased to see him and had smiled at him when she handed him the lemonade, but then she had moved away to sit where he was unable to see her. He was too modest to realise that Cathy had moved so that she might watch him unobserved.

Mrs Ward had been pleasant at first, he thought, but there had definitely been a chill in her manner when he left and Cathy had turned away her head as she said goodbye to him. Could it be that she and her mother had welcomed him automatically but then decided that he was impudent, barging in uninvited, or even that he had gone there looking for thanks? His face grew hot at the thought.

Familiar as he was with his mother's unreasonable moods it seemed quite likely to him that he had offended Mrs Ward in some way. Certainly he could never take up Mr Ward's invitation to call again while he was so clearly unwelcome to his wife and perhaps to Cathy. And yet he had felt so sure that there was a closeness between them... Perhaps it was just that he had thought so often about her since that first meeting.

He tossed and turned during the night, thinking of Cathy and wondering how he could contrive to see her again. A church clock was striking three when he suddenly thought of the Mersey Wheelers. What if he joined the club? He could see Cathy and gradually get to know her, and if she didn't welcome his attentions he could quietly drop out without causing any embarrassment.

The following night was his Red Cross night and he sought out a fellow member, Jack Carmody, whom he knew sometimes helped as a leader in the Albany Boys' Club, to ask about the Mersey Wheelers.

'The Cycling Club,' Jack said. 'I've been out with them once or twice myself. Sydney Townsend is the organiser.'

'I'd like to join,' Greg said. 'Is that possible?'

'Oh, yes. They're mostly young people about sixteen but Sydney's really keen and he'd welcome a new member.'

'He wouldn't think I was too old?' Greg said diffidently.

'Not at all. They are mostly the boys from the club and their friends, but Sydney's twenty-two and the leaders who often go along are about that age. As I say, I've been out with them myself. Sydney's a bit pompous but he's a good chap.'

Jack promised to see Sydney and fix things up, and Greg went home satisfied that he had started things moving. But he was too impatient to see Cathy to wait for news from his friend.

He knew by now that she worked in Crown Street. He walked through it one night but only succeeded in seeing her leaving Finestone's with a group of friends. The glimpse of her only made him more eager to speak to her again and the following night he waited in a turning off Seymour Street until he saw her approaching, then stepped out as though by accident just as she reached him. Only one girl accompanied her. Cathy and Greg greeted each other and then stood still, smiling shyly.

The girl looked curiously at Greg then said loudly, 'I'm in a hurry, Cathy. I'll see you tommorer.'

'Yes, all right,' she said vaguely, still looking at Greg and the girl laughed and ran off.

'Where are you going?' Cathy asked Greg innocently.

'Er – to er—' he said, then laughed. 'Really I'm not going anywhere. I was just hoping to see you.' They began to walk along slowly. Cathy could think of nothing to say and presently Greg said diffidently, 'I hope your mother wasn't annoyed that I called at your house.'

'Oh, no,' Cathy said. 'Why should she be?'

'I just thought—' Greg's face grew red. 'I thought she seemed – I thought I'd annoyed her.'

Now Cathy's face grew red with embarrassment. How could she repeat her father's words about Mary, and her mother's reaction to them? Instead she said quietly, 'How did you know which was our house?'

Greg explained about the red-haired little girl and Cathy chuckled.

'Sarah Burns,' she said. 'She's so *nosy*. She talks to everyone and finds out everybody's business. Her mother goes mad because she's entirely different, really quiet.'

'She asked me if I was a copper,' Greg said with a grin. 'I'd been hanging round so much hoping to see you.'

Cathy smiled with delight, her eyes like stars, and impulsively Greg took her hand and squeezed it as they walked along. He told her that he had asked Jack Carmody to enroll him in the Mersey Wheelers, and asked if she would mind if he joined.

'Of course not,' she said. 'Mam won't let me go on Sunday's run but I'll be going on the next one. We really enjoy them, me and Norah.'

'I know most of the members are younger than me,' Greg said. 'But Jack Carmody has been on some of the runs, he says, and other leaders who are about my age. He's going to let me know at the next Red Cross meeting, and perhaps come himself.'

'I think I remember him,' Cathy said. She smiled to herself, thinking that Norah would be pleased. She had really fallen for Jack Carmody but had given up hope of seeing him again.

It seemed only minutes before they arrived at Egremont Street. Mabel Burns arrived from the opposite direction at the same time.

'Hello, Cath,' she exclaimed, glancing with frank curiosity at Greg. He raised his hat and said a formal goodbye to Cathy before walking away. 'Who's the feller?' Mabel asked, linking her arm through Cathy's.

'He knows our Mary,' Cathy said, and Mabel promptly lost interest and began to talk about her baby brother. Cathy felt that she wanted to hug the thought of Greg to herself for a while before she was obliged to answer questions about him.

Greg felt that he wanted to shout or sing but he managed to restrain himself and walk steadily along, until at the bottom of Plumpton Street he came face to face with Mary.

'Mr Redmond,' she exclaimed, and Greg raised his hat, stammering: 'Miss Ward. Er – good evening.'

'Good evening. You're rather out of bounds, aren't you?' Mary said with a teasing smile, but Greg was still too exhilarated by his meeting with Cathy to concentrate and could only say lamely, 'Er – yes, I am.'

He could think of nothing else to say, and finally Mary said coolly, 'My regards to your mother.' He raised his hat again and walked rapidly away.

She strolled on, smiling to herself. It was not unusual for young men to be too overcome to speak when she smiled at them, and she put Greg's hurried departure down to this and to his lack of social experience. Probably not had much experience with girls to judge by his shyness, she thought, but she was satisfied to see that he had found out which way she walked home from work, and contrived to waylay her. She had no doubt that he would soon find a way of meeting her again.

Cathy had said nothing about meeting Greg, and neither did Mary when she arrived home, merely took off her hat and fluffed up her hair, smiling at her reflection in the overmantel mirror with a satisfied air.

'Everybody seems pleased with themselves tonight,' her father remarked as he came through from the back kitchen. 'You look like the cat that got at the cream, Mary, and our Cathy came in as though she'd lost sixpence and found a shilling. She says it's because she's feeling so much better. What's your excuse?'

'Do I need an excuse to look pleasant?' she demanded.

Her mother looked up from where she was serving the meal. 'I'll remind you of that sometime,' she said drily.

The following day was Saturday. Cathy finished work at two o'clock but she knew that she would not be able to meet Greg on his busiest day of the week. Her mother had been adamant about missing the ride on Sunday, but Norah had said that she would stay at home too.

'I don't mind, honestly,' she told Cathy. 'If it's a nice day we can go for a walk. I don't care as long as we're out.'

'Come to our house for tea,' Cathy said. 'Mam told me to ask you if you weren't going on the run.'

Norah agreed eagerly. 'I love coming to your house,' she said. 'A whole day with my da is more than I can stand. You don't know how lucky you are, Cath, to have a father like yours.'

Cathy squeezed her friend's arm in sympathy. On the rare occasion that she had been to Norah's house she had been appalled by the way her father behaved. Once she had been there when Norah's mother had forgotten to buy her husband's tobacco, and he had roared at her and hammered on the table while Norah's mother cowered before him. Another time he had flung his meal on the floor because, he said, it was cold. His violence and his loud bullying voice terrified Cathy, and she wondered how Norah could bear to live in the same house as him. Norah told her once that when her brothers were younger, her father had regularly taken them upstairs and beaten them savagely with his belt while her mother wept downstairs and Norah clung to her.

The sons had left home as soon as they were old enough, and now only Norah remained at home. Her father never struck her but he criticised everything she said or did. Once when she and Cathy had returned after ten o'clock from a concert, Norah had found the door locked when she reached home.

'You know what a cold night it was,' she told Cathy the following day. 'I'm sure I'd have frozen to death if Ma hadn't crept down to let me into the kitchen when he was asleep.'

'But what did he do when he found out?' asked Cathy.

'Oh, Ma had to come down again in the morning to let me out and bolt the door after me. I'd been in the kitchen all night so I was warm enough, and I stayed in the privy until he went to work.'

'While I was warm in bed, and it was my fault we were late,' Cathy said remorsefully. 'If it happens again, Norah, come to our house for the night.'

'Thanks all the same,' she said, 'but I wouldn't cause trouble for anyone else. That's why I didn't go to our Sam's house last night.'

'I don't know how you keep so cheerful,' Cathy exclaimed.

Norah laughed. 'He never picked on me while the lads were there,' she said. 'It's only since Tommy and Teddy joined the Army that he's started on me, because there's no one else except Ma. Sam's warned him what he'll do to him if he ever hits her, and Dad knows he means it too.' She laughed and nudged Cathy. 'Don't look so worried, Cath. He works long hours and Ma and I enjoy ourselves when he's not there.'

Cathy did worry though, and often thought how important it was to marry the right man, and not one who would become a monster like Norah's father or Mary Mellor's husband. Mrs Mellor had told her once that she was at school with Norah's mother.

'A lively pretty girl she was too,' she said. 'Like Norah is now, but that swine bullied the life outa her.'

Sunday was a sunny day and Norah and Cathy walked along the Landing Stage, their arms around each other's waists.

Cathy felt very close to her after Norah had said again how lucky her friend was to have such parents. How brave and cheerful Norah was in spite of her unhappy home. Cathy could keep the news of Greg from her no longer, and told Norah all that had happened.

'You're a dark horse!' Norah exclaimed. 'I knew he came to your house to ask about you, but I thought it was just an excuse to see Mary again.'

'Norah!' Cathy exclaimed indignantly. 'I told you he came to ask how *I* was. Why should he have come to try to see Mary? Mind you, she thought the same thing and so did my dad, I think,' she added honestly.

'And what did you think?' asked Norah, chuckling.

'I don't know. The way he looked at me… but then I thought he might be interested because he did the dressing on my head, and Mary seemed so sure.'

'She was wrong, evidently,' Norah said. 'If he made an excuse to meet you coming home from work, and he wants to join the Wheelers.'

'With Jack Carmody,' Cathy said, looking teasingly at her. 'He's asked Jack to arrange it anyway, and he said Jack Carmody might come out with the club again.'

They walked in silence for a few minutes, both busy with their own thoughts, until Norah said suddenly, 'Watch out for your Mary, Cath. Greg sounds just the sort of fellow who'd suit her. About the same age, tall and handsome, not to mention the most important part – he's got his own business.'

'Mary wouldn't!' Cathy exclaimed. 'Anyway, he's got some say in the matter, too, you know.'

'Yes, but if Mary really makes a play for a fellow he hasn't got much chance,' Norah said. 'It's not just her looks, she's crafty too. Remember poor Bertha.'

Cathy remembered, and thought about Isabel too, although she had loyally kept that affair to herself. She said staunchly, 'Mary wouldn't do anything to hurt me, and I don't think Greg would be so weak-willed either.'

'I hope not,' Norah said. 'But I felt I should warn you, Cath. You really like Greg, don't you?'

'Oh, yes,' Cathy said fervently. 'Wait till you meet him, Norah. You'll like him too. He's like my dad in many ways.'

'Then I *will* like him,' Norah said, laughing. 'I can't wait until next Sunday.'

Cathy had hoped to see Greg waiting for her when she left work on Monday, but he had been detained by a customer until it was too late, and late on Tuesday a commercial traveller had to be dealt with. On Tuesday night he saw Jack Carmody at the Red Cross meeting and learned that he had been enrolled in the Mersey Wheelers. The following Sunday the run was to Old Swan and Prescot, Jack told him.

Greg was determined to see Cathy on Wednesday after work, and he hastened off in good time to meet her. He had thought his mother knew nothing about his previous absences from the shop but she had been looking out of the flat window on the second occasion and had seen him walking away up London Road.

A bell had been connected so that she could ring the shop from the flat to summon Greg if she needed him. She rang it immediately. The shop manager, a stout elderly man, came hurrying upstairs to find Mrs Redmond lying back on the sofa, holding a bottle of smelling salts.

'Mr Gregory has just stepped out for half an hour on business, Madam,' he said. 'Can I help?'

'A glass of water please, Mr Braithwaite,' she said feebly. 'I feel a little faint.' When he returned with the water, she asked casually, 'This business. Do you know what it is?'

'In connection with repairs, I think, Madam,' Mr Braithwaite said. He had worked for the Redmond family for nearly forty years and knew far more about them than they realised.

'I see,' Mrs Redmond said. 'Don't mention to my son that I needed to ring for him, please. I wouldn't wish to worry him.'

Mr Braithwaite bowed and left her, allowing himself a secret smile before he returned to the shop. He said nothing to Greg and neither did Mrs Redmond, but she stationed herself at the window at the same time on Monday and Tuesday. She was there on Wednesday when Gregory strode away up London Road, and still there twenty minutes later when Mary left the shop and crossed over London Road.

'So that's it,' Mrs Redmond said aloud. 'That's what's going on. She's missed him and come here looking for him, the brazen hussy.' She flung herself back in the chair and wept.

The truth was that Mary had become impatient at what she saw as Greg's slowness, and determined to hurry things along. She took from her secret hoard a bracelet lent to her by Isabel and never returned, and broke the safety chain on it. Denby's had begun to close early on Wednesday's so Mary walked up to Lime Street Station and in the ladies' cloakroom washed her hands and face, then combed out her hair and arranged her hat at a becoming angle before walking to the shop in London Road.

She had arrived minutes after Greg had left, unseen by Mrs Redmond who was looking in the direction Greg had taken.

Mary's quick glance around showed her that Greg was not in the shop, but she went to the fatherly figure of Mr Braithwaite and smiled appealingly at him as she produced the bracelet. He placed a chair for her in front of the counter and disappeared into a back room with the bracelet. Mary meanwhile turned her attention to a young man who was tidying a showcase.

'I thought I might see Gregory Redmond,' she said.

'He's just stepped out on business, Madam,' the young assistant said.

Mary smiled up at him. 'He's very interested in the Red Cross, isn't he?' she said.

The young man drew closer to her. 'Yes. He should have been a doctor, you know,' he confided.

Mary gazed into his eyes. '*Should* he?' she murmured, fluttering her lashes.

The young man was lost. 'Yes,' he said recklessly. 'He was training for it, but his father was up to his eyes in debt when he died, and Mr Gregory had to come into the business instead.'

He glanced behind him but, there was no sign of Mr Braithwaite and the shop lad was chasing a dog from the door, so he continued: 'His uncle would have paid for him, I believe, but it was Mrs Redmond. She quarrelled with her brother-in-law so that was out, and she wanted him – Mr Gregory, I mean – here to dance attendance on her. I'm sorry for him, straight I am.'

Mary leaned closer to him. 'What happened about all the debts?' she asked. 'It could have been a tragedy for all the staff, couldn't it?'

'It could indeed,' he agreed in a low voice. 'Luckily the uncle and the solicitor sorted matters out before *she* quarrelled with them.'

'So the shop's pulled round now?' Mary asked, and when he nodded she said sweetly, 'I'm so glad, for *your* sake.'

Mr Braithwaite returned to the shop and the young assistant moved hastily away to another counter.

'I'm so sorry for the delay, Madam,' Mr Braithwaite said. 'The man had some difficulty because the chain had broken off and pulled a link out of place. It must have caught on something.'

Mary smiled at him. 'Thank you so much,' she said. 'I'm very fond of this bracelet.' She took her purse from her pocket but Mr Braithwaite waved it away.

'Our pleasure, Madam,' he said. 'Perhaps we will have the pleasure of serving you on another occasion.'

'I'm sure you will,' Mary said. 'You're very kind.'

She rose and walked gracefully from the shop after including the young assistant in her dazzling smile, well satisfied with the result of her visit even though she had not seen Greg.

Chapter Twelve

Greg arrived at Finestone's shortly before Cathy emerged. Her eyes lit up when she saw him waiting for her. They lingered behind the girls who were rushing away from the building, and walked slowly along, holding hands, as Greg told her about his plans for Sunday.

'A monsoon wouldn't keep me away,' he said fervently. All too soon, it seemed, they arrived at Egremont Street and Greg asked if he might see her again the next night.

'I was held up these last two but I'll be here tomorrow night, if you're sure you don't mind, Cathy.'

'I'll look forward to seeing you,' she said honestly, but people were approaching so she said goodbye hastily.

All the following day, as she sat at her sewing machine, Cathy thought about Greg, longing for six o'clock when she would see him again. But when she left Finestone's he was nowhere to be seen. She began to dawdle along, wondering whether she had mistaken the meeting place, when he arrived, breathless.

'Cathy,' he gasped, 'I'm terribly sorry – I'll have to go right back. Mother rang down to the shop for me. She was so upset, quite hysterical. She'd been reading letters Father had sent her, and looking at photographs of him.'

'Then you must go right back, Greg,' Cathy exclaimed. 'Is there anyone with her?'

'No. She thinks I've gone to the chemist for a draught for her.'

'Then go, quickly,' she urged, and he squeezed her hand before running back down the steep street. Cathy walking on, disappointed that their meeting had been so brief but thinking sympathetically of his mother's grief. Her soft heart was touched by the thought of Mrs Redmond's sorrow at her husband's death and the realisation of how much she must miss him.

Imagine if it was Dad, she thought. How would Mam or any of us bear it? It must be hard for Greg too when he has to try to comfort his mother while he still has his own grief to bear.

Her mind was filled with sad thoughts but she tried to throw off her despondency before she reached home in case it aroused comment from her mother. She had still not said anything to her parents about Greg, and the longer she left it the more difficult it seemed to tell them about him.

Later that evening when Cathy was in Josie's house, Mary, usually the more secretive of the two sisters, spoke about Greg to her parents.

Lawrie had grazed his hand on the wheel of his wagon, and he commented jokingly to Sally that he could have done with the young chap who dressed the cut on Cathy's head, to see to the graze for him. Mary was sewing a button on a skirt but she looked up.

'He should have been a doctor, you know,' she said.

'He certainly shaped like one,' Lawrie said. 'He did a great job on Cathy's head. What stopped him being a doctor?'

'His father died, leaving a lot of debts, so he had to go into the business,' Mary said. 'His uncle would have paid for the training but Mrs Redmond quarrelled with him.'

Her parents exchanged glances but said nothing then. Later in bed, Sally said quietly to Lawrie, 'Our Mary seemed to know a lot about the Redmond lad.'

'That's what I thought,' he agreed. 'I liked the lad anyway, so I'm not grumbling.'

'Neither am I. Let's hope she's found someone to suit her at last and will settle down.'

'I told you she would,' said Lawrie. 'There you are, Sal. All that worrying for nothing.'

'It's a wonder he hasn't been here though,' she said. 'All her other fellows call for her.'

'Well, perhaps it's a sign that she's serious about him,' Lawrie argued.

'M'm, maybe. I'm not so sure as you, Lawrie, but I hope she *is* settled with him. I really liked him, too.'

Mary said no more about Greg during the following days but she seemed full of high spirits, and Sally was sure that he was the cause.

Cathy came out of Finestone's on Thursday night looking around hopefully, and was delighted to see Greg waiting for her. He came over and took her hand, smiling down at her.

She said immediately, 'How is your mother, Greg?'

'Much better,' he assured her. 'I've asked her not to look out photographs and letters as they upset her so much, and she's promised not to.'

'It must be very hard for her,' Cathy said, 'but perhaps as time goes on—'

'I hope so,' he said. 'You're very kind-hearted, Cathy.' He squeezed her hand. 'Mr Braithwaite in the shop is rather unsympathetic. Mother has rung down to the shop for me three times today, and Braithwaite told me I should be more firm with her. He said Father spoiled her and I shouldn't do the same.'

'Of all the cheek!' Cathy exclaimed. 'It's easy for him to talk. He doesn't know what it's like to be a widow.'

'He means well,' Greg said. 'He's been with us for about forty years and he treats me like a son, but I did rather resent his saying that about Mother. I suppose it's true in one way – Father was a very indulgent husband. My uncle said that too, but it only makes it harder for Mother now.'

'I'm sure it does,' agreed Cathy. 'But if Mr Braithwaite has been with you so long he must be quite old himself, and old men get funny ideas, don't they?'

'Yes. I shouldn't get annoyed with him,' Greg said. 'I owe him a lot. I didn't know anything about the business so he's been a tower of strength to me.'

'Did you find it very hard, learning the business?' she asked gently.

Greg shrugged. 'It was the whole thing,' he said. 'I felt as though the sky had fallen in on me. I'd always wanted to be a doctor and it was all mapped out. I was to train at Guy's and was working hard to qualify for entrance there – I'd have made a good doctor, Cath, I know I would. Then my father died, and everything changed.'

'It must have been terrible – losing your father at that age.'

'Yes.' Greg hesitated. 'I felt – if he'd lived longer, we might have got to know each other better.' Cathy was silent, uncertain what to say, and he continued, 'You see, it wasn't like your family, Cath. I was away at school, and even in the holidays Mother and Father were often abroad so I didn't see much of them. I stayed with my aunt and uncle, and they have a son a few months older than me, and three daughters, so they were really more like my family. This may seem odd to you, but in a way, when Mother and my uncle quarrelled, I missed him more than I missed my own father. Do you think that's strange, Cathy?'

'Not at all,' she said. 'I can see how it was for you. It must have been a dreadful time.'

'We didn't live over the shop then,' Greg said. 'Father owned three shops but when he died so suddenly things were in rather a mess. Mother was always delicate, you see, so he often had to take her abroad, then we had a large house near Neston on the Wirral, which cost a lot to keep up.'

'So when did you come to live over the shop?'

'When my uncle, who was my father's executor, and the solicitor sorted things out. They decided that the house would have to go, and two of the shops, and we would keep the shop on London Road and have the empty rooms over it done up and furnished for Mother and me to live in. It meant of course that she lost all her friends just when she needed them most, and she felt very bitter towards my uncle but I'm sure he was doing what he thought was best for us.'

They had reached the corner of Egremont Street and Greg said ruefully, 'I'm sorry, Cathy, I talked about myself all the way home. It's just that I've never had anyone to talk to and you're such a sympathetic listener. Forgive me.'

'Of course,' she said, and smiled shyly. 'I'm very interested.'

'We'll talk about you all day on Sunday,' he said. 'I'm looking forward to it no end.'

'Your mother will be all right?'

'Oh, yes. I've arranged for a lady from the church to visit her, and she said she's pleased to know I'll be out in the fresh air.' They smiled at each other.

'Till Sunday then. Ten o'clock at the corner of Low Hill.'

'Till Sunday,' Greg echoed, watching her as she walked lightly away. Reluctantly, he turned to walk back to the shop, thinking of the scene with his mother when he had first mentioned the outing with the Mersey Wheelers.

She had paid little attention when he spoke about Jack Carmody, but when he said that he had asked Jack to enroll him in the cycling club, she had begun to weep.

'So I'm to be left alone all day,' she wept. 'Your father asked you on his deathbed to look after me, and this is what you do. I'm glad he didn't live to see what an ungrateful, selfish son you are.'

'That's not fair, Mother,' he protested. 'I do my best but I think I'm entitled to a day out now and again. I'll ask Miss Nugent to stay with you.' His mother had continued to cry and reproach him until he walked out of the room in a fury. When he returned, she had changed completely.

'I'm sorry, dear,' she said. 'I was upset but you are quite right. I'll be pleased for you to have a day in the fresh air away from the shop. You must go ahead with your plans.'

Now Greg reflected on the feeling of relief which had swept over him, and decided that he had sprung his plan too suddenly on his mother.

It was fortunate for his peace of mind that he was not aware that she was busily making her plans.

Rain fell heavily on Friday night and Saturday morning, but on Saturday afternoon a fresh wind sprang up and sent the clouds scudding inland. Sunday dawned bright and sunny.

'Isn't it a lovely morning?' Cathy said when she called for Norah. 'Everything looks as though it has been washed.'

Norah smiled at her glowing face. 'I suppose you'd think it was lovely if it was raining cats and dogs,' she said quizzically. 'As long as you saw Greg.' Cathy smiled and blushed but made no reply as they rode along to the meeting point at Low Hill.

They were early and only a few members had arrived. Greg was not among them. Cathy looked eagerly down Prescot Street, hoping to see him riding up, but the road was empty. She and Norah stood on the outskirts of the group, holding the handlebars of their bicycles and frequently glancing down the hill. Only Jack Carmody appeared.

He greeted the rest of the group then moved nearer to Cathy and Norah.

'I have a message for you from Greg Redmond, Catherine,' he said quietly. 'I called there but they were waiting for the doctor – his mother has had a heart attack. He asked me to tell you how sorry he is that he can't join us.'

Cathy was unable to speak and Norah said quickly, 'Is she very bad?'

Jack Carmody shrugged. 'I didn't see her,' he said. 'There was a rather hysterical friend there but Redmond was very concerned about the message for Catherine.' He raised his cap and moved off to join Sydney. A few moments later the Wheelers set off.

Cathy was grateful to Norah for staying close to her, and giving her time to recover before she needed to speak to the others. It was a pleasant ride but Cathy noticed little of the beauty around her as she rode along, listening to Norah's easy chatter, and wondering what was happening at Greg's home. Her feelings were divided between bitter disappointment on her own behalf and concern for Greg and his mother. She longed to be with him and comfort him. They stopped at Old Swan, and settled down under the trees to eat their lunch.

Sydney announced that after lunch those who wished could continue on to Prescot a few miles further up the hill, and the others could explore Old Swan and the nearby district of Knotty Ash.

Cathy and Norah were sitting eating their sandwiches when Jack Carmody joined them.

'We don't often see you out with us,' Norah said.

He smiled. 'I came today to give moral support to Greg Redmond. I thought he was a bit worried about being older than most of the members, so I came along too.'

He looked at Cathy and said teasingly, 'I didn't know he had a special reason for joining.'

Cathy blushed but said nothing and Norah remarked that it was a shame that after all Greg had been unable to come.

'I hope his mother is not very ill,' she added. 'It sounds serious.'

'I doubt it,' Jack said drily.

'You think he was just making an excuse?' Norah said.

'Oh, no, but I just wonder about the heart attack. I may be misjudging the lady, but it's amazing how often she's ill on Red Cross nights, so Greg can't turn up. I wasn't surprised this morning that he was prevented from coming.'

'But why doesn't he just ignore her if she's only pretending?' Norah asked.

Jack smiled at her flushed, indignant face. 'It's not as simple as that,' he said. 'People can actually induce heart attacks through hysteria. It's sometimes hard to tell whether it's genuine or not, and there's always the possibility that you may be wrong.'

'But don't you learn that sort of thing in the Red Cross?' asked Norah.

'Not exactly, and of course it's different when it's someone close to you. Redmond seems to believe in her illness and, as I say, it may be real. If he doesn't, he's too loyal to say so anyway.'

Sydney came over to them. 'Are you coming on to Prescot, girls?' he asked.

'"Does the road wind uphill all the way?"' said Norah, striking a pose, and Jack countered with, '"Yes, to the very end."' Seriously though, it's an interesting little town. Birthplace of Kemble, and Nelson's friend Hardy lived there. There's a Pre-Reformation church too. Can't we tempt you?'

'Last chance this year,' Sydney added, but Norah shook her head.

'No, thanks. Too steep for us, isn't it, Cathy? We'll just explore Knotty Ash.'

The Prescot contingent rode off, and Cathy and Norah set off with them but turned aside to ride to Knotty Ash. Cathy appreciated Norah's tact and kindness in saving her from the need to talk to the others and refraining from any comment on Greg's mother.

'Jack Carmody's nice, isn't he? Not very discreet but nice,' was all that Norah said.

The sun shone and the air was sweet with the scent of honey-suckle in the hedges they passed, but Cathy felt that the beauty around them only made her heart heavier. She tried to look and act as though she were enjoying herself, feeling that it was unfair to spoil Norah's day out by being miserable. Strangely, after a while she found that her efforts to convince Norah made her feel more cheerful herself.

In Knotty Ash they dismounted and leaned their bikes against the wall while they wandered round the old churchyard, reading the inscriptions on the gravestones.

'Look at this,' Cathy said to Norah. "Isabella, devoted wife of Samuel and loving mother of all her children". And six of the children died within seven years of her death.'

They paused by another gravestone to read the names of five children who had died in infancy, then, most poignant of all, a later inscription which read: 'March 1862, Michael Horatio, lost at sea aged fourteen years. The only surviving child and the joy and hope of his sorrowing parents. "Though He slay me yet will I trust in Him!"'

Cathy shivered, feeling cold as she read the words so eloquent of almost unbearable grief. Norah slipped her hand through her friend's arm.

'How did they bear losing all those children?' she said. 'Come on, Cath. We shouldn't be glooming here on a lovely day like this.'

'No, we shouldn't,' Cathy agreed, leading the way to the bicycles, but she felt less sad than when she entered the churchyard. Perhaps the evidence of real grief had put her own disappointment in perspective.

They cycled downhill and came to a farmhouse on the corner of the lane, a row of terraced cottages beside it. Narrow arched passage-ways ran between some of the cottages and Norah dismounted.

'Let's go down here,' she said.

'They belong to the cottages,' Cathy protested, but Norah was already halfway down the passage, wheeling her bike. Cathy followed meekly. It led to a cobbled square and another group of cottages, and as they emerged an old woman popped out of one of the doors giving on to the square.

'Oh, I'm sorry,' Norah said, smiling at her. 'We thought this lane might lead somewhere. We're trying to find somewhere where they serve teas.'

'Nay, theer's nowt theer, lass, only fields,' the old woman said. 'Whee're tha from?'

'Liverpool.'

'Liverpool,' the old woman echoed in amazement. 'By th' eck, love, you're a long way from whoam and wantin' a cup of tea. Come in, do. I'll mek tha a cup.' She turned and went into the cottage and the girls propped their bicycles against the wall and followed her.

'I wasn't hinting for you to make us a cup of tea,' Norah said, looking uncomfortable. 'We just thought – a teashop.'

'Nay, a cup of tea's nowt,' the woman said. 'Tha must be clemmed. Sit thee down. It'll not be a minute.'

She bustled about making tea in a big brown teapot, and putting a plateful of buttered scones on the table.

'Help thaselves now. Don't wait to be pressed,' she said.

The scones were hot from the oven and Cathy said shyly, 'They're lovely, but weren't they meant for somebody else?'

'Nay, love, my daughter-in-law or some of the children might coom in, but theer's plenty.'

'Is that your daughter-in-law?' Norah asked, indicating a sepia portrait of a girl taken in profile as she held a rose against her cheek. 'She's pretty, isn't she?'

'Not if tha saw her face on,' the old woman said frankly. 'She's a good girl, but she skens like a basket of whelps.'

The girls looked puzzled and the old woman suddenly crossed her eyes. 'Like that,' she said with a chuckle.

Cathy and Norah were uncertain what to do about payment when they had finished the meal, but when Norah put her hand in her pocket the jingle of money made the old woman whip round.

'I hope as tha's not thinking of leaving owt,' she said. 'If I can't give folk a cup of tea wi'out money passin' it's a poor do. Eh, I enjoyed the jangle with thee, I did that.'

'Well, thank you very much,' Norah said, and Cathy added, 'We really enjoyed talking to you, and the scones were lovely.'

They left with an invitation to call at any time and began to ride back to Old Swan to join the others.

'Wasn't she nice?' Cathy said. She suddenly began to laugh. 'The way she described her daughter-in-law. "She skens like a basket of whelps".'

'It's a good description of a squint though,' Norah said. 'When you think of the tiny puppies they sell behind the market, all cross-eyed until they're old enough to focus.'

'Funny that it's so near Liverpool yet the people talk so different. Real Lancashire. I wonder just where people stop talking Liverpool and start talking like that? Wasn't she a nice old woman though, and she'd had such a hard life.'

'Yes. Widowed before she was thirty and with five young children to keep on the little she could earn.'

'I'm glad the children are good to her now,' Cathy said. 'But I suppose they enjoy visiting her. She's such a cheerful woman.' She sighed suddenly. 'I wonder how Greg's mother is? Do you think Jack Carmody was right, Norah, and her illness is just imaginary?'

'It seems like it if she's sick whenever he wants to go out,' Norah said. 'You'd think he'd be able to tell though, with Red Cross training and all.'

'I suppose he can never be sure, as Jack said. There's always the chance that it might be real, and if he was unsympathetic then he'd never forgive himself.'

'Pity she's not more like that old woman,' Norah said. 'It'd do her good to have to turn to and look after someone else instead of leaning on her son.'

This was so uncomfortably close to what Cathy had been thinking herself that she tried to change the subject.

'I've enjoyed myself today, Norah, thanks to you. I didn't think I was going to but I did.'

'That's good. No use upsetting yourself over a fellow like that.'

Cathy's face grew red. 'What do you mean?' she said. 'A fellow like that?'

'Tied to his mother's apron strings. He'll never be any good to you, Cath.'

'But he's not tied to his mother's apron strings. He just feels responsible for her. His father asked him to look after her when he was on his deathbed, so Greg feels it's his duty to look after her.'

'To look after her, but not to let her rule his life,' Norah said. 'You couldn't rely on him if she decided to be ill whenever he arranged to see you.'

'It's too soon to decide that,' Cathy said. 'That's only what Jack Carmody thinks about it.' She was beginning to regret having told her friend so much and Norah seemed to realise it because she only said, 'It's your business, Cath. I only wanted you to see what you might be getting into, before you got too fond of him.' Cathy smiled at her and said nothing, but she thought ruefully, Too late for that, Norah. Too late from the first moment I saw Greg.

She knew that whatever happened in the future nothing could change her feelings for him.

Chapter Thirteen

Later, when Cathy left Norah and rode home, she tried to remember Mrs Redmond as she had seen her on the day when Greg carried her into the room over the shop, but her memories were confused. She could vaguely remember a tiny woman, richly dressed, who complained about her heart, and Mary talking to her and bringing in some reference to her rich uncle and aunt in Aigburth. But all that Cathy could picture clearly was Greg's face as he bent over her.

When she reached home her mother and Mary were both out and her father was asleep on the sofa. He woke and told her that her mother had left her meal ready, then he nodded at the mantelpiece.

'There's a note there for you, love,' he said. 'A young lad brought it.'

Cathy snatched up the envelope and tore it open. It contained a note from Greg.

> Dear Miss Ward,
>
> I hope you enjoyed the day. I can't tell you how sorry I was to miss it. My mother recovered quite quickly from her attack, but she plans to stay in bed for a few days.
>
> There is a concert in aid of the Red Cross to be held in the Assembly Rooms on Wednesday night. Will you be free to attend it?
>
> Yours truly,
> Gregory Redmond.

Her father had gone into the back kitchen and Cathy sat down clutching the note, a happy smile on her face.

She was still sitting, holding the note and smiling, when her father came back into the kitchen. He looked at her enquiringly.

'Good news, love?'

'It's from Greg Redmond, Dad,' she said eagerly.

'Greg – oh, the lad who bandaged your head.'

'Yes, he wants me to go to a concert with him on Wednesday,' Cathy said, looking at him with shining eyes.

'You and Mary?' he asked.

'No, Dad, *me*. Nothing to do with Mary,' she said with a touch of resentment. 'He was going to come on the run today but his mother was ill.'

Lawrie sat down and began to fill his pipe to give himself time to think. 'He belongs to your Club then? I didn't know that,' he said.

'He's only just joined. This should have been his first time out but his mother had a heart attack.'

'I see,' her father said, feeling that he was seeing much that he had been blind to before. He made a great play of lighting his pipe, his mind working furiously. What was going on? If that young fellow was playing fast and loose with his girls, he thought with the beginnings of anger, but then he remembered the young man sitting nervously in the kitchen and decided that he was not the type for that. One of the girls must have got hold of the wrong end of the stick and it was more likely to be Cathy. He hoped fervently that Sally would come home before Mary. She would know how to deal with this.

'What does he say about the concert, love?' he said gently.

'Just asks if I'm free,' Cathy said, still smiling. 'Here you are, Dad. You can read it.' She held out the note to him.

Lawrie read the stilted little missive with relief. So that was it! No word of love in the note, and he didn't even ask outright to take her to the concert. It looked as though the young fellow was trying to reach Mary through Cathy, but what a damnfool way of going about things! Here was his poor child, happy and excited, believing that Greg was courting *her*.

'He's a bit old for you, pet, isn't he?' Lawrie said cautiously.

Cathy flashed back, 'Only four years, but he's had a lot of responsibility with having to take over after his father died. That's made him seem older.'

'Aye, and being an only child and his mother at odds with her family – he's got a lot on,' her father said. 'You'd be better off with a lad of your own age, love.'

She was looking at him in amazement. 'How do you know all that, Dad?' she asked, disregarding his other remarks.

'Our Mary told us. Seemingly he told her all about himself,' Lawrie said.

'But I heard all he said when we were coming home,' said Cathy. 'She must have got all that out of his mother. I didn't hear all they were saying, only our Mary bragging about Uncle Albert's house.'

She smiled at her father's worried expression. 'It's all right, Dad. Ellen's sister was married when she was sixteen, and really in some ways Greg's very young. He's so shy.'

Lawrie got up and began to poke the fire, moving the fire irons about agitatedly, longing to hear Sally's step in the lobby. 'Eat your tea, Cathy,' he said, and fled to open the front door and peer down the street. As though in answer to prayer, Sally appeared walking with Peggy Burns.

'Sal,' he said, stepping out of the door to detain her by the front gate.

'You're in your stocking feet, and on those flags!' she exclaimed. Then, at the sight of his face, she suddenly gripped his arm. 'Lawrie, what's wrong? The girls?'

'They're all right,' he interrupted. 'At least – stay here a minute.'

'Peggy had tactfully hurried into her own house, and Lawrie quickly whispered about Cathy and the note.

'I *thought* she was excited about the run,' Sally said. 'All the time she took getting ready… but she said nothing about him. It's not like her to keep things dark.'

'I didn't know what to say to her, Sal. I mentioned that he was a bit old for her but she flared up. I'm glad you're home, love.'

'I'm sure you are,' she said ironically, before walking slowly into the house.

Cathy's meal was still untouched and Sally looked with dismay at her pink cheeks and shining eyes, and the note still clutched in her hand.

'Did you have a good day, love?' she asked, playing for time, but Cathy said immediately, 'Yes, Mam, but Greg couldn't come.'

'I didn't know he was supposed to,' she said. Cathy blushed, wondering why she had found it so hard to tell her parents about Greg. Now that she had broken the ice by telling her father she was only too anxious to talk about Greg, but her parents seemed unresponsive. Presently Cathy glanced at the clock, and said that she would slip down to see Norah.

Her mother raised no objection and Cathy went out, still carrying the note.

'So what do you think, Sal?' Lawrie asked when she had gone.

'I think it's Mary who's deluding herself.'

'But the fellow met her from work and told her all about himself,' Lawrie said. 'I think he's trying to reach Mary through Cathy and I'm worried about the poor child being hurt.'

'Why should he do that?' demanded Sally. 'He meets Mary and tells her his life history, according to her. He had plenty of chance to ask her out at the same time – no need to go all round the mulberry bush working it through Cathy. No, I think she got it right when she said Mary got the information from Greg's mother.'

'But Mary's so sure he's interested in her,' Lawrie said. 'She must have *some* reason. And Cathy's said nothing until now.'

'I know it's not like her,' Sally agreed, 'but there's been something ever since that Sunday. I've wondered once or twice when she came in from work if she was starting with brain fever because of that knock on the head, she seemed so strange.'

'I didn't see any difference in her, but it's a queer business altogether,' Lawrie said, shaking his head. 'Surely Mary's been out with enough fellows to know when one's keen.'

'It's Mary who's interested,' Sally said firmly. 'All that other stuff – well I've heard her fairy tales before. He's joined the club with Cathy, and now he's asked her out. You can't get away from that, Lawrie.'

'I don't know what to think, I just don't want Cathy to get hurt. She's too young for this sort of thing.'

Sally made a gesture of impatience. 'Of course she's old enough. How many lads had Mary been out with by the time she was Cathy's age? Cathy's just cast in a different mould to Mary, that's all. What worries me is – does Mary know that he's interested in Cathy? We'll have to keep her out of the way, especially while she's so excited, until we can talk to Mary.'

Cathy, tired by the day's cycling and her excitement, was in bed and asleep by the time her sister returned from visiting friends with Sam. Sally tried tactfully to find out just how things stood between Mary and Greg, but with little success.

Later she reported to Lawrie, 'You just can't get a straight answer from our Mary. She twisted about, hinting and bluffing, until in the end I told her straight out about Greg inviting Cathy to that concert. She still tried to fool herself that he was after her.'

'You see, Sally. Mary must have some idea of his feelings even if she can't just spell it out in black and white. That stiff little note could mean anything.'

'For God's sake, Lawrie, will you face facts? You're as bad as she is, and for the same reason. You can't believe anyone can see her without falling for her.' They were silent for a while then Sally said briskly, 'Anyway, I've put her right, and she'll have time to get used to the idea before she speaks to Cathy.'

'What idea? I think I'd better see this young fellow and put him straight, Sal.'

'But he probably doesn't realise we thought that about Mary,' she protested. 'I'm not talking about that. It's this idea of him and Cathy courting. She's far too young and she's never been out with another lad. I don't want her to get hurt.'

'I don't think Greg Redmond would hurt her. I like the lad.'

'So do I, and if Cathy was a few years older I'd be glad to see them courting, but she's too young. She's got time to change her mind half a dozen times before she settles, and she wouldn't just flit from one to another like Mary. You know what she's like, Sal. She'd get all worked up and upset if she had to tell a fellow she'd changed towards him.'

'I can see what you mean, Lol. Cathy's certainly different from Mary – as stubborn as a mule for one thing, and too soft-hearted for her own good, but what if she's met the right one now? It can happen,' she said with a slight smile.

'Don't we know it?' Lawrie said, giving her a kiss. 'It only seems five minutes since we met and here we are worrying about our girls courting. But I don't like the idea of Cathy pairing off. I think they should still go round in a crowd then there's no harm done if they change their minds.'

'Don't forget he's invited her to this concert on Wednesday.'

'Yes, well, you'd better tell her I want a word with him,' Lawrie said.

Sally sighed. 'I hope Mary was listening when I tried to tell her about the concert. Surely she must realise now that it's Cathy he's interested in.'

'I hope she won't be too upset,' Lawrie said. 'Let's hope it wasn't the lad himself she was interested in, so much as the jewellery business.'

Greg waited anxiously for Cathy's response to his note. When he reflected on his failure to turn up for the ride, coming so soon after his curtailed meeting with her on Thursday night, he worried she might decide he was unreliable and have nothing more to do with him. He had tried to convey how he felt in the letter, but after starting then tearing up numerous efforts he had finally sent the brief note, hoping he would have an opportunity to explain more fully in person.

He was feeling angry and disillusioned with his mother. He had wondered whether her illness had been genuine on other occasions, how the bouts occurred so fortuitously whenever he arranged to go out, but he'd told himself that her illness was caused by a fear of being left alone, and that she truly believed herself to be ill. Two things had changed that opinion.

On Sunday morning when his mother had collapsed, he had been alarmed and concerned and had sent for the doctor immediately in spite of his mother's protests.

'Never mind the doctor. Don't leave me, Gregory,' she had moaned, and Miss Nugent had dashed about hysterically, offering impossible remedies and shaking with terror. Greg had turned away from his mother to speak to Miss Nugent but had turned back in time to surprise a calculating expression on her face. She had closed her eyes immediately and begun to moan feebly again, but Greg felt as though cold water had been thrown in his face.

The doctor who arrived was not their usual family doctor but his young assistant. Greg felt that his mother might have refused to let him attend her if Miss Nugent had not been there, anxiously insisting she needed medical help.

Greg was waiting in the living room when the doctor left his mother's bedroom. The young locum smiled reassuringly. 'No cause for alarm,' he said. 'The patient must rest and avoid excitement.'

'Was it a heart attack?' Greg asked. The doctor pursed his lips and stroked his beard before replying.

'Strictly speaking, no,' he said. 'The lady is of a nervous disposition. Has something alarmed or distressed her this morning?'

'Yes,' Greg said bluntly. 'I arranged to go out for the day.'

'I *see*,' the doctor said. 'But she was not alone. Is that her companion?'

'No, just a friend whom I asked to stay with my mother. I may say that something like this has happened on other occasions when I've arranged to go out,' he said. He felt disloyal but his anger at the calculating look was still fierce. The doctor looked thoughtful.

'You are an only son, I take it.'

'Yes. My father died four years ago, and my mother has found it hard to recover from the loss.'

'Hmm. Has she many friends?'

'No, very few. We lived in Neston until my father's death, and Mother has not made many friends since we came to live here.'

'Then I think it would be wise if her circle of friends was enlarged. Perhaps she could interest herself in charitable work – plenty of scope for it.' He glanced round the luxuriously furnished room.

'I'll suggest it,' Greg said doubtfully.

The doctor picked up his hat and gloves. 'A word of advice,' he said. 'When you make arrangements, don't discuss them with your mother beforehand. Better if she has less time to worry about your plans.'

And to make her own, thought Greg, but said quietly, 'Thank you. My mother has had a lot to bear since my father's death, and she has always been delicate.' He felt that he owed it to his mother to make excuses for her, but the doctor only said, 'Quite, but sometimes one must be cruel to be kind. It is unwise for your mother to be so dependent on you.'

On Monday morning Cathy was up early for work, humming happily as she washed and dressed, but when she came downstairs Sally said immediately, 'I hope you are not thinking of replying to that note yet, Cathy.'

'Well, yes, or Greg might meet me from work.'

'Then don't make any arrangements until your dad has seen him.'

'But I thought Dad liked him,' Cathy said, looking downcast.

'He does, but he wants a word with him,' Sally said. 'Dad's very easy with you girls but he won't let anyone ride roughshod over him. Drink your tea and get off to work. You'll be late.'

Although Cathy knew that her mother often spoke more sharply than she intended in the morning, she was alarmed by the warning about her father. All day as she sat at her sewing machine she turned the words over and over in her mind, and was relieved to see Greg waiting for her when she left work.

He also had spent a troubled day, wondering whether he had done the right thing in sending the note. He knew little about girls and had had no opportunity for learning what was acceptable when courting. He feared that he had blundered in sending the letter. As soon as she began to tell him what her mother had said, he interrupted her.

'I'm sorry, Cath. I've been wondering all day if I'd put my foot in it, sending that note. I wasn't thinking properly. Do you think your father's annoyed?'

'I don't know,' she said doubtfully. 'Dad's not strict usually but when he puts his foot down, he means it.'

'What did your mother say exactly?' Greg asked, and when he heard of Sally's remark about riding roughshod he looked worried.

'I've gone about things the wrong way,' he said. 'Do you think – if I apologise to your parents, tell them I just didn't know the right thing to do – do you think they'll forgive me. Let me see you again?'

'It's not as bad as that,' she assured him. 'Dad's not like some other girls' fathers. Like Ellen's father and Mr Ashton and Mr Hancock in our street. They're all strict but they don't really take much notice of the family. Dad takes an interest in me and Mary. We can talk to him.'

'I noticed that the night I called on you,' he said, 'how different he was. Fathers are usually very aloof.'

'Don't worry, Greg,' she said. 'He won't shout at us, but he'll explain properly.'

'Will you ask if I can see him tomorrow night?'

'Yes, all right, and I'll put a note through the shop door tomorrow morning,' she promised. They parted in Islington, Greg returning to the shop while Cathy walked the rest of the way home alone.

She arrived before Mary, and as soon as she had finished her meal, Sally sent her in to Peggy Burns with a message. Mary had said nothing about her conversation with her mother to Cathy who was blissfully unaware of her sister's interest in Greg. Sally meanwhile was determined to keep the girls apart as long as possible, until she could see how affairs would turn out. She had dropped a hint earlier in the day to Peggy Burns, who asked Cathy to help with the children. She was always happy to spend time with the Burns children, and by the time she had undressed the baby for bed, and fed him and Ben with bread and milk, Mary had been home and gone out again.

Cathy found Mrs Burns a receptive listener when she talked about the outing to Knotty Ash, and when Peggy asked if the cut on her head was quite healed she was able to bring Greg's name into the conversation and tell the neighbour shyly all about him, and the invitation to the concert.

'He sounds a nice lad,' Peggy said. 'Your mam and dad like him, don't they?'

'Yes. At least I thought they did, but Dad seems vexed about the concert, Mam says. I think he doesn't realise I'm grown up, Mrs Burns. He said Greg was too old for me, just because he's twenty, and I should find a lad of my own age.'

'He doesn't seem very strict with Mary,' Peggy said. 'Was he strict with her when she was your age?'

'I don't think so,' Cathy said. 'Our Mary was always out with different lads, even years ago. She had to make them call for her though, so Mam could see what they were like.'

'You should be glad, Cathy, that your mam and dad take such good care of you,' Peggy Burns said. 'There's many a girl goes wrong for the want of it. For all your Mary goes out with so many, they all know they've got to treat her with respect.'

'I don't have those sort of problems,' Cathy said, smiling ruefully. 'It's because Mary's so beautiful lads flock round her.'

'No more than what you are in a different way,' Peggy said. 'You're both nice-looking girls.'

Cathy laughed. 'Mrs Malloy said that once, but she said Mary was more striking-looking.'

'I like your colouring better,' Peggy said. 'Maybe I've seen enough of red hair with all the copper nobs in this family. Every one of them with the same ginger hair as their father.'

'Norah said Mary's hair was ginger one time, and Mary said her hair was called Titian after a man who painted girls with hair that colour.'

'She's got a good opinion of herself,' Peggy Burns said with a sniff. 'And that's another way you're different. You want to think more of yourself, Cathy. You're a proper looker, and it seems as if this feller's fell for you, anyhow.'

When Cathy went back to her own home her father had returned from the meeting he had gone to from work. He said immediately, 'I want to see Greg Redmond, Cathy. Did your mam tell you?'

'Yes, Dad,' she said. 'I told Greg, and he said can he come and see you tomorrow night?'

Lawrie looked taken aback. 'By God, that was quick off the mark,' he said. 'Does he know why I want to see him?'

'I told him it was about the concert.'

'It's about more than that,' Lawrie said, then a thought seemed to strike him. 'You told him – when did you see him?'

'After work. He came to meet me, to find out about the concert,' Cathy said. 'I said I'd put a note through the letter box on my way to work if it was all right tomorrow night.'

Lawrie glanced at Sally, then said firmly, 'Tell him to come here tomorrow night, and don't make any more arrangements without asking me or your mam.'

He put his pipe back in his mouth and turned back to the papers he was studying, and Cathy and her mother made supper in silence. Cathy was pondering her father's remarks, and her mother seemed anxious to have the supper ready early.

'Come on now, Cathy,' she said as soon as the supper was ready. 'Eat up, and drink your cocoa and get to bed. You look tired.'

'Our Mary's not even in yet,' Cathy said, but she ate her supper quickly, then said goodnight to her mother.

When she went to kiss her father goodnight, he said, 'Hold on a minute, love,' and went to his coat pocket. Sally sighed impatiently, but he took out a small parcel and gave it to Cathy. 'I had my Sunday overtime,' he said, 'so I got this for you.'

It was an amber bangle, and Cathy exclaimed in delight as she slipped it on her arm. 'Oh, Dad, it's lovely,' she said, her eyes shining.

Her mother clicked her tongue. 'Yes, and sugared almonds for me and a bottle of scent for Mary. I thought you were going to spend your share of the overtime on something *you* wanted, Lawrie.'

'This is what I want,' he said with a grin. 'A bangle, sugared almonds, and a bottle of scent. What else would I want?'

They all laughed, but Sally said again, 'You look tired, Cathy. Hurry up to bed now.'

She went upstairs, and when she was in her nightdress slipped the bangle on her arm again and went to look at her reflection in the pier glass in her mother's bedroom.

For a while she looked with pleasure at the amber bangle circling her rounded upper arm, then she pulled the folds of her nightdress closely around her and studied her reflection more carefully. Was she a nice-looking girl, as Mrs Burns and Mrs Malloy had told her, or were they only trying to console her because she was so plain compared to Mary?

The mirror showed her a girl not as tall as Mary, and with a gently rounded figure in contrast to her sister's fashionably large bust and tiny waist. Her brown eyes and dark curls were more ordinary, she thought, than Mary's glorious red-gold hair and sparkling blue eyes, but even Cathy could see that the cleft in her upper lip and chin, and the deep dimples when she smiled, were attractive.

I'm not as beautiful as Mary but I'm not ugly, she decided. And, anyway, Greg likes me. Smiling at the thought, she went back to her own room, and fell asleep almost immediately.

Downstairs her mother was saying quietly, 'You nearly gave me heart failure there, Lawrie, keeping her back when I was trying to get her off to bed before Mary comes in.'

'I wanted to give her the bangle,' he excused himself. 'I wanted to soften it a bit, like, telling this lad they can't start courting.'

'I know,' Sally said. 'But I want to keep her and Mary apart as long as I can, to give Mary time to get used to the idea that she can't have Greg.'

'And Cathy's meeting him from work,' Lawrie said. 'I think it's a good job I can give him a talking to tomorrow. The sooner the better.'

'But don't be too hard, Lawrie,' Sally urged. 'He strikes me as a sensitive sort of lad. We don't want to stop it altogether, and we don't want to put ideas in his head, either.'

'Leave it to me, Sal. I'll spell it out for him and clear the decks, that's all.'

Chapter Fourteen

Cathy put a note through the shop door as she had promised, and at eight o'clock Greg arrived to see her father. He looked pale and nervous. When Cathy opened the door, she kissed him impulsively before showing him into the kitchen where her mother was sewing and her father sat by the fire.

Greg had expected to meet angry parents, but they greeted him with easy friendliness. Lawrie said casually, 'Take your coat off, lad, and sit down.'

Sally stood up and put down her sewing. 'Come and give me a hand, Cathy,' she said, walking into the scullery and shutting the door to the kitchen.

'I won't beat about the bush,' Lawrie said immediately. 'I believe you've asked Cathy to a concert.'

'Yes, I'm sorry. I should have asked your permission first,' Greg said breathlessly.

'Don't worry about that,' Lawrie said. 'I'm not one for rules and regulations, although mind you I like things done properly, but I want to clear the decks. I don't want either of my girls to be hurt.' He paused, and Greg said quickly and earnestly, 'I'd never do anything to hurt Cathy, Mr Ward.'

Lawrie nodded his head, seeming to think that more than one question had been answered. 'About this concert. Now if you and Cathy go to places like that, people are going to start pairing you off, and Cathy's far too young for that. She won't be sixteen until June.'

'But what can we do?' said Greg. 'We've met each other *now*, so even though Cathy's young – can't we see each other?'

'You don't get my drift, lad,' Lawrie said. 'I mean because Cathy's so young she might change as she grows up a bit more. I don't want you to seem so settled that you couldn't break up without causing a lot of talk. And I know what she's like. She'd carry on rather than hurt your feelings or have people feeling sorry for you.'

Greg smiled tenderly. 'I know what you mean, Mr Ward,' he said. 'But couldn't we go out together, and then if Cathy changed her mind I'd accept it and tell her I didn't mind. I would, honestly.'

'I don't doubt you, lad, but other people might make it awkward for either of you to change your minds.'

'I'll never change,' Greg said. 'We've only met a few times but I *know*, Mr Ward.'

Lawrie laughed. 'That takes me back,' he said: 'When I met Cathy's mam I went in to ask her da if we could go out together, but I was worse than you. I finished up asking him if we could get married. Gave him the shock of his life.'

He chuckled, then said more seriously, 'Mind you, Sally was older than Cathy is now, and she'd had a lot of responsibility and trouble that Cathy hasn't had, thank God. Anyway, you'd better stick to going about in a crowd for the time being, and see how things go.'

'What about the concert?' Greg said diffidently. 'Should I get another couple of tickets and ask your other daughter and Sam Glover to come with us?'

'No, no,' Lawrie said hastily. 'Leave it the way it is, but make sure people know you're just friends. And you'd better cut out the meetings after work, just in case of talk.'

Greg looked startled but said quietly, 'Very well, Mr Ward, but later on—'

'Yes, later on, lad, I'll be pleased to see you together. I've nothing against you, I just want Cathy to grow up a bit. You've got plenty of time ahead of you.' He went to the scullery door and opened it. 'I've put a light to the parlour fire, Cath, if you want to go in there with Greg.'

When they had gone, Lawrie turned to Sally. 'By God, I nearly sailed into deep water there, Sal.' She looked alarmed and he said quickly, 'Nothing to worry about, but when I said they shouldn't go out on their own he asked if he should get tickets for the concert for Sam and Mary! I told him to leave things as they are, but I was brought up short, I can tell you.'

'It's a wonder you didn't think he was trying to reach Mary through Cathy,' Sally said, but he shook his head.

'No. Cathy's the one, no doubt about that, Sal. I just hope Mary doesn't get upset about it.'

'How did you leave it with him then?'

'I told him Cathy was too young to start courting seriously and I wanted them just to go about in a crowd for the time being.'

'I hope you haven't jumped the gun, Lawrie,' Sally said anxiously. 'He mightn't have had any idea of being serious.'

'He has,' Lawrie said, 'but he saw my point. I tell you, Sal, I like that lad. Him and Cathy are two of a kind.'

'I think so too,' she said. 'I'd better tell Mary about the concert, though, and let her know how things stand.'

–

Mary was not at home when Greg arrived the following night, but when he and Cathy left the house she was walking home alone and saw them strolling along arm in arm. They were too engrossed in each other to notice her, and she hurriedly turned down a side street and walked away from the house until she'd had time to recover from the shock. Although her mother had warned her that Cathy had been invited to the concert Mary had felt sure that there was some mistake until she had seen them together.

It's this Red Cross thing, she decided finally. He's interested in Cathy because he dressed the cut on her head, and he's asked her out now as a little treat because she has been ill.

As usual Mary was soon able to convince herself that what she wanted to believe was the truth, and she quickly felt cheerful again.

Meanwhile Cathy was floating on a cloud of happiness. She felt that she was correctly dressed, and was warmly welcomed by various members of the Red Cross to whom she was introduced by Greg. She was unaware that most of them shared Jack Carmody's view of Greg and his mother, and were delighted to see that Greg had managed to assert himself. She thought that they were charming, friendly people and was blissfully happy to think that she was accepted by them.

Jack Carmody joined them in the interval when refreshments were served, and Cathy's only regret was that Norah was not with them. When the concert was over they walked home with their hands clasped, both so full of happiness that it seemed difficult to keep their feet on the ground.

'The first time we've really been out together,' he said when they stopped to say goodnight. 'I hope it's the start of our lifetime together, Cath.'

'Oh, Greg, I feel so happy,' she exclaimed. 'I'm sure I'll never be as happy as this again. I feel as though I'd like to die now while I'm absolutely, perfectly happy.'

He looked at her in alarm, and she laughed. 'I don't want to die really, Greg. You know what I mean, don't you?'

He laughed and agreed, and after they had kissed goodnight several times, they parted. Cathy went straight to bed, but she was too excited and happy to sleep and lay for hours going over and over all that had happened, like a miser counting his gold.

Greg was hurrying along, oblivious to his surroundings, when he came face to face with Mary and a young man. She greeted him with undisguised pleasure and introduced him to Sam.

'Did you enjoy the concert?' she asked.

'Oh, yes,' Greg said.

'It would be a treat for Cathy,' Mary said patronisingly, 'to be taken to a concert by an older man instead of hanging about with young boys. It will cheer her up after her accident.'

Sam was looking at her in amazement but Greg only smiled happily, in such a state of bliss that her words entirely failed to register with him. Unaware of this, Mary stood close to him, smiling up into his eyes, and he said happily, 'Yes, Cathy enjoyed it too.'

'What was on the bill?' asked Sam.

'I don't remember,' Greg said vaguely. He held out his hand to Mary and she shook hands with him, thinking, Even his handshake's so firm – not like Sam's limp clammy hands.

'I hope I see you again soon,' she said, smiling encouragingly at Greg, and he said eagerly, 'I hope so too.' He was delighted that Cathy's sister seemed to approve of him.

Sam said loudly, 'Goodnight, then.' Greg said goodnight and moved away, and Mary glared at Sam and refused to take his arm as they walked along.

'Do you *have* to be so uncouth?' she said angrily. 'Suddenly blurting out goodnight in the middle of a conversation.'

'But he'd shook hands with you, Mary,' Sam bleated, abandoning his attempt to be masterful.

'There are ways of doing things. But, of course, if you don't know by now you never will,' she said cuttingly.

'I never know when I'm doing right with you,' he grumbled.

'Isn't that what I've just said,' she demanded. 'Anyway, now *I'll* say goodnight.'

They had reached her house and Sam said pleadingly, 'Can't I come in, Mary?' But she flounced into the house and shut the door, leaving him standing disconsolately outside.

Sydney had organised a visit to the Roller Rink on the Saturday night, as one of the winter social events of the cycling club, and Mary overheard Cathy telling her mother about it. She decided immediately that she would make Sam take her there on the same night, giving her the opportunity to make it clear to Greg that Sam was simply a friend, and giving Greg the chance to ask her out. She was still convinced that he was simply being kind to Cathy, and that only shyness and the belief that she and Sam were courting had prevented him from asking to take her out.

How eagerly he had responded to her hint about seeing him again, she thought, until as usual Sam had blundered in and spoiled things. As soon as he had served his purpose she'd get rid of him, she decided, letting her mind roam happily over the idea of showing Greg off to her friends.

'Are all the cycling crowd going tonight?' she asked Cathy. 'Can they all skate?'

'Most of us can,' Cathy said. 'You went with someone last year, didn't you, Mary?'

'Yes, but Sam wants to learn,' she said carelessly. 'We'll go the same night as you, and some of you can help him, and me, because I only went once.'

Cathy readily agreed, pleased for Sam's sake that for once Mary was prepared to consider his wishes. She was longing for Saturday night; all the more because Greg had abided by her father's wishes and had not been to meet her from work.

He was waiting at the top of Brunswick Road with Norah and her two cousins, Charlie and George Benson, when Cathy arrived with Mary and Sam. Norah looked annoyed when she saw Mary, but Cathy and Greg were oblivious, walking along in their own happy dream, holding hands. Mary set out to charm all of them and by the time they reached the Rink even Norah had to admit that she could be fascinating when she wanted to be.

Sydney was waiting outside with other members of the club and Cathy introduced Mary and Sam, and told him that it was Sam's first visit and only Mary's second to the Roller Rink.

'It's only a question of balance,' Sydney assured them. 'Any of our members will be pleased to help you.'

Mary smiled at him vaguely, privately deciding that there was only one member who would be allowed to help *her*. When they had been fitted with skates, Sam attempted to take Mary's arm but she drew away from him.

'We need to skate with those who can do it first,' she said, looking up at Greg appealingly. He glanced ruefully at Cathy but crossed arms with Mary and skated off. She found it more difficult than she expected to keep her balance, but she had a natural grace which soon helped her to get the rhythm. She still leaned heavily on Greg, though, and looked up frequently into his face, smiling disarmingly.

Cathy had taken Sam under her wing, but knowing she could not support him as Greg was supporting Mary she took him first down Mug's Alley, where he could grip the wooden barrier to save himself from falling and bringing Cathy with him.

'You're doing well, Sam,' she encouraged him.

He mopped his face. 'It's warm work, Cath,' he said, looking wistfully at the men who skated alone or with arms crossed with a girl. They had returned to the group and Mary and Greg skated up in time to hear Sam say, 'How long do you think it will take me?'

Whether he had relaxed his grip on the barrier or whether it was the sight of Mary was uncertain, but the next moment Sam's skates slipped. He made a desperate and ungraceful effort to save himself but failed and fell flat on his back, his arms and legs awkwardly splayed out.

'It will take *you* forever,' Mary snapped contemptuously.

The others looked at her indignantly and Charlie and Greg helped Sam to his feet. He looked red and uncomfortable, and Charlie said quickly, 'Don't worry, Sam, I was more on my back than on my feet the first few times, but it comes all at once.'

'It's only balance,' Norah said. 'Come on, Sam. Come with me and Charlie.' Norah and her cousin skated off with Sam between them. Greg quickly seized Cathy's hand and they skated away. The other members of the group paired off and left Mary standing alone, supporting herself on the outside barrier.

Almost immediately a young man skated up to her.

'Care to try?' he asked, holding out his arm, but Mary snapped, 'No, thanks,' and turned away haughtily. He shrugged and skated off, and she stood, a lonely figure, trying to look unconcerned. She realised that she had made a mistake in being unkind to Sam in Greg's hearing, but there was no chance of repairing the damage until they all returned.

Cathy saw Mary standing alone and was worried.

'Our Mary's on her own, Greg,' she said. 'Should we go back?'

'Oh, Cath, we've only just got together,' he said. 'She'll be all right.' A few moments later they skated past Mary again, still standing alone by the barrier.

'Someone will ask her up soon,' Greg said, seeing Cathy glance at her, but her soft heart was touched by Mary's effort to look unconcerned.

'She must be feeling awful, Greg,' she said. 'She hates to be conspicuous and she only came for Sam's sake. We'll have to go back to her.'

He sighed but agreed and they skated back to Mary.

'Try it with two of us to support you, Mary. It's much easier,' Cathy said. Mary smiled brilliantly, quite happy while one of the two was Greg.

Meanwhile Sam was making good progress with Norah and Charlie. 'There you are, Sam. You're getting the hang of it fine,'

Norah encouraged him. 'You'll probably pick it up quicker than Mary. She's too sure of herself.'

They looked at her, skating past with Greg and Cathy, and smiling up at Greg.

Charlie said tactlessly, 'Maybe she won't want to learn too quick.' Norah frowned at him and he added quickly. 'She might be afraid of a fall.'

Sam was too intent on making his feet move smoothly to be disturbed by Charlie's remark but Norah looked thoughtful.

I wonder if that's what she's after, she thought, noting Mary's languishing glances at Greg. I'll kill her if she tries to cut Cathy out. She can't bear anyone but herself to have a feller.

When they skated round again Norah was pleased to see that now Mary was on one side of Greg and Cathy on the other so that Cathy and Greg could hold hands.

'She's throwing all her weight on Greg,' Charlie said, following Norah's glance. 'She's not even trying.'

Sam looked over. 'She doesn't like to put herself out,' he agreed.

Norah was delighted. Was Sam seeing sense at last? Gawky though he was, she felt that he was worthy of someone better than Mary, someone who would appreciate his good qualities.

His moment of insight was short-lived. When they all came together again, Mary smiled brilliantly at Sam. 'You're doing very well,' she said, and immediately he was grinning with delight.

'It's good fun, isn't it?' he said. 'Should we try together now?'

'Oh, no, Sam, we're not nearly steady enough,' she said. 'We'd bring each other down, unless... Will you take Sam and me, Greg?'

He could only agree, and skated away with Mary on one side of him and Sam on the other.

Norah was furious. 'The cheek of her,' she fumed to Cathy, 'monopolising Greg like that. She knows he's your lad.'

'She doesn't really,' Cathy defended her sister. 'I haven't said anything to her, not even about the concert.'

'She shouldn't need to be told,' Norah said. 'She's got eyes in her head, hasn't she? She's only got to see the way he looks at you to know, but there's none so blind as those who don't want to see.'

'It's only that she feels safe with Greg, Norah,' Cathy protested. 'He's much taller than most of the others.'

'Now the minute they come back, you go off with Greg and *stay* with him,' Norah instructed her, but when Charlie asked Cathy to skate she went off with him. Norah skated with a brother and sister from Egremont Street, and found willing listeners when she criticised Mary.

'Cathy's so soft,' Norah declared. 'She won't hear a word against their Mary and anyone can see what a scheming hussy she is.'

'I've never liked her,' Jinny Ashton said. 'You'd never think her and Cathy were sisters, they're that different.'

'I told Cathy to stay with Greg when he comes back,' Norah said. 'But she's gone off with our Charlie now. She wouldn't hurt his feelings by saying no when he asked her but she might be away when Greg gets back. She's too soft for her own good.'

When Greg returned with Mary and Sam, Cathy was still skating with Charlie, but Greg knelt down and pretended to adjust his skate until she returned. Immediately he rose to his feet and they skated away, their bodies close and their hands tightly clasped, for the short time that remained.

When they left the Rink, the group gathered outside to hear Sydney's plans for future events.

'The next event will be a lantern lecture on a trip up – or down – the Amazon River. It will be held at the Albany Boys' Club and ladies will not be admitted, I'm afraid.'

Cathy looked at Greg in dismay, and he said quickly, 'What about another visit here? I think everyone enjoyed it.'

There were murmers of agreement, and Sydney nodded his head.

'We could meet here again a week today if you wish, but it won't be on the calendar of events for the Boys' Club. My responsibility is to the boys themselves.'

'Quite so,' Jack Carmody said smoothly, 'but I for one will be here at the same time next week, and so will Greg, and everyone who wishes can meet here.'

When the group split up and moved away, Mary carefully manoeuvred to take Greg's free arm. The pavement was too narrow to allow four people to walk abreast without blocking the way for those walking in the other direction, and Sam had to keep falling back to allow people to pass.

For most of the journey home he trailed behind them miserably but Mary held Greg's arm firmly, chattering on various topics, including the jewellery trade.

'That reminds me,' he said. 'I'm sorry I wasn't in the shop when you called. I hope you've had no more trouble with the bracelet.'

'No, it was something quite simple,' she said hurriedly. She turned on Sam. 'Why do you keep shuffling along behind me?' she snapped.

'I had to let that lady pass, Mary,' Sam mumbled. She gave an impatient exclamation, but they had reached Egremont Street, and Greg resolutely removed his arm from Mary's.

'We'll leave you and Sam to say goodnight,' he said. He moved away with Cathy, saying over his shoulder, 'Goodnight Mary. Goodnight, Sam.'

'When did she go in the shop?' Cathy asked as soon as they were alone.

'A few weeks ago. I was looking at the repairs book and Mr Braithwaite mentioned it. I think it might have been when I was meeting you from work. Didn't you know about it?'

'We often don't see each other for days,' Cathy said hastily. 'If I've gone out when she comes in from work, or the other way round.' Even to Greg she would not admit that it sounded like Mary's scheming.

'It's going to be difficult to arrange to go out in a crowd, Cath,' Greg said. 'If it was summertime, we could go on the ferry or go for walks or rides with a crowd, but not now. Sydney's only really concerned about the Boys' Club.'

'Well, he only let girls in the Wheelers because lads asked if their sisters could join,' Cathy said. 'So we can't blame him.'

'I was hoping a lot of events would be arranged, but he's got other plans,' Greg said. 'The Rink seems the only hope.'

'It wouldn't be so bad if you could meet me from work,' Cathy said. 'But Dad won't even have that, will he?'

'No, but I couldn't have done it very often anyway,' Greg said. 'I'd be taking advantage really if I went out often near to closing time. There's a lot to do, putting valuable stuff in the safe and checking the takings and so forth.'

'Did Mr Braithwaite complain?' Cathy asked.

'Oh, no. No one complained but they were all delayed. Even the shop lad was late getting away because he had to wait to put the shutters up. My mother rang down for me too that night I walked home with you, and Braithwaite had to go up to her.'

They walked in silence for a few minutes, then Greg stopped and put his arms around her.

'I'll think of some way,' he murmured, kissing her and holding her close. 'That night at the concert was perfect, wasn't it? There'll be other concerts, and we'll get a crowd to go. I'll ask Carmody, and perhaps Norah and some of your other friends. Maybe Mary and Sam would go, too.'

Cathy drew away. 'I think they've got their own friends. Mary and Sam, I mean,' she said stiffly.

'I suppose so,' Greg agreed. 'Poor Sam. He's head over heels in love with Mary, isn't he?'

'Yes, but I don't think she'll marry him, even though they've gone out together for so long. He's such a gawk, although he's a nice fellow.'

'And Mary's such a charming girl,' Greg said. 'I imagine that Sam's not the only one "Suffering from Cupid's dart", as the song says.'

'It's very late,' Cathy said. 'Mary must have gone in. I'd better go too.'

They kissed hastily and Cathy went into the house. Her mother was alone in the kitchen and Cathy said in surprise, 'Where's our Mary?'

'In bed. She came in ten minutes ago,' her mother said. 'Your dad's in bed too, luckily for you. Where have you been.'

'We walked round the block. I thought we'd only been a few minutes,' Cathy said. She drank a cup of tea quickly, and went upstairs but Mary was either asleep or feigning to be. Cathy climbed into bed without speaking to her then found it impossible to sleep.

Her thoughts went back and forth over the events of the evening. She thought of Norah's angry remarks about Mary monopolising Greg. Could it be true that Mary was trying to take Greg away from her? Surely she wouldn't do that to her own sister, whatever had happened with Bertha and Isabel. Greg had seemed very willing to go off with her too, she thought angrily, but then her sense of justice made her admit that he could not have refused without outright rudeness.

Yet he had made that remark about Mary being a charming girl. And this business about her going in Redmonds' shop…

I'm going to tackle her about that, Cathy vowed. The sly cat! And Greg saying that he couldn't have met me from work, anyway. I'm sorry I spoke about it, seeing that it suited him to have it stopped. Not fair to the staff, and his old mother ringing down for him.

Cathy shed a few angry tears, covering her face with the sheet in case Mary woke.

He worries about the staff, he worries about his mother, he worries about Sam, he worries about everyone but me, she thought, deliberately fanning her anger. But then she remembered Greg's arms around her and his kisses, and for a while was filled with warm and loving thoughts.

But in the small hours doubts returned to plague her, and in the morning she looked pale and heavy-eyed after her troubled night.

Her mother looked at her searchingly. 'You didn't have much to say about the Roller Rink last night. Did you enjoy it?'

'Yes, we're going again next week. It's the only way I'll be able to see Greg again,' she added resentfully.

'Your father's only thinking of your own good,' Sally said sharply. Cathy looked sullen, but said nothing.

Although Sally had defended Lawrie's ruling to her daughter, later when she went in to have a cup of tea with Peggy Burn, she admitted that she was worried about it. 'I can see what his idea is,' she said. 'He thinks that if they get too settled as a courting couple, they won't be able to break it off without a lot of talk if they change their minds. But I think he's wrong.'

'Do you think they will change their minds?' Peggy asked.

Sally shook her head. 'No, I don't. You know what a stubborn little madam Cathy can be when she makes up her mind.'

'I think there's more to it than that, Sal,' Peggy protested. 'I seen Cathy going out with that lad from your house one night and I thought they looked real happy and well suited. Why doesn't Lawrie like him?'

'He does, Peggy, and so do I. It's just that Lawrie thinks that it'd be better if they went about in a crowd, but Cathy said this morning they'll only be able to see each other for such things as going to the Roller Rink.'

'And even there, they'll all pair off,' Peggy said shrewdly, 'unless fellas have changed since I was a girl.'

Sally laughed. 'I'll have to have a word with Lawrie,' she said. 'What tickles me, Peggy, I'd only just met him and he went to ask me da if we could get married.' She sighed. 'Fellas have got short memories.'

'If Cathy likes the lad, and you and Lawrie haven't got nothing against him, it'd be a shame to break it up,' her neighbour advised. 'And that's what could easy happen.'

'Girls are a trial,' Sally said. 'We've been worrying because Mary won't settle, and now we're worrying because Cathy's settling too soon. There's always something.'

'Your Mary'll soon settle when she meets the right feller,' Peggy comforted her.

'Mary'll never break her heart over a lad,' Sally said, 'but Cathy takes things so much to heart. But you know, Peggy, though Mary may be a bit hard on lads, she'd never do anything to hurt her dad or myself. Mrs Malloy used to say she was a bit wild but she had a feeling heart, and I think it's true.'

She stood up. 'I'd better get back,' she said. 'I feel better after having a talk with you, anyhow.'

'There was a fellow we learned about in school,' Peggy said. 'Must've been a king. I remember the picture of him in our books sitting in a chair with his crown on, telling the sea to stop coming in.'

'King Canute,' Sally said, smiling.

'Aye, well, tell Lawrie about him, will you?' Peggy said, with a grin. 'Tell him he's got about as much chance as Canute.'

Cathy had gone straight from work to a meeting with Rosie Johnson, and Lawrie was at work, so Sally sat alone sewing in the kitchen when Mary returned from work.

'Did you enjoy the Roller Rink?' she asked.

'Yes, it was good,' Mary said, with a faint smile.

'Cathy seemed a bit doubtful about it, I thought,' Sally said, but Mary said nothing, only looked down, smiling to herself. 'What about Sam?' her mother pressed her.

'As clumsy as usual,' Mary said scornfully. 'He's hopeless.'

'So you won't be going next week then?'

'*I* will,' Mary said. 'He can please himself.' Sally bit off a thread and looked at Mary's complacent smile. 'I'm going to have a word with your dad about Greg and Cathy,' she said. 'It won't work just meeting in a crowd.'

Mary looked puzzled. 'I don't know what you mean.'

'Of course, you were out on Tuesday,' Sally said. 'But I thought Cathy would have told you. Dad told Greg that he and Cathy could only go out in a crowd – he doesn't want them to be paired off as a courting couple because Cathy's so young.'

'But that's ridiculous,' Mary said angrily. 'Who was pairing them off, for Heaven's sake? Dad's making a fool of himself.'

'Don't speak about your father like that!'

Mary flounced out into the scullery. She opened the door into the yard and stood breathing deeply, indifferent to the chill of the damp, foggy air.

Why were older people such fools? Her father acting stern and only putting ideas in Cathy's head, and forcing Greg into an impossible position. Probably by the time he realised what her father was getting at, it would be too late for him to say that there had been a mistake. His feelings for Cathy were being blown up out of all proportion by Mam and Dad. Why did they always think they knew best?

Like the time they had given Alfred Jones his marching orders because they said he was flashy. Maybe he was, but he always treated her well, and with respect. Yet they had welcomed Jimmy Meeson, and look what happened with him.

Mary thought of the sunny day in spring when she had gone with Jimmy on a char-a-banc drive from Crosby to Sefton Church. They had wandered away from the others, through a little wood and into a meadow, to sit and kiss, while she teased then withdrew from him as usual. This time it had been different. A hot tide of feeling seemed to sweep her along, and within minutes they had thrown off their clothes and come together in ecstasy.

I liked it, Mary thought. I enjoyed it, and wouldn't mind a bit being married. But of course she hadn't told Jimmy that.

Instead she had wept and he had apologised and tried to comfort her, saying he would marry her if things went wrong. A porter! Yet it had been a comfort to think of those words when for four terrible days her period had not arrived. She recalled the relief when at last she had come on at the fifth day, and her vow never to run that risk again.

She had quickly discarded Jimmy, and her mother had said she was sorry! And they still think they know how to run our lives, Mary thought with contempt.

Chapter Fifteen

The week that passed before she could see Greg again seemed interminable to Cathy, all the more because she was plagued with doubts.

Did Greg want to see her more frequently, or did the present arrangement suit him? She often thought of how he had spoken of it being difficult to leave the shop to see her, and his admiration for Mary. Her feelings of inferiority to her sister, and memories of Mary's behaviour at the Roller Rink and on the way home, constantly troubled Cathy. She lay awake for hours every night, worrying.

Several times she tried to ask Mary about her visit to the shop but she was adept at slipping away from confrontation, while still managing to drop frequent hints which suggested that she had seen Greg since the visit to the Roller Rink.

Cathy grew pale and quiet, and her father watched her thoughtfully. Matters came to a head on the night of the next visit to the Rink. Norah was unable to go as her father had been laid off work and refused to let her leave the house, but even without any prompting from her friend, Cathy could see how Mary schemed to stay close to Greg.

Cathy walked with Mary and Sam to the meeting place in Brunswick Road, but was pushed aside as Mary greeted Greg effusively and took his arm. Greg took Cathy's hand and slipped it through his other arm, and as they walked along he tried to tell Cathy quietly how much he had missed her, but Mary bombarded him with questions so that he had to keep turning to her to answer.

As soon as they met Sydney and the others outside the Rink and went inside, Mary impudently claimed Greg as her partner, laughing up at him as she said gaily, 'Come on, teacher. Finish the lesson you started to give me last week.'

Cathy refused to look at Greg as he skated off with her sister. She bent down to fiddle with her skate so as to hide the tears of mortification which filled her eyes, and Sam bent down beside her. 'Me and you are in the same boat, it looks like, Cath,' he said. 'Will you skate with me, or would you rather not? I know I'm awkward.'

'Don't be so humble, Sam!' Cathy exclaimed. She stood up. 'Think more of yourself. You're worth ten of any of them here. At least you know your own mind. I'd like to skate with you.'

Surprised and pleased, he took her hands and they skated away. Whether her words had given Sam confidence, or whether Cathy's anger gave her extra power was uncertain, but she and Sam whizzed around the floor, passing Greg and Mary and finally coming back to the barrier, flushed and triumphant, to applause from club members gathered there.

Mary and Greg returned, and he came and stood beside Cathy and attempted to take her hand but unluckily at that moment a young man who was a presser at Finestone's skated up to them.

'Hallo there,' he said. 'I thought youse two had fell out. I 'aven't seen you waiting round our place lately.'

'No, Greg can't spare the time from the shop,' Cathy said crisply. He looked at her in amazement, but she turned away and said to Sam, 'Another go?'

'That's right. Keep ahead while you're winning,' Charlie Benson said, and Cathy and Sam skated off again.

Now Greg was angry, too, and when Mary held out her hand he skated off again with her, a grim expression on his face. What does she want me to do? he thought angrily. I've kept to her father's rules and now that's a fault, it seems. And it's another fault to skate with her sister, he thought, remembering the expression on Cathy's face as she had looked at him and Mary. She should be glad that *someone* in the family welcomes me.

Mary laughed up at him. 'Don't look so fierce, Greg,' she said teasingly. 'It's only one of Cathy's tantrums. She starts them for nothing at all.'

'That doesn't sound like her,' he said defensively.

'Oh, we keep hoping she'll grow out of them,' Mary said carelessly. 'She may change when she grows up, I suppose.'

Greg said nothing, but looked thoughtfully at Cathy as she skated by with Sam. Was this what Cathy's father had been trying to tell him?

He looked dismayed and puzzled, and Mary smiled her secret smile as she skated along, leaning heavily on him. Cathy was now skating with Jinny Ashton and the two Benson brothers so Mary and Greg continued to skate together.

Jack Carmody had been watching the by-play and as soon as Mary and Greg stopped for a rest, skated up to Mary.

'Come along, Miss Ward,' he said. 'I'll teach you the figure of eight.' He pulled Mary on to the skating rink, and Greg moved to stand beside Cathy. Her sudden anger had faded away, leaving her looking pale and unhappy. A rush of tenderness swept over him.

'Will you skate with me, Cath?' he asked. She nodded, and they crossed arms then held hands and skated off without a word. I don't care whether she's moody or not, Greg thought, she's Cathy, and there's no one else for me. I'd rather have Cathy with moods than anyone else without them.

Aloud he said quietly, 'What I said about leaving the shop, Cath. I think I said the wrong thing, put it badly. You know I'd have wanted to meet you, no matter what, if your father hadn't forbidden it.'

'I could see there were problems, though,' she said stiffly.

'Nothing that I couldn't have overcome for the sake of seeing you,' Greg said earnestly. 'I thought you knew that, Cathy.'

And what about Mary? Cathy longed to say, but was unable to bring herself to. So she had to accept Greg's explanation about meeting her from work, pretend that it was the only cause of their tiff, and all was well again.

She smiled at him but she still felt deeply unhappy and uncertain about his relationship with Mary. Even though she realised that her sister had made the first advance, she felt that Greg had responded too readily. And what about the meetings that Mary had hinted at? Cathy's doubts were intensified when they all met again at the barrier.

Jack Carmody and Mary were the last to arrive. She immediately clutched Greg's arm and cried dramatically, 'Oh, Greg, save me from this figure of eight fiend. Don't let him take me again.'

They all laughed and Sydney said pompously, 'You don't know how fortunate you are, Miss Ward, to be coached by Jack. He's our most skilled skater.'

'I'm sure he is,' Mary said, still clinging to Greg, 'but it's too strong for me. Come on, Greg, a little gentle exercise to restore my nerves.'

Mary was still the centre of attention, and it was impossible for Greg to refuse. Cathy could only watch in impotent rage as her sister drew him on to the rink and they skated off.

Sam appeared beside Cathy. 'Looks like Mary'd rather have him for a partner than me,' he said mournfully.

'Then why don't you *do* something?' she muttered fiercely. 'You're a man. It's easier for you.'

'I will,' he said, squaring his shoulders, and when Mary and Greg returned he said loudly, 'Come on, Mary. It's my turn now,' and took her hand.

She shrugged and made a face at Greg. 'After the Lord Mayor's coach came the dust cart,' she said, before being pulled on to the rink by Sam.

'The damn cheek. If I was him I'd trip her up,' Charlie Benson exclaimed.

'And leave her lying there,' added his brother. Jinny Ashton nudged him and indicated that Cathy could hear them, expecting the usual outburst from her if anyone criticised Mary, but she was staring ahead of her with a stony expression on her face, and said nothing.

Greg bent over her and said quietly, 'Will you leave now with me, Cath?' She looked up at him and nodded.

The others were moving off to skate but Greg said quietly to Sydney, 'Will you excuse us and explain to the others? Cathy and I are leaving now.'

They went out into the street and he took her arm.

'What is it, Cath?' he said urgently. 'Things seem to be going wrong between us. Are you still vexed with me?'

'No. It just doesn't seem the same,' she said. 'I—I'm just not sure of anything any more.'

'But you're sure of me, Cath. You know I love you. I'll always love you. Do you mean you've changed your mind?'

'*No!* But things are happening, and being said. I just don't know,' Cathy said in a low voice. Her pride prevented her from continuing, but Greg understood.

He was a shy and modest young man and had truly believed that Mary was simply showing approval of his courtship of Cathy by being friendly, but she had shown her hand too clearly that evening for any man, no matter how modest, to make any mistake.

'Will your father be at home?' he asked. 'I've got to talk to him, Cathy.'

'He'll be in bed. He's on the early shift this week.'

'I'll come tomorrow then. I'm going to ask him to change his mind. Ask him if we can have things on a proper footing so everyone knows how things stand with us. He might refuse, Cath, but I've got to try.'

She smiled up at him tenderly. Her doubts had been set at rest without Mary's name being mentioned and when Greg put his arms about her and kissed her, she responded passionately, eager to atone for her lack of trust.

When Cathy went indoors her mother greeted her with relief. 'I'm glad you're home,' she said. 'I've got a real bilious headache. I didn't say anything to Dad or he'd have stayed up for you and sent me to bed instead. Where's Mary?'

'She'll be in soon,' Cathy said. 'Greg and I left early. Can I get anything for you, Mam?'

'No. If I can just put my head on the pillow I'll be all right,' her mother said, pressing her hand to her forehead and appearing not to notice Cathy's words. 'Don't forget to damp down the fire and lock the door, love.'

She went upstairs and Cathy sat down to wait for Mary. At first she sat in a happy dream, thinking of Greg's loving words and kisses, but presently she began to remember Mary's behaviour and her lying hints that she had been meeting Greg, and she determined to confront her sister as soon as she arrived.

Suddenly Mary burst into the kitchen and before Cathy could speak she raged at her: 'How did you get him to leave early? Came over faint, I suppose. It's a wonder you haven't got him here bathing your head.'

'You know that sort of trick better than I do,' Cathy flashed back. 'It was Greg who wanted to leave early. He got tired of you throwing yourself at him.'

'Why, you—' Mary began, taking a step towards Cathy, but then she stopped and gave an artificial laugh. 'Really, you're pathetic. All that sulking and carrying on tonight just to attract attention, and he was fool enough to fall for it. I felt quite ashamed of you.'

'I was ashamed of you,' Cathy retorted. 'I always thought fellows fell for you because you were beautiful but I see the truth now. See how much scheming goes into it as well.'

'What do you mean by that?' Mary said angrily.

'You know what I mean. The way you carried on with Greg at the Rink and when we were walking there. And taking the bracelet to his shop.'

'And why not? The shop's open for business, isn't it?' Mary drawled.

'Yes, but why Redmond's out of all the jewellers in Liverpool?' Cathy demanded. 'You know very well you only went to see Greg.'

'Is that what he thinks? Does he think all his customers go there to see *him*? Is that what he's been telling you?' Mary sneered. 'He *has* got a good opinion of himself.'

'He didn't say anything, but I know why you went and so do you,' she retorted hotly.

'Really, Cathy, I don't know whether he's a plausible liar or you're thick, but you seem to believe everything he tells you. Whatever that vain creature thinks, I simply went to have a bracelet repaired.'

'And where did it come from – the bracelet?' Cathy exclaimed, suddenly losing control of her temper. 'From your hoard in the fireplace?' She stopped, aghast, as astounded as Mary at the words which had seemed to spill from her mouth.

Mary's face had grown pale, and she stood over Cathy, her eyes narrowed. 'So you've been rooting and prying round have you? You sly little cat!'

'I haven't,' Cathy protested. 'I saw you one night. I don't want to know about it. I've never looked there.'

'It's my business, d'you hear? My business! But I suppose now you'll go running to Mam and Dad with the tale.'

'You know I won't,' Cathy said, bursting into tears and running up to the bedroom. She sat on the side of the bed, her hands over her face as she rocked back and forth, crying bitterly. Why had she said that? Where had the words come from? She had believed that the thought of Mary's hoard was deeply buried in her mind, and yet these words had burst from her.

I don't want to know anything about it, she thought, and I don't want to know anything about *her*. Behaving like that, and saying those things about Greg! I'll never speak to her again, never!

Still angrily crying she threw off her clothes and climbed into bed, huddling on the edge to be as far away as possible from Mary.

She slept heavily, exhausted by emotion, but when she woke she was surprised to feel quite calm. The row with Mary had brought to a head not only her doubts of the previous weeks but also the vague uncertainties of years.

Now she felt that she could see clearly many things about her sister that she had refused to acknowledge before. The blindly adoring younger sister Cathy had been, had gone for good. Although she had no desire for any further quarrels with Mary, she felt that she wanted nothing more to do with her.

She thought lovingly of Greg, and looked forward to the future with him. When she went downstairs she found that the kitchen was cold and the fire only smouldering. 'Oh, Mam, I forgot to damp down the fire!' she exclaimed.

'So I found out,' her mother said drily. 'It was out but Dad lit it again before he went to work. You forgot the door too.'

'Is your head better?' Cathy asked.

'Yes, thank God. I think it was that mutton we had that caused it. Hurry up, Cathy, you'll be late.' But Cathy was already hurrying, anxious to leave the house before Mary came downstairs.

After she returned from work Cathy told her father that Greg was going to call to see him. 'Take him in the parlour when he comes,' was all that Lawrie said, but Greg was surprised at the ease of his interview with Cathy's father.

He had mentally marshalled all his arguments, but had only said diffidently, 'I'm afraid I've come to ask you to change your mind, Mr Ward,' when Lawrie interrupted him.

'Aye, and if you hadn't come, lad, I'd have sent for you. I'm not one of those fellows who won't admit when they've made a mistake.'

'We've kept to your ruling,' Greg said, 'but it's awkward in the winter. There aren't many places to go in a crowd, only the Roller Rink, and perhaps people's houses.'

'Yes, and you'd be pairing off there, I suppose,' Lawrie said.

'Even in a crowd,' Greg said hesitantly. 'It's difficult. Cathy and I know our – our plans – our hopes, but other people don't realise.'

Lawrie glanced at him sharply, but Greg said no more.

'Aye, I can see it could be awkward,' Lawrie said easily. 'Cathy's mam didn't agree with me from the start. Maybe women have more sense about this sort of thing. D'you know what Mrs Burns next door called me – King Canute.'

They both laughed, but then Lawrie said seriously, 'I was thinking of what was best for Cathy, but I thought I was doing what was best for you, too, lad. I know how hard a long courtship can be, and I didn't have to wait as long to get married as you will. That's if you stay together.'

Greg flushed. 'Cathy'll be safe with me, Mr Ward,' he said indignantly. 'And staying together – I know I won't change, but if Cathy does I'll make it easy for her. I don't think she will, though.'

'I don't think so either, when I weigh it up,' Lawrie said. 'She's not one for changing her mind. Too stubborn, her mam says. Mary's the one for moods and changes, but still, it wouldn't do for us all to be the same. I'm not doubting you, lad, just giving you a word of advice. Watch your step because it won't be easy, that's all I'm saying.'

'Thank you, Mr Ward,' Greg said. 'I'll bear it in mind. It's all right, then, for Cathy and me to go out together?'

'Yes, but don't monopolise her,' Lawrie said. He stood up. 'Right then, we'll get a bit of supper then I'm off to my bed. I'm up at four o'clock.'

'Do you mind if I go for a walk with Cathy instead,' Greg said, 'to tell her what you've said?' Lawrie agreed, and as soon as they had left Sally said, 'Well? You sorted it out then? Cathy told me why he came.'

Lawrie told her what had been said and added generously 'I think you were right and I was wrong, Sal, but no harm done, I think.'

'Just as well to let them know the difficulties,' Sally said. She sighed. 'Doesn't seem five minutes since they were babies, her and Mary. The years go too fast.' Lawrie leaned back in his chair stirring his tea and looking at the fire. 'Have they said anything about last night, her or Mary?' he asked.

Sally looked alarmed, 'No, why do you ask?'

'Just something he said, about wanting other people to know about him and Cathy. Could have meant anything or nothing. I like that lad more and more, Sal, every time I see him.'

'So do I,' Sally said, but she spoke absently, and later when Lawrie had gone to bed, and Greg had gone home, she detained Cathy in the kitchen.

'How did you go on at the Roller Rink last night?'

'It was good,' Cathy said quickly. 'But I was sorry that Norah couldn't go.'

'Why did you leave early?' her mother demanded, looking searchingly at Cathy.

'Just to walk home on our own.'

'What about Mary? I didn't hear her come in.' But Cathy just said that Mary had come home shortly after her and Greg.

Sally was not satisfied, especially when she saw the tell-tale blush on Cathy's face, but decided to let the matter rest for the moment.

Chapter Sixteen

Sally had been determined to question Mary, and to find out more about what had happened, but before she had the opportunity, something happened which drove all thought of her daughters' estrangement from her mind.

Peggy Burns' brother and the sons and husbands of many of the neighbours worked at Bibby's oil cake mill in Great Howard Street, and on November 24th a terrific explosion there caused the deaths of twenty-three men. One hundred and thirteen were seriously injured, and thirteen of these later died.

Peggy's brother was killed outright, and Sally went immediately to try to comfort her. As usual her sympathy, deep and sincere, was also practical. She took over the running of the Burns household so that Peggy could go to her widowed mother, and they could grieve together and comfort each other.

Sally had the baby's cot put beside her own bed for the two nights that Peggy was away, and Mabel Burns took the toddler, Ben, into her own bed, so that the little ones scarcely missed their mother.

'Mabel's a good girl,' Sally told Lawrie, 'and young Sarah must be a good help to Peggy – she's so quick and handy – but Jimmy Burns is absolutely helpless. I'm sure you'd have made a better shape if you'd been left with a family.'

'He's never been to sea, love,' Lawrie said. 'That's where you learn to look after yourself. He's a good handyman though.'

When Peggy returned she was pleased to find her children well cared for and her house running smoothly.

'I can't thank you enough, Sal,' she said. 'It made all the difference to me mam, having me staying with her. Our Ritchie had been such a good son to her and she thought the world of him.'

She wiped away tears and Sally said sympathetically, 'It must be hard for your mam. Wasn't your dad killed in an accident too? This must have brought it all back to her.'

Peggy snorted. 'That was different,' she said. 'Mam shed no tears over him, believe me. She was made up.'

Sally looked shocked and Peggy said quickly, 'You might think that's hard but you don't know the life she had with him. She was

147

married for eighteen years and she never had more than a few weeks in all that time when she wasn't carrying a baby. She was married when she was sixteen and had our Henry, then ten months after she had me, then ten months after me another girl, and that's the way it went on. She only reared five of us out of the lot.'

'She's had a hard life then, and a lot of sorrow.'

'She told me once she was glad when she had a stillborn because otherwise she knew she'd most likely lose them anyway. Three died in one week from measles,' Peggy said. 'I know I've got seven myself but I've had a couple of years between each one. And Jimmy's a very different man to my father.'

'Your children are all healthy too,' Sally said. 'That's a lot to be thankful for.'

Sally felt that later Peggy might regret speaking so freely, yet she thought that if it had helped to keep her mind off her brother's death, she could only listen and hope that Peggy realised she would never repeat her confidences.

'My father was a drunkard,' Peggy said. 'He drank every penny he earned, pawned anything he could lay his hands on for drink. I remember once he pawned his docker's hook for fourpence ha'penny. Mam begged him for three ha'pence to get a tin of condensed milk for the baby, because she had no milk and the poor little thing had cried all day with hunger. He went out and drank the fourpence ha'penny and the baby died in the night.'

'What did you *do*?' Sally exclaimed. 'About your father, I mean.'

'We didn't do anything,' Peggy said. 'I know, Sally. Sitting here now I think, "Why didn't I snatch the money off him, or get some milk off the neighbours or something?" But then, my mam was too ill and frightened and I was only a kid. We were all hungry and cowed down.'

'I wasn't criticising,' Sally said quickly. 'I can see how it was, but the poor child.'

'I worried about it for years,' her neighbour said, 'but then Mam told me it would have died anyway. It was sickly – it didn't starve to death.' Sally was unconvinced. She knew that often, when she lay awake at night, she would be haunted by the thought of the starving baby, but she said nothing.

'Mam did cleaning when she could,' Peggy said. 'Me and our Katie scrubbed steps and the lads turned their hands to anything to earn a copper, or we'd have starved. We had to keep it dark from the old fellow though or he'd have had it for drink.'

'Drink's a curse.'

'It is. You can see why me mam was glad to see the back of him. He was drunk when he fell in the dock and drowned. He'd met our Henry coming home with his first pay packet – he'd started work in a sawmill, and me dad took his wages. Henry said he was made up that he was drunk on his wages when he drowned. We were all bitter, I suppose.'

'I'm not surprised!' Sally said. 'But looking at your mam now, I'd never have thought she'd been through all that.'

'That's what I mean, Sal. The way she is now she could stand up to him, but she was too dragged down then with childbearing and hunger and fear, I suppose, to do anything about it. I wouldn't have got married and left her the way she was then, but she soon got on her feet once she got rid of him. I knew she was all right when I heard her laughing with the woman next door about him. He was buried by the parish and me mam said, "I'd dance on his grave – if I knew where he was buried." Me poor mam! And now to have to face losing our Ritchie.'

Sally came home a little later, but often over the following weeks as she went about her housework she thought of Peggy's story and marvelled at it. To think that she had endured such a childhood, yet although very small she was never ill and had borne seven healthy children. Sally sighed as she thought of her own stillborn son, and of Lawrie giving young Ben Burns a ride on his foot, or holding his head down to allow the baby to pull his hair. Did he ever think of the little son they had lost, who would have been a lad of ten now? she wondered.

An air of sadness hung over the whole neighbourhood. So many men had been killed or injured in the explosion at Bibby's and the fire that followed it. Weeks later six motherless children died in a house fire and the father later hanged himself, and Mr Ashton of Egremont Street was badly injured on the docks.

'Why do these things always seem to happen just before Christmas?' Sally said to Lawrie. 'Bad enough at any time but even worse near Christmas.'

She had even more cause for grief when Emily arrived to spend the holiday at home, looking thinner and frailer than ever, and not seeming to have benefited at all by her stay at the sanatorium. Sally went to Aigburth to see her and was deeply offended by Albert's manner.

'I only stopped to speak to the maid when she brought my coat and he practically hustled me out,' she told Lawrie, tears of mortification filling her eyes at the memory. 'If it wasn't for seeing Emily I'd never set foot in the house again.'

'I suppose he's on edge, worried about Emily,' Lawrie soothed her. 'You'll have to make allowances for him, love.'

'And so was I upset,' she said, 'but I gave Albert no cause to treat me like that. Another thing worried me. Mary told me Isabel had a new friend and she wasn't wanted now, but one of those women from the church was at Emily's and she said something about, "Poor Isabel. You couldn't expect her to forgive Mary." I'd have asked what she meant but Emily hadn't heard her luckily, and the woman went just afterwards so I couldn't tackle her on her own.'

'Why don't you ask Mary?' Lawrie said.

'I did,' Sally said grimly. 'She put on her usual act. Opening her eyes wide and looking as though butter wouldn't melt in her mouth. "I don't know what you're talking about, Mam." I'll find out though, I'm determined.'

'Probably just a girls' quarrel. Those old cats from the church are troublemakers.'

'No, there's something, and our Cathy knows what it is. She was there when I spoke to Mary, and you know the way she colours up. She won't tell tales but she couldn't get out of the room fast enough. There's something going on between those two as well. I wonder if Greg's at the bottom of it.'

'For God's sake, Sally, all that was sorted out,' Lawrie protested, but she was not convinced. 'No, there's something,' she insisted. 'But I'll never get it out of Mary. She's as deep as a drawn well.'

Mary and Cathy avoided each other as much as possible. It was easier now that Cathy was so often out with Greg, or Norah, or attending meetings with Rosie. Mary had discarded most of her admirers when she moved into Isabel Willard's circle, and was dismayed to find that they were not replaced when she stopped visiting Aigburth. Only Sam who had hung on with dogged persistence was still available and much as he sometimes annoyed her she kept him at her side as a stopgap. Fortunately for him, Mary had not yet realised that it was because she and Sam were seen as a courting couple that other young men had not asked her out.

Mary was furious when she realised that Cathy and Greg were now accepted as a couple, but her feelings were not only of anger. Although her father was right in thinking that she was originally attracted to Greg because of his background, and perhaps because she was piqued by his lack of response to her, she found to her dismay that she really cared for him.

His tall figure, handsome face and deep pleasant voice, caused sensations and longings in her that she had never before experienced. She had done more to encourage him than she had ever done with a man, and how galling it was to realise that all the time he had only been interested in her sister.

Of course I'm fond of Cathy, Mary told herself, but what does a man like Greg see in her? She's so shy and tongue tied with strangers, and she makes friends with all sorts of unsuitable people. She's never tried to improve herself but just sails through life without a care except when she's getting involved in ridiculous causes like the Suffragists or attending meetings where people rant about injustice. Really, she's quite unsuitable as the wife of a gentleman, Mary thought, and not even pretty. Well, pretty perhaps but not beautiful like me. Surely Greg will soon see his mistake and turn to me, so suitable in every way.

No matter how much Mary tried to whip up her anger or hope for a change, it did nothing to blunt her disappointment or ease the ache in her heart when she saw how Greg looked at Cathy, with his heart in his eyes.

The fact that Sam looked at her in the same way meant nothing to Mary and she was even more impatient with him when she compared him with Greg.

Christmas passed quietly and sadly although the adults made an effort to throw off their cares to make Christmas happy for the Burns children.

Cathy and Mary felt obliged to speak to each other and show at least a surface friendliness, partly because of the season of goodwill and partly because of their mother's evident doubts about them. But both of the girls felt that the old affection between them had gone for ever.

On New Year's Eve 1911, Mary's frustration and misery seemed to reach a peak. She had been invited to a party at the house of Sam's cousin, and Cathy and Greg were going to a party at Jack Carmody's house.

Sally had made dresses and capes for both girls. Mary's was of blue tussore, cut low at the neck and with a full skirt; her cape was dark blue with a military collar. Cathy's dress was brown with cream embroidery on the shaped waistband and on the Chinese Mandarin collar, and she had a brown cape lined with cream silk.

The girls were in the parlour waiting for Greg and Sam to arrive, and admiring themselves in the overmantel mirror. Cathy twirled around so that the full skirt of her dress swung out. 'Josie's Gran says we're dressed above our station in life,' she said. 'But I don't care.'

She looked at Mary's elaborately dressed red-gold hair and her blue eyes which were the same colour as her dress.

'You look lovely, Mary,' she said impulsively, too happy to remember the rift between them.

Mary looked again at her reflection in the mirror. And much good it will do me, she thought despairingly, with only Sam to go out with. If only she was going out with Greg.

Before she could answer Cathy, Greg and Sam arrived at the same time, and Mary's unhappiness grew as she compared Greg's handsome face and tall figure with the weedy Sam.

Greg smiled down at Cathy as he lovingly draped the cape about her shoulders, while Sam fumbled with Mary's, his clumsiness increased by her evident impatience as she tapped her foot, eyes glittering.

By the time that her parents came into the room to survey the girls proudly and wish them a happy evening, Mary felt ready to burst with suppressed fury. Sally watched them go with foreboding. 'I'm worried, Lawrie,' she said, as they returned to the kitchen. 'Our Mary's in a queer mood tonight. I don't like it.'

'It's just your fancy, love,' he said easily. 'They both look as pretty as pictures.'

'I know *that*,' Sally said impatiently. 'It's just Mary's moods that worry me. And the way she speaks to Sam. I wonder he puts up with it.'

'He's a bit too much of a doormat,' Lawrie agreed. 'But Mary must be fond of him, the time she's been going out with him.'

'She's keeping him to fall back on,' Sally said shrewdly. 'She'd cast him off quick enough if someone she liked better came along.' She sighed. 'I can't help but worry about her, Lawrie.'

Sally would have worried a great deal more if she had been able to follow her daughter. After leaving Cathy and Greg at the end of Egremont Street, Mary and Sam walked on in silence. The streets were thronged with merrymakers and the crowds thickened as they approached Commutation Row, but Sam seemed unable to prevent Mary being jostled and suddenly her fury reached boiling point.

On a sudden impulse she slipped away from him, using her elbows ruthlessly to push through the crowds until she was widely separated from Sam. She could hear him bleating, 'Mary, Mary, excuse me, excuse me,' as he tried to follow her but she worked her way through to the edge of the crowd near the fountain.

The next moment she was away, skimming up Islington to Kempston Street and the home of a widow who was the head of the workroom at Denby's.

Mrs Richards was known as the Merry Widow because of her many men friends and the raffish parties she gave. Although Mary had often been a willing listener to Mrs Richard's risqué stories, she had been offended when she was invited to one of her previous parties.

Now a trip to the Merry Widow's house suited her mood and she was welcomed with open arms by Mrs Richards, who was already tipsy. 'Come in, come in,' she screeched. 'Come and meet the lads and lasses.' Most of the people there seemed long past the age when Mary would have described them in such terms, but there were a few younger men, and she was determined not to find fault but to enjoy herself.

A glass was thrust into her hand and she joined a group who were standing round the piano, singing. For a while she basked happily in the admiring glances of the men. As time went on more and more people arrived and Mary found herself pushed away from the piano and sitting on a sofa, a glass of strong punch in her hand, beside a flashily dressed elderly man.

'Where have you been hiding, m'dear?' he asked, putting his arm around her shoulders. 'I must scold Bella for hiding a pretty little girl like you.'

Mary smiled uncertainly and took a sip from the glass, but the man tipped it up so that the fiery liquid coursed down her throat. She could feel it burning, and choked and coughed. 'What did you do that for?' she demanded, but the man only laughed.

'Nothing like a little drink to put you in the mood,' he leered. 'My word, you're a stunner when you flash your eyes like that.' He squeezed her shoulder. 'I can see that you're a lively sort of girl,' he said. 'Eat, drink and be merry, that's what I say.'

'So do I,' Mary cried recklessly as the drink seemed to burst like a bubble in her head.

'Here, Bella, another drink!' the man shouted. Mrs Richards came over, winking and wagging her finger at him. 'Now don't you go getting her drunk, you naughty man,' she said, but she handed another brimming glass to Mary.

A younger man appeared beside them. 'Come on, Bella, who's your friend?' he said, eyeing Mary. 'Introduce me.'

Bella Richards introduced him as Stanley and gave only Mary's Christian name before she moved away. Stanley plumped himself down on the other side of Mary.

'Don't be encouraging old Humphrey,' he said. 'You're too sweet a fruit to fall to him.' The older man glared at him.

'Clear off,' he said fiercely. 'I saw her first.'

'Now, now, Humphrey, give young blood its chance,' Stanley said. Humphrey's arm was still about Mary's shoulders, but

Stanley took her hand and pressed it against his knee and Mary began to feel nervous.

She forced a laugh. 'That's enough,' she said, 'you're like two dogs fighting over a bone.' She tried to rise but Humphrey's arm pressed more heavily on her shoulders and Stanley began to pull her hand closer to the crotch of his trousers. Mary tried to attract Mrs Richards' attention, but she was standing with her arms round two men, eyes closed, singing raucously and swaying in time.

'You're a sweet li'l filly,' Humphrey was murmuring. 'Lillie Langtry's not in the same class for looks.' Stanley was still tugging at her hand.

Mary had just decided to scream to attract Bella's attention when someone shouted, 'Quick, everybody out! It's just on midnight!' All the party surged into the street and Mary managed to escape from the two men and place herself near to Bella Richards.

A roar went up from the merrymakers as twelve o'clock struck, and all the ships on the river sounded their hooters, the Clan Line ships sounding above all the others.

The crowd linked arms for 'Auld Lang Syne' and when it finished Mary could see Stanley being kissed by a girl with a painted face and feathers in her hair.

'That's one of them street walkers from next door,' Bella said indignantly, but Mary was relieved to see the young man safely occupied.

Humphrey had disappeared so Mary felt safe enough to allow Bella Richards to draw her back into the house. She joined the group round the piano, determined not to leave them again, but after a while the punch and the heat of the room made her feel lightheaded.

She slipped into the hall, closing her eyes as she gulped fresh air coming from the open front door, but suddenly she was seized and pushed into the dark space between the stairs and the hatstand. Humphrey leaned drunkenly against her, mumbling, 'Li'l friend, give us a kiss.' She tried to push him away but his grip tightened so that her dress was torn from her shoulder.

'My dress,' she yelled, pummelling at him with her fists and shouting for Bella but the noise in the house drowned her cries.

Humphrey sagged heavily against her, smiling foolishly. 'Li'l spitfire,' he muttered. 'Pay for it.' He took a sovereign from his vest pocket and dropped it down the front of her dress, following it with his hand and clutching her breast.

Mary screamed and struggled to escape but she realised that she was trapped in the corner, so she changed her tactics and stopped resisting. 'All right. We'll go upstairs,' she said.

He leered at her. 'Thass better,' he said thickly, attempting to stand upright.

'I'll have to go to the closet first,' Mary said. 'All that punch.'

'All right,' he mumbled, staggering backwards, and she escaped to the lavatory in the backyard, trembling with fright but with her brain working quickly. She took the sovereign from inside her dress, then unbuttoned the leg of her drawers and slipped it inside before buttoning up again.

She could hear Humphrey calling her but there was a bush growing between the door of the lavatory and the gate into the back entry. She hid behind it while carefully drawing back the bolt on the gate and slipping into the entry.

It was pitch dark and she was unable to see the filth there but with one hand she held up her dress while with the other she held the torn shoulder of her dress together as closely as possible. The crowds in the streets had dispersed and she sped along, shivering with cold and fright.

She had hoped to slip into the house unobserved but her father was at the door looking anxiously down the street for her. Mary burst into tears as she reached him, and he put his arm around her and drew her into the house.

'What happened, love?' he was asking when Sally rushed down the lobby to meet them, and Mary flung herself into her mother's arms.

'Oh, Mam, I got separated from Sam and a man grabbed me and tore my dress,' she whimpered.

'Where's your cape? Have you come through the streets like that?' Sally cried. 'Enough to give you your death.'

'Where were you? I'll find him and bloody kill him!' Lawrie shouted, snatching up the poker, but Mary clung to her mother, weeping, and Sally held her close, comforting her and saying to Lawrie, 'It's no use. You'll never find him. Get her a drop of brandy.'

He flung down the poker, face congested with anger, and went into the parlour, returning with a small glass of brandy. 'Drink this, love,' he said to Mary. 'Never mind, you're safe now at home, but where the hell was Sam?'

'I don't know,' she said, sipping the brandy, but suddenly a wave of nausea overcame her, and she rushed out to the lavatory and was violently sick. When she returned to the kitchen her mother had her nightdress warming by the fire. 'The bed'll be warm, love,' she said.

'Cathy's been in for a while. Thank God nothing worse happened. Get undressed now and into bed, and I'll bring up a hot drink for you.'

Her father had tactfully disappeared so that Mary could undress in the warmth of the kitchen, but she pretended to misunderstand her mother and, seizing her nightdress, rushed from the room, saying, 'Thanks, Mam.'

Cathy appeared to be asleep and Mary undressed quickly. She slipped the coin from her drawers, then with a quick glance at her sister she knelt by the fireplace and took out the brick to secrete the sovereign. Cathy had been awakened by the commotion downstairs, but something furtive in Mary's manner as she entered the bedroom made her close her eyes and pretend to be asleep.

The chink of coins made her open her eyes, but when she saw what her sister was doing she quickly shut them again. I don't want to know, she thought. I don't want to know anything about it.

Mary flung on her nightdress and slipped into bed, shivering and pressing close to Cathy for warmth, until her mother came up with hot milk.

'You didn't say what happened to your cape, Mary,' she said. 'This didn't happen at the party, surely to God.'

'No, we were in the street,' Mary said, prudently being vague about the time in case her mother saw Sam before she did. 'That's how I got away. I ran off and left it in his hand, I think. I don't really know, Mam. I was so frightened.'

'Never mind, love, you're safe home now. Try not to think about it and get to sleep,' Sally said, taking the empty cup, and tucking the bedclothes around her.

'I'm sorry, Mam, after all the work you put in on that cape,' Mary whispered, but her mother said again, 'Never mind, love. All the same, I'll have a few words to say to Sam Glover when I see him. I thought I could trust him to look after you.'

She went out and within minutes Cathy heard her steady breathing and was amazed to realise that Mary was sleeping. She turned her mind firmly to thoughts of Greg, and soon she too had happily fallen asleep.

Chapter Seventeen

The next morning when Mary left for work, Sam was lurking about at the end of the street. He came towards her but before he could speak she said angrily: 'A fine one you are, Sam Glover! Leaving me to get knocked about in that crowd. I was hysterical – ready to collapse when I got home.'

'I couldn't help it, Mary,' he protested. 'One minute you were there and the next minute you'd gone. I looked everywhere for you, honest.'

'You didn't look everywhere or I wouldn't have had such a dreadful experience. My clothes nearly torn from my back by drunken men.'

Sam's mouth fell open. 'You were attacked?' he gasped.

'I got away, but no thanks to you. You'd better not show your face at our house. My dad's furious with you.'

'I'm very sorry, Mary. You know I'd give my right arm to protect you. I was like someone demented looking for you,' he said. 'I even ran to Duke Street in case you'd found your way to the party but nobody'd seen you. I tried everywhere, and then I went to your house but the lights were out so I was afraid to knock in case you were all in bed.'

They were near to Denby's by this time, and Sam tried to detain her. 'Can I see you tonight?' he asked humbly. 'Nothing like this will ever happen again, I promise you.'

Indeed it won't, thought Mary, but aloud she said impatiently, 'No, I'll have to give Mam and Dad time to cool down. I'll let you know.' She waved airily and walked away leaving Sam gazing after her with a miserable expression on his face.

Mrs Richards was also waiting to see her, looking belligerent, but Mary attacked first. 'A fine friend you are!' she said. 'You didn't take a bit of notice when I was shouting for help and that filthy old man attacking me.'

'Humphrey—' Mrs Richards began, but Mary interrupted her.

'Yes, Humphrey. He tore my dress to ribbons. I was lucky to get home unmolested, the state I was in. My mother and father were horrified.'

'Humphrey reckoned he was the loser,' Mrs Richards said. 'He was carrying on shocking. Said he gave you a pound and you ran away with it.'

'I'll have the law on him,' Mary exclaimed, allowing her voice to rise and panting with simulated anger. 'Wait till I tell my father. Who is he? Where does he live? My dad will kill him for saying a thing like that.'

'Now, Mary, don't get excited,' Bella Richards said in alarm. 'I'm only telling you what he said. He kept saying, "She took my sov and scarpered." I thought you should know.'

Mary opened her eyes wide in an expression that her mother would have recognised. 'He was trying to push something down the front of my dress, and put his hand down too. It might have been money – I was too frightened to notice and anyway my dress was too badly torn to hold anything. I tell you my father was rushing out with the poker when he saw the state of me, but if he hears this – well!'

'That's what must have happened,' Mrs Richards said hurriedly. 'Humphrey was drunk anyway and the sovereign must have dropped on the floor and someone's swiped it. Just forget it, dear.'

'How can I?' Mary said. 'He's making out I'm no better than those girls next door to you. My dad would make it hot for him if he knew, and I think I should tell him. He knows a lot of influential people – lawyers and clergymen and people like that – through his work with destitute children.'

'Don't say anything, dear,' Bella urged. 'I'll deal with Humphrey.'

'But how many people did he say it to? Did he say my name?'

'He only knew you as Mary. I'll soon put him right,' Bella said. 'Just forget it, dear, to oblige me.'

'Well, I don't want to cause trouble. It was good of you to invite me to your party. As long as people know the truth, and he's sorry for what he did to me.'

Mrs Richards patted her arm. 'I'll see to that, dear,' she said. 'Friends again?'

Mary smiled at her and went to her position in the shop, thinking how easy it was to fool people, and also with pleasure about the addition to the hoard concealed behind the bedroom fireplace.

For a while she refused to let Sam call for her, hoping that her parents would forget about the events of New Year's Eve if they were unable to question him.

Sally had been pondering them however, and she said to Lawrie, 'I think we might have have been wrong to blame Sam for not looking after our Mary. Ten to one that madam gave him the slip and then got more than she bargained for.'

'I think you're wrong there, Sal. He's such a gawk he'd let himself be pushed away from Mary, and once she was on her own, well, there's some queer creatures about. I believe her.'

'You would though, wouldn't you?' Sally said tartly. 'You'd believe her if she said black was white. It's funny how her cape turned up. She just *happened* to know the one who found it – and hardly a mark on it.'

'I think you're a bit hard on her, Sal.' I just wish she'd find someone with more gumption than Sam.'

'I still haven't got to the bottom of that business about Isabel either,' Sally said. 'I've never managed to see that woman again at Emily's to ask her.'

'What's happening about the sanatorium?' Lawrie asked, anxious to change the subject.

'Albert wanted her to go back, but for once Emily got her own way and she's staying at home. It didn't do her much good anyway,' Sally said with a sigh. 'She looks so ill, Lawrie.'

'Perhaps she'll pick up a bit now she's home,' he said. 'And you'll be able to see more of her. That should do her good.'

'I don't know what's got into Albert though. He's bobbing round all the time I'm there, watching me like a hawk. I wondered how he could be home so much in the daytime, but I found out yesterday that he's only home the day I'm there. He must find out when I'm coming.'

'It must be just chance,' Lawrie said. 'Why would he want to stay off just because you're seeing Emily?'

'I don't know,' Sally said, 'but it's not chance. Perhaps he thinks I'll turn her against him.'

'Don't worry about it,' Lawrie said. 'And don't stop going. It does Emily good to see you, and he'll soon get over his mood.'

'I won't,' Sally said. 'It'd take more than him to keep me away from Emily, but I'm fed up with mysteries.'

Sally still felt that Cathy and Mary had changed towards each other, although on the surface they seemed friendly enough. Mary managed to hide her bitter jealousy when she saw Greg and Cathy together, and Cathy was particularly happy at this time.

Norah had been invited to the New Year's Eve party at Jack Carmody's house, and since then she and Jack had been going out together. Cathy was delighted. She liked Jack and she knew that Norah had cared for him for a long time. She felt that they were as well matched as herself and Greg, and the four of them spent many happy hours together.

Now that her father had given permission for her to see Greg frequently, Cathy thought that the future was set fair for all of them, and she pictured a time when she and Greg, and Norah and Jack, were married. She had been thinking of this when she called to see her friend one night, so her shock was all the greater when she arrived at the house.

As usual she had watched for Norah's father to leave, but when Mrs Benson opened the door she cast a scared glance along the street. 'He said she wasn't to see nobody, Cathy. Just come in for a minute.'

Cathy exclaimed in horror when she saw Norah's face. Her left eye was closed and her lips cut and swollen. Both sides of her face were badly bruised.

'Norah, what happened?' Cathy gasped. But Norah only shook her head, indicating that she was unable to speak through her swollen lips.

'It was him,' her mother whispered. 'He got told she was courting with a Catholic. He went mad and battered her.'

'Jack,' Cathy said. 'Is Jack a Catholic? What difference does it make anyhow?'

Norah's mother stood by Cathy, nervously twisting the strings of her apron. 'You'd better go,' she said. 'If he comes back – he said she hadn't got to see no one.'

Anger exploded in Cathy. 'I'm not surprised,' she raged, 'to do that to Norah. No wonder he doesn't want anyone to know! He should be lynched – just because Jack's a Catholic.'

Mrs Benson's thin cheeks flushed and she put her hands on her hips. 'I know your father's got funny ideas, Cathy Ward,' she said, 'but any other father in Liverpool would have done the same as her father done. She asked for it, going with a pape.'

I don't believe it! Cathy thought, but only bent over Norah and put her hand on her friend's shoulder. 'I'll watch my chance to see you again, love,' she whispered. 'Never mind.' She went out anxiously, speeded by Mrs Benson who looked up and down the street before she left. Cathy felt stunned with shock as she walked home, and sad that she could do nothing to help Norah.

Her parents were both in when she reached the house and she poured out her tale of Norah's injuries. 'And her mother seemed to take her father's side,' she finished indignantly.

'Poor Norah,' her mother said. 'I'm afraid it's only the start of her troubles too. What about Jack's family?'

'I don't know anything about them,' Cathy said. 'But he's an awful nice fellow, Mam. I thought Norah's mam would be made up with him, but she seemed to think Mr Benson was right. She said any father would have done the same, and Norah asked for it going with a pape.'

Her father gave a snort of disgust. 'Yes, and if he was a Catholic he'd have battered her for going with a Protestant! What the hell's wrong with them? This town's torn apart by religion.'

'If you can call it religion,' Sally said. 'I remember my da giving the pay out about it one time when Emily was little. I'd taken her out for the day and we got mixed up with an Orange procession. A crowd of Mary Ellens were waiting for them at the top of Langsdale Street, and when the procession got by St Francis Xavier's one of them lifted a placard up with a kipper on it: 'Cured at Lourdes'. It was all the Mary Ellens were waiting for. I thought they were going to kill each other.'

'It gets me down,' Lawrie said. 'People should be standing together to get a better life for their children, and they waste their time fighting each other.'

'A pape. That's what Mrs Kilgannon used to call Mrs Mal, wasn't it?' Cathy said thoughtfully.

Sally sighed. 'Ah, Mrs Mal,' she said. 'She had the last word about them. She said that the ones that had the most to say, Catholic or Protestant, never put foot inside a church, and she was right. What will Norah do about work?'

'She couldn't go the way her face is,' Cathy said. 'She'll just have to stay in the house, I suppose. I don't think Mrs Benson wants me to go there, but I'm going to see Jack and tell him, then I'll tell Norah what he says.'

'Keep out of Mr Benson's way though, love,' was all that Sally said. She was tempted to tell Cathy to keep out of it altogether, but she was as indignant as her daughter and as sorry for Norah.

Sally was right in her forecast that it was only the start of Norah's and Jack's troubles. Jack's family were devout Catholics, all daily Mass attenders, and they watched him narrowly for signs of backsliding. Norah's parents were not churchgoers, but they were horrified at the idea of her having any contact with the Scarlet Woman, as her father described the Catholic Church.

'I'd rather see you dead than mixed up with one of *them*,' he declared, and Jack's mother told him he was breaking her heart.

'It's crazy,' Cathy said to Norah when they were able to meet again. 'It's like people having wars over religion. Surely everyone's trying to get to the same Heaven.'

'I know,' Norah said. 'Would you believe that Jack's mother was pleased when she first heard about me, just because she thought with the name Norah I must be a Catholic.'

'"What's in a name?"' Cathy quoted, but Norah was too ruffled to respond.

'That's the crazy part. My grandmother *was* a Catholic before she was married, and my mam named me after her. You know, Cath, I always liked Jack but this is sort of forcing our hands.'

'How do you mean?'

'I wanted to go out with him for a while, see if we were really suited and how things went with us. I didn't think of being really serious or planning to be married for years and years, but the way they're carrying on we'll have to make up our minds before we're ready.'

'But I thought you liked him,' Cathy said. 'I mean, I thought you were sure.'

'I *do* like him, and I think Jack really likes me, but we're not like you and Greg. I don't know, Cath. Maybe I *am* sure – oh, I don't know what I'm doing or saying. I feel so mixed up,' Norah said despairingly.

'Is it very bad?' Cathy asked.

'It's terrible. Between my dad threatening me and my mam nagging, then Sam and the other lads coming down shouting at me, I just feel like running away,' Norah said. 'I'd just give in if it wasn't for Jack, but he's having a bad time too.'

'His family can't threaten him, surely,' Cathy said.

Norah shrugged. 'No, but there's more than one way to skin a cat. His father's dead, but his mother cries every time she sees him, and his sisters are the same. His brother tells him there's plenty of good Catholic girls in the parish, so why go out with me?'

'The cheek!' Cathy exclaimed indignantly. 'I'd stay together just to show them.'

'That's what I'm afraid of,' Norah said quietly, then pulled Cathy round to face her. 'Enough of my troubles,' she said. 'What about you and Greg? Are you still walking into lamp posts?'

Cathy giggled and blushed. She and Greg had taken a lot of teasing when they appeared, both with bruises on their faces, and confessed that they had been walking along with their arms round each other, so oblivious of their surroundings that they had walked into a lamp post.

Cathy had tried to hide her own happiness while Norah was encountering such difficulties, but now her friend smiled at her. 'Cathy,' she said, 'you're like a bottle of champagne that's ready to burst its cork and froth all over the place, and Greg's no better. Don't try to keep it in because of me and Jack. I'm made up that everything's going well for you, Cath, honest.'

Cathy hugged her, feeling that such a generous and loving girl should not have to face such troubles.

Mary's feelings were very different to Norah's. She bitterly resented Cathy's happiness. She found it impossible to crush down her own feelings for Greg, and to see him with Cathy was like having salt rubbed into a wound.

Now that she went out less frequently with Sam, she was again asked out by other men, and something in her manner, a new boldness and recklessness, made her attract a different type of young man.

Also unknown to Mary, the knowledge that she had been at Bella Richards' party emboldened some men to ask her out who would not previously have dared. Most of them were indignantly refused but sometimes her unhappiness made her rash, and one night she accepted an invitation to the theatre from a man who worked in the Dispatch Department at Denby's.

She dressed carefully for the occasion and the man whistled in admiration when she met him. 'My word, you look a stunner,' he said admiringly. 'Real classy.'

Mary smiled at him although, as she always did nowadays, she compared his flashily dressed, stocky figure and coarse voice with Greg's, and a tide of misery rose in her.

At the theatre, as soon as the lights dimmed the man's hands began to rove about her body and at first Mary made no protest. What does it matter? she thought drearily, and there was always the hidden shameful knowledge that she enjoyed it up to a point.

Made bold by success, the man began to explore further. Mary suddenly drove her elbow into his ribs.

'Leave off,' she hissed. 'I've come to see the show.' Sulkily he complied, but when they left the theatre he called a cab and bundled her into it. 'Blacklow Grove,' he said to the cabby.

'Where's that?' Mary asked.

'Where I live, darling,' he said. 'Where we can have a bit of fun.' He grabbed her and twitched up her skirt, cursing when he discovered several petticoats beneath it.

She struggled and pulled away from him, and he said coarsely, 'Like breaking into a bank. I'll soon have them off.'

'Oh, no you won't,' Mary said furiously. 'Stop this cab *at once*.'

The cabdriver glanced back and the man said quickly, 'Take no notice of her. She's being coy.'

Mary leaned forward. 'Stop this cab or I'll scream for a policeman,' she said.

'Here, I don't want no trouble,' the driver said, pulling up. Mary jumped out and the man thrust some money at the driver and followed her.

'What's the game?' he said. 'You come out with me, didn't you? What's all this hoity toity bit?'

'You've got a cheek,' Mary said breathlessly. 'I came out to go to the theatre, not be taken to your house without a by your leave.'

'*I've* got a cheek?' he said. 'Wharrabout you? You went to Bella Richards' party, didn't you?'

'Because I didn't realise,' Mary said. 'I told her what I thought about the scum at that party.'

'Oh, did yer,' he jeered. 'Them scum are straighter than what you are. Letting a fellow pay out for theatre seats and a cab, then going sour on him.'

'I wasn't aware that I was invited on those terms,' Mary said haughtily. 'I'm used to gentlemen.'

He laughed coarsely. 'And yer've never had their hands up yer skirts? Come off yer high horse! A feller can always tell.'

Mary stepped into the road and raised her hand imperiously at an approaching cab. The man made to follow her into it, but she glared at him so ferociously that he recoiled. 'Eastbourne Street, please,' she said to the cabdriver determined that the man would not learn her address.

She paid off the cab in Eastbourne Street and walked the rest of the way home, thankful that she had taken the precaution of carrying money on her. She felt soiled and degraded by the experience. The man's words 'A feller can always tell' kept returning to her, and her misery and desperation increased.

Her parents were deeply disturbed by her moods. Her father thought that Mary was upset about the incident on New Year's Eve, and his feelings swung between anger at the unknown man and concern for Mary. He hated to see his much loved, brilliant daughter unhappy, and did all he could to try to cheer her.

Mary loved her father and tried to respond to his efforts and to show pleasure at the small gifts he bought for her from his overtime pay, but sometimes she felt that she wanted to scream at him.

Sally sensed that the trouble lay with Greg, and watched anxiously as Mary exerted all her charm on him whenever Cathy was out of the way. She was relieved when Greg's attention returned to Cathy as soon as she appeared.

She told herself that it was as natural as breathing with Mary to behave like that with any man, and that Greg only responded out of politeness because Mary was Cathy's sister, but often when she woke in the small hours, Sally lay awake worrying about her family being torn apart. Only Cathy, lost in her golden dream, seemed unaware of the tension in the house.

Chapter Eighteen

In March Sally had another cause for worry. She was bending over the washtub one Monday morning when there was a knock at the door, and she opened it to find two young girls on the step. They looked vaguely familiar but it was only when the older girl spoke that she realised who they were.

'Myfanwy!' she exclaimed.

The girl said quickly, 'Yes, and this is Bronwen who worked for Mrs Deakin too.'

'Of course, come in,' Sally said, then in sudden alarm she exclaimed: 'Emily – Mrs Deakin. Is she all right?'

'Haven't seen her for a long while,' Myfanwy said, as Sally ushered them into the kitchen and shut the door to the steam-filled scullery. 'Sit down, girls,' she said, taking off her sacking apron.

'Sorry to trouble you, we are, Mrs Ward,' Myfanwy said, 'but Bronwen, she's in trouble, see.'

Bronwen began to cry with loud gulping sobs. 'Oh dear, love, I *am* sorry,' Sally said. 'But never mind. You're not the first and you won't be the last.' She stood up and moved the kettle nearer to the fire to make tea, her panacea for all evils. At Myfanwy's next words she sat down abruptly.

'Mr Deakin it was, see, got her into trouble.'

'Albert!' gasped Sally. 'Oh, no. My poor Emily.'

'It's true, Mrs Ward,' Myfanwy said, but she looked alarmed at Sally's pallor and dashed to get her a drink of water.

'Sorry I am to give you such a shock, Ma'am,' the maid went on, 'but we didn't know what to do. Couldn't go to the house with her in such bad health, poor lady, so we came to you.'

'I'm glad you did. You're good, thoughtful girls,' Sally said faintly as she sipped the water. Some colour came back into her face and she said more strongly, 'Does *he* know? Mr Deakin.'

'Yes, indeed. Tell Mrs Ward, Bronwen,' Myfanwy ordered. But the other crouched lower in the chair, weeping even more bitterly, and Myfanwy began the tale. Bronwen had come from her Welsh village to work at the Grange a few weeks before Emily went to the

Sanatorium and she had not seen Albert very often. 'Kitchenmaid she was, see,' said Myfanwy. 'No use to cry, girl. Tell Mrs Ward.'

Bronwen, still weeping, said that she had shared a room with another maid, Elsie, who had been given permission to sleep at home after her day off. Bronwen had gone to bed at the usual time and was fast asleep when she was wakened by Albert climbing into her bed. He put his hand over her mouth, and with the other hand tore at her nightdress.

Bronwen wept so bitterly and became so incoherent when she tried to tell what followed that Sally became alarmed.

'Don't upset yourself, love,' she said, putting her arm around the weeping girl. 'You'll harm the baby. We can guess what happened.'

'Always one for touching, he was,' Myfanwy said. 'Ruby – you remember Ruby, Mrs Ward? Mister Macfeely, she called him. Got worse, too, and dirty talk whispered.'

'So it's nothing new?' Sally said. 'He's just got worse. Doing that with Bronwen, I mean.'

'Tried it with me one night when I was on my own,' Myfanwy said. 'But I was awake. Hit him with a chair, didn't I, and left next day.'

'But didn't you tell anyone?' Sally asked.

Myfanwy shrugged. 'My word against his, see, and him such a respectable man. Cook was deaf, and Mrs Smith, the housekeeper, she would be deaf too for any trouble. I asked for my wages and left.'

'And did you go home for a while?' Sally asked.

'No indeed. I had a friend, a nurse in the Southern, and she got me a job in the Nurses' Home.'

Sally had made tea, and she poured it and cut fruit cake for the girls while she thought about what to do.

'And when did this happen to you, Bronwen?'

'Months ago,' the maid whispered. 'When madam was away.'

'And you didn't tell anyone?'

'No. Ashamed I was, and he didn't come again. Elsie came back see,' Bronwen said, weeping again. 'I never thought of a baby. Sick I was, and Cook told me. Put my wages on the table and said to go.'

'She came to me,' Myfanwy said quickly. 'We're from the same village, and Ruth my friend the same. Lives out now, Ruth, so Bronwen stayed in her room. In the bed when Ruth is out of it, isn't it, but the landlord is getting nosy.'

'You couldn't go home, love?' Sally asked, but Bronwen looked alarmed and clutched Myfanwy's arm.

'No. The shame, see,' Myfanwy explained. 'Her brothers and her dada in the choir, and her mam pillar of the chapel.'

'I see,' said Sally, thinking that if it was her girl the chapel and the choir could go hang. But it was obviously different for these girls.

Myfanwy explained that there was an empty room in the house where Ruth lived, and if they could take it Bronwen could stay until a month before the baby was due. Then Ruth knew of a Home where she could go to have the baby, and it would be adopted from there. It was just a question of paying for the room.

Sally stood up and took out half a sovereign and some silver from the handleless teapot on the mantelpiece.

'Take this for now,' she said. 'Don't worry, I'll get it back from Mr Deakin and fix something up for you. When is the baby due?'

'Beginning of June,' Myfanwy said. 'Sorry to bother *you*, Mrs Ward, but—'

'I'm glad you did,' Sally said. 'You know my sister, Mrs Deakin, has been so ill. A shock like this would kill her.' Tears filled her eyes and she turned away from the girls to hide them, but Bronwen saw and said timidly, 'Sorry I am, Ma'am, very sorry.'

Sally wiped her eyes. 'You were good girls to keep it from her,' she said. 'I brought her up, you see, and I worry so much about her.'

'I know. That's why we came to you, Mrs Ward,' Myfanwy said. 'Wouldn't upset Mrs Deakin for the world. Always good to me, she was. She knew I was homesick and let me have time off to see other Welsh girls in Liverpool. Bring them to the kitchen when she took over the housekeeping.'

'And Mr Deakin. You're sure he knew about the baby?' Sally said.

Bronwen's face was already red and blotched with tears but she began to cry again, and Myfanwy said tartly, 'Come on now, Bronwen, no more tears, is it?'

She stood up and Sally helped Bronwen into her coat. 'I don't doubt you, love,' she said. 'I just can't believe that Albert would be so cruel as to turn you out if he knew. Perhaps he thought you weren't sure?'

Myfanwy shook her head. 'He knows, Mrs Ward. Went to his works we did, and the gatekeeper sent us away. Said Mr Deakin's orders.'

'I see,' Sally said. 'Can you come again? I'll talk about this with my husband and see what he thinks.' It was arranged that Myfanwy would come again on her day off in the following week, and Sally said to Bronwen, 'Don't worry any more, love. Think about the baby. You don't want to harm it, do you? Everything will be all right.'

As Bronwen led the way down the lobby, Sally said quietly to Myfanwy, 'It's a good thing she has a friend like you, poor child.' Myfanwy sighed. 'Feel to blame, don't I? Never thought of him trying it with another girl.'

'There's no one to blame but him,' Sally said firmly. 'Don't worry. Mr Ward will see him.'

The girls left and Sally went out to her neglected washing. The fire was nearly out under the boiler and when she went into the backyard for more coal, Peggy Burns' head popped up over the wall. 'Ready to come in for a cup of tea?' she asked.

'I can't, Peg,' Sally said. 'I've still got my clothes in the boiler. I've had visitors and I'm all behind, and Lawrie's on early. He'll be home before I can turn round.'

'Do you need a hand?' Peggy asked.

'No, I'll soon catch up, thanks,' Sally said, and Peggy said cheerfully, 'Righto, I'll drink your cup of tea as well as my own.' She disappeared and Sally took in the coal to shovel it under the boiler, thankful to have an understanding neighbour. She felt that she must be alone for a while to recover from the shock of the news that the girls had brought, and to sort out the tangle of her thoughts.

The clothes were soon boiling up again and she made herself a fresh cup of tea and sat by the fire to drink it, feeling sick and shaky. My poor Emily, she thought, her throat tight with tears. After what she went through with Walter, if she heard this it would kill her!

Sally's hands were shaking and she put down her cup and saucer. God, these old men, she thought with disgust. It seemed they were everywhere, preying on defenceless young girls. Thank God mine never went into service so we've been able to look after them.

Lawrie was on early shift so was soon home and Sally poured out the tale to him. He was as shocked and disgusted as she had been, and he thought of something which had not occurred to her. 'This Mr Macfeely business… I wonder how long that's been going on. If I thought he'd touched our girls—'

'Oh, Lawrie, surely he wouldn't dare!' she exclaimed. 'I don't like the idea of him being near them now but surely he would never have dared to touch them.' She looked so agitated that he said quickly, 'No, he wouldn't, Sal. He'd know they'd tell us and what would happen to him. The meanness of him though, to take advantage of young girls like that away from home. He should have been taking their father's place, looking after them.'

'What will you do?'

'I'll go and see him at the works,' Lawrie said. He was striding round the kitchen, his face red with anger, and when he seized his cap and said he would go right away, Sally was alarmed.

She knew that while his indignation and anger was fresh he would be more likely to knock Albert down than to deal with the matter quietly and discreetly, and there was always the danger that the news of any scenes might get back to Emily.

'Don't go now, Lawrie,' she pleaded, but he was opening the door. 'I'll catch him if I go now,' he said. 'God, Sally, when I think! It could have been one of ours if we'd let them go into service.'

Sally rarely used any feminine wiles on Lawrie but now she leaned back in the chair and closed her eyes.

'I could do with you here,' she said. 'This has been a terrible shock. I gave Myfanwy some money so they'll be all right for a while.'

He hesitated then put his cap back on the dresser. 'I suppose it has been a shock, love,' he said. 'But you'll be glad they came to you instead of Emily, though.'

He sat down, clasping his hands between his knees, and Sally said fervently, 'Indeed I am. They're good girls. Myfanwy's a real little mother, the eldest of a big family she told me once. She'll look after the other little girl.'

Lawrie clenched his teeth. 'I'd like to give that feller a bloody good kick!' he exclaimed. 'The rotten swine. I'd like to get if off my chest today, Sal.'

'Don't, Lol,' she begged. 'I don't want you to go out. And, anyway, if there's any trouble our Emily might get to hear of it.'

He sighed but agreed. His shift at work changed the following day and soon after eight o'clock in the morning he was on his way to Albert's box works. Sally had pleaded with him to remember Emily and not make it impossible for her to see her sister, and Lawrie had promised to restrain himself.

When he came back he said immediately, 'Don't worry about Emily, Sal. I've told him that she hasn't got to know anything about this, and you're to be able to see her whenever you want, and he's agreed.'

'Thank God. What did he say?'

'What could he say? I told him there was more than one girl who could give evidence against him. He started moaning about how hard it was with an invalid wife and all that, but I told him, if he'd gone with a prostitute I'd have understood, but he took advantage of a young girl, under his own roof too.'

'When you think of what could have happened to that girl!' Sally exclaimed. 'Did he ever think of that after he threw her out?'

'Don't you worry, Sally, he'll think of it now,' Lawrie said grimly. 'I put the fear of God in him. He won't try that caper again, and I've told him her friends can cause trouble for him if he doesn't do something for her. He says he'll give me a hundred pounds for her. I reckon that should be eighty pounds for her to keep her until the baby's born, and a bit to start her off in another job, and ten pounds each for Myfanwy and the nurse – Ruth, wasn't it? They must have been keeping her out of their own pockets.'

'He's getting off lightly, I reckon,' Sally said. 'I was thinking while you were out. I know now why he turned so nasty with me. He must have thought I was quizzing the maid and would find out about this.'

'I've warned him what I'll do to him if he does anything else to upset Emily,' Lawrie said. 'I was disgusted. It was like sticking a pin in a balloon the way he tried to bluster then just collapsed. You can go and see Emily tomorrow or any time you like, love. He'll keep out of your way.'

Sally said nothing to Mary or Cathy about the incident but the ubiquitous Sarah Burns had been around when Sally was showing the girls out, and she said to Cathy, 'Who were them girls who came to see your mam? Welshies they sounded like, and one of them was whingeing.'

'Old friends,' Cathy said quickly, but as soon as a possibility arose she asked her mother about the girls.

'It was Myfanwy and another Welsh girl,' her mother said, 'but don't ask me why they came, because it's none of your business.'

'I'm not a child,' Cathy said indignantly.

'I don't care how old you are, it's not your business,' Sally said. 'How did you know about them anyhow?'

'Sarah Burns told me,' said Cathy.

'Sarah Burns!' Sally exclaimed. 'She's a nosy little faggot. It's a good job for her that her mother didn't hear her.'

Mary had heard the conversation, and later Lawrie, always more indiscreet than his wife, dropped a remark about his visit to the box factory. The two girls put two and two together and later in the bedroom Mary said lightly, 'Sounds as though Uncle Albert has been a naughty boy.'

Cathy was sitting up in bed, her arms round her knees as she looked out dreamily at the moonlight on the roofs of the houses opposite. She shrugged. 'Not for the first time,' she said curtly.

She was astounded at Mary's response. She threw down her hairbrush and gripped Cathy's arms. 'Did he touch you? Did he?' she demanded. 'I'll kill him if he did.'

Surprise made Cathy imprudent. 'No,' she stammered, 'but he touched you, didn't he?'

Mary turned away and picked up her brush. 'How do you know?' she said in a low voice.

'I saw him, a long time ago. I'd stayed with Aunt Emily then I went into the garden and saw you and Uncle Albert, so I ran away.'

Mary said nothing but sat with her head bent, picking at the bristles of her hairbrush. After a while Cathy said timidly, 'Didn't you mind?'

'I don't know,' Mary said. 'I suppose I was flattered, and a girl in the shop said her uncle did far worse things so I thought it was usual.' She said nothing about money and Cathy sat with her hands round her knees, uncertain how to proceed. Then Mary began to brush her hair, and Cathy lay down and said goodnight.

She knew, and felt that Mary realised that she knew, that Mary must have been aware that the incident with Uncle Albert was wrong, but now that seemed less important to Cathy than the fact that her sister had felt so protective towards her. A feeling of warmth spread through her as she remembered how swiftly and fiercely Mary had reacted to the idea that Albert might have touched her young sister.

For a while she felt her old love for her sister, but a few weeks later Mary's behaviour reawakened Cathy's mistrust.

Greg's mother had been invited to spend Sunday with a lady from the church, and Sally had invited him to come for his midday dinner with the family. When he arrived Cathy was at the Mellors' house helping Josie with some sewing, but Mary took Greg into the parlour and produced a small box with a broken hinge. 'I've broken this,' she said in her low husky voice, 'but I'm sure *you'll* be able to fix it for me.' She stood close to him, smiling up into his eyes.

Greg flushed. 'Yes, certainly, only too pleased,' he stammered.

She put the little box in his outstretched hand, and left her hand lying in his, still smiling up into his face.

They were standing together, Mary still smiling with beguiling helplessness and Greg looking pleased and flattered, when Sally walked into the parlour. She said good morning to Greg then said crisply, 'Why are you bothering Greg with that box, Mary? You know your father could have fixed it for you.'

'No trouble, Mrs Ward,' Greg was saying, when Cathy came running across the road and burst into the parlour.

'Sorry I was out, Greg,' she said. Her cheeks were pink, her eyes bright, and she was bubbling with laughter as she launched into an account of Josie's struggles with the dress.

'She said she looked deformed in it, and no wonder! She'd tacked the front where the back should be and put both the sleeves in the wrong way. You never saw anything like it, but we had a good laugh anyway and we soon sorted it out.'

Greg had turned to her, smiling, but suddenly Cathy became aware of the tension in the room. She looked from her mother's stern expression to Mary's voluptuous figure so close to Greg, who was still holding the small box in his hand. A cold finger of fear touched her and her smile faded.

'I'm glad you were able to fix it for Josie,' her mother said, then jerked her head at Mary. 'Come and give me a hand with the dinner,' she said. 'I thought you'd done the cabbage.'

Mary looked sulky but she followed her mother out of the room and Cathy sat down on the sofa, She felt that suddenly the brightness of the day was dimmed, but Greg sat down beside her and took her hand, and with an effort she smiled at him. 'Has your mother gone to Anfield then?' she asked.

'Yes. Mrs Cottam and her daughter came for her quite early,' he said. 'They suggested going to Morning Service then straight on to their house.' He glanced self-consciously at the box he still held in his hand, and slipped it into his pocket. 'Mary asked me to fix this, but I'll do it at home,' he said. His face coloured as he spoke and Cathy felt sick at heart, but tried to smile.

'Josie's gran was creating about us sewing on a Sunday,' she said. 'She's supposed to be deaf, but Josie only whispered to me, "Take no notice of her," and the next minute she gave Josie such a clout across the head! She said she'd be cross-eyed for a week.'

Greg gave a shout of laughter, and suddenly put his arms around Cathy and hugged her. Thankfully, she raised her face to his for a kiss. I'm imagining things, she told herself, ready as always to hope for the best, and when her mother called them she went quite happily into the kitchen for her dinner.

Her father had been working but was at home for the meal which passed cheerfully although Sally seemed quiet and withdrawn. After dinner Greg helped the girls to clear away while their mother went upstairs to lie down, and their father stretched himself on the sofa to read his newspaper.

Cathy had started to wash the dishes as Mary and Greg carried them through from the kitchen. She was humming happily when suddenly she glanced into the shaving mirror her father kept propped above the sink. It reflected Mary glancing provocatively at Greg as he passed her a dish. Cathy swung around. 'We'll go for a walk on the "Sticks" as soon as these are finished, Greg,' she said loudly.

'Yes, all right,' he agreed. 'It's a bit windy out but nice and sunny.'

'I think I'll come with you,' Mary said airily. Cathy snatched the dish from her hand and Greg hurriedly returned to the kitchen.

'It's manners to wait to be asked,' Cathy hissed furiously but Mary only shrugged.

'I didn't know I needed an invitation to walk along the Landing Stage.'

'Would you like it if I tacked on to you and Sam?' Cathy said angrily.

'I'd be *delighted* if you tacked on to me and Sam,' Mary said, laughing and following Greg into the kitchen. She went over to her father. 'Will you come for a walk on the "Sticks" with me, Dada?' she said, using the old pet name.

Lawrie looked up in dismay. 'I'm tired, chick,' he said. 'Four o'clock start this morning. Can't you find someone else to go with you?'

The girls had kept their voices low as they quarrelled in the scullery and Lawrie had heard nothing, so it was quite by chance that he glanced at Greg who felt obliged to say, 'Cathy and I are going to the Landing Stage, Mr Ward, Mary can come with us.' He was careful not to look at her so missed her triumphant smile as she went back into the scullery.

Cathy was standing motionless, her hands in the bowl of water and her eyes full of angry tears, but when Mary flounced back, she blinked them away and flung up her head proudly.

'I got my invitation, you see,' Mary said gaily, but Cathy looked at her with contempt.

'I heard,' she said. 'Is that how you get all your invitations? I can't say I like your methods.'

Mary grew red with fury then shrugged and turned away. 'Won't do you any good, you know,' she said. 'Trying to keep him in a glass case.' She sauntered back into the kitchen, and her father held up his stockinged foot apologetically. 'I'd have liked to come with you, pet,' he said, 'but my feet are aching.'

'Don't worry, Dad,' she said. 'I'll be all right with Greg.' She smiled brilliantly at him and he hurriedly dumped the cruet on the dresser and went back into the scullery to help Cathy.

When they left the house, Cathy could see that Mary was manoeuvring to walk between herself and Greg so she quickly took his arm and crooked her other arm for Mary to hold. I can be crafty too, she thought grimly, but Mary ignored Cathy's arm and placed herself on the other side of Greg, holding his free arm and smiling at him.

They had just set off when there was a loud 'Cooee' from Josie who had come out on to the step of her house.

'Where a' y'going, Cath?' she called.

'The Landing Stage,' Cathy called back. 'Want to come?'

'Yes. Hold on a minute,' Josie shouted, dashing back into the house and reappearing wearing her hat and coat. She linked her arm through Mary's who stared straight ahead, her face set.

'I'm glad to get outa our house,' Josie said. 'Me gran's done nothing but moan.'

'Is she still going on about the sewing?' asked Cathy.

'No, she's found half a dozen other things to moan about since then,' Josie said. 'Eh, Greg, you're doing all right. One lad and three girls.' She gave a loud screech of laughter and Mary wrinkled her nose in disgust.

As they walked four abreast they were obstructing other walkers and when an approaching couple had to step into the road, Josie tugged at Mary's arm. 'We'd better walk ahead, Mary,' she said. 'People can't get past.' Greg withdrew his arm from Mary's with alacrity, and she was forced to walk ahead with Josie, who chattered on, seemingly unaware of Mary's stony silence.

Cathy hugged Greg's arm and he smiled down at her. God bless Josie, Cathy thought. That couldn't have worked out better if I'd planned it. When they reached the Landing Stage, her sister took Greg's arm again and they walked along in a foursome, but Mary's pleasure was again spoiled by Josie, who said loudly, 'Eh, Mary, we'd do better on our own. We'd have a better chance to click if we wasn't with these love birds.'

'I came for fresh air, not to click, as you call it,' Mary said icily, but Josie laughed, unabashed.

'Listen to her,' she said. 'Lady Muck. You could 'a got fresh air in your backyard if that's all you were after.' Mary turned her head away haughtily but she still held Greg's arm.

At his suggestion they walked down to the end of the Landing Stage to where an old woman sold apples from a barrow. He bought some which they ate sitting on a low wall, looking out over the river.

The wall seemed clean, scoured by the fresh breezes which blew from the Mersey, and Cathy and Josie sat down without hesitation, but Mary would only sit down when Greg spread his handkerchief on the wall. She drew him down beside her and leaned close to him, asking him about the ships which were in the river, and looking into his eyes.

Cathy trembled with anger but told herself fiercely that she trusted Greg. But do you trust Mary? a small voice seemed to ask.

A seagull swooped low over a group of Norwegian seamen who stood a few yards away from the wall, and a bird's droppings landed on the collar of one of the men. He raised his fist and shouted at the bird. As it flew away, its raucous cry sounded like derisive laughter. The seaman's companions fell about laughing as he yelled strange oaths after the departing bird, and all the people nearby, including Josie, laughed too.

Only Mary and Greg seemed oblivious to the little comedy as they sat close together, their faces only inches apart, looking out over the shipping and glancing at each other from time to time as Greg named the ships.

Cathy was torn between misery and anger: anger at Mary's blatant efforts to monopolise Greg, and misery at his apparent readiness to respond to her. Anger predominated, and when they stood up, Cathy took Josie's arm, leaving Greg to follow with Mary. If that's what he wants, he can have it, she thought. But every step she took, unable to see him, was agony to her.

Mary strutted along, leaning heavily on his arm and looking up at him coquettishly, but Greg was strangely silent. He scarcely replied to her remarks and hurried her along when she tried to dawdle, so that they kept close behind Cathy and Josie. Josie looked back occasionally to make a laughing remark, but Cathy looked steadily ahead. At one point Josie gave a loud shout of laughter and Mary said crossly, 'Really, that girl is so common. I wish Cathy was more discriminating in her choice of friends. She should be trying to improve herself and drop creatures like that.'

'Cathy's the faithful sort,' Greg said quietly.

Mary went on, '"Show me your friends and I'll tell you what you are," my mother always says.'

He said nothing, and Mary suddenly remembered how meaningfully her mother had looked at her as she quoted the saying, and wondered uneasily how much Sally suspected about Bella Richards and the rest of her new circle.

Chapter Nineteen

When they reached the house, Josie ran off across the road, calling cheerfully, 'Ta ra then. Watch out for seagulls.'

Greg tried to detain Cathy but she walked into the house, leaving him to follow with Mary, who ran up to their bedroom. When Cathy and Greg went into the kitchen they found that Sally was downstairs.

'You've baked, Mam!' Cathy exclaimed. 'You didn't stay long in bed.'

'Long enough,' her mother said offhandedly. 'So Josie went with you? I heard her calling you.'

She omitted to say that she had come downstairs as soon as they had left, to ask Lawrie what was happening. He could only tell her that Mary had asked him to go for a walk with her, but he was tired and Greg had suggested that she went with him and Cathy instead. Sally said nothing of her worry and speculation about the two girls but now she looked anxiously into Cathy's face.

'Yes, she said she was glad to get away from her gran.'

'I don't blame her,' said Sally. 'Poor Mrs Mellor. She has her share with that old woman. Nothing suits her.' She bent and opened the oven door, and while her face was hidden said with assumed carelessness, 'I see Mary went right upstairs. Is she all right?'

'I don't know,' Cathy said. And I don't care either, she thought. Something of it sounded in her voice and Sally darted a glance at Greg who was standing awkwardly by the door. 'Sit down,' she said. 'Tea won't be long. The fresh air should have given you an appetite.'

He sat down and Cathy said to her mother, 'I'll just wash my hands and do the butties.' She disappeared into the back kitchen.

Lawrie was sitting on the sofa, yawning. He smiled at Greg. 'Might have done me good to go out with our Mary,' he said. 'I feel more tired since I had a doze.'

Cathy grimaced to herself when she heard her father's words. That would have spiked Mary's guns, she thought, then misery swept over her again. Greg, she thought. How could he? I know Mary tries those tricks with every fellow she meets, but for Greg to fall for them like that... Sitting so close with their faces nearly touching, while she buttered him up asking about ships that she probably knows more about than he does! And Greg looking into her eyes, telling her the names of ships as though there was no one else there but them. Cathy could feel an almost physical pain as she remembered the scene, and anger swept over her again.

Making a fool of me too, she thought. Good thing Josie didn't notice their antics while I sat there ignored like one of Lewis's dummies.

Her hands trembled as she cut and buttered bread but by the time she had finished she was able to walk calmly into the kitchen, avoiding Greg's eyes as she put the plate on the table.

When the meal was ready Sally went into the lobby and called upstairs to Mary. She had evidently spent the time in washing herself and changing her blouse, and her hair had been brushed and re-arranged. Cathy immediately felt conscious that she had worn the same blouse all day, and that her hair had been blown about by the fresh wind off the river.

They sat down at the table and Cathy took a chair beside her father and away from Greg. Lawrie smiled fondly at Mary. 'My word, you look nice, love,' he said. 'You look as though you've just stepped out of a bandbox.'

'And well she might,' Sally said tartly, 'dolling herself up while Cathy and I do the work.' Lawrie looked surprised, and Mary darted a venomous glance at her mother before turning to smile at Greg. An uncomfortable silence fell, and when he bit into a piece of celery the noise sounded like a pistol shot in the silence.

It seemed to rouse Lawrie who said quickly, 'Awkward stuff to eat, celery. Did you ever hear Mrs Mal's tale of the young man who came to tea when she was in service, and the cream cake?'

'I don't remember that one,' Sally said.

'I'll bet Cathy knows it, don't you, love?' Lawrie said, but she shook her head, unable to speak.

'Mrs Mal was in service, you see,' he went on, 'and this young man came courting one of the daughters of the house. Very smart clothes and a la di dah way of talking, but Mrs Mal said she had her doubts about him.'

'You couldn't fool her,' Sally said with a smile.

'She must have been a bit nosy even then,' Lawrie said. 'Because she was a nursery maid, but she offered to help the parlourmaid so she could get a look at the lad. The way Mrs Mal put it they didn't have their tea round a table like Christians, but had to balance a cup and saucer and plate on their knees.'

Sally sighed. 'D'you know, Lawrie, it's like listening to her talking when you say that.'

'Anyhow,' he continued, 'this lad picked up a cream cake off his plate and bit into it, and all the cream shot out of the other end. He'd just been talking in a posh voice but when the cream shot out he shouted, "Bloody Hell!" Mrs Mal said they all sat there like pillars of salt, and her and the other girl had to clear up the cream and get out quick while they could keep the laughter in. She said they ran to the kitchen and screeched with laughter, and the others in the kitchen were going mad to know what was up but they were laughing too much to tell them.'

'Ah, Mrs Mal,' Sally said. 'I wish you'd known her, Greg. I wonder what happened to the young man?'

'God knows,' Lawrie said, 'but he wouldn't get far with his courting after coming out with a mouthful like that. So see you watch your tongue, Greg, or I might show *you* the door like that poor young man.'

'Well, there's many a slip between cup and lip, as they say,' Mary said sweetly. She looked at Greg as she spoke, the sideways provocative look from under lowered lids that Cathy had often seen her use to good effect on others. She shook with rage. She felt as though she would choke if she tried to swallow and her father suddenly noticed her distress.

'Cathy's the one who could tell you about Mrs Mal, Greg,' he said. 'You were always good pals, weren't you, chicken?'

She was still unable to speak and he went on, 'Mrs Mal thought the world of her, and Cathy did a lot to make her happy especially after she came to live with us. Well, she had a full and happy life, and a peaceful end free from pain so we couldn't have wished anything different for her.'

'Yes, she had a peaceful end,' Cathy said. Her voice was husky but no one seemed to notice. Her father smiled at her. She tried to smile in return then looked to where Mary was offering the plate of bread and butter to Greg, leaning towards him and looking provocatively into his flushed face.

He took a slice of bread and butter mechanically, without taking his eyes from her face, and she smiled and passed the tip of her tongue over her parted lips. Greg seemed mesmerised, gazing at Mary like a rabbit at a stoat, and a black tide of jealousy rose in Cathy. Her hand tightened round the handle of the knife which lay beside her, and her mother said sharply, 'Pass that plate, Mary. Your dad wants a butty.'

Mary passed the plate to her father, and Greg turned his head and picked up his knife and fork as though released from a spell.

Cathy clasped her hands beneath the table to hide their trembling, and bent her head. Her food was untouched. After a quick glance round the table her mother ignored Cathy and talked to Greg about the opening of the St Paul's Eye Hospital by Lord Derby.

Mary ate her meal slowly and daintily, a complacent smile on her face while Cathy struggled to compose herself and hold back the tears. She was determined that Mary would not see her distress, and to calm herself she tried to remove herself in spirit by thinking about Mrs Malloy.

She remembered her old friend saying once, 'Don't upset yourself and fall out with your friend over Mary, girlie. She's a born mischief maker. Don't be giving her the satisfaction of causing trouble.' But she could draw little comfort from that memory.

Cathy's anger at Mary's behaviour was swamped by bitter hurt at Greg's response to her. I trusted him. I thought he was different, she thought, but she's cast a spell over him. He hasn't even looked at me.

She peeped across the table to where Mary was leaning against Greg, her breast pressing against his arm and her face close to his, as she asked him to pass the salt. Cathy remembered a snatch of conversation she had overheard at a tram stop: 'She can make "Good morning" sound like "Come to bed".' Suddenly she realised what the speaker had meant.

Sally had gone into the back kitchen for custard. Now she banged the jug down on the table. 'Rhubarb pie, Gregory?' she asked. Lawrie looked up in surprise. 'You're getting your full title today, lad,' he said, laughing. 'Must be because it's Sunday.' Greg made no reply, but looked red and uncomfortable.

There was a loud knock on the door and Lawrie went to open it. He came back with a telegram in his hand and handed it to Greg who read it quickly. 'My mother is staying the night with her friends,' he said. 'They'll bring her home tomorrow.'

'That's good. You won't have to rush home then,' Lawrie said. 'The lad's waiting for a reply.' Before going to the door Greg looked across at Cathy, but she said nothing and sat with her head bent. When he returned to the table it was Mary who welcomed him, smiling deeply into his eyes.

When the meal was over, Sally said briskly, 'I've put a match to the parlour fire for you and Greg to sit in there, Cath. Mary will help me to clear away.'

Cathy had knocked a fork to the floor, and as she bent to retrieve it she saw Mary's and Greg's clasped hands were resting on his knee. By the time she sat up again, Greg had withdrawn his hand and was nervously fumbling at his collar with it. Cathy heard her own voice saying loudly, 'I'll help, Mam.' Without knowing what she was doing, she found herself standing in the scullery.

'Just put those dishes in the bowl, and go in the parlour,' her mother said. 'The water's not hot enough for them yet anyway, and Mary can do them when it is.'

As though in a dream Cathy walked into the parlour and Greg followed her. She sat down in the green plush armchair beside the fire, and sat staring into the flames, her head turned away from him. He hesitated by the door then sat down in the armchair facing her.

'Are you cold, Cath?' he asked nervously.

'No,' she said, glancing at him briefly, then turning back to look into the fire.

'Will – will you sit on the sofa?' he said, but she made no reply and they sat in silence for a while.

Cathy was still struggling to hold back tears, swallowing fiercely and making herself think of a book she was reading or a meeting she had been to with Rosie – anything to take her mind off Greg and help her control herself.

Suddenly he came over to where she was sitting and dropped on his knees beside her chair. 'Cath,' he said urgently. As she turned to him and he saw that her eyes were bright with tears, he flung his arms around her. 'Oh, Cath,' he said in distress, 'I don't know what's happened – what's gone wrong today. It should have been such a lovely day.'

She held herself stiffly within the circle of his arms while the tears flowed. Neither of them spoke; Cathy because she was too proud to admit why she was upset, and Greg because he was afraid of making matters worse.

In the kitchen Mary and Sally had cleared away and washed the dishes. Mary was about to go out of the kitchen when her mother stepped in front of her and firmly closed the door into the lobby.

'Where do you think you're going?' she said grimly.

Mary opened her eyes wide and said innocently, 'Into the parlour. Why?'

'Isn't Sam coming?'

'Yes, but I don't think we'll go out,' Mary said, shrugging her shoulders. 'He can join us for a few songs round the piano.'

'If you stay in, *Madam*, you can stay in the kitchen,' Sally said. 'You know fine well that for once Greg can stay without worrying about his mother, and you're not going to spoil it.'

Mary gave a long-suffering sigh. 'I thought Dad didn't want them to be on their own,' she said. 'I can't do right.'

'Don't waste your soft soap on me, Mary. I've got you weighed up, milady, and well you know it.'

The doorbell rang and Mary flounced out to open the door, then returned with Sam in tow. 'You're not welcome to stay in,' she said to Sam, then ran upstairs and reappeared wearing her hat and coat. 'Come *on*,' she said, and he smiled sheepishly at Sally and Lawrie before following her out of the house.

'What was all that in aid of?' Lawrie asked.

'*She* knows,' Sally said, 'and I'm not having it.'

'I don't know what all the fuss is about,' Lawrie said. 'Why can't the four of them have a bit of a sing song together? Mary's only trying to do what she thinks I want.'

'Honest to God, Lawrie, sometimes I think you walk round in blinkers!' Sally exclaimed. 'Cathy and Greg not speaking to each other, and neither of them touching the meal, and Mary either making up to Greg or sitting there like a cat that's swallowed the cream. Making that crack about "Many a slip" too!'

'Well, by God, you can make something out of nothing all right. I'm not blind but I didn't see any of that,' Lawrie said. 'Mary's right about one thing. She can't do anything right as far as you're concerned.'

They glared at each other and Sally rattled the poker furiously in the bars of the grate. 'And you can't see a fault in her,' she snapped. 'She can twist you round her little finger the same as all the others, but I tell you this – she's not going to break Cathy's heart to satisfy her vanity, not while I can stop it.'

She dashed into the back kitchen, gripping the edge of the sink and blinking away tears as Cathy had done earlier in the day. After a few minutes Lawrie followed her.

'Don't be upsetting yourself, girl,' he said. 'You worry too much. You can't live their lives for them.'

Sally swallowed. 'I *am* worried,' she said. 'I can see this family being split in two. Greg's a nice lad, but I wish they'd never met him.'

Lawrie slipped his arm around her. 'Maybe Greg and Cathy have had a bit of a tiff, but I'm sure it's nothing to do with Mary. They'll soon get over it.'

Sally sighed. 'I hope you're right,' she said. 'I'll bet poor Sam's getting the rough edge of her tongue now, the mood she was in.'

'Yes, and here's us nearly falling out too. I suppose you'll blame Mary for that!'

'And I'd be right,' Sally said grimly, but she went back into the kitchen and sat down while he made a fresh cup of tea.

Meanwhile Cathy and Greg had heard Sam's knock, then the closing of the front door as he and Mary left the house. Cathy had been determined not to give her sister the satisfaction of knowing that she had quarrelled with Greg, but as soon as Mary had left the house Cathy said firmly, 'You'll have to go. I've got a headache and I want to have an early night.'

Greg looked dismayed. 'But – can't we talk, Cath?' he pleaded.

Cathy was adamant. 'No, I don't feel like talking. I'm going to bed.' Her face was blotched with tears, but her composure and her air of quiet dignity made her seem years older than the girl who had run laughing into the parlour a few hours earlier.

Greg tried to protest but she looked at him so implacably that he shrugged, and went into the lobby for his hat and coat. Cathy followed him, pulling the parlour door closed behind her so that he could not return there. He was forced to go to the kitchen to say goodnight to Sally and Lawrie.

'Off already?' Lawrie said in surprise, and seemed about to say more until a glance from Sally stopped him.

'Cathy has a headache,' Greg said awkwardly. 'Thank you for your hospitality, Mrs Ward.'

'You're welcome, Greg,' she said, and Lawrie said cheerfully, 'Any time, lad.'

Cathy led the way down the lobby and opened the front door, but when Greg bent to kiss her she turned her head so that the kiss landed on her cheek.

'When can I see you?' he asked urgently.

'I don't know. Goodnight,' she said. He turned away, muttered 'Goodnight', then walked swiftly away.

Cathy sped upstairs to pour water into the washbowl and sluice it over her face. Deliberately she whipped up her anger by thinking of her miserable day, finished by Greg stalking away from the door. I don't care if I never see him again, she told herself, bathing her face over and over again until she felt calm enough to go downstairs.

In the kitchen her mother was darning socks and her father reading a newspaper. Cathy said quickly, 'I've got a bit of a headache, Mam. I think I'll go up.' Sally gave her one quick glance but only said quietly, 'There's a cup of tea in the pot. Would you like it?'

'No thanks, I'll have a drink of water.' She went into the scullery and drank a cup of water, hoping to steady herself enough to behave normally until she could reach the sanctuary of her bed, then she went back and kissed her parents goodnight.

They both behaved as though there was nothing amiss, although her father dropped his paper and patted her cheek as she bent over him, and her mother kissed her more warmly than usual.

Cathy fled to her room to change into her nightdress and dive into bed within minutes, free at last to let the tears flow as hurt and disillusion tore at her.

I'll never forgive him, never! she thought, sobbing into her pillow. Strangely, her anger against Mary was in abeyance as distress at Greg's behaviour mounted in her. Deliberately she let scenes from the day pass through her mind: Greg with his face close to Mary's as they talked about the ships in the river, then walking arm in arm with her; Greg at the table, gazing at Mary as though he was bewitched and holding her hand beneath the table. I thought he was different, she thought, weeping. I thought there was such a bond between us that he'd never be tempted by Mary or anyone else.

Her pillow was soaked and she sat up and turned it over angrily. I'm not going to cry any more, she told herself. He's not worth it. Let him have Mary if that's what he wants. I'm finished with him.

But even as she thought this she knew in her heart that she would always love Greg, whatever his faults.

Chapter Twenty

Greg strode away from the house, confused and unhappy, his mind and body in a ferment. How could he love a girl as deeply as he loved Cathy, and yet be aroused by someone like Mary? He thought of Cathy, of the closeness between them and the way their minds were so completely in tune. What a difference she had made to his life. It had been like stepping out of shadow into sunshine to know her, to feel the warmth of her personality and her happiness, yet they had been able to talk seriously about subjects that interested both of them.

I love everything about her, he thought, and yet... Mary's soft breast pressing against him, her tongue flickering over her lips as she gazed into his eyes, had aroused sensations in his body that he had never known.

He veered away from his homeward path to go down to the waterfront and stand leaning on a bollard, staring unseeingly at the heaving water. What's wrong with me? he thought despairingly. Am I some sort of a freak? If only there was someone he could talk to.

He remembered just before his father's death staying with his aunt and uncle. There he had had a conversation with his cousin. Charlie was the same age as himself and they had talked about 'wet dreams' and Charlie's passion for his housemaster's daughter.

And that was the last time I've been able to talk like that with anyone, Greg thought bitterly. His father's death had meant Greg's leaving school, and the company of boys his own age, and being thrust into a position of responsibility among men older than himself.

His mother's quarrel with his uncle had cut him off from Charlie, and her incessant demands had left him no free time to make other friends.

Why did I allow it? he thought. Because I'm weak, that's why. Letting her manipulate me; always having to scheme to get away, and then often having to stay at home because of her imaginary illness. Letting her make me put off meeting Cathy on one flimsy pretext after another.

He glanced up at the bulk of a ship anchored in the river, and remembered Mary pressing against him as she asked the names of the ships, and manoeuvring to keep him away from her sister. His contempt for himself grew.

No wonder Cathy despised him! He remembered her stony expression as she turned away from his kiss, and groaned aloud.

I'm not good enough for her anyway, he thought wretchedly. Dominated by my mother, dancing like a puppet on a string to Mary's tune, I'm just a weak fool, not fit for a girl like Cathy.

There was no one to tell him that he was too hard on himself or that he was confusing diffidence and good manners, coupled with a sense of duty, with weakness. He turned away from the river and walked home, in the depths of despair.

It was strange to walk into the house and not hear his mother's querulous voice demanding: 'Is that you at last, Gregory?' He threw himself down in a chair, without removing his coat or lighting the gas mantle. He sat for hours, thinking of the past four years of his life and worrying about the events of the day.

Had other men experienced this? he wondered. Loving one girl deeply and permanently, yet feeling their body respond to another. There was no one he could ask. He thought of Jack Carmody but dismissed the idea immediately. Jack was a good fellow, a lively companion, but too indiscreet to confide in. Norah once said that whatever went in through his ears came out through his mouth, and it was true.

Why had he never felt this arousal with Cathy? Was it because she was so young and innocent, or because he was sexually immature? I responded quickly enough to Mary, he thought grimly.

He thought about her. She had always been flirtatious with him as she was with any man, but today had been different. He remembered when he had casually put his hand on his knee as they sat at table, Mary's hand was already on his knee, stroking it, then her hand had covered his. He had snatched his hand away but been unable to control the trembling of his body.

Did Cathy notice? Greg wondered. Did her parents? He grew hot at the thought. He hoped that Cathy's innocence had protected her from knowing, and that she had been hurt only by his neglect of her during the day.

Oh, Cathy, he groaned, what the hell is wrong with me? A church clock struck two and he stood up, shivering and stiff with cold, and went to bed.

He fell deeply asleep. When he woke a few hours later, the soul searching and distress he had endured seemed to have cleared his mind and he could put the events of the previous day in perspective.

He decided that he had been weak and stupid to respond as he had to Mary, but nothing had actually happened. To her it had been only a brief whim, he was convinced, a way of passing a boring day. The incident was only significant because Cathy had been hurt by it.

From now on he would be different, firm with his mother and in control of his own life. He would insist that his mother invited Cathy to tea and make it clear to everyone that he was deeply in love with her, that they were a courting couple who would marry as soon as it was possible.

He began to plan for that future. He would take more interest in the shop, build up the business so that he could provide for his mother as well as himself and Cathy when he married.

His mother constantly complained about having to live over the shop instead of in her own home, so he would make enough to buy her a small house and provide her with a companion. Then he would feel that he had fulfilled the obligation laid on him by his father and he and Cathy could marry and live over the shop.

He felt full of energy and as quietly confident as he had last felt when as a boy of sixteen he had planned to excel as a doctor. Circumstances had changed all that, but he could still make a success of life for himself and for Cathy.

As for Mary, he would treat her politely but distantly as Cathy's sister, and forget that she had ever been able to a make a fool of him. He sat down and wrote to Cathy, asking when he could see her again but not mentioning Sunday. He felt that he could explain and apologise better face to face. He sped through the deserted streets and put the letter in the Wards' door.

Sally had put the envelope on the end of the dresser when Cathy came down. She snatched it up eagerly, and tore it open.

It contained a single sheet of paper, and Cathy read the words on it with disbelief. Only a message asking her to meet him; no word of apology for his behaviour on Sunday.

In a sudden burst of temper, she flung the letter into the fire then tried to snatch it out again. She was too late.

'What are you playing at?' her mother exclaimed. 'You're lucky you didn't burn your hand.'

'I—I changed my mind,' Cathy muttered.

'So I see. You're getting too ready with your moods lately,' her mother said sharply. 'You think everything should be the way you want it.'

'*I* do?' Cathy exclaimed in amazement.

'Yes, you do. And another thing – don't expect people to be perfect, because you're far from perfect yourself.'

Cathy was too stunned to reply. Mary had came downstairs before she found her voice.

'You're going to be late too,' Sally greeted her eldest daughter. 'It's ridiculous the time you spend dolling yourself up. You could do with a few children round your feet to take your mind off yourself.' Mary made a face to Cathy behind her mother's back, but she looked away without responding. Mary went down to the outside toilet.

'Don't forget,' Sally said quietly to Cathy, 'Greg must have taken the trouble to write that letter last night and drop it in here.'

'I know, Mam,' Cathy said. 'I'm sorry I burned it.'

'That poor lad must think this is a madhouse, after coming from such a quiet home,' Sally said. 'The moods and tantrums of yours and Mary's must have him bewildered.' She handed Cathy her parcel of sandwiches. She kissed her mother swiftly. 'Thanks, Mam,' she said, before leaving for work. They both knew that she was not referring to the sandwiches.

Cathy pondered on the events of Sunday as she sat at her machine. Her mother seemed to be on Greg's side, she thought, but then Mam didn't know all that had happened. Yet the more she thought of the incidents, the more her anger with Mary grew, as she remembered her sister's blatant attempts to monopolise Greg. How could he have ignored her without being openly rude?

I'm to blame too, Cathy thought, letting Mary cause trouble between us. She felt that the day would never end, so that she could go home and write to him.

Greg had swiftly put his plans into action. As soon as he returned from Egremont Street, he took out the shop books and studied them. When the staff arrived he was already downstairs with a plan for the rearrangement of the window drawn up.

He had expected opposition from Mr Braithwaite but the old man seemed pleased, and agreed that the fresh display would attract more interest. Greg told him that he had studied the books, and thought that there were ways to improve trade.

'I'd like to see the travellers myself, too,' Greg said diffidently, but Mr Braithwaite was enthusiastic.

'I'm glad to hear it, Mr Greg,' he said. 'I remember when your father was a young man he had a lot of good ideas. That's why we were able to expand and open other shops.'

'I don't know that I'll be able to do that,' Greg said with a smile, 'but I hope we can improve trade here.'

'I'm sure we can. We've only been ticking over as you might say,' Mr Braithwaite said.

Greg glanced up quickly. 'I suppose you could say the same about me. This must have been difficult for you, and I've only just realised it. When my father died, to have me brought in nominally in charge but knowing nothing, and not trying very hard to learn.'

The old man shrugged. 'We kept our jobs, which was more than the chaps in the other shops did. And you did what was required to keep things going.'

'Well, it'll be different now. I'm really going to work at it,' Greg said.

Mr Braithwaite nodded his head. 'I know you've had a hard time, Mr Greg, and this wasn't what you wanted, but my father used to say, "If you want to be a farmer and you can't, make sure you're the best ploughman in the parish."'

Greg laughed. 'I get the message.'

They were interrupted by a commotion at the front of the shop as Mrs Redmond arrived home. Greg went out to greet her and to invite her friends upstairs, but they declined, saying that they had another appointment. They drove away looking relieved, Greg thought, and he escorted his mother upstairs.

The daily cleaning woman was in the kitchen, and Greg asked her to make tea for his mother. He went back to where she lay in her chair, dabbing her forehead with eau de cologne. 'Mrs Drew will make tea for you, Mother,' he said. 'I'm going back to the shop.'

'That's not necessary, surely, Gregory. Let Braithwaite look after things. I need you here.'

'I'm needed in the shop, Mother,' he said firmly. 'Mrs Drew will look after you.' He turned on his heel and went out leaving his mother looking after him with her mouth open.

He worked hard throughout the day, but whenever there was a lull, thoughts of Cathy filled his mind. He remembered the implacable glance she had given him, and the set expression on her face as she turned away from his kiss, and wondered if things would ever be the same between them. Cathy had told him herself that her mother considered her obstinate.

He was tempted to try to meet her from work, but felt that it might be too soon for her to decide to forgive him, and that it would be better to wait for her reply to his letter.

Cathy had half hoped to see Greg waiting for her outside work, but in one way she was relieved that their first meeting would not be under the eyes of the other girls leaving work. She had convinced herself that he was quite blameless, but as her anger with Greg diminished, her bitterness towards Mary grew.

She was determined not to speak to her, but she wondered how Mary would behave and what their mother would say.

Cathy found that her worry was unnecessary. Her mother served the meal silently, seeming to be lost in her own thoughts, and paying little attention to Cathy or Mary.

Myfanwy had called during the morning to tell Sally that Bronwen's baby had been born on the previous Saturday. Myfanwy assured Sally that Bronwen and the baby were both well, and very well cared for in the Mother and Baby Home. Bronwen had entered a month earlier. But she seemed worried, and eventually told Sally the reason.

Arrangements had been made for the baby to be adopted at two weeks old, and the adoptive parents had been at the Home soon after the baby was born to see it.

Papers had been given to Bronwen to sign but she had flatly refused.

'Says she's going to keep the baby,' Myfanwy said. 'Won't listen to sense no way.'

'Poor child, it's only natural,' Sally said, but Myfanwy was unsympathetic.

'Had it too soft she has,' she declared. 'Me and Ruth doing the worrying, and her – no worry about money, lying in bed. Wouldn't clean her room, nothing.'

'It doesn't sound as though she could look after a baby,' Sally said. 'And what about money? Does she think Mr Deakin…? Mr Ward promised the hundred pounds would finish it.'

Myfanwy shook her head. 'Hasn't thought about anything, that's the trouble. Like a toy the baby is to her, the fool! But it's not the fools who get hurt, Mrs Ward. Poor Ruth's in trouble because she fixed it up, see, And the couple – everything ready, nursery, toys… everything.'

'It's a sad business altogether,' Sally said, 'but a good home like that for the baby seems the best solution. Bronwen's only a child herself. If she makes a fresh start, she's got all her life before her to have other children she can look after properly.'

'Will you come and see her, Mrs Ward? Talk sense into her. Distracted we are, me and Ruth,' Myfanwy said.

Sally promised reluctantly, knowing that she would find it hard to persuade the girl to part with her baby although it was the only realistic solution.

Her fears that Emily might hear of the affair made her too worried and abstracted to notice the tension between Mary and Cathy. Mary pretended to be unaware of her sister's silence, and chattered about a girl who had started work at Denby's.

'Elizabeth Fairburn, her name is. Isn't that a lovely name? Her family have paid a premium for her, and you know those girls usually keep themselves to themselves, but she's really friendly. Asked if she could sit with me at the lunch break.'

Cathy was tempted to ask whether Elizabeth had a young man, and if so if she had been warned about Mary, but she said nothing, and avoided looking at her sister.

Later when Mary had gone to Janey's and her mother had gone to help to settle old Mr Ashton for the night, Cathy took out the pen and ink and notepaper. She sat for a while pondering what to say, wishing that she had kept Greg's note to re-read. Finally she wrote as briefly as he had, suggesting a meeting by the Necropolis at seven o'clock, on Tuesday.

She ironed a blouse and darned a pair of stockings while she waited for her mother to return before posting the letter, her thoughts dwelling lovingly on Greg as she mechanically performed her tasks.

As soon as her mother returned Cathy put on her hat and coat. 'I'm going out for a while, Mam,' she said. 'I might call at Norah's.'

'Don't be too late,' her mother said, making no reference to the letter in Cathy's hand. She ran lightly down to London Road and put the letter through the house door by Redmond's shop. It was a mild, pleasant evening, and she hoped that Norah's father would be out and that she could come for a walk, but when she turned into the street he was standing by the front door, his pipe in his mouth and his thumbs in the armholes of his waistcoat.

When he saw Cathy he took the pipe from his mouth and scowled at her. Cathy walked past, smiling nervously at him. Poor Norah, she thought, to be under the thumb of such a man.

For weeks she had only been able to see her friend for snatched meetings. Mr Benson had given orders that Norah was to stay indoors after she returned from work, and her mother had changed from ally to jailer.

'It must be because she's afraid of him,' Norah had said to Cathy. 'I couldn't bear it if Mam turned fully against me. We've always been so close. I'd run away if it wasn't for her.'

Cathy had agreed with Norah, hoping to console her, but privately she had no doubt that Mrs Benson was as adamant as her husband in her belief that Norah and Jack must part.

Jack Carmody had gone to the house to try to reason with Mr Benson, but he had been threatened with violence by Norah's brothers if he tried to see her again. She had sent him a note by Cathy begging him to keep away as she knew that her father and brothers meant what they said, and she feared for his safety.

Cathy felt miserable as she walked home, thinking of the difficulties that Norah and Jack faced and wondering what the outcome would be. It seemed to make her own worries insignificant by comparison.

The following morning Cathy was amazed to receive a letter from Teddy Benson, who with his twin brother Luke was in the Army and stationed on Salisbury Plain.

> Dere Cathy,
> I hope you don't mind us riting to yuo but me and Luke is worried about our Norah. She sed in her letter as the old feller battered her for going with a cathlick. We carnt rite to her but tell as we said keep outa his way as hees a bad old man. We wasn't going to come home no more but tell her well comand fix him if he batters her agann. We now its an anging matter in Liverpool going with a cathlick but differint in other plases, dussnt matter.
> Yours respeckly,
> Teddy and Luke Benson.

Cathy felt a lump in her throat as she read the untidy scrawl. At least *someone* is on Norah's side, she thought. She made up her mind to get the letter to her as soon as possible and to write to the boys herself, suggesting that they enclosed a note for Norah when they wrote again, instead of sending a message.

She put the letter away carefully, but it was forgotten when she thought that by now Greg would have read her own letter and that she would see him that evening.

Cathy had thought of the events of Sunday so often that although she remembered the broad outlines of the day, she was confused about the undercurrents and unsure how much she had imagined.

I'm going to forget it, she decided. I'm not having any more to do with Mary, but I'm not going to think any more about Sunday, and I'm not going to talk about it.

Greg was waiting by the Necropolis, studying the gravestones of long-dead people when she arrived. He took her hand and they stood for a moment in silence. Then he began, 'Cathy, I'm sorry—'

She laid her finger over his lips. 'Isn't it a lovely evening?' she said, smiling at him. He smiled back, then tucked her hand in his arm. They began to stroll along.

'About Sunday,' Greg began again, but Cathy interrupted him.

'I don't want to talk about Sunday. It's water under the bridge now.'

'I won't talk about it then,' he said gravely, 'but I'll just say – I did a lot of thinking on Sunday night, and I've decided I'm going to be different. I'm going to stop drifting.'

'Drifting?' she echoed.

'Yes, drifting. I haven't been pulling my weight in the shop,' he said. 'I've behaved like a child with my mother, too, which hasn't been good for either of us. Everything will be different from now on.'

'I see,' Cathy murmured, trying to hide her surprise. Whatever she had expected Greg to talk about, it was certainly not his plans for the shop. He sensed her bewilderment and squeezed her hand. 'I just thought hard about the future, Cath,' he said. 'Our future. I tried to see myself as others see me and I decided that they saw a weak-kneed fool, drifting aimlessly along.'

Cathy began to feel annoyed. 'I suppose you just drifted into going out with me then?' she said, more sharply than she intended.

'No, Cath, *indeed* not,' he protested. 'I'm putting this very badly. I mean, I've had the luck to meet a perfect girl, and I've got to try to make myself worthy of her.'

'That's *much* better,' Cathy said, laughing up at him mischievously. 'You said that quite perfectly.'

Greg laughed too, and drew Cathy into a convenient doorway while he kissed her tenderly. 'Oh, Cath,' he murmured, resting his cheek on her hair. 'If I lost you, my life wouldn't be worth living.'

They stood for a while, locked in each other's arms, then Cathy said quietly, 'No danger of that, Greg. You worry too much.'

'I suppose I do,' he agreed ruefully. 'But, Cathy, if you knew how much you mean to me! It's been like a new life for me since I met you.'

A few people had glanced curiously at them so they stepped out of the doorway and began to stroll along.

'I walked round for a while on Sunday night,' he said, 'and tried to plan ahead.'

'For the shop?'

'That as well,' he said, 'but I was trying to plan our future. At least what I hoped would happen if you still – still – if you hadn't changed your mind.'

'What were the plans?' Cathy said, determined not to talk about Sunday.

'I wondered if your father would agree to us getting engaged on your sixteenth birthday,' Greg said.

She shook her head. 'He wouldn't, Greg. Not officially engaged. And what about your mother?'

'Don't worry about her,' he said, slipping an arm around her and kissing her again. 'The plans I'm making for the shop are really plans for us. It makes enough to keep Mother and me, but I want to expand so that when we marry I can provide her with a house and companion, and we can have our own home.'

'I hadn't thought of all that,' Cathy confessed. 'I'd just thought about getting married.'

He kissed her again. 'If I work hard now, Cath,' he said, 'I'll feel as though I'm bringing all that so much nearer. You're sure your father won't agree to the engagement?'

'Quite sure,' she said, 'but it doesn't matter, does it? As long as we know our plans.'

They strolled on, talking them over, then Cathy told Greg about the letter she had received from Norah's brothers.

'I saw Jack Carmody passing the shop last night,' Greg said. 'He looked absolutely haggard.'

'Isn't it all ridiculous, Greg? Why can't people be sensible?'

'I suppose they will one day,' Greg said, 'but in the meantime this religious business is ruining many lives. Jack used to be such a light-hearted chap, too. It's a shame.'

'Norah looks ill,' Cathy said. 'Mind you, I'm not surprised. Cooped up indoors in this lovely weather. Her father's a horrible man.'

'It's not just him, though,' Greg said. 'Jack's getting no peace from his family. He was telling me about it at the Red Cross. I think they'll have to give in and stop seeing each other, Cath.'

'They can't see each other now, not openly, but I think it'll all be too much for them,' she said with a sigh.

Without realising it they had turned down towards the river and before long were standing near the spot where Greg had stood in such despair on Sunday night.

He said nothing of that to Cathy, only marvelled at his good fortune at being so swiftly forgiven by her, or at least being treated as though there was nothing to forgive.

She's a girl in a thousand, he told himself, vowing that he would never again do anything that would hurt her, or cause a rift between them.

Chapter Twenty-One

Greg was determined to make his mother accept Cathy as his future wife, and the following evening he forced the issue. He sat down facing her.

'Mother, you remember Cathy Ward who was injured on Bloody Sunday? You know that we've been going out together since then, don't you?'

'I know nothing of the sort!' she exclaimed. 'What time is it, Gregory?'

'Never mind the time,' he said. 'Mother, I want you to invite Cathy here. I'm sure that when you know her better you'll love her.'

Mrs Redmond closed her eyes and moaned faintly. 'Not now, dear,' she said. 'Don't bother me. I don't feel well.'

'You always say you feel ill when I try to talk about Cathy, but you *must* meet her. Eventually I hope she'll be my wife.'

Mrs Redmond burst into tears. 'How can you be so cruel to me? It's that girl – she's turned you against me. You never used to speak to me like that, Gregory.'

'Mother, don't get upset. I only want you to *meet* Cathy. You'll love her, I promise you, and you've often said you wished you had a daughter.'

His mother covered her ears. 'Don't talk about her,' she sobbed. 'What would your father say? His last words were to tell you to look after me.'

She began to sob even more loudly and to utter small screams and cries of distress. Greg tried to take her hand. 'Mother, Mother,' he said. 'Don't get so upset.'

She pulled her hand away and began to rock back and forth, still screaming and sobbing, and he became more and more alarmed as her hysterics increased and her face became purple. Nothing he could do or say seemed to have any effect, and at last in panic he ran down to the street door to seek help.

They had few neighbours as many of the flats above the shops were used for business, but a widow and her two middle-aged daughters lived opposite above their millinery shop.

The daughters were just entering their front door, and Greg ran across and asked for help. They called upstairs, 'The lady over the road is taken ill, Ma. Stay there, we're going over.'

They went over with Greg, and fluttered about Mrs Redmond, trying to soothe her, but still she screamed and cried, even louder now that she had a larger audience. The next moment the milliner waddled in.

She went up to Mrs Redmond, and without saying a word gave her a sharp slap on each cheek. The screams stopped abruptly and Mrs Redmond sat open-mouthed, staring at her.

'The best cure for yisterics, dear,' the milliner said in a satisfied tone. 'You'll be better now. Girls, make her a cup of tea.'

Greg watched in fascination as his mother was handed a face cloth and towel and told to wipe her face. She obeyed meekly, and then she was handed a cup of tea by one of the 'girls' and ordered to drink it by their ma.

'Often has the yisterics, does she?' Ma asked him.

'Er, my mother's, er, nervous,' he said.

'Well, if it happens again you know what to do. See how it worked. Same as with my niece Dolly. What was she like, girls?' Ma appealed to them, and they said in chorus, 'Dreadful, dreadful. Bundle of nerves.'

'Yes, came to stay with us, Dolly did. Used to cry and scream just like that, and lie on the floor drumming her heels too, but I cured her, didn't I, girls?' They nodded in unison. 'Yes, Ma cured her,' they said.

'Couple of smacks, a jug of water over her one day when she was really bad, and she was as right as rain. Started again when she went home but I'd told my sister what to do, and Dolly was all right after that. Never fails. Your ma'll be all right now. Come on, girls.' She waddled out, followed by the 'girls' and by Greg, who thanked her warmly.

When he returned his mother was still sitting with a stunned expression on her face. 'Gregory, those dreadful people. Where did they come from?'

'The shop over the road, Mother,' he said, deliberately misunderstanding her.

'I mean how did they come into my drawing room? Surely you didn't invite them, Gregory.'

'They were very kind and helpful,' he said firmly. 'I could do nothing to calm you. I didn't know the treatment for hysterics then.'

She darted a glance at him, and he looked back at her blandly. 'I won't talk about the invitation for Cathy now as you've upset yourself so much,' he said. 'We'll talk about it tomorrow.'

'*You've* upset me, you mean,' she said, but there was a new meekness in her tone.

I should have done this long ago, thought Greg. Better for both of us if I had, but everything will be on a better footing now. He was so sure that he had solved his problems outright, it was fortunate for him that he was unable to foresee how long his troubles with his mother would last.

For the moment all was well, and the next night he was able to persuade her to write inviting Cathy to tea on the following Sunday.

He had not seen Cathy to tell her of the scene with his mother as she had been busy helping Sally with her sewing orders. She had had such a rush of mourning orders from the families of men lost on the *Titanic* in late April that all her other work had fallen behind. She was anxious to complete her orders to leave her free to visit Emily before she went to see Bronwen.

On a previous occasion she had been to see her sister at The Grange soon after a meeting with Bronwen, and had found it hard to dismiss from her mind the memory of what had happened in that house. Emily, whose senses had become more acute since her illness, had noticed something in Sally's manner and asked what was wrong. She wanted to be sure that she avoided that danger this time.

She went to see Emily the next day, and felt a stab of fear when she looked at her sister's hands, which looked almost transparent.

Emily smiled at her cheerfully. 'Tell me all your news, Sal,' she said, and Sally told her about her sewing orders, and about Mary and Cathy.

'It seems such a long time since I've seen them,' Emily said wistfully.

'I don't like to send them at the weekend,' Sally said. 'I think Albert wants you to himself after working all week.'

'He would love to see them too,' Emily said. 'Poor Albert! He's so good to me, and he worries so much, Sal. Did you see the cane bathchair he bought me?'

Emily was lying on a sofa which had been wheeled on to the terrace outside the drawing room, and Sally looked over the balustrade of the terrace to where a cane wheelchair stood on the garden path.

'Albert wheels me round the garden every day when he gets home from business,' Emily said proudly. 'I'm so lucky, Sal. Nothing is too much trouble for him. He's always thinking of little treats for me.'

Sally was silent, thinking with amazement how different Emily's view of Albert was to the way she and Lawrie regarded him. Truly, no one knew the truth about anyone else, or all that went on in a marriage.

'Would you like me to wheel you now?' she asked Emily.

'No, thanks, Sal. I'd rather just sit and talk,' she said. 'The ladies from the church don't come so often, so we'll have some peace. Does Mary ever go to the church now?'

'No,' Sally said. 'But you know Mary. Now she's full of some new girl at work. This one's in a tennis club at West Derby so I suppose that'll be the next thing.'

Emily smiled. 'And Cathy courting,' she said. 'The years go too fast, don't they, Sal?'

'They do,' she said with a sigh.

'But you like the young man, don't you? Perhaps he could come with the girls to see me. I'd love to meet him,' Emily said.

Sally hesitated. 'I'm sure he'd love to meet you, too. Mary could come another Sunday, perhaps.'

She stared down at her hands, tightly clasped in her lap, then glanced up to find Emily looking at her with a puzzled expression on her face. Before she could stop herself, Sally began to pour out her troubles to her sister. 'Oh, Emily,' she said, 'I don't know what to think! Cathy and Greg seem so well suited and happy, but there's something – our Mary doesn't seem to accept it. I'm sure she's in love with Greg.'

She burst into tears and Emily held out her arms and drew Sally's head on to her shoulder. 'Don't cry, love,' she said gently. 'You might be mistaken. What makes you think that?'

'The way she behaves, making a dead set at him,' Sally wept. 'And it's causing trouble between them, her and Cathy. And Cathy and Greg too, I think.'

Emily held her close and kissed her cheek, and Sally clung to her for a moment, then sat up and wiped her eyes.

'I'm sorry, love,' she said, her voice thick with tears. 'I shouldn't be upsetting you. I don't know what made me—'

'Sally, don't shut me out,' Emily begged. 'Who can you talk to if not to me? You know I love the girls as if they were my own.'

'I know,' Sally said. 'I didn't tell you, but at first Mary thought it was her that Greg was interested in. So did Lawrie and I for that matter, but we soon realised it was Cathy.'

'But surely that was all sorted out,' Emily said. 'You told me about Lawrie wanting Cathy just to be friends with Greg and then changing his mind. I remember you told me about your neighbour calling him King Canute.'

Sally smiled as Emily had hoped she would, then she said seriously, 'That had nothing to do with Mary at least.' She stopped and looked thoughtfully at Emily. 'Do you know, Em, I'm just wondering if deep down Lawrie was thinking that Greg might switch to Mary, and that's why he didn't want Greg and Cathy to get too serious. I'm sure Lawrie himself didn't realise it, but it might have been at the back of his mind.'

'But why should he think that?' Emily said. 'You told me that Lawrie was very happy about Cathy and Greg, and thought they would be happy together.'

'Yes, but it's not like him to be looking for difficulties in the future, is it? He's usually looking on the bright side and sure that everything's going to turn out right. There must have been some sort of doubt in his mind, even if he didn't know it himself.'

'But that was all a long time ago,' Emily said. 'Cathy and Greg have been courting for about nine months, haven't they? Mary must have realised her mistake by now.'

'Yes, but she hasn't given up hope. I'm sure. Last Sunday...' She stopped, and Emily urged her to go on.

'You're not upsetting me, honestly,' she said. 'I want to know all your worries, as well as all the good things you tell me.'

'I don't know what to tell you, because I'm not sure myself,' Sally said. 'I may be imagining the whole thing.'

'What does Lawrie think?' Emily asked.

'He thinks I've got a down on Mary, but it's not true, Emily. I hope I am wrong, but it seemed to me Mary was making a dead set at Greg all day, and it's not the first time. It seems as though every time Cathy's out of the way, she's doing her best to flirt with him.'

'And what about Greg?' said Emily.

'I can't honestly blame the lad. He doesn't encourage her and I know he truly loves Cathy, but I don't know... It's hard to know what to do for the best.'

'Don't worry any more, Sal,' Emily comforted her. 'Who knows what's round the corner? Mary could meet her Prince Charming tomorrow, and you'd wonder why you worried.'

She began to cough and Sally looked alarmed. 'I've tired you, love, with all my rabbiting,' she said remorsefully, but Emily shook her head. The coughing bout was soon over and she insisted that she felt better than she had done for a while.

'You look better,' Sally said. It was true. Emily looked more animated than when her sister had arrived and there was more colour in her cheeks.

'It's because we're talking about something else besides illness,' she said. 'I get so sick of the subject. Now I've got something different to think about. But don't worry, things will work out with the girls.'

Sally rose. 'I'll go now though, love,' she said, 'so you can rest before Albert comes home. I'll come again in a couple of days and make arrangements for the girls to call.' She kissed her sister. 'I feel better myself since our talk. Thanks, Emily.'

She walked home, thinking over the conversation and making up her mind to take Emily's advice and stop worrying.

She hoped that she had not upset Emily by her tears, and that it was true that she felt better. Whatever came over me, Sally thought, to cry like that? She remembered Peggy Burns talking about a neighbour who was forever crying. 'Her bladder must be near her eye,' Peggy had said, and Sally smiled now at the memory. Peggy's a case, she thought, but she'd have to say the same about me, if she'd seen me in Emily's.

She watched Cathy and Mary closely for a few days, but she was reassured by what she saw. It was impossible for them to avoid each other altogether, and although Cathy still felt bitter towards Mary she was too proud to show how badly she'd been hurt, so on the surface they seemed friendly.

Cathy felt that the fateful Sunday had marked a turning point in many ways. She felt that she had changed. She was no longer a carefree girl floating along in a cloud of bliss, unaware of much that was happening round her, with only vague, happy dreams of the future.

She wondered why. There was little that she could pinpoint about that day to have caused such a change, only undercurrents, yet all their relationships had been subtly altered.

Greg was different too. More forceful and decisive, full of plans for the future, definite plans. There was a difference in the way that he held and kissed her too, Cathy thought, but preferred not to think too deeply about that. His manner towards Mary was pleasant but formal, and sometimes Cathy felt that it could never have been any different.

Mrs Redmond had written to Cathy to invite her to tea. She was very nervous about meeting Greg's mother again, but Mrs Redmond was on her best behaviour. She welcomed Cathy, and offered a cheek to kiss.

'It's a treat for me to have a visitor,' she told Cathy plaintively. 'Shut away up here, I see so few people. Very different to when I had my home at Neston.'

'But it's very nice here,' Cathy said shyly. 'Such big rooms.'

'But above the business, and on the road! No garden, not even a front door. I often wonder what my poor father would think about it. He was a solicitor, you know, dear. If he'd lived he'd never have allowed me to marry into trade, let alone live above the business.'

'Perhaps we'll be able to find you a house soon, Mother, when business improves,' Greg said cheerfully. Cathy was relieved to see that his mother's comment, implying that she had married beneath her, had not hurt him.

Mrs Redmond told Cathy at length about her many health problems while Greg served the tea which the daily woman had left ready and Cathy listened sympathetically.

She knew that Mrs Redmond imagined many of her symptoms but she had read that it was said of Dr Johnson's friend, Mr Thrale, 'He believes himself to be ill, and that belief is in itself an illness'. Cathy felt that these words applied to Mrs Redmond and she was ready to make allowances for her, because she wished so much to be friendly with Greg's mother. Her first visit was brief, but she and Greg both felt that it had been a success.

Chapter Twenty-Two

Mary secretly felt ashamed of her behaviour on that Sunday, especially when she remembered how her mother had looked at her with anger and contempt. A devil gets into me, she admitted to herself ruefully, and she tried to believe that she was glad that she had not caused serious trouble between Cathy and Greg.

It was hard for her not to feel bitter jealousy when she pictured Greg holding Cathy in his arms, but she made a determined effort to crush down her longing for him.

She found it easier because of her growing friendship with Elizabeth Fairburn, and the wider social scene she was now becoming a part of.

They seemed unlikely friends. Elizabeth, dark and stocky, with strong features, hated her middle-class background and the restrictions it imposed on her, and had strong views on men's dominance over women. Ironically, Mary longed for just the sort of life that Elizabeth was struggling to escape from.

Mary was astounded to learn that Elizabeth had needed to fight hard to be allowed to work in Denby's, and that it was only a compromise instead of the enrolment in the Liverpool College of Art that she had really longed for.

Mary would have thought herself in Heaven to have a home like Elizabeth's, full of heavy mahogany furniture, rich velvet curtains and Turkey carpets, and crowded with a profusion of small tables bearing shell boxes and silver-framed photographs. To have a cook and three other servants and, most of all, to stay at home and fill her days with visiting, shopping, tennis and Bridge... yet Elizabeth hated it and fought to be free!

The two girls held different views on almost every subject, but Mary was too pleased to have become Elizabeth's friend ever openly to disagree with her.

Her appeal to Elizabeth lay in her flawless beauty. Elizabeth loved to design clothes for Mary and choose suitable materials for them. The clothes were plain and the colours more subdued than Mary would have chosen, but when they were made up everyone agreed that they were perfect for her.

Elizabeth had introduced Mary to many of her friends, and together they attended social occasions in the evenings and went to the Tennis Club on light summer evenings.

'I don't mind going to these things at night,' Elizabeth confided. 'As long as I can live my own life during the day.'

Mary felt that working in Denby's could hardly be described as freedom but she said nothing. She had learned her lesson from the business with Isobel Willard and was quiet and subdued in her behaviour towards the young men, using her charm only on the other girls or the older ladies who helped with tea making or scoring, though she hoped to attract one of the young men, at some time.

One of the unattached young men of the group or perhaps the brother of one of the girls she became friendly with, she thought. But although they were polite and friendly, none of them asked her out.

Most of them were the sons or the grandsons of men who had risen in the world, and they chose their brides very carefully. They would never risk their hard-won position by marriage to the daughter of a railwayman, no matter how charming.

Mary enjoyed her visits to the Tennis Club, although the invitations she hoped for did not materialise, and she was asked out by other young men in her own circle, so Sam was again relegated to her rare free evenings.

She was more circumspect in her choice of escorts since her fright at the New Year's party and with the packer from Denby's, but the nondescript young men she went out with only increased her hunger for Greg.

He came to tea on alternate Sundays now, and he and Cathy spent the other Sunday with his mother. Mary was careful not to show her feelings when he visited her home.

She was confident that she had succeeded in hiding them and on the surface she and Cathy were the best of friends. They sometimes went together on a Sunday morning to visit their Aunt Emily, and had a few mutual friends, but they never exchanged confidences now.

One of the mutual friends was Beattie, the mother of twins whom the girls had visited on the day of the strike meeting when they had met Greg. Cathy sometimes visited Beattie with Greg, and he was fascinated by the twin baby boys. Never having seen babies at close quarters before, he was astounded by everything they did, and Beattie and her husband were charmed with him.

Mary was also a frequent visitor to Beattie's house, and it was there that she met a young man, Edwin Stubbs, and began to go out with him. Beattie shared a house in Baker Street with an older couple, who were friendly with the Stubbs family who lived a few doors away.

Edwin was an only son, with five adoring sisters and a strong sense of his own importance and in the honour which he, a shipping clerk, bestowed on Mary by asking her out.

She had met his mother and two of his sisters when she was visiting Beattie and they had arrived to call on the couple who shared the house. She had been annoyed then by the way that they looked her over, and talked about Edwin.

'I think they expect me to fall down and worship him too,' Mary said when they had gone. 'It's not my way, Bea.'

Beattie laughed. 'No, you're more used to people doing that to you,' she said. She was a plump, pleasant girl, happily married and delighted with her babies, and fond of both Mary and Cathy. She shared a love of books with Cathy, but for Mary her feelings were more protective. She felt that stodgy Edwin was unworthy of a girl like her.

The affair lasted only a short time, as Mary was too independent by nature to tolerate his behaviour for long. He often arrived late to take her out, and always decided where they would go, then spent most of the time talking about himself.

One evening he arrived half an hour late, offering no apology, and when they left the house he raged because his trousers were splashed with mud by a passing cart.

'I suppose you think *I* should have walked on the outside of the pavement,' Mary said. 'It would be on a level with your standard of manners.'

'What do you mean?' he spluttered.

'You were half an hour late,' she said. 'Why?'

'I got held up,' he said sullenly.

'Indeed. And that's all the explanation you can give, and no apology.'

'For half an hour? Plenty of girls'd be glad to wait longer than that for me, and not shopgirls either.'

'Then you'd better go out with them,' she said, standing still. 'I don't put up with those sort of bad manners.'

'It's a pity about you,' he said angrily. 'What do you know about manners, working in that shop.'

'Manners are learnt at home,' Mary flashed. 'That's where I learned mine, although the people at Denby's could teach *you* a few.'

Edwin's face was purple with rage. 'You, you—' he spluttered. 'Talking about *my* manners! My mother said you were a forward hussy, and my sister said you didn't show proper respect to them.'

'I can see why you're so uncouth,' Mary retorted. 'Brought up in a family who are vulgar enough to talk like that about other people's guests.'

She turned on her heel. 'I've wasted enough time with you,' she said cuttingly.

Edwin was nearly speechless with indignation but managed to gasp, 'You've got a cheek! A shopgirl, and me a shipping clerk. Wait till I tell them.'

Mary looked him over contemptuously, then laughed her clear bell-like laugh and walked away.

So that's that, she thought. She felt exhilarated by the quarrel and her rout of Edwin, and too full of energy to go tamely home. Janey was out, she knew, so she decided to go to see Beattie. Too bad if she came across any of Edwin's family. She could easily deal with them, she thought.

Beattie was alone, knitting placidly while her babies slept and her husband visited his mother. She welcomed Mary, waving her pink knitting. 'I'm expecting again,' she said cheerfully. 'I'm going to make a pink jacket and bonnet and hope for a girl, this time.'

'I wish you luck,' Mary said. She told her about her quarrel with Edwin, and Beattie chuckled when she heard of Mary's comments on his mother and sisters. 'You're well out of it, Mary,' she said. 'He was unworthy of you, and if you'd married him, you'd have had the whole family like a millstone round your neck. Is it back to Sam now?'

'For the time being, while I look around,' Mary said airily.

After a while Beattie put down her knitting and made supper, then the two girls sat talking in low voices. The fire had burned low, and the only sound in the quiet house was of ash dropping into the ashpan, and the ticking of the clock.

Beattie became confidential, talking about her husband Bill, and their hopes and fears for the future. 'I've been lucky, meeting Billy, because we're just right for each other. I wish you could meet someone, Mary. What sort of man would you really like?'

She sat looking in the fire, and playing with her bracelets as she dreamily described her ideal man.

'That sounds just like Greg Redmond,' Beattie said shrewdly. 'I suppose he would have been just right for you.'

'He would,' Mary admitted with a sigh. 'It's a funny thing, Bea. All the men I've been out with, yet the one I could really fall in love with has to choose Cathy.'

The dim room in the quiet house encouraged confidences, and Mary found herself telling Beattie what had happened on the Sunday of Greg's visit, even to the way that she had felt when she pressed close to him, and the fact that she was sure of Greg's response to her.

Beattie listened silently, except for a few sympathetic murmurs, and at the end she heaved a sigh, 'What a shame,' she said quietly. '"If only". The saddest words anyone can say.'

Mary sighed too. 'It's no use, Bea, I know that. I thought at first he'd made a mistake and would soon realise it, but he seems besotted with Cathy. They've gone about together so long now and even that Sunday didn't seem to make any difference with them. That was his chance to break with her if he wanted to, but she even visits his mother now.'

'But are you sure he'd have turned to you even if he broke off with Cathy?' Beattie asked gently.

'Maybe not,' Mary said with a shrug, 'and yet, he did feel something for me, I could tell. If the chance had been there he'd have taken me – and I'd have let him,' she added defiantly.

'And you'd both have hated yourselves afterwards,' Beattie said. 'You know that's true, Mary. Cathy appeals to the romantic and chivalrous part of him, but you appeal only to his baser instincts.'

Mary made a gesture of protest but said nothing, and Beattie went on, 'I'm not saying this to hurt you, Mary, but only because I'm your friend and I think it's better for you to face facts.' A tear splashed on Mary's hand and she took out her handkerchief and wiped her eyes.

'I know what I'm talking about,' Beattie said. 'I'll tell you something, Mary, something I've never told anyone else, only Billy. I'm older than you, you know – I'm twenty-eight. Did you never wonder where I worked before Denby's?'

'I didn't think about it,' Mary said.

'I was a teacher in a small church school in a village in Derbyshire,' Beattie said. 'After my mother died I lived alone in the schoolhouse, and being as it was a church school some of the children were in the choir, so I often saw the choirmaster. Always with the children there, or the vicar, or in church though.'

She sat looking in the fire and Mary prompted her. 'Go on. What was he like?'

'He was eight years older than me and married, happily married. One night he came to my house with some music. Mary, I don't know what happened but suddenly we were in each other's arms. We were like lunatics, like animals. We came together there on the floor with the door unfastened, the curtains not drawn. It was madness. Anyone could have looked in or walked in on us.'

'But they didn't,' said Mary.

'No, they didn't. But when it was over, he cried. Said he'd never forgive himself. He loved and respected Celia, his wife.'

'And do you think that was true?' Mary said. 'How could he if he did that with you?'

'I know it was true. I'd seen them together. We swore it wouldn't happen again, but it did. The second time we met by chance in a wood and came together and after that it was like a hunger in the blood, and we had to see each other.'

'But in a village. Didn't anyone know?' Mary asked.

'Not for a long time. Outwardly we were just the same, the prim schoolmistress and the respectable choirmaster,' Beattie said bitterly. 'But we'd look at each other, perhaps in church, and know that we had to get together. Then it would happen – a travesty of love. Frantic, screaming, clawing at each other. I look back now and I can't believe it.'

Mary sat in stunned silence, then her friend went on: 'If only I had left then! I should have done. I was free to. He had his job, his position in the church, his wife and family. All his roots were there but I was born in Lancaster, I could easily have gone.'

'But you did. You must have done,' Mary said.

'Yes, but too late. The whispers started. It came out Celia had known from the beginning but had said nothing, hoping he'd come to his senses. I was asked to leave. No reference, of course. I loved teaching but it was closed to me. I came here and got that job in Denby's stock-room.'

'But the man?' Mary said hesitantly.

'Oh, he stayed. I was blamed. Men! They've been the same ever since Adam,' Beattie said bitterly. '"The woman tempted me." Shifting the blame.'

'But I meant, didn't you miss him, miss the lovemaking?'

'No. That was the awful thing. When I got away from him, I realised that I didn't even like him. I despised him, yet if I'd stayed I couldn't have resisted going with him.'

Mary looked at Beattie, at her soft blurred features and plump figure.

'I can't believe it,' she exclaimed. 'You seem the most unlikely person. So placid always.'

Beattie shrugged. 'I know, but don't ever think it can't happen – it can. I was lucky, I met Billy, and by a bigger stroke of luck he understood and forgave me. He told me he'd met a tramp once who'd been an MP, wealthy, happily married and everything, and thrown it all up for some woman, only to finish up as a tramp.'

'Well, I've never heard of anything like that before!'

'No, but you've touched on the fringes of it with Greg,' Beattie said. 'Keep away from him, Mary.'

'Oh, it wasn't anything like *that*,' she said rather huffily. 'I just thought he was suitable.' She glanced at the clock. 'Is that the time? I'd better go.'

'You won't ever repeat what I've told you, will you?' Beattie said earnestly. 'I just didn't want someone else to make the same mistake, especially a friend.'

'No, indeed,' Mary said. She smiled. 'No one would believe it of you anyway.'

She left and walked home, thinking of Beattie's tale and deciding that she didn't believe it either. It's from one of these books she reads, Mary thought, Marie Corelli or someone like that. Cathy reads them and probably tells yarns to people too.

She remembered Beattie's words, that she appealed to Greg's baser instincts, and felt annoyed. I wish I hadn't told her so much, she thought. I think I'll stop going there. I don't want that conceited Edwin to think I'm hoping to meet him again, anyway.

After the brief affair with Edwin was over, Mary spent most of her free time with Elizabeth Fairburn, and Sam was re-instated for an occasional evening.

Her moods and tantrums had ended it seemed, and her mother saw with relief that even at home now, her behaviour was composed and quiet.

Sally had spent a wakeful night after her visit to Emily. Although Emily had assured her that she had not been upset or worried when Sally confided her fears for her daughters, and had in fact seemed better when she left her, at two o'clock in the morning she was convinced that she had harmed her sister.

She's not well enough to bear my worries, Sally thought, and to have me crying over her. I should be trying to cheer her not worrying her.

Sally knew by experience that if she woke during the night, worries which had seemed trivial during the day assumed frightening dimensions, but she was unable to dismiss her fears and fall asleep.

The following morning her worries seemed more manageable but she thought constantly of Emily, and decided that she would call to see her again, instead of going to see Bronwen.

Emily was surprised and delighted to see her and they spent a pleasant afternoon together. Sally was careful to talk only of pleasant matters and to make it clear to Emily that her worries about Cathy and Greg and Mary had no foundation.

She told Emily that Cathy had been invited to visit Greg's mother, and promised to let her know the outcome of the visit.

'I'm not very keen on what I've heard about her,' Sally said frankly. 'Cathy hasn't said anything, but her friend Norah said one time that Mrs Redmond was always fancying that she was ill, especially if Greg wanted to go out.'

'One of those, is she?' Emily said. 'Cathy'll have to be firm from the start. How is the affair going with Norah and that Catholic lad?'

'Trouble all the way,' Sally said. 'The families are only driving Norah and Jack together, if they could but see it.'

Albert arrived home early as Sally was about to leave. She became hot and flustered at the thought of his guilty secret but he greeted her civilly, without any sign of discomposure, and Sally wondered if he knew of the birth of his son.

On Monday morning she rose early to get ahead with her washing so that she could visit the Home later, but Myfanwy arrived before she finished.

'I was going to the Home,' Sally said, but Myfanwy said briefly, 'No need, Mrs Ward. Baby's been adopted.'

'It's for the best,' Sally said, 'although it's hard on Bronwen.'

'Bronwen!' Myfanwy burst out angrily. 'Made a proper fool of us, hasn't she?' She said something in Welsh then added, 'Angry I am, Mrs Ward. Poor Ruth being blamed. Matron thinking she's in on it, and Ruth knowing nothing.'

She poured out the tale while Sally listened in amazement. Bronwen had annoyed the staff of the Home and been told to leave. She had arrived at Ruth's room with the baby. Ruth had taken her in and spent a nightmare few days trying to conceal them from the landlord.

She had been puzzled by Bronwen's insistence on keeping the baby as she seemed unwilling or unable to care for him, but one day a heavily veiled lady had arrived at the room.

'The one who wanted to adopt him,' Myfanwy said. 'Let her see him, take a fancy to him in the Home, Bronwen did, then put on the act. So, the lady comes, Bronwen cries, says she's heartbroken but she can't keep him, and the lady takes the child.'

'But why? I don't understand,' Sally said.

'Feels guilty taking the baby, doesn't she? Gives Bronwen money to go away, make a fresh start, baby will have every care – de dah, de dah.'

Sally had been making tea and she stood with the teapot in her hand, staring open-mouthed at Myfanwy. 'Who'd have thought it?' she said finally. 'She seemed such an innocent little girl. Still, in the end it all worked out, and at least the poor baby has a good home.'

'Oh, yes, and the lady has her child, and Bronwen has her money,' Myfanwy said bitterly. 'And poor Ruth, she has the bad name, and me too for being mixed up in it.'

A sudden thought struck Sally. 'Do you think she told the truth? About Albert, I mean?'

Myfanwy nodded. 'Yes, that was true. Remember he tried it with me, but he soon stopped when I fought back and screamed. Encouraged him maybe, she did, but it happened.'

'At least she was good enough to come to me instead of upsetting Mrs Deakin,' Sally said.

'More to that too, it's come out now,' Myfanwy said with a shrug. 'My idea, and she agreed, but it turns out she'd been stealing from The Grange. Told to go for that really, and couldn't go back.'

'Stealing?' Sally said. 'Stealing what?'

'Small things, trinket boxes, ornaments, that sort of thing. Into the apron pocket, and sneaked out to sell. Said she was trying to get something together for when she left. So many lies, you see, Mrs Ward. One tale contradicts the other.'

'And Mr Deakin knew about it?' Sally said.

'Yes. Threatened her with the police if she made trouble, she said, but she's such a liar. Main thing is, she won't dare to go back so Mrs Deakin will never know anything.'

'Thank God for that anyway,' Sally said. 'What will she do now?'

'Go away somewhere. Better be a long way from me and Ruth, I told her. Don't worry about Bronwen, Mrs Ward. She'd live where others would starve.'

'And that poor baby!' Sally said. 'It looks as though he'll be better off away from her.'

'Yes, longing the lady was for a baby, and comfortably off. A good home, he'll have, plenty of loving, and never know what he came from.' Myfanwy stood up to go.

'Sorry I ever bothered you with it, Mrs Ward,' she said, but Sally smiled at her. 'Don't say that, love. You were thinking of my sister and I appreciate that. Come and see me any time, and bring Ruth. I'll always be glad to see you.'

When Myfanwy had gone, Sally went back and finished her washing, pondering on what the girl had told her. At least Emily was safe from ever hearing about the affair, she thought thankfully, and perhaps Albert had not been as wicked as she had thought.

But Bronwen to have turned out to be so devious! I never really took to her, Sally decided, even though I was sorry for her. Poor Ruth and Myfanwy suffering for Bronwen's cunning schemes, though. But at least they can feel that they did what they thought was right at the time, and will learn by this experience.

Sally had confided in Peggy Burns, without going into too much detail about the affair, and when her neighbour came in later for a cup of tea she told her of the outcome.

'Just as well that girl can look out for herself,' Peggy said. 'Although it's a pity about the others. You can stop worrying anyhow, if the girl goes away to make a new start. Emily will never hear anything.'

'I think of how my girls would be in that situation,' Sally said. 'They'd be absolutely lost. Not like Bronwen.'

'Yes, it would finish Cathy,' Peggy said. Sally noticed that she said nothing about Mary. She glanced at Peggy then decided against saying anything. Perhaps Peggy spoke only of Cathy because she was the same age as Bronwen, not because she thought Mary would be cunning enough to survive.

Chapter Twenty-Three

Cathy was very happy now, all the niggling doubts about Mary laid to rest and the love between herself and Greg growing ever stronger and deeper. The thought of him lent a glow of happiness to all she did.

He was working hard to improve the shop and expand the business, and he and Cathy were full of hopeful plans for the future.

When she was not with Greg, Cathy spent much of her time at the Victoria Women's Settlement in Everton. She greatly admired the Warden, a Scottish lady, Elizabeth McAdam, but her idol was Eleanor Rathbone who was on the committee of the Settlement.

Miss Rathbone was a member of a wealthy Liverpool family. Ever since childhood Cathy had heard her father speak approvingly of the Rathbones and their work for the poor and needy of the city. Eleanor's father, William, had organised the district nursing service to tend the sick poor in their own homes, and all the family had played their part in different schemes to help the poor.

Eleanor Rathbone was particularly interested in the plight of widows with young children, left destitute by the father's death. She was also an enthusiastic Suffragist, and Cathy never forgot a meeting at which Miss Rathbone declared that the reason that widows were so badly treated was because they were women and therefore without a vote which they could use to demand justice.

After that Cathy attended every meeting at which Miss Rathbone spoke, and worked even harder for Women's Suffrage.

She came away from these meetings full of enthusiasm, expecting her father and mother to agree with her when she repeated the arguments she had heard, but she got little sympathy from either of them.

'Surely you believe women should have the vote, Mam?' she said one night. 'They're just as intelligent as men.'

'Yes, but women haven't got time to read papers or go to meetings like men,' her mother said, 'so they don't know who to vote for.'

'Women should know what's happening in the world,' Cathy exclaimed, but her mother only laughed. 'Wait until you're married with a few children round you. You won't be gallivanting off to meetings, I can tell you.'

On other occasions, especially when there were reports of Suffragettes breaking windows or disrupting meetings, Sally was disapproving. 'It's unwomanly,' she said. 'I don't approve of them being badly treated in jail, but I don't think they should carry on like that.'

'But women have been trying to get the vote for forty years,' Cathy argued. 'The Pankhursts and women like them are getting some notice; anyway. And you've got to admire their courage, Mam.'

'Foolhardiness, I call it! I hope you're not thinking of getting up to any of these capers, Cathy.'

'Mam, I'm a *Suffragist*,' Cathy said. 'Even Rosie is still a Suffragist, working in peaceful ways. She says the Suffragettes want the vote for middle-class women but the Suffragists want it for *all* women.'

No matter how much Cathy argued she felt that her mother was not convinced, and believed that the talk of Votes for Women would be quickly forgotten by Cathy when she was married and had less time to 'gallivant'.

Even her father treated the matter lightly, although he agreed with Eleanor Rathbone's fight for help for widows. Cathy felt that secretly he was shocked by the women's militancy and agreed with her mother that it was unwomanly. She was hurt and dismayed to find that for once they disagreed about something that meant so much to her.

Only to Greg could she pour out her feelings, sure of his support and interest. She went to meetings with Rosie Jackson now because Norah was not allowed out by her father, except when accompanied by her sister-in-law.

Norah still managed stolen meetings with Jack, during working hours or when she managed to lose her jailor, but so many years must pass before they could defy their families and marry that the outlook for them seemed hopeless.

Cathy was a willing carrier of messages between Norah and Jack, and she did all she could to cheer her friend, but she could see little hope of happiness for them.

Sometimes after leaving her, Cathy felt almost guilty about her own happiness and had a superstitious fear that it was too good to last. Usually she spent at least two evenings each week with Greg, and they had every Sunday together.

Mrs Redmond was invited to spend the day with friends on alternate Sundays, and on those days Greg came to Cathy's home for his meals.

Afterwards they walked out, or took a trip on the ferry if the weather was fine, or sat in the parlour, their arms about each other as they talked, always in accord, or sat in silence, happy just to be together.

On the Sundays when Mrs Redmond was at home, Cathy was invited to visit her. As the months passed, she realised this was where the obstacle to her happiness would lie.

Although Greg's mother greeted her effusively, Cathy soon realised the falseness of her smiling greeting, and every visit became an ordeal. She had to be constantly on the alert in case her innocent remarks were twisted to imply something entirely different, and to brace herself for the venomous stabs of Mrs Redmond's retaliation.

They were usually delivered when Greg was not in the room, or in such a way that it was possible to believe that she was merely being tactless. Greg seemed to believe that his mother simply spoke without thinking.

At first Cathy tried to believe this also. Open and honest herself, she found it hard to believe that anyone would show such ill will to someone who had done nothing to provoke it and had come in friendliness.

'Mother's a bit tactless,' Greg said awkwardly after a few of these visits, 'but I know she likes you, Cath, and when she really knows you, she'll be as crazy about you as I am.'

She tried to reassure him. She could see that he was uneasy about his mother's behaviour, and was flattered by his belief that no one who really knew her could resist her.

Nevertheless, she always finished the visit seething with anger and felt a hypocrite when she kissed Mrs Redmond goodbye.

She said nothing at home about Mrs Redmond's behaviour, but confided in Norah. 'She says such nasty things, but when I try to remember them they seem different. It must be the way she says them.'

'What sort of things?' Norah asked.

'She asked me if Mam had been in service, then she began to talk about servants she'd had. She said in that tinkling voice, "Some of them try to ape their betters. They manage a kind of veneer but it soon cracks." Then she looked me up and down and said, "After all, I always say, you can't make a silk purse out of a sow's ear."'

'That was downright rude enough for anyone to realise,' Norah said indignantly. 'Greg must be blind and deaf if he didn't see she was being catty.'

'He'd gone out for the tea tray,' Cathy said, 'and she's so crafty. I'd just told her that Mam hadn't been in service so if I pulled her up she'd say, "What do you mean? You'd just told me your mother wasn't in service." She was trying to make out that we weren't good enough for them.'

'She's got a cheek!' Norah exclaimed. 'Has she met your mam?'

'No, but I tell you what, Norah. Her father was a solicitor and Grandad was a shipwright, but Mam's more of a lady than she'll ever be. She wouldn't invite people to her house and then insult them.'

'I don't know why you go.'

'I don't want to hurt Greg or make things awkward for him by refusing, and if I did I'd have to tell him why.'

'I think he should know,' Norah said, but Cathy shook her head.

'No, I don't want to make trouble between Greg and his mother. This can't last forever. She'll get fed up when she realises she's getting nowhere with her catty remarks.'

As time passed there seemed little sign of alteration in Mrs Redmond's behaviour. Outwardly she was still as gushing and falsely sweet towards Cathy, yet she managed to plant her venomous barbs at every visit.

Over and over again Cathy vowed that she would never visit again, but she realised that Greg was torn between his duty to his mother and his urge to defend Cathy, and she was unwilling to force an open rift.

For a while he went on hoping that his mother was simply tactless, and even when he was forced to realise her malice towards Cathy, was uncertain how to deal with it.

The easy way out would have been to stop the visits, but always in his mind was the memory of his father's dying request that he should look after his mother. He felt that the only solution was to try to change his mother's attitude to Cathy.

She gave him the opportunity one day when she criticised Cathy's involvement with the Suffragists.

'Cathy is doing what she believes to be right, and I agree with her,' he said firmly. 'Look, Mother, you must understand that I won't listen to any criticism of her. I'm hoping that she'll soon be my wife.'

His mother ignored his last comment. 'So I'm not allowed to speak!' she exclaimed.

'Not in that way about Cathy, and you must stop making nasty remarks when she visits you, too.'

'Nasty remarks,' she cried. 'I make that girl very welcome and if she's told you anything different she's telling lies.'

'Mother, I've *heard* you,' Greg said. 'Anyone but Cathy would have quarrelled with you long ago. It's got to stop.'

Mrs Redmond began to weep. 'I knew it,' she wailed. 'I knew that girl would turn you against your mother. You worry about her, but what about your duty to me?'

Greg tried to harden his heart, but the sight of his mother's tears unnerved him. He felt that her resentment of Cathy was caused by fear of a lonely future and he tried to reassure her. He sat down beside her and put his arm around her. 'Don't cry, Mother,' he said gently. 'Cathy wouldn't try to turn me against you. She's very sympathetic because she knows how hard it is for you to be without a husband. There's no reason why we can't all be happy together.'

'Oh, Gregory, you foolish boy,' she wept, but for some time refrained from criticising Cathy to Greg and made no malicious remarks during Cathy's next few visits to her.

Gradually however her animosity towards Cathy, which had been unchanged but hidden, began to show itself again. Armoured by Greg's love and the knowledge that they had discussed the problem of his mother, Cathy was usually able to ignore her barbs but sometimes it was impossible not to be hurt by them.

The weather during the summer of 1913 had been unpredictable with cold wet days followed by spells of humidity and thunderstorms. One sultry Sunday in July, Cathy walked unwillingly towards the Redmonds' flat. The streets were dusty and the air oppressive with the threat of thunder. Cathy felt in no mood for Mrs Redmond's antics.

The old girl had better not start anything today, she thought, or I'll have something to say! I just won't put up with it.

Mrs Redmond was so mild in her conversation at first that Cathy thought she had sensed it would be unwise to be provocative, but before long the innuendoes began.

Greg was in a buoyant mood. He had been working on the shop books and been amazed and delighted to see the improvement in the profits. 'If this goes on, we should be able to expand,' he told them jubilantly. 'Perhaps take over next door if they decide to move to Church Street. Those brooches you suggested have been selling like hot cakes, Cath.' He put his arm round her and hugged her.

Seeing it, Mrs Redmond lost her temper. 'I never interfered in business,' she said. 'My husband always told me not to bother my pretty little head about it.'

Cathy was prepared to let that pass but Greg said swiftly, 'It might have saved him a lot of worry if you *had* concerned yourself more, Mother. I'm glad of Cathy's support.'

'I hope this means we can leave this dreadful place, Gregory, and take a house over the water,' his mother said. She looked disparagingly at Cathy. 'If we can return to our rightful place and our old friends perhaps you can meet a suitable girl for your wife, dear.'

Cathy and Greg both jumped to their feet, and Cathy said furiously, 'Someone like you, I suppose, to kill him with worry?'

At the same time Greg was saying angrily, 'You've gone too far this time.'

Mrs Redmond seemed unperturbed. She gave her tinkling laugh. 'Don't be silly,' she said chidingly to Greg. 'You must have known that this was just an interlude.'

'*What* was just an interlude, as you call it?' he said wrathfully.

She patted her hair and smiled. 'Living here, dear, and going about with this little girl. *I* knew we'd go back to our rightful place, sooner or later.'

Cathy had snatched up her jacket and moved to the door. Greg barely paused to snap at his mother, 'I'll speak to you later,' before taking Cathy's arm and going out with her.

They hurried down the stairs and walked rapidly along the road, both too tense and angry to speak. Cathy was near to tears. When they reached Islington Greg drew her into a convenient shop doorway and put his arms around her.

'Cath,' he said, holding her close to stop her trembling, 'I can't tell you how angry I am, and how ashamed. Don't be upset, love.'

'But why, Greg? Why does she hate me? I wanted to be friendly with her.'

'She doesn't hate you, Cath. She'd be the same with any girl.'

'Even one from her own class,' Cathy said bitterly, then tightened her arms about Greg's neck and kissed him. 'I'm sorry, love, I shouldn't have said that. You can't help this.'

They clung to each other in silence then Greg said softly, 'Are you all right, Cath?'

She nodded. 'Yes. Are you?'

'Yes, but I think I've got to do something about this,' he said. They were both calmer but his jaw was set. 'We've tried to humour her but that's finished. I've made excuses for her – to myself, I mean, but not any more.'

A plane tree grew outside a house near the corner of Soho Street. When they started to walk along, Greg stopped there and took Cathy's hand.

'Cath, it's two years next month since we met,' he said gently. 'Do you think – will you become engaged then?'

She looked up into his face, at his steady grey eyes and his firm cleft chin, and a rush of love for him made her voice tremble as she whispered, 'Yes, please.'

She buried her face in his shoulder, suddenly shy, and he held her tightly in his arms. 'Oh, Cath, I do love you,' he said, and she raised her head and kissed him.

'And I love you,' she said. 'Just think, two years ago we didn't even know each other.'

'We'd have met sooner or later,' he said confidently. 'We were meant for each other. I'll have to ask your father's permission, though. Will he be in now?'

'I think so,' Cathy said, and they strolled along, anger forgotten, as they made plans for their future.

'I've got to make a success of the business,' Greg said. 'I'll have to find a house and a companion for my mother. I still have a duty to look after her – that's all it is now, Cath, a duty – but I'm going to make sure that she's settled well away from us when we're married.'

'I couldn't live under the same roof as her,' Cathy said. 'I'd be taking a hatchet to her before long.'

'Don't worry,' he said grimly. 'I'm going to tell her my plans and make sure that I earn enough to carry them out.'

Lawrie was at home when they arrived and Greg said immediately, 'Will you allow us to get engaged next month, Mr Ward? It'll be two years then since we met.' Lawrie looked taken aback. 'Two years eh?' he said. 'That's gone quick.' He rose to his feet and held out his hand to Greg, smiling at Cathy. 'Welcome to the family, lad. Happy to have you aboard.'

Sally came down the lobby and Cathy flung herself at her mother. 'Mam, we're getting engaged next month,' she cried.

There were smiles and kisses all round and Lawrie brought out a bottle of rum. 'Pity our Mary's not in,' he said, 'but we can't wait for her.'

He added hot water and sugar to the rum for Cathy and Sally, and all drank a toast to the future. 'I feel dizzy,' Cathy said later when they were sitting in the parlour. 'It must be because I was so angry before and now I'm so happy.'

'It's the rum,' Greg teased her, but he confessed that he felt the same.

'You've still got to face your mother,' Cathy reminded him. 'She's going to be very angry.'

'She can be,' he said tersely. 'I know all her tricks and I'm ready for any of them.' He frowned. 'I must seem very disloyal, talking about her like this, but that business today was the last straw. She's never going to turn her spite on you again, Cath, I'll make sure of that.'

In the kitchen Lawrie and Sally were discussing the same subject in low voices. 'I think there's white water ahead with his mother,' Lawrie said, and Sally agreed.

'Did you notice he didn't answer me really when I asked him what she would think?' Sally said. 'Only said that she would be lucky getting a daughter-in-law like Cathy.'

'Yes. I wonder if something happened there today? They were back very early,' Lawrie said.

'That's the only thing that worries me,' Sally said, 'but I think Cathy will be able to cope with her and Greg will watch out for Cathy.'

Mary accepted the news of the engagement with equanimity and smiled as she congratulated them, but the sight of the half hoop of diamonds on Cathy's finger cost her a pang, especially as her hopes of meeting an eligible young man at the Tennis Club had come to nothing.

On September 14th 1913 Mary was twenty-one years old. She was at the peak of her beauty, and although many of her former escorts were now married or engaged, there were always fresh admirers to pay court to her. Mary, however, was determined not to commit herself to anyone who failed to reach her picture of the ideal man. Occasionally, especially since Cathy's engagement, she felt alarmed at the swift passage of time, but was sure that somewhere there was a man who could fulfil all her dreams. She intended to be ready when he appeared.

On a Sunday in late October, Mary had arranged to visit the Museum with Elizabeth Fairburn. It had been a foggy morning but the fog had dispersed and the sun had come out when the girls walked into town.

Near the steps of the Museum Mary saw her father talking to two men, one of whom she had met. He was a partner in a law firm and like her father belonged to a group which distributed soup to destitute people sleeping under the Overhead Railway at night.

Lawrie proudly hailed Mary and Elizabeth and the lawyer introduced the man with him as a Canadian to whom he was showing the sights of Liverpool. Clive Walden, the Canadian, had arrived in England only a few days earlier, he told them. He had been born here and taken to Canada as a baby, and this was the first time he had returned.

The Canadian was a tall man with high cheekbones and blue eyes. He had tightly curling fair hair and a heavy moustache over his full red lips. Something in his glance encouraged Mary to give him the bold challenging look which she had not used for some time.

In later years it was Lawrie's greatest grief that it was through him that his beloved daughter met Clive Walden, but on this day he was pleased and proud to see the Canadian's open admiration of Mary.

The girls had said that they were about to visit the Museum and Lawrie was on his way home from a meeting, but after a few minutes' conversation when they were about to part the Canadian said breezily, 'I haven't seen your Museum.' He turned to Lawrie. 'With your permission, sir, I'd like to ask the young ladies to show me round. I'd be proud to escort them.'

Lawrie nodded, too taken aback to speak, and the girls blushed and smiled. The next moment Clive had shaken hands with Lawrie then the solicitor, thanking him for showing him around, and was walking up the steps of the Museum between Mary and Elizabeth.

Lawrie and John Bagshaw, the solicitor, were left staring at each other in amazement.

'Er – rather different, Canadians I find,' John Bagshaw said. 'Very – er – forth-right. Very decisive.'

'He certainly didn't let the grass grow under his feet,' Lawrie said with a grin.

The solicitor smiled. 'Every excuse, of course. Your daughter is a very beautiful young lady, Mr Ward. I imagine this is not the first time this has happened – that someone has been bowled over, I mean – but Walden's approach – er – very unconventional.'

'Do you know him well, Mr Bagshaw?' Lawrie asked.

The other man shook his head. 'Only professionally,' he said cautiously. 'I knew his uncle, now deceased, quite well.'

They parted, Mr Bagshaw to hail a taxicab and Lawrie to walk home, smiling to himself at the effrontery of the Canadian, and Mary's composure as she was whisked away.

Sally was not so pleased when she heard about the encounter.

'Sounds a bit impudent to me,' she commented. 'Still, our Mary knows how to deal with hardfaced fellows.'

Mary's method of dealing with Clive was to adopt a ladylike and modest air as they walked round the Museum, and then to insist that she must go home with her friend.

'Elizabeth's mother expects me for tea,' she told him demurely.

A less experienced man would have thought that he had been mistaken in the bold look he had earlier received from Mary, but Clive had understood her signal. She reinforced it by glancing provocatively at him beneath lowered lids several times before they parted, after arranging a visit to the theatre on the following night.

Chapter Twenty-Four

It was hard for Mary to sit composedly in Elizabeth's house sipping tea, listening to her mother and aunts gossiping, while she was so full of excitement about the Canadian and all that had happened at the Museum.

She was relieved when eventually Elizabeth asked if they might be excused, and took Mary up to her bedroom. They looked through Elizabeth's clothes and Mary admired her new shoes, then her friend said, smiling, 'What will you wear tomorrow night, Mary?'

'I thought the bronze silk.'

'It would be quite perfect,' Elizabeth said enthusiastically. 'There you are! I knew you'd have occasion to wear it.'

Mary smiled. 'You know my mother didn't think I should accept that dress length from you, but when she saw your design I think she just couldn't resist making it up.'

They laughed and Elizabeth took a for cape from the wardrobe.

'Would you like to borrow this?' she asked. 'No one need ever know.'

'Oh, Elizabeth, it would be perfect!' Mary exclaimed, 'But your mother—?'

'We'll smuggle it out,' Elizabeth said. 'She needn't know. I tell you what – I'll bring it into Denby's tomorrow.'

She brought out some designs she had recently completed and Mary was charmed with them. 'Why don't you show them to someone in Denby's?' she asked, but Elizabeth shook her head.

'No, I don't want them meddling with my work,' she said firmly. 'Some day I'll design exclusively and pick and choose my clients. I hope I can find someone to model who'll make them look as good as you do, Mary.'

Later she walked home alone, her mind racing with plans for the following night. She had no worries about her clothes, but planned her campaign to capture Clive as carefully as any general drawing up battle plans.

She must encourage him enough to show that his courtship would be welcomed, but not so much that she would seem too easy a capture. She knew by experience that men never valued what was obtained too easily, and had an uneasy feeling that she would need to be extra careful with Clive.

He seemed an experienced man of the world, very different to the young men with whom she usually flirted. He might easily be the one who called the tune.

When she arrived home, she found her mother alone.

'You're early,' she greeted Mary. 'I believe you met Dad by the Museum.'

'Yes, by the steps,' Mary agreed. Her mother glanced at her, seeing the simmering excitement in her flushed cheeks and bright eyes. 'What about this Canadian then?' she said bluntly. 'Your dad said he walked round the Museum with you and Elizabeth.'

'Yes, he did,' Mary said. Then, unable to contain her excitement, burst out: 'Oh, Mam, he's a real gentlemen, and he's asked me to the theatre tomorrow night.'

'Tomorrow night. That was quick work!' Sally exclaimed. 'Is he coming here?'

'No, I'm meeting him at the theatre,' Mary said. 'I've told you, Mam,' she went on before her mother could speak, 'it's usual. Fellows think you're trying to trap them if you bring them to meet the family right away.'

'Then it's up to you to put them right,' her mother said. 'To tell them it's because your father wants to know who you're with.'

Mary looked sulky but Sally went on, 'A decent man will think all the more of you if he knows your family looks after you. We only try to do our best for you, love.'

'I know, Mam,' Mary said. 'But I can look after myself, and anyway Clive is a real gentleman. Very well mannered.'

Sally smiled at her. 'What will you wear?' she asked practically.

'My bronze silk. Elizabeth thinks it'll be very suitable, and she's lending me her fur cape.'

'That's kind,' Sally said. 'Have you brought it home with you?'

'No, she's wearing it herself tonight,' Mary said glibly, 'but she'll bring it in to work tomorrow.' She implied that Elizabeth had her mother's permission and Sally asked no more questions.

A little later she went next door to see Michael Burns who was ill, and Mary ran upstairs to inspect her clothes and get everything ready. She washed her hair and was sitting before the fire drying it when Cathy and Greg came in.

'Your hair!' Cathy exclaimed. 'I thought you only washed it on Fridays.'

'I did, but I'm going out tomorrow night so I've done it again. I want it just right,' Mary said.

Her hair hung like a shining curtain as she held her head forward, the firelight striking bright lights from it as she brushed it.

She flung it back and looked at them. 'I'm going to the theatre with a Canadian,' she said triumphantly. Before they could ask any questions Sally came down the lobby and Mary let her hair fall forward again, but later in bed with Cathy she talked about Clive Walden, too excited to keep her news to herself.

Gradually over the past months the girls had slipped back into their old habit of confiding in each other, although not as freely as in the past.

Cathy hated to be on bad terms with anyone, particularly Mary, and when the latter made overtures of friendship had responded, pushing the thought of her sister's trickery to the back of her mind. The deep uncomplicated love and trust of their childhood had gone forever, Cathy felt, but on a shallower level they were friends again.

Now she sat up in bed, her arms around her knees, as Mary shook out the bronze dress hanging behind the door.

'That's beautiful, Mary,' she said. 'It really suits you. Would you like to borrow my topaz necklet?'

'Yes *please*,' Mary said. 'Elizabeth is lending me her fur cape too. I'll feel like the belle of the ball.'

'And you'll look it too,' Cathy said. 'What's Clive like – to look at, I mean?'

Mary fluttered her eyelashes and pressed her hand to her heart, pretending to swoon. Cathy laughed. 'As good as that?'

'Better,' Mary said emphatically. 'He's very tall, with fair hair all in little curls, blue eyes and a heavy moustache. But his clothes – Cathy, they must have cost a fortune.'

'You needn't worry. You'll look just as well dressed,' Cathy said staunchly. Still Mary looked uneasy.

'I *am* a bit nervous,' she admitted. 'He seems such – such a man of the world. I could tell just from talking to him that he travelled about and mixed with all sorts of posh people. I hope I don't make a fool of myself, Cath.'

'Don't be daft,' she said. 'You were able to talk to him all right today, weren't you? It sounds to me as though he was smitten at first sight, the way he went into the Museum with you and then asked you out. You've got nothing to worry about, Mary.'

'He *is* interested, I'm sure, Cath. He hardly looked at Elizabeth, or at the things in the Museum for that matter. It was just an excuse to come in with us. He kept staring at me all the time.'

'There you are then,' Cathy said. 'And you'll look as well-dressed as anyone there.'

Mary smiled then blew out the candle and climbed into bed.

'How was Tinkerbell, by the way?' she asked. Tinkerbell was the name they had invented for Mrs Redmond, after Cathy had told Mary how much she detested her tinkling laugh. Often Cathy felt better able to disregard Mrs Redmond's most wounding remarks when she thought of discussing them with Mary and laughing about 'Tinkerbell'.

'Tinkling away,' she said now.

'I hope you didn't take any notice.'

'No, I didn't, I just wish Greg wouldn't worry so much,' Cathy said. She gave a huge yawn and snuggled down under the bedclothes. Minutes later both girls were asleep.

On Monday evening excitement made Mary look even more beautiful than usual and Clive pursed his lips in a soundless whistle of admiration as she stepped from a cab and walked towards him.

He took her arm and she walked proudly beside him into the theatre to be escorted by the manager to the best seats in the house. Clive took her wrap and laid a large box of chocolates on her knee. She smiled brilliantly at him. He was wearing evening dress and smelled of expensive soap and bay rum. Mary felt that she should pinch herself to be sure that she was not in a beautiful dream.

He leaned close to her, smiling into her eyes, and she felt the pressure of his arm against her and braced herself for roving hands when the lights went down. Instead, he leaned back in his seat and watched the play.

In the interval he asked her about herself and she talked about her job in Denby's, and managed skilfully to bring in references to her uncle's home in Aigburth and his box factory in Islington.

He already knew that she had a ladylike friend in Elizabeth who also worked in Denby's and Mary felt that she was giving a good impression of her background. He would have to know about her humble home if all went as she hoped, but time enough for that, thought Mary.

In return he told her as much of his background as he intended her to know. She heard that he had been born in England and taken to Canada as a baby, and had now returned to claim his inheritance after the death of his uncle, his only surviving relative.

'Will you be going back to Canada?' she asked artlessly.

Clive laughed. 'I doubt it,' he said. 'I'm completely without ties, you see, so I can live wherever I choose.' He smiled at Mary and she smiled back, trying to hide her pleasure at his reply.

When the play was over, he carefully draped Mary's borrowed cape about her shoulders. 'May I suggest supper?' he said. 'It's still quite early.'

She agreed and he directed the cab he had called to take them to an ornate building near Duke Street. The interior was thickly carpeted and lit by pink-shaded lamps. Mary moved as though in a dream as her cape was whisked away and they were conducted to a small table in an alcove.

'How did you know about this place?' she asked. 'I've lived here all my life and I didn't know about it.'

Clive smiled his enigmatic smile. 'I have friends,' he said, and Mary felt that the subject was closed. He asked to see her again the following night but she refused, saying that she had a previous engagement. She thought it was wiser not to be too easily available to Clive but she had an uneasy feeling that he saw through her little ploy.

It was arranged that he would take her to a concert at Saint George's Hall on the Wednesday evening, and Mary returned home in great excitement to tell her parents and Cathy of all she had learned about him.

Cathy was delighted at Mary's success, not least because it meant that she felt more free to show her own happiness. While Mary had been so discontented and unsettled, and Norah so unhappy, Cathy had felt that she must be careful not to make her own happiness too obvious.

She had confided in Beattie one night, and told her that she tried to keep her ring out of sight when she was with Mary or Norah, but Beattie had told her not to be daft.

'It's Mary's own fault that she hasn't got a ring herself,' she said. 'She could have one off Sam tomorrow, but if she wants to wait for bigger game it's her own lookout. And Norah – I think she's being stubborn and stupid carrying on with that feller when it's causing so much trouble.'

'But they love each other,' Cathy protested. Beattie snorted, but luckily one of the children claimed her attention and the subject was dropped.

Later, when Cathy was leaving, Beattie returned to it.

'Don't let Mary or Norah spoil your pleasure in your ring, Cathy,' she said. 'Remember, it's their own choice the way things are.'

'I don't think either of them begrudge me my happiness *or* the ring,' Cathy hastened to say. 'It's just – I feel I've been so lucky, and I don't want to rub it in when they're in a bad patch. It isn't spoiling it for me though.'

Now, at least as far as Mary was concerned, Cathy felt that she was free to show her happiness as much as she liked. Strange, she often thought in later years, how they had all accepted immediately that the affair with Clive was permanent and that Mary had gained her heart's desire.

She seemed to be ablaze with triumphant happiness each time she returned from an evening with Clive, and all the family were affected by it. They rejoiced in her happiness and were relieved to be free of her moods which had unsettled everyone when things went badly for her.

Now it seemed as though Mary bore a charmed life and all her problems were solved as though by magic. She had been able to keep Elizabeth's cape for the concert at St George's Hall but then it had to be smuggled back into Elizabeth's home. Mary had wondered what she could do for other evenings out, until her mother arrived home from The Grange with a fur cloak of Emily's for her to use.

Sally now went to see Emily on three afternoons a week. While her sister rested on a sofa, Sally sat beside her, sewing and telling her of all that had happened in the family. One afternoon she spoke of the kindness of Elizabeth and her mother in lending the cape to Mary, and Emily said immediately, 'But it will have to go back, won't it? Listen, Sal, I have an evening cloak that Mary could use until I'm well enough to go out in the evening again.'

The sisters still kept up the fiction that her illness could be cured but Sally's heart was heavy as she listened to Emily's brave words and looked at her frail body and hollow cheeks. She forced a smile though and told Emily that Mary would be delighted.

'She's got that blue cloak I made for her but it's not really stylish enough for the places she's going to with Clive,' she said. 'Supper clubs no less, as well as the concerts and theatres, but what will Albert say?'

'If it's what I want, he won't mind,' Emily said, smiling.

Mary was ecstatic when she saw the fur and wrote immediately to her aunt to thank her. Now all her problems were solved, she thought. Although her mother frequently said that Mary and Cathy had three times as many clothes as their friends because of her skill with her needle, Mary had always longed for more.

Now particularly she felt that she needed them. Fortunately, Elizabeth's uncle, a ship's master, had recently returned from the Far East with bales of beautiful silks and Elizabeth had managed to obtain several dress lengths for Mary from them. She had sketched out designs which Sally had made up, and even Mary, usually so dissatisfied with her lot, had to admit that she was lucky to have such a generous friend and talented mother.

Sally had to put aside some of her sewing orders to make the dresses for Mary because her days were so fully occupied but Cathy helped her with the most urgent orders.

As well as visiting Emily three afternoons a week, Sally was also helping Peggy Burns, whose children had each fallen sick in turn. One morning when Sally went in to her neighbour's house, she looked quite distraught with her hair falling untidily round her white face and her eyes red-rimmed. She looked despairingly at Sally. 'We've hardly had a wink of sleep with them,' she said. 'I just don't know what to do.'

Sally bent over Michael who lay coughing on the sofa, his face red and eyes glittering with fever.

'When our Cathy had pneumonia, Lawrie bathed her face with cold water and it seemed to bring the fever down,' she said.

'But, Sally, with a cough like that! I've tried to keep him well wrapped up,' Peggy protested.

'I know. I was the same with Cathy, but the wet cloth did seem to help her,' Sally said. She had taken a spare pillow in with her and some butter moistened with honey. Now she slipped the pillow beneath Michael's head and coaxed him to take some butter and honey.

The baby had kept up a thin wailing punctuated by bouts of coughing but the two women managed to get him to swallow some of the butter and honey. Both children briefly stopped coughing but Michael still tossed and turned uneasily on the sofa.

'Try the wet cloth, Sal,' Peggy Burns said suddenly. 'I'm that desperate I'll try anything.'

Sally moistened a cloth with cold water and gently wiped Michael's face. He sighed and lay more quietly. Peggy watched eagerly. 'It seems to be working, doesn't it?' she said.

'It should bring the fever down,' Sally said. 'Let me take Ritchie while you have a rest, Peg.'

She took the baby from Peggy's arms and walked about, trying to soothe the fretful child while Peggy sat down near Michael.

'To think I ever grumbled because he was such a bundle of mischief,' she exclaimed. 'I'd give anything now to see him running round wild again.'

'He will,' Sally encouraged her. 'Look at the way the others have thrown it off.'

'Just look at him though, Sally. There's not a pick on him and he was such a bonny little lad,' Peggy mourned.

The baby had fallen asleep and Sally laid him down on Peggy's knee, then tidied the hearth and made a pot of tea for them. The other children arrived home from school and twelve-year-old Chrissie began to bustle about helping her mother, so Sally returned home taking four-year-old Ben with her.

Her worries about Emily had receded while she was busy next door, but they soon came back in full force.

Later when she sat at the table with Lawrie and the girls, with Ben sitting on cushions piled on a chair beside her, Sally could eat nothing. She busied herself helping the child so that no one would notice, but after the meal when Lawrie and Mary had gone out and Cathy was sitting with Ben on her knee, reading him a story, she suddenly broke off and leaned towards her mother.

'What's up, Mam?' she asked. 'You didn't eat a bit of your tea.'

Sally had been sitting with her knitting in her lap, staring into the fire. Now, she started and picked up her knitting.

'Are you worried about—?' Cathy said, nodding meaningfully at the wall between their house and the Burns'.

Sally shook her head. 'I was thinking about your Aunt Emily,' she said. 'She hasn't got an ounce of flesh on her bones, Cath. I've never seen her look so ill.'

'Don't worry, Mam. Aunt Emily's been ill for years, hasn't she, yet she's kept going. You know what they say about creaking gates lasting longest.'

'I hope you're right, love,' Sally said with a sigh. 'I dread the winter months, though.'

Ben was looking from one face to the other and Cathy said quickly, 'I know, Ben, let's see what you can draw.'

She took a pencil and an empty sugar bag from the dresser drawer and opened out the bag for the child to draw on. When he was occupied she said to her mother, 'I met Mrs Drew today – the woman who cleans for Mrs Redmond. She was calling her for everything! She said Mrs Redmond talks to her as if she's muck, and carries on as if she's got a houseful of servants.'

'It's a wonder Mrs Drew stays,' said Sally.

'She said she wouldn't if it wasn't for Greg, and I think she needs the money too. She told me to make sure though that we didn't live with Mrs Redmond.'

'By God, Cathy, that's the last thing you should do!' Sally exclaimed.

Cathy laughed. 'No danger,' she said. 'Greg feels responsible for her but he's going to find a small house and a companion for her and we can live over the shop. I don't care how hard up we are as long as we're on our own.'

'It never really works out, living with other people. We seemed all right living with your grandad until Mary was born, then he used to interfere about the way we brought her up,' Sally said.

She looked at Cathy, bending over Ben and guiding his hand, and said softly, 'Another few years and, please God, Cath, you'll have a few of your own round you.'

Cathy blushed and smiled but her face was tender as she smoothed the child's hair. 'I'm looking forward to it, Mam,' she said quietly. 'How do like the idea of being a grandma?'

'Very much,' Sally said emphatically.

She was smiling now and seemed to have forgotten her fears for Emily, and later when she took Ben home she found a great improvement in the Burns. Both the sick children were asleep and Jimmie Burns was sitting at the table eating his meal. Peggy looked quite different to the desperate woman of a few hours earlier.

Her hair was neat and she was wearing a clean apron. She greeted Sally with a smile as she took Ben from her.

'They've slept right through,' she whispered. 'I don't know whether it was the honey or the wet cloth.'

'Probably it just reached its peak last night,' Sally said, 'but they both look better and so do you.'

'I've told her she's gorra look after 'erself an' all,' Jimmie said. 'She doesn't want to go knockin' 'erself out.'

Sally was tempted to say that her neighbour would find life easier if he did more to help but she held her tongue. Peggy seemed to be satisfied and her children were all helpful.

Sally spent a more peaceful night, comforted by Cathy's words about creaking gates and by the improvement in the two small invalids next door.

Chapter Twenty-Five

Clive was living in the house left to him by his uncle, being looked after by the couple who had acted as caretakers since his uncle's death. Mr Bagshaw had introduced him to many local people. Mary fumed when Clive told her of the invitations he received to 'At Homes' and musical evenings.

'They've all got marriageable daughters,' she raged to Cathy, 'and they're after him like a pack of wolves.'

'But you're the one he's asking out,' her sister argued. 'So why worry?'

'Yes, but I'm at work during the day and they're free to chase him at any time,' Mary said. 'I'll go mad if anything goes wrong now, Cath.'

'I don't see why it should,' Cathy said. 'He must be interested to ask you out so often. Why don't you ask him to come here for you?'

'He's used to such posh houses though, Cath. I'd feel ashamed – but don't let Mam know I think that.'

'Of course not, but there's nothing wrong with this house,' Cathy said. 'It's not posh but it's not a slum and he might like to see an ordinary house. You can't be ashamed of Mam and Dad anyway.'

Mary stopped brushing her hair and sat looking thoughtful. 'It's a risk,' she said, 'but still – nothing venture, nothing win, as Dad says.'

'Do you really like Clive?' Cathy asked. 'As a man, I mean?'

'Apart from his money, you mean?' Mary said. 'Yes, I do. I like his looks and his manners and I love being looked after properly when we go out. I can't believe my luck – if I can only bring it off!' Cathy said nothing and Mary suddenly flung down her hairbrush. 'I'm going to ask him here,' she said with decision. 'It might move things on a bit.'

Clive had arranged to take Mary to the theatre on Saturday night, and he had told her that he also had tickets for a Sunday afternoon concert at the Assembly Rooms. Mary told her mother that she intended to ask Clive to call at the house for her on Sunday, and Sally immediately began an orgy of cleaning.

'No need for that, surely,' Lawrie protested, when Sally emptied a cupboard and began to put fresh paper on the shelves. 'He's not going to examine the cupboards.'

'I might have to open it for something while he's here,' she said. 'Anyhow, I'll feel better knowing everywhere's clean.'

'Has Mary said much about him?' Lawrie asked.

'Not much, except that he's a real gentleman. And of course she's made up with all the trips to The Empire and The Star, and the suppers afterwards.'

'Aye, that'll never upset her,' Lawrie said with a grin. 'I'd only just met him that day when the girls walked up but he seemed a pleasant sort of fellow. Nice manners.'

'I think she doesn't want to say too much until she's more sure of him,' Sally said shrewdly.

'He seems to be just the ticket for her,' Lawrie said, 'but I'm glad she's bringing him here. I'd like to have another look at him and weigh him up before she gets in too deep with him.'

'I'm a bit nervous about him coming here,' Sally admitted 'With him having travelled about and lived in posh houses. Mixed with posh people too.'

'That doesn't make him any better than us,' Lawrie declared. 'I don't care if the King of England comes here. This is a respectable, well-conducted family and we're as good as anyone.'

'I didn't say I was ashamed of the family,' Sally said sharply. 'I said I was nervous of meeting him, that's all.'

Lawrie stood up and moved the kettle nearer to the fire. 'I'll make a cup of tea,' he said. 'Sit down and drink it, Sal. Don't get yourself all worked up about this fellow. Mary doesn't seem to be worrying about the place, does she?'

'No, and she won't be bringing him back for a meal. I thought she would but she says he's made arrangements for meals out so they won't be back until late.'

'There you are then,' Lawrie said, pouring the tea. 'That's a bit less for you to worry about. Come and sit down now, love, and drink this.'

On Sunday Mary was waiting in the parlour, looking composed and elegant, when her father opened the door to Clive and ushered him into the parlour. Sally was hovering in the lobby and Lawrie drew her into the parlour and introduced Clive.

He bowed before shaking hands with Sally who was suddenly overcome with nervousness and unable to speak, but the next moment Cathy came into the parlour and was introduced.

'I've read about Canada,' she told Clive, 'about Prince Edward Island in the Fall and how beautiful it is.'

'It sure is,' he said. 'The colours of the maples when the leaves turn – wonderful.'

'Is it near Toronto?' asked Cathy.

He smiled at her. 'Not really, but I left Toronto after my parents died, and travelled about for a few years.'

Mary had glanced out of the window and now she exclaimed, 'Clive, is that your cab outside?'

'Yes, I told him to wait,' he said casually. They all looked at each other in amazement and Mary rose to her feet. 'In that case we'd better go,' she said, drawing on her gloves.

'No hurry,' Clive said, but he too stood up and picked up his hat and gloves, then shook hands with Sally. 'Very proud to make your acquaintance, Ma'am,' he said, and Sally blushed and murmured, 'Pleased to meet you.'

Mary kissed her mother and told her that it would be late evening when she returned, while Clive shook hands with Cathy then Lawrie who escorted them to the door.

The cab driver held the door and Clive handed Mary into the cab and stepped in after her, watched by most of the neighbours from behind their curtains.

Lawrie returned to the parlour, laughing. 'The state of our Mary,' he said. 'Not a feather out of her. Letting him hand her into the cab to the manner born.'

'Did I make a fool of myself?' Sally asked anxiously, 'I just lost my tongue when he bowed, then I blurted out "Pleased to meet you" when he was going.'

'What's wrong with that?' Lawrie said. 'He'd just said he was pleased to meet you.'

'You were fine, Mam,' Cathy assured her.

'I was glad when you came in and talked to him about Canada,' Sally said.

'I've seen the day when you'd have been hiding in the backyard till he'd gone,' Lawrie said with a grin. 'You've come out of your shell, Cath.'

'Maybe I've just got more nosy,' she said, laughing. 'I was dying to see what he looked like, and anyway I thought it might have seemed rude if I didn't come in. He's nice though, isn't he? Very easy to talk to.'

'He seems a real gentleman like Mary described him,' Sally said. 'Very well-dressed and well-mannered.'

'And tall and handsome,' Cathy added. 'He's just the man Mary's always wanted. I hope it goes right for her.'

'Aye, he seems just the ticket,' Lawrie agreed, privately deciding to find out more about Clive now that he could see how the wind was blowing.

A little later Peggy Burns called over the backyard wall to Sally. They never visited each other on Sundays when the families were at home. Sally said anxiously, 'Is something wrong? The children—?' but Peggy laughed.

'No, they're all fine,' she said. 'I just wondered how you got on with Mary's beau. I saw them going off.'

'Peggy, I hardly opened my mouth!' she said. 'He gave a sort of bow when he shook hands with me and my wits left me. Good job Lawrie was there, and our Cathy came in and talked to Clive about Canada.'

'What did you think of him?'

'He seems very nice,' Sally said. 'A real gentleman but not stuck up or anything, very friendly. Lawrie says they're like that from the Dominions, not snobbish like English people.'

'He looked very posh, but so did Mary. You must be proud of her, Sal. Such a beautiful girl, and so ladylike.'

Sally coloured with pleasure. 'She pays for dressing, as Mrs Mal used to say. The clothes always look well on her.'

'A few in this street got their eyes full,' Peggy said, 'Mrs Mellor was very nearly through the parlour window, and Josie and one of the daughters-in-law were peeping from behind the bedroom curtains.'

'Mary still gets letters from Frank Mellor,' Sally said. 'Mrs Mellor'd go mad if she knew but Mary never encouraged him. She only wrote to him once or twice, just to be polite.'

'He's got a cheek!' Peggy said. 'Mary can do a lot better for herself than Frank Mellor, no matter how it turns out with the new feller.'

Lawrie appeared at the scullery door. 'You two'll get your deaths standing there,' he said. 'Why didn't you come in here in the warm, Peggy?'

'I can talk better standing on a bucket,' she said with a grin. Sally laughed too. 'The rim on this one's cutting into my feet,' she said glancing down at the upturned bucket she was standing on, and Lawrie went back into the house, shaking his head.

Sally followed after a few minutes and a little later Greg arrived to take Cathy to visit his mother. The fortnightly visits had been resumed after Greg and Cathy became engaged and Mrs Redmond was now less openly hostile to Cathy, although she still planted a barb at every opportunity.

Lawrie had been teasing Sally about her cleaning when Greg arrived. He winked at Greg and said, 'I'd take the huff on if I was you, Greg. You're lucky if you get a clean cup when you come here, but this fellow Clive was in the house only a few minutes and my wife cleaned everywhere for him.' He opened a cupboard door. 'Look at that – fresh paper and all! You never get that sort of treatment, do you?'

'No. I look for the red carpet every time I come,' Greg said solemnly, 'but it's never down.'

'Take no notice of them, Mam!' Cathy exclaimed. '*I* know why you cleaned everywhere. It's like having your best clothes on – it makes you feel more sure of yourself.'

'How did it go, anyway?' Greg asked.

'Oh, he was very nice,' Sally said. 'A very smart-looking man, and very polite. He had a cab waiting at the door so he was only here for a few minutes.'

'Gave the neighbours a treat anyway,' Cathy said. But later, when she was walking along with Greg towards his home, she suddenly shivered.

He looked down at her in surprise. 'Are you cold, Cath?' he asked.

She shook her head. 'No, someone just walked over my grave,' she said. They walked on in silence for a few minutes then she said suddenly, 'I'm not sure about Clive.'

He refrained from pointing out that she had only seen Clive for a few moments, seeing by her expression that she was deeply disturbed. 'What do you mean, love?' he asked gently.

'I can't say, exactly. It's just a feeling. He's all I said, tall and handsome and polite, but there's *something*. Like the time we went to a house one day and there was that man there who was more like a woman.'

'But there can't be anything like that about Clive if he's so keen on Mary.'

'I know. I'm not saying he's like that but he gave me the same sort of creepy feeling.'

'Don't worry Cath. Your mam and dad seemed to think he was all right.'

'He probably is, and I'm just imagining things. There's only you I can tell though, Greg. Other people might think I was envying Mary.'

'I hope you're not,' he said, squeezing her arm. 'I'd be very upset.'

'You know I'm not,' Cathy said, resting her head on his shoulder. 'I don't envy anybody in the world now.'

'I expect people are envying me,' he declared, and they strolled along whispering words of love to each other. In later years, though, Cathy often remembered her instinctive distrust of Clive.

Lawrie carried out his plan to ask Mr Bagshaw for further details about Clive but the solicitor could tell him very little.

He could only say that Clive came of a respectable family but his father had been the 'black sheep' in his youth, and had been sent to live abroad. He had eventually settled in Toronto with his wife and child, and Mr Bagshaw presumed that he had made good there.

Clive's bachelor uncle had been Mr Bagshaw's friend as well as his client, and the solicitor told Lawrie that he thought Clive resembled his uncle.

'A very upright man,' he said. 'But lonely. All his family were dead, and when Hugh himself died I made enquiries in Canada for his heir.'

Mr Bagshaw had found that the parents were dead and had been unable to trace Clive at first. Fortunately he had responded to a newspaper advertisement, and come home to claim his inheritance: a house in Neston on the Wirral and a 'substantial' sum of money. The solicitor was too correct to divulge the amount, but Lawrie was chiefly interested in Clive's character and he was satisfied with what he had heard.

It was not surprising that Mr Bagshaw had been unable to trace Clive in Toronto. A few years earlier he had covered his tracks very carefully when he hurriedly left the city to escape men demanding payment of gambling debts, two furious husbands and his discarded lover.

It had seemed like fate when another occupant of the sleazy lodging house where Clive was living had brought in food wrapped in a newspaper on which he saw Mr Bagshaw's advertisement.

Clive felt it was his second chance and he had come to England determined to lead a settled respectable life, among the people who had known and respected his family.

Mary – pretty, vivacious, and with a hint of sensuality – had attracted him immediately. He soon realised that her background was humble in spite of her ladylike appearance and manners, and at first hoped to seduce her rather than marry her. Two things made him change his mind.

The first was her determined resistance to him, which made it clear that only by marriage could he possess her.

The second was the danger his quick wits perceived when he began to move in local Society among more eligible young ladies.

Mr Bagshaw had evidently dropped a hint that Clive hoped to marry and settle down in his uncle's house, and while the local families were prepared to welcome Clive, the older people also remembered his father. If he asked to marry one of their daughters enquiries would be made about his past, by people who as ships' masters or the occupants of good positions in large shipping offices in Liverpool were far better placed than Mr Bagshaw to find out about his life in Toronto.

Clive knew that they could still stir up a hornet's nest about him, and he began prudently to decline invitations to musical evenings and other local events. Time enough for them when he was safely married, he thought.

He now called at Mary's home when he was taking her out, and all that he learned of her family pleased him. She seemed to be almost as lacking in relations as he was himself, with only an uncle, fully occupied with his sick wife, parents and sister. Her father had neither the money nor the family connexions to make enquiries about him.

In any case, Clive felt, the welcome they gave him showed that they were too anxious for a good match for Mary to make any difficulties. He was unaware that the same welcome was extended to everyone who entered the Wards' house.

His hunger for Mary grew every time he saw her. She responded eagerly when he kissed her and allowed him to run his hands over her shapely body but any attempt to go further was indignantly resisted. 'I like a girl with spirit,' he said after one of these occasions, and Mary smiled demurely, but she was a little uneasy about other remarks he made. 'I fancy marrying a virgin,' he said once and another time when she had fought herself free of him and slapped his face, 'I'll enjoy bringing you to heel'.

It was how they talked in Canada, Mary persuaded herself, and was excited by the hint about marriage.

A few weeks later Clive took her to the theatre and then to the supper in a softly lit, secluded alcove in the club. After the meal he drank brandy, leaning back in his chair and looking at her through half-closed eyes. Then he put down his glass and leaned forward to take her hand.

'I think it's time we got married, honey,' he said.

Mary wasted no time on a show of reluctance or surprise, knowing that Clive would see through it instantly. She only smiled into his eyes and said softly, 'Oh *yes*, Clive.'

He intended them to marry as soon as possible without the formality of an engagement, but had seen how enviously Mary eyed Cathy's engagement ring. Now he drew a ring case from his pocket and snapped it open.

Her eyes widened with delight when she saw the large emerald set round with diamonds. Eagerly she held out her hand for Clive to slip it on her finger.

'You like it?' he asked, smiling at her radiant face.

'It's beautiful,' she breathed, turning her hand this way and that so that light flashed from the stones. 'What time is it?'

He pulled out his gold hunter. 'Just after eleven.'

'Can we go home now and show them?' she asked eagerly. 'I can't wait until tomorrow.'

Clive laughed indulgently. 'Of course, honey,' he said.

'And you'll come in with me? My dad will expect you to ask his permission.'

He frowned and she added hurriedly, 'Only a formality, but if it keeps them happy—'

He shrugged. 'Anything you say, honey. I'm still fogged by your English customs.'

Sally and Lawrie knew what had happened as soon as Mary called them into the parlour to see Clive. She kept her hand hidden but her eyes were brilliant with excitement and her parents were smiling as they followed her.

Clive bowed to Sally then held out his hand to Lawrie. 'I believe I have to ask your permission, sir, to marry your daughter.'

Lawrie shook his hand, then glanced at Sally. 'If that's what you want, Clive, and what Mary wants, we're very pleased to have you in the family.'

Mary flung her arms round her mother and kissed her, then kissed her father and held out her hand. They exclaimed in wonder at the ring and Clive stood smiling indulgently at them.

'We must drink to this!' Lawrie exclaimed. He brought glasses from the kitchen, and a bottle of port and one of rum, but as he was about to pour the drinks Cathy and Greg arrived.

There was renewed excitement when they were told the news and Mary showed them her ring.

'It's beautiful,' Cathy exclaimed, hugging Mary and kissing her then turning to Clive. Greg put his arm around Mary and kissed her, and even in the midst of her excitement she felt a stab of pain as she felt his lips on hers, and looked up into his grey eyes. Forget him, she told herself fiercely. It's Clive now, Clive!

Greg turned to shake hands with Clive and Mary flung up her head. 'You're just in time to drink our health,' she said. Her voice was slightly unsteady but she glanced at her ring and seemed to draw strength from it.

'There's only one thing worries me,' her father said. 'Are you thinking of going back to Canada, Clive?'

They all waited anxiously for his reply but he said breezily, 'No, sir. I aim to settle down now in the family home. I've done enough travelling.'

'Aye, Mr Bagshaw told me he had a bit of a job to find you,' Lawrie said.

'Yes, I left Toronto when my parents died,' Clive said, opening his eyes wide in a way which suddenly reminded Sally of Mary when she was telling lies, but he went on, 'I thought I'd see a bit more of the country but that's all over now.' They all looked at each other with relieved smiles and Lawrie handed round the drinks.

'Let's wish Mary and Clive long life and happiness,' he said, raising his glass.

It was arranged that Clive would call for Mary on the following day which was Sunday and take her to see his house. 'I want Mary to look around and see if she wants any changes,' he said. 'I'd like us to marry real soon.'

The following day was dry but cold, and just before Clive arrived for Mary a weak sun struggled through the clouds. 'It's a nice day for looking at the house,' Mary said with satisfaction. 'Everything's going right for me now.'

She returned in the evening even more pleased and excited. The house was perfect, she told the family, and she and Clive had fixed their wedding day.

'Easter Saturday, April 11th,' she announced triumphantly. 'There's no need to wait any longer. The house only needs new curtains and covers and some decorating. Clive says he'll take me to Paris for our honeymoon.'

Cathy and Greg were sitting together on the sofa, and she stifled a sigh. How lovely, she thought, to be able to arrange to marry whenever you liked. To have no problems to solve, and a house, and plenty of money available for any plan, even a Paris honeymoon.

But then she looked at Greg and knew that she would never wish to change places with Mary or anyone else, no matter what the circumstances.

Chapter Twenty-Six

Sally hastened to see Emily the following day, knowing how pleased her sister would be to hear Mary's news, but when she arrived she found Emily asleep, and the nurse who had attended her to Scarborough sitting beside the bed.

She put her finger to her lips and followed Sally out of the room.

'What's happened? Is my sister worse?'

'She had a slight haemorrhage during the night,' the nurse said. 'Doctor has been and he'd like her to go back to the Sanatorium before the fogs get any worse.'

'I thought she seemed a bit better in herself the last few weeks,' Sally said, but the nurse pursed her lips.

'She doesn't want to go away again, that's the trouble, and she's trying to put the best side out. Mr Deakin thinks she should go to the San. Of course, while she's ill here his nights are disturbed sometimes,' she said with a sniff.

'But what's best for Emily?' Sally asked. 'And what's going to happen?'

'Well, I've suggested that she goes to a small nursing home I know of in Southport,' the nurse said. 'It's only about twenty miles further up the coast, but she'd have the sea air and be away from the smoke and the fogs and yet near enough to have visitors.'

'I think that's a good idea,' Sally exclaimed. 'It'd be better for Emily and I could get to see her often. It's less than an hour on the train.'

'It's a very good place for anyone with tuberculosis,' the nurse said.

'I'm sure you're right,' Sally said. 'But what about Mrs Deakin? What does she feel about the idea?'

'It seemed to calm her,' the nurse said. 'She got very upset at the thought of going back to Yorkshire. I think she was worried about not being able to see you.'

'I could go to Southport as easily as come here,' said Sally. 'And Mr Deakin?'

'He's lying down. He didn't go into work.' The nurse looked quizzically at Sally, but she only said, 'I mean about the Southport idea.'

'He likes it. Mrs Deakin would be looked after there day and night, and he wouldn't have to worry. She wants to stay home for Christmas but that's only ten days away and it'll take that long to make the arrangements.'

She had been peeping into Emily's bedroom from time to time and now she exclaimed, 'Ah, you're awake, Mrs Deakin. Here's your sister come to see you. I'll just tidy you up first.'

She shut the bedroom door firmly on Sally. When she was admitted she found Emily propped up in bed wearing a pretty bedjacket, and with her hair brushed and plaited. There was a hectic flush on her thin cheeks but she smiled and held out her arms.

'You had a bad night, love,' Sally said, kissing her.

'Yes, and I disturbed everybody,' Emily said. 'I rang for Mrs Noble and she called Albert, and got one of the young maids up to help. It's not fair on them.'

'You shouldn't worry about that,' Sally said. 'They know you can't help it and it's worse for you. Albert will be only too glad to do anything for you, I'm sure. You'd look after him if it was the other way round.'

Emily agreed rather doubtfully and they discussed the Southport scheme.

'It's a lovely place,' Sally said. 'We've taken the girls there for a day out a couple of times. The air will do you the world of good, and when the weather's nice I'll wheel you to look at those lovely shop windows on Lord Street.'

'I'll have to take my bathchair,' Emily said, but Sally was pleased to see that she was smiling.

She told Emily about Mary's engagement, and promised that the young couple would come to visit Emily before she left for Southport. 'Mary's dying to show you her ring,' she said. 'Cathy and Greg will come to see you too, and we'll all visit you in Southport.'

When Sally left, she was relieved to see that Emily looked better, brighter and happier.

'You've given her something nice to think about,' the nurse whispered approvingly as she showed Sally out. 'Something to look forward to.'

Mary readily agreed to take Clive to visit her aunt and uncle and show them her ring.

Her brief uncertainty about her power over Clive had been replaced by her usual confidence, and she told Cathy that the Easter wedding had been her idea.

'Clive was all for getting married in January,' she said, 'but I stood out for Easter.'

'Why?' Cathy said, thinking privately that she would have expected her sister to make sure of Clive as soon as possible.

'I want to enjoy being engaged,' Mary said airily. 'I need time to get my clothes ready, and anyway I'm not giving the cats at work the chance to say I had to get married in a hurry.'

'They'd soon find out they were wrong, wouldn't they?' Cathy said.

Mary shrugged. 'I wouldn't be there then,' she pointed out.

Cathy had been gradually accumulating a 'bottom drawer' since her engagement, embroidering tablecloths and pillowcases and making dainty underwear. Mary had admired the nightdresses she had made, with drawn thread work round the neck through which Cathy had threaded narrow blue ribbon. Now she asked Cathy to make similar ones for her.

She made no other provision for a bottom drawer. 'Clive's house is full of linen and china and anything we can possibly need,' she told the family gaily. 'And he will buy anything I want.'

'But you don't want to go there empty handed, surely,' her mother said. 'I should think you'd feel better if you'd made some effort yourself.' Mary dismissed the idea.

Mrs Redmond had been invited to spend Christmas with her friends from the church, and Greg was to join the Ward family for Christmas dinner.

Sally also rather nervously invited Clive but he declined, saying that he was spending Christmas in Paris with a friend.

'Is his friend a Frenchman?' Sally asked Mary.

'No, he belongs to Clive's club in Liverpool,' Mary said. 'He said he met this man when he was staying there and they both thought they'd like to spend Christmas in Paris.'

Sally said no more. She knew that Clive stayed at his club in Liverpool after an evening out with Mary, instead of making the cross-river journey to his house on the Wirral. Although she was surprised that he was prepared to be apart from Mary at Christmas, she was relieved that there was no need for her to entertain him.

Before he left Clive gave Mary a gold locket, similar to the one which Greg had given Cathy, but heavier and more ornate. He also gave her a jewellery box which played 'Greensleeves' when the lid was lifted, and Mary was amazed and delighted to find that it contained fifty gold sovereigns.

'He's certainly not mean,' Sally said to Lawrie. They were both uncertain whether it was right for her to accept such a gift, but Mary and Clive seemed to have no doubts.

'After all, they *are* engaged,' Sally said finally. 'But every penny of it will go on her back, you see.'

Sally was less concerned about Mary's affairs than she might have been because she was now spending so much time with Emily. Mary and Clive had visited her and she told Sally that she was delighted at Mary's good fortune.

'He's just the man for her,' Emily said. 'He can give her the sort of life she's always craved, and he's a smart, handsome man into the bargain.'

'She's really fallen on her feet,' Sally said. 'That lovely house, and fully furnished too.'

'She must feel it's a dream come true,' Emily said, but Sally shook her head.

'She just takes it all for granted,' she said. 'Says she always knew she'd meet someone like Clive.'

'Lovely to be young and confident,' Emily said with a small sigh. 'I was glad to see Cathy and Greg too. He's a nice lad.'

'One of the best,' Sally agreed. 'The only drawback there is that flaming old mother. She's a real blood sucker. Want, want, wanting all the time, Cathy says, dragging the lad back when he's trying to get on.'

'Still, you must be happy to see both your girls settled now, Sal,' Emily said wistfully.

'I am,' she said, 'I'm very lucky. If you can just get your health back in Southport, love, my cup will be full.'

'You'll come often to see me, won't you?' Emily said anxiously.

'Of course I will, and stay for the whole day too.'

Emily smiled. 'Then I *will* soon be better,' she declared.

Sam Glover still hung about hoping to see Mary even though she had discarded him. Cathy was anxious to break the news of Mary's engagement to him before he heard it elsewhere. She intercepted him at the first opportunity.

'Hello, Sam, how are you?' she said.

'Fine. How's Mary?' he asked eagerly. She slipped her hand through his arm and walked along with him. 'Did you know she'd met a Canadian?' she asked.

'Yes, I saw them together,' he said miserably.

'He came to England because his uncle died and left him a house and some money,' Cathy said. 'He's really fallen for Mary, Sam, and he's asked her to marry him.'

She felt his arm stiffen but he only said quietly, 'And she said yes, I suppose?'

'Yes, she did, Sam, and with him being a Canadian, and not having any relations, and having all this from his uncle like – I think they'll get married quite soon.'

They walked in silence for a few minutes then he said in a muffled voice, 'How soon, Cath?'

'Easter,' she said gently. 'He's given her an engagement ring.'

'She likes him then?' Sam said. 'You think she'll go through with it?'

'I think she will, Sam,' Cathy said. They had reached a corner of the street where they stopped and Cathy withdrew her arm. Sam held out his hand and with a dignity which Cathy had not expected said quietly, 'Thanks, Cath. It was good of you to tell me like this.'

'I thought it was better for you to know, Sam. I didn't want you to hear it from anyone else,' Cathy said. She might have said something about his starting afresh and meeting someone else but a glance at his face decided her against it, and she simply shook his hand and left him.

She went in the back gate of the house and into the outside privy where she had taken refuge to shed so many bitter tears for Mrs Malloy. Now once again she leaned against the whitewashed wall and wept for the end of Sam's dream, and for his suffering because of his faithful love for Mary. But her sister was too excited to spare a thought for Sam.

Mary had lost no time in spending the money in the box. She had bought material and Elizabeth had designed several gowns to be made up in Denby's workroom. From an exclusive small business in Bold Street, Mary had ordered underwear and nightdresses.

The nightdresses were threaded with ribbon like the ones that Cathy was making for her, but in addition they were lavishly trimmed with lace, and each had a matching peignoir edged with swansdown.

Greg's Christmas gift to Cathy was a scarf and a brooch in the form of a letter C outlined in diamond chippings. Cathy saw Mary eyeing the brooch and wondered how long it would be before she acquired one in the shape of the letter M, larger and more showy than Cathy's. She felt only a mild irritation, however, and told herself that imitation was the sincerest form of flattery.

Everyone seemed pleased by Mary's good fortune. To the girls in Denby's it was like a fairy story, and made them believe that their own dreams could come true. The neighbours were pleased for Sally's sake.

A few such as Mrs Bennet and Mrs Mellor might say that Mary Ward was no better than she should be, going out with so many lads, and that Clive might get more than he bargained for in marrying her. All agreed, though, that Sally was a good neighbour, always ready to do a good turn and no gossip, and she deserved to have her girls well married.

Peggy Burns was truly delighted and gazed in wonder at Mary's ring and her other gifts from Clive. 'You've properly fallen on your feet,' she said admiringly. 'I've never seen a ring like that before except in a shop window.'

Peggy was suitably impressed by all the details she was given of Clive's house, and Mary decided that she was quite a nice woman, although she had previously thought her rough and outspoken.

'I wish I could see mine as well settled,' Peggy said with a sigh to Sally when they were alone. 'When I think of that one our Robbie's courting, and the feller our Mabel's hanging after, I could go mad!'

'They're young yet,' Sally consoled her. 'They could change a few times before they settle.'

'Our Robbie's nearly nineteen and this one's properly got her hooks into him. I don't know what he sees in her. A little weaselly thing she is, buttering everyone up, but she doesn't fool me.'

'Robbie's not soft. He'll see through her.'

'I don't know, Sal, she's so smarmy. But I told him, I've seen it all before – a girl telling a feller he's God's gift to wimmin, then once she's got her marriage lines giving him the life of a dog.'

'No use worrying, Peg. I know I'm the wrong one to talk, the way I've worried about mine, but it all works out in the end. Not much we can do about it anyway, only rear them to know right from wrong and hope for the best.'

'Has your sister gone to Southport yet?'

'Yes, that reminds me. I'm going for the whole day tomorrow. I'll take some sandwiches and get a cup of tea while she's having her lunch, as they call it, and go back to see her in the afternoon. Will you be able to nip in and keep the fire going for Lawrie and the girls coming in?'

'Of course, and I'll get anything from the shop or do any cooking you want,' Peggy said. 'I'll be only too glad to after all you've done for me.'

Sally was pleased to find Emily happy and comfortable in the small nursing home recommended by the nurse. She began to spend two days a week with her, at first sitting with her in the morning then going out to have a cup of tea and a sandwich before returning in the afternoon. But soon the matron/proprietor invited her to have her lunch with her sister which gave them even more time together.

Sally was surprised to find that Albert only visited Emily on Sundays. 'I thought he would have stayed in Southport,' she told Lawrie. 'He could travel in quite easily each morning, and it wouldn't matter if he was late, seeing that he's the boss.'

'He likes his comfort,' Lawrie said. 'I suppose it suits him better to stay at home, and Emily doesn't mind, does she?'

'No, she seemed to take it for granted he'd stay in Liverpool, but fancy being so near and only seeing her once a week.'

'Ah well, nowt so queer as folk, as they say,' Lawrie said.

Time flew for Sally because she was so busy with her visits to Southport and helping Mary shop and make preparations for the wedding.

The weeks before Easter passed almost too quickly for all of them. Cathy and Lawrie felt that they wanted to grasp at the flying days before Mary was gone from the house forever.

'I'll visit you and you can come and see me,' she told her father, but he knew that life would be different after Easter.

Even for Mary the weeks went too quickly, although she had never been so happy. Her stock of clothes was growing every day and she had money to buy all the small luxuries of ribbons and gloves that she had always craved.

Clive still took her regularly to the theatre or concerts, and at the weekend she visited his house and saw the improvements she had suggested taking place.

He had told her to change anything she wished but most of her efforts had been resisted by the caretaker's wife who acted as housekeeper. Mary had objected to the huge shabby old leather armchair in the morning room. Mrs Stewart had folded her arms. 'That was Mr Walden's favourite chair,' she said grimly. 'I can see him sitting there now. He liked this room because it was so sunny and he spent most of his time here, sitting in that chair.'

Mrs Stewart also resisted Mary's suggestion that some of the clutter should be cleared from the numerous small tables dotted about. 'They're mostly family photographs, madam,' she said.

'I'm afraid to suggest anything,' Mary said to Clive when the housekeeper had left them.

He said easily. 'Don't worry, honey. Do as you like. I'll get rid of them when we're settled in, and you can choose your own staff.'

Mary felt a thrill of delight. Choose her own staff! With fresh confidence she decided that the sunny morning room should be her own sitting room, and ordered fresh curtains and covers in other rooms too. Something in her manner seemed to warn Mrs Stewart who became much more eager to please, but Mary was determined that she must go.

The caretakers were absent and Mary and Clive were alone in the house one day when his kisses became fiercer and the pressure of his arms forced her back on to the sofa. His body was lying heavily on her, while he attempted to force his tongue into her mouth.

She twisted her head away and managed to push him off, saying pleasantly, 'Not yet, Clive.'

Not while she was so near her heart's desire. To allow him to take her now might make him change his mind about marrying her. She was afraid that he would insist but he released her, saying with a bark of laughter, 'You'll keep! I'll enjoy you all the more for the waiting.'

Several times she feared a repetition when he kissed and caressed her after an evening out. She was relieved when he left her without protest as soon as she resisted.

She was unaware that he visited a discreet establishment in town before returning to his club, and one of the 'girls' suffered rough treatment from him because of his arousal by Mary.

These were only small ripples on the surface of her happiness, and she felt flattered that Clive desired her so much.

Mary had decided that she wanted a quiet wedding, with only her family, Elizabeth, Mr Bagshaw and his son and daughter-in-law present. Clive gave his hearty approval to the idea.

Sally worried about entertaining the lawyer and his relations, but Mary told her that Clive was arranging for the wedding breakfast to be served in the Adelphi Hotel.

'It's usual with his class of people,' Mary told her mother, 'especially as there'll only be a few of us. Clive will pay for it.'

'I don't think that's right,' Sally said. 'We've got a few pounds now in the Savings Bank and some money in the teapot. We'll pay for the wedding breakfast.'

'Oh, Mam, you've worked for years to get that money together,' Mary exclaimed. 'That old handless teapot has been there since we were little children. I'm not letting you spend it all for this, especially when it's nothing to Clive.'

Lawrie also demurred at the idea of Clive's paying for the meal but Mary managed to persuade them that it was the best plan.

'I must admit, I'm glad I haven't got to worry about those posh people coming here,' Sally told Cathy. 'I'd been wondering if I could put the table in the parlour, so I'm glad to do it this way. I'm a bit worried about not asking any of our friends to the wedding though, Cath.'

'Why don't we have a party for them here at night?' she suggested. 'Mary says they'll be leaving for Paris right after the meal, so we'd have plenty of time to get it ready.'

'That's a good idea!' Sally exclaimed. 'Everything's sorting itself out nicely. I'm just going to stop worrying.'

Mary was determined to be married in church, and Greg, who was best man, introduced her to the vicar of the church at which his mother worshipped. The vicar readily agreed to marry Mary and Clive after she had talked to him, vaguely but charmingly, about attending church in Aigburth with her invalid aunt.

'I thought you'd have liked a big wedding, Mary,' Cathy said that night when they were in the bedroom.

'I thought it would be too awkward, with Clive having no relations. And then you know what Mam's like. She'd have had any rag tag and bobtail here. Better to stick to just the family and the couple of friends.'

Cathy sighed. 'The weeks are going too fast,' she exclaimed. 'I can't believe you'll soon be gone and we'll never talk like this again. We'll miss you terribly. I know Dad and Mam are dreading it.'

'I'll come home often,' Mary said, 'and you can all visit me.'

'Yes but it'll be different. You'll be a married woman,' Cathy said. She smiled wistfully. 'Remember years ago when we were only children really, you said you'd marry a rich man and live in a big house and I could come and visit you.'

'Vaguely,' Mary laughed. 'It was always my dream, and now it's coming true.' She sat smiling at her reflection in the mirror and Cathy said goodnight rather sadly and lay down to sleep.

Chapter Twenty-Seven

The weather was unsettled for the days before Mary's wedding, with a boisterous wind which threatened to blow cyclists from their machines, and frequent squalls of rain, but late on Good Friday the wind dropped, and the sun shone for Mary's wedding on Easter Saturday.

It shone into the bedroom where Sally and Cathy were helping Mary to dress. As Sally looked at Mary's glowing face, her lips parted in excitement, she was suddenly overcome by a storm of tears.

'Oh, Mary love,' she said, taking her daughter in her arms and kissing her. 'Be happy.'

'I will, Mam,' she said with such touching confidence that Sally wept afresh.

'Don't cry, Mam,' Cathy urged her. 'You'll make your eyes all red.' But she was near to tears herself.

In later years Sally wondered if it was some presentiment or mother's instinct which had made her shed tears on Mary's wedding day.

Now she wiped her eyes and she and Cathy carefully helped Mary into her wedding dress of gold-embroidered ivory brocade. It had been designed by Elizabeth in a medieval style, with a heart-shaped neckline and hanging sleeves tapering to a point. The shaped waist emphasised Mary's figure.

Clive's wedding gift of pearls was about her throat, and she wore a Juliet cap of the brocade on her bright hair, studded with pearls. She carried a sheaf of creamy lilies with gold stamens.

Her father was waiting in the lobby as she walked regally downstairs. She looked so breathtakingly beautiful that he was unable to speak and could only cup her face in his hands and kiss her gently. 'You look beautiful, love, beautiful,' he said at last.

He looked past Mary to Sally, and as their eyes met saw traces of her tears and knew that they had been shed for their lovely wilful daughter, so dearly loved, who was leaving their care now and starting a new life. God grant her happiness and watch over her, he prayed silently.

'A lovely sunny day. A good omen,' he said aloud. 'You all look beautiful. I'm proud of all my girls.'

They smiled at each other, then Sally and Cathy kissed Mary and left for the church. The neighbours clustered near the door exclaimed at the sight of them. Cathy as Mary's only bridesmaid wore a dress of palest peach, with a Juliet cap of the same material, and carried a posy of spring flowers. Sally wore a brown silk dress and a straw hat.

'Yiz look the 'eight of fashion,' Mrs Bennet said, and there were appreciative murmurs from the other neighbours.

A few minutes later they gasped with astonishment when a white motor car with white ribbons on the bonnet drove up and stopped in front of the house. 'It's with him being a Canadian,' they told each other, but they were silent with awe when Mary came out of the house with her father and stepped inside.

As the car moved away, Mary suddenly kissed her father. 'Thanks, Dad. Thanks for all you've done for me,' she said, 'I'm sorry I've worried you.' A tear lay on her eyelashes and her father gently wiped it away.

'Not a bit of it,' he said. 'Thank *you*, love, for all the – the happiness.' He turned his head away and swallowed then said gruffly, 'Don't forget. We're always there if you want us.'

Mary blinked. 'You'd think it was a funeral we were going to instead of a wedding,' she said gaily.

Cathy and Sally were waiting in the church porch to fuss about Mary, adjusting the folds of her dress before Sally slipped into the church and the organ began to play.

Mary walked gracefully down the aisle with her hand on her father's arm and her head held high. Cathy walked demurely behind her. Even now in her moment of triumph, as Mary approached Clive and Greg waiting at the altar, she felt a pang as Greg's glance passed quickly over her and fell with loving pride on Cathy. But she gave no sign of it, only smiled brilliantly at Clive.

Although Mary had said she wanted a quiet wedding she was surprised at the number of people who were in the church. Clive had arranged for the choir and the organ, and sent masses of flowers to decorate the church. He had also arranged for the church bells to be rung, and when they emerged a crowd had collected outside the church.

Mary and Clive drove off in the white car, and other vehicles were waiting to take the other wedding guests to The Adelphi.

Sally felt nervous when she entered the hotel, overawed by its magnificence, but she hid her feelings under her usual air of quiet dignity, and chatted pleasantly to Mr Bagshaw and his son and daughter-in-law.

The meal was served in a private room, and the wine which Clive pressed Sally to drink helped her to relax and enjoy the delicious food and unobtrusive service. Toasts were drunk but the speeches were short and soon the guests moved to another room.

Cathy and Greg stood together. He took her hand. 'You look beautiful, Cath, absolutely beautiful,' he said. He smiled into her eyes and then looked over at Mary. 'She looks like a queen, doesn't she?'

Mary was standing with Clive, laughing up at him teasingly as they talked to the Bagshaws. Cathy said impulsively, 'I *do* hope she'll be happy, Greg. They look well matched, don't they?'

'They make a handsome couple, right enough,' he agreed, 'and Mary'll be able to hold her own in any company.'

'We'll miss her though,' Cathy sighed. 'It all seems to have happened so quickly – it only really hit us this morning that she was going. Mam was in tears and Dad and I weren't far off.'

'Never mind. She'll visit you and you'll be able to visit her often.'

Clive had taken a bedroom at The Adelphi and soon Mary went up, accompanied by her mother and Cathy, to change into her travelling clothes.

'A month in Paris,' young Mrs Bagshaw said to Elizabeth. 'Paris in the spring – so romantic! I do envy them.'

'Yes, so do I,' Elizabeth said. 'All the great fashion houses, and the spring collections.'

'Of course, you design Mrs Walden's clothes, don't you?' Mrs Bagshaw said with a hint of condescension in her voice.

Elizabeth made no reply but looked towards the door, where Mary had appeared in a blue outfit which exactly matched the colour of her eyes, a large hat in the same colour on her red-gold hair. There were kisses and a few tears before she and Clive departed on the first stage of their journey to Paris.

The guests soon dispersed, and back at Egremont Street Cathy and her parents were glad to be kept busy preparing the party for their friends and neighbours.

'I wish we'd been able to have the wedding breakfast here,' Sally said to Cathy. 'I felt as though Mary'd gone from us right away in that posh hotel and with those people.'

'But it would have been awkward, Mam. You'd have been worrying about the Bagshaws, even for things like going down the yard to the privy.'

'I suppose I would,' Sally agreed. 'And it all went off lovely, didn't it? In the church and in the hotel everything was perfect. Even the sun came out.'

'It was just right for Mary,' Cathy said dreamily. 'Just what she's always wanted and what she should have. I couldn't imagine her married to Sam or any of the others after seeing her today.'

'Oh, Cath, I hope she'll be all right. It's such a different world.'

'Not to Mary. She's mixed with posh people like Isabel and Elizabeth and their families, and she was always quite at home in The Grange even when we were very young. Greg says she'll hold her own anywhere.'

'She'll do that all right. Nothing daunts Mary,' Sally said with a touch of her old sharpness, but she looked happier as she laid out the food for the party.

Soon the house was filled with neighbours and friends, who willingly accepted glasses of port or spirits from Lawrie to drink the health of Mary and Clive.

Sally had invited several of the girls from Denby's, including Janey Powell, and Cathy went to talk to her.

'Mary looked beautiful,' she said.

'Yes, I seen her,' said Janey. 'We was outside the church. We seen that Elizabeth Fairburn there an' all. I suppose we wasn't posh enough to be invited.'

'Mary wanted a quiet wedding because Clive's got no family,' Cathy said. 'Just our family, and Elizabeth because she designed the dress, and Clive's lawyer and his family.'

Janey looked mollified. 'Aye, I seen there was only the few of you,' she said. 'Was The Adelphi very posh?'

'Yes, and the food was lovely,' Cathy said. 'But I think we'll enjoy ourselves more tonight.'

Most of the guests had managed to see the bride and her family, either setting off from the house or at the church, and they all agreed that Mary and Cathy had looked lovely.

'Your Mary was a credit to the street,' Mrs Mellor declared. 'Yer wanna tell her that when yer see her.'

'I'll bet that's all Mary's worrying about,' Josie giggled to Cathy, 'being a credit to the street!'

The only drawback to Cathy's enjoyment was the number of times she was asked when she and Greg planned to marry.

Sometimes it seemed to her that their wedding day was moving ever further away. No matter how hard Greg worked to make enough money to provide his mother with a separate home, her extravagance always frustrated his efforts, and Cathy was determined that not even for his sake could she share a home with his mother.

Mrs Redmond had become friendly with another member of the church, a spoiled and selfish widow like herself. Mrs Duval's family welcomed the friendship and willingly entertained Mrs Redmond every second Sunday. It gave them a brief respite from her complaints and demands, and they were delighted to arrange for the two ladies to go on holiday together.

Both insisted that the holidays were not for enjoyment but in the hope of improving their health. They had spent a week at Buxton 'taking the waters', and another week at Brighton, and now they were considering a visit to a German spa. In vain Greg tried to persuade his mother that they were unable to afford it, especially as she spent so much money while she was away.

'The Duvals are in a different category from us as regards money, Mother,' he told her. 'You can't possibly keep up with Mrs Duval and I'm sure she understands that.'

'So you want me to suffer pity as well as everything else,' she cried. 'I go away for the sake of my health, not to enjoy myself, but you don't care. You don't care how much I suffer.' She began to weep, saying, 'If only your father had lived to care for me.' Greg stood up and walked over to the window, waiting for her to compose herself, but she wept ever more bitterly.

He sat down beside her. 'Mother, don't get upset,' he urged her. 'I'm only telling you how things are. The business is improving but it takes time.' But she refused to be comforted.

'When I think of Annie Duval's family, how they do everything they can to make her happy, and then my son – so selfish and ungrateful. You begrudge me any comfort, Gregory.'

'Mother—' he said helplessly, but she ignored him. She had been careful not to indulge in hysterics since 'Ma' had advised Greg how to deal with them, but now she wept for long enough to prevent any further discussion about finances.

Mrs Redmond had curtly declined an invitation to Mary's wedding, without giving any excuse, but Cathy felt that she knew the reason and had told Greg not to give his mother any details about the wedding, either before or after it.

It was with chagrin that Mrs Redmond was told about the wedding by her cronies at the church and by the vicar. He described the guests as 'most superior people' and praised the bridegroom's generosity in the offering he had made to the church funds and the arrangements for flowers, choir and church bells.

'You didn't tell me the wedding would be like that, Gregory,' she complained.

'Like what, Mother?' he said brusquely.

'Properly conducted. Acceptable people there, and Miss Hawkes said the reception was at The Adelphi.'

'What difference did it make? You said you were unable to accept the invitation, so it didn't matter what it was like.'

'Don't be obtuse, Gregory,' Mrs Redmond said sharply. 'I wasn't prepared to go among those people and any riff raff they might invite, but if I'd known all this—'

Greg's expression was grim. 'Please don't refer to Cathy's family as "those people", Mother,' he said. 'Mary chose that sort of wedding chiefly because Clive is a stranger in England. When Cathy and I marry it will be different and we'll have all our friends and relations there.'

His mother snorted. 'A lot might happen before that day, Gregory – if it ever comes.'

Cathy suspected that her mother knew the reason for Mrs Redmond's refusal of the invitation, and was hurt by it, and her anger grew at the thought of the insult offered to her parents and Mary. Greg prudently said nothing about his mother's comments after the wedding but Cathy felt that she would be unable to talk to her without showing her anger.

She was due to visit Mrs Redmond on the Sunday following the wedding but she told Greg that she had decided not to go.

'I don't see why I should,' she said. 'She didn't bother to come to the wedding.' But as usual when Cathy attacked his mother, Greg defended her.

'She doesn't have any social life now, Cath,' he said. 'She finds it difficult to mix with people except for a few old friends in the church.'

'She'd have come if she'd known people like the Bagshaws were the only ones there apart from us, and the reception was at The Adelphi,' Cathy said shrewdly. This was so near the truth that Greg coloured, and Cathy became more angry.

'It'll be a long day for Mother if she's alone,' he said.

'You can stay with her if you're worried about her being lonely,' Cathy said. 'That'll suit her, and it'll give me a chance to ask Norah to tea.'

'Very well,' he said stiffly. 'If that's what you want.'

Later she shed angry tears but was too proud to retract her words. I'm playing into her hands, she told herself, but she asked her mother if she could invite Norah to tea on Sunday.

'Of course, love, if that horrible father will let her come.'

'She's let him think that she and Jack are finished,' Cathy said. 'They couldn't go on the way they were, but they're both determined not to go with anyone else, and to get married as soon as she's old enough to do it without her father's consent.'

'It'll be hard for them,' Sally said, shaking her head.

'They can still pass messages to each other by me and Greg.'

'His mother won't mind him coming here, will she?' said Sally. 'It's the Sunday you're supposed to go there, isn't it?'

'He's not coming here. He's staying with her,' Cathy said. Sally said no more but looked troubled as she glanced at Cathy's flushed face.

Norah had enjoyed more freedom since ostensibly parting from Jack, and was delighted to be invited to Cathy's home for tea on Sunday.

'You look better, love,' Sally told her when she arrived. 'You've got to swim with the tide sometimes.'

Norah smiled but said nothing. Later she told Cathy that her life was not much easier, even though she had agreed not to see Jack. 'They still watch me like hawks,' she said. 'I've only given in for the sake of peace, but I'll finish up with him, you see.'

'Never mind,' Cathy comforted her. 'The years will soon pass, and you'll know you're getting nearer all the time to when you'll be able to marry Jack.'

'I'll never feel the same about me mam, Cathy. I always thought it was the two of us against my dad but she just ganged up with him over this. After the way he's always treated us, too.'

'It's a shame that in a way you've lost her over this. If Jack hadn't been a Catholic you'd never have found out she could be like that.'

'The trouble is, Jack's family are as bitter against us as mine, and he worries so much about his mother. She's always whingeing and saying he's breaking her heart, and he gets real upset about her.'

'It's the same with Greg's mother,' Cathy confided. 'He's so soft with her and always making excuses for her. I can't stand her.'

'Didn't your mam invite her to the wedding? I thought she'd have been there with Greg being best man, and she's such a snob it would've been just her cup of tea.'

'She was invited all right, but she refused,' Cathy said grimly. 'I'm sure it was because she didn't know it was going to be so posh, and I wouldn't tell her anything about it or let Greg. It shouldn't have made any difference.'

'Does she know now?' Norah asked.

'Greg said her friends at the church had told her about it, but of course he wouldn't tell me what *she* said then. He's always covering up for her and giving in to her.'

'You'd think he'd be bitter against her after the way she almost ruined his life.'

'He used to say he was, but he wasn't really. Now, the more I say about her, the more he sticks up for her. We met Florrie who used to look after him when he was little and took her to tea on her afternoon off, and when he was paying the bill she whispered to me that his father had spoiled his mother and I should make sure Greg doesn't do the same.'

'But you think he does?'

'*He* doesn't think so, but really he gives in to her about everything, except about going out with me. We were talking one night, not arguing about her, just talking, and he told me he thought she was a fairy princess when he was little. Florrie used to put him to bed and his mother would come to say goodnight to him before she went out. He went all dreamy telling me about it – about her bending over him, and her clothes and her jewels and her beautiful scent.'

'And not doing a hand's turn for him,' Norah said. 'Sounds to me like Florrie was more his mother.'

'D'you know they sent him away to school when he was seven?'

'Seven,' Norah echoed. 'God, Cath, he wasn't much more than a baby. Think of little Michael Burns – he's seven, isn't he?'

'Greg just laughed about it. He said he was a real cry baby; used to cry every night for Florrie at first.'

'Well, that speaks for itself, doesn't it? If he cried for Florrie not for his mother.'

'He was never long at home after that, really. When he was older, his mother and father were often abroad while he had his school holidays, so he stayed with his aunt and uncle, until his father died and he had to leave school and live with his mother.'

'The cheek of her to expect so much after not bothering about him when he was little!' Norah said indignantly.

'She doesn't think so. She was just sorry for herself, as far as I can make out. She fell out with Greg's uncle because he had to sort things out and sold their house and two of the shops, and got the rooms over the London Road shop fixed up for her. But I think there were so many debts it was the only thing to do.'

'Does Greg ever see his uncle?'

'No. He'd like to, but thinks it would be disloyal to his mother. I'm going to ask him to our wedding, though.'

'What will Lady Redmond think about that?' Norah giggled. 'Perhaps she won't come if they do!'

'I wouldn't care,' Cathy said, 'but I suppose Greg would be upset.' She sighed. 'Things are never straightforward, are they, Norah?'

'They were for Mary,' Norah pointed out.

'Only because Clive had no family,' Cathy said, and they both laughed. Sally called them into the kitchen for tea, but before they went Cathy flung her arms round her friend and hugged her. 'I *have* missed talking to you, Norah,' she said. 'I don't like to talk about Mrs Redmond to Mam, in case it worries her.'

'Don't worry about that horrible woman,' Norah said, hugging Cathy in return. 'Greg's just naturally soft-hearted and she plays on that, but you wouldn't want him any different, would you, Cath?'

'No, I think he's perfect as he is,' she agreed, laughing as they went into the kitchen. It was a cheerful meal and afterwards as they cleared away, Lawrie said to Norah, 'It was a brainwave, you coming to tea today, love. Got us over our first Sunday without Mary.'

'Have you heard from her yet?' Norah asked, and he laughed. 'Not yet,' he said easily. 'But Paris is a long way off and I suppose she's busy enjoying herself. It's a lovely place, by all accounts.'

It was well for Lawrie's peace of mind that he knew nothing of what was happening to Mary in Paris.

Chapter Twenty-Eight

Paris enthralled Mary. She was charmed by its air of gaiety, the blossoming trees, the crowds of elegant people, and their loud, rapid speech.

She squeezed Clive's arm as they drove along a wide boulevard to their hotel. 'Isn't it exciting?' she breathed. 'Isn't it *foreign*?'

He laughed indulgently, pleased to see her so impressed.

Clive had engaged the bridal suite in the luxurious hotel and when they were shown up to it Mary's happiness was complete. There were flowers everywhere, and an ice bucket on the table holding a bottle of champagne: 'Compliments of the Management'.

Clive filled two glasses and they toasted the future before Mary explored the suite. The bedroom was larger than the drawing room, with a bathroom opening from it. Mary exclaimed at the sight of the ornate bath, and Clive demonstrated how the handles above it could make hot water gush from the tap.

They went back to the bedroom and as she stood before the mirror and lifted her arms to remove her hat, Clive put his hands over her breasts. 'That's the most erotic thing a woman can do,' he said, nipping her neck with his teeth.

Mary smiled vaguely, not quite sure what the word erotic meant, but they were interrupted by a knock on the door. The chambermaid stood there. Clive spoke to her in fluent French then turned to Mary. 'She'll unpack for you, and draw your bath,' he said. 'I'll see you later.'

He went out and the woman bobbed her head at Mary and began to unpack her suitcases.

Mary shook her head and shrugged when the woman spoke to her, to indicate that she spoke no French, but she was able to indicate which clothes she intended to wear and they were laid out on the bed. When the chambermaid had gone Mary locked herself in the bathroom and luxuriated in the warm, scented water of the bath.

Clive returned just in time to dress for dinner, and later heads turned as they swept into the dining room to be shown deferentially to their table by the head waiter. Mary glanced around the dining room at the elegant women and well-dressed men then at the reflection of herself and Clive in a nearby mirror. *None of them make such a handsome couple as us,* she thought complacently.

She felt that nothing now could mar her happiness and pride in her new husband. She looked forward to their first night together, knowing that she enjoyed making love and confident that she could convince Clive that she was a virgin by pretending to be nervous and shocked. *It was all like a beautiful dream,* she thought, not knowing how soon the dream would become a nightmare.

She went up to their suite before Clive and was in bed wearing her prettiest nightdress when he arrived. He had been drinking steadily all evening. His face was red and his eyes glittered as he lurched over to the bed.

'You can get that off,' he said thickly, pulling at the neck of her nightdress. He began to throw off his own clothes and then leaned over her again. 'Get it off, I said,' he snarled.

She turned her head in disgust at the smell of his breath and this seemed to infuriate him further. He tore furiously at her nightdress then turned away and fumbled in a box in the drawer, while Mary slipped out of her torn nightdress, keeping herself modestly covered by the sheet and averting her eyes from his naked body.

He turned back to her, holding a leather strap in his hand.

'Might as well begin as we mean to go on,' he said with a throaty laugh.

When Mary looked back on the night that followed, her main feeling was one of disbelief. How could the urbane, well-mannered man turn into this obscene creature, grunting and dribbling as he attacked her? Why had she never suspected what lurked beneath that gentlemanly appearance?

Towards morning he fell asleep and she crept from the bed into the bathroom and locked the door. She was too agitated to try to select the right handles to fill the bath, but ran water into the washbowl and began frantically to wash her body.

His teeth had drawn blood on her neck and shoulders and breast, and she could feel the stinging weals on her back and buttocks, but the pain meant nothing to her. It was the feeling of being soiled and degraded that made her wash herself over and over again.

Her hands, she thought, and her mouth… At the memory she turned and vomited into the lavatory then turned back to the washbowl to scrub obsessively at her hands and to rinse out her mouth and even rub soap on her tongue. Would she ever feel clean again?

She crept into the bedroom to gather some clothes and dressed herself with trembling hands. Afterwards she crept through the bedroom to sit huddled in a chair in the drawing room, trembling and shaking. What can I do? What can I do? she thought distractedly, but was too upset and agitated to think clearly. She could only crouch in the chair, thoughts tumbling chaotically round her mind.

Dada, Dada. She wept as she thought of her father and wondered whether to send him a telegram but she rejected the thought immediately. No one must know. She couldn't bear them to know.

A sound at the bedroom door made her crouch even lower in the chair, then she heard the chink of china and Clive's voice speaking in French. She heard the bedroom door close, then Clive began to call her name with more and more impatience.

Eventually she went to the connecting door, keeping her eyes averted from the sight of him sitting up in bed, holding a cup.

'Oh, there you are,' he said offhandedly. 'Coffee?' She shook her head, still keeping her head averted, and crept back to the chair.

A little later she heard the sound of water running and then splashing as Clive took his bath, but she could only huddle in the chair, feeling that this must all be just a dreadful dream from which she would soon awaken.

He came to the door of the drawing room, impeccably dressed and showing no sign of the excesses of the night. To Mary this made everything even more unreal. How could he look so ordinary? she thought wildly. But he said in his normal, pleasant voice, 'Come along, Mary. Don't be silly.'

He pulled a gold watch from his pocket and snapped it open. 'Breakfast time,' he said. 'Make yourself presentable.'

Even the thought of food made her feel sick, and she dashed to the bathroom, retching and vomiting, then scrubbing out her mouth. How could she ever bear to put food in her mouth again? she thought.

Clive made an impatient gesture. 'Come along,' he repeated.

'I can't,' Mary whimpered, but he came to the bathroom door and said with a steely note in his voice, 'Wash your face and make yourself presentable, *at once*.' Mary found herself meekly obeying him.

Mechanically she washed her face and brushed and pinned her hair. The mirror showed how pale she was, with dark shadows under her eyes and with bite marks showing on her neck above her dress. With shaking hands she tied a scarf about her neck to hide them.

'That's better,' Clive said approvingly, and took her elbow as they went down to the dining room. She shuddered at his touch but walked meekly beside him and sat down at the table.

Her thoughts were still too confused and the struggle to contain her nausea too great to allow her to pay any attention to others in the room, but urged by Clive she eventually managed to drink a cup of coffee.

They were about to rise from the table when the reality of her situation suddenly became clear to Mary, and she was overcome with a feeling of such shock and horror that she shook until her teeth chattered.

Clive leaned over the table. 'Pull yourself together,' he said, in the steely tone he had used earlier, and once again Mary obeyed him. He escorted her back to their rooms, then left her, saying pleasantly, 'Dress yourself suitably, my dear. We'll drive round the sights of Paris, then after lunch – perhaps some shopping?'

Mary had walked beside him with her teeth clenched, holding herself rigidly and feeling that any sudden movement would make her break apart. Alone in the rooms she realised that her body was drenched in perspiration and her clothes were clinging to her, so she washed then changed her dress for one with a high-boned neckline.

Clive smiled approvingly when he returned. 'Excellent, my dear,' he said, and once again they walked through the public rooms of the hotel. Mary glanced about her furtively, noticing that many of the women wore dresses with high necklines or scarves about their throats. Was it just fashion, she wondered, or did these women too have to suffer misery and degradation from their outwardly civilised husbands?

She still shrank from any contact with him and in the carriage drew as far away from him as possible.

'You're being ridiculous,' he said coolly. 'Behaving like an ignorant child. It's time to grow up.'

A flash of her old spirit came back to Mary. 'That's not growing up,' she said. 'It's being degraded.'

'Nonsense,' he said. 'The girls in Estelle's think nothing of it.' He laughed at her puzzled face. 'Estelle's, my dear, is a high-class Liverpool brothel. You didn't imagine I returned to my celibate couch while you paraded your maidenly scruples, did you?'

Mary sat in stunned silence. What next? she thought. How many more shocks were to come? She saw nothing of the sights of Paris as they drove on, but Clive recovered his good humour and became once again the pleasant urbane man she had known in Liverpool.

Later as they walked through the beautiful shops Mary began to wonder if she was going mad. She caught sight of their reflections in a window, a handsome, well-dressed man with an elegant woman on his arm. We look so *respectable*, she thought wildly. Did I dream that last night? Am I losing my mind?

Clive bought her handkerchiefs and perfume, and treated her with the courtesy and consideration he had shown her since they met, and she began to wonder if the behaviour of the previous night had been caused by a temporary brainstorm. Her hope was in vain.

Mary sometimes felt that the most frightening aspect of her life during the next few weeks was that she never knew what to expect from Clive. During the day his behaviour was irreproachable, and he gave no indication of what would happen at night.

Sometimes, to her relief, he would be absent for most of the night gambling, and several times he came to bed at the normal time then simply wished her goodnight and fell asleep.

Many other nights, though, were a repetition of the first, sometimes revealing yet more horrors for Mary to endure. Nothing availed her against Clive when he was in this mood. To struggle against him only encouraged him, and tears and entreaties were ignored.

They had been married for nearly three weeks when one night she found a chink in his armour and nearly paid for it with her life. Mary could neither eat nor sleep and she had become thin and pale, all her bright beauty dimmed, but she had begun to recover from the first shock and to think more coherently.

In her first confused state she had thought that other men in the hotel behaved as Clive did, and that she was merely an ignorant girl out of her depth among sophisticated people. Now she realised that was not true. Clive was the one who was different, a madman who was cunning enough to play the part of a civilised man during the day and revert to his true self only at night.

This thought was in her mind when she was enduring yet another night of suffering and humiliation. When he put his face close to hers and began to whisper obscenities, she hit back at him. 'You're a pervert,' she screamed. 'A filthy pervert.'

The next moment his hands were round her throat and he was shaking her violently. 'Don't say it, don't say it!' he yelled. 'Don't call me that.' His hands tightened viciously around her throat and she could feel herself choking and the blood pounding ever louder in her head. She tried to pull feebly at his hands but the relentless pressure increased and her eyes seemed to be starting from her head. Then she felt as though she was falling into a pit.

The next thing she was aware of was being held in Clive's arms while he said urgently, 'Mary! Mary darling, open your eyes.' But she could only make strange crowing noises as she tried to gulp air into her lungs.

'Mary, Mary,' Clive kept repeating in a distraught voice. 'Forgive me, forgive me.' Her tongue felt enormous and she still fought for breath, but she managed to open her eyes. Clive wept with relief.

Mary leaned back, supported by his arm, feeling weak and dizzy while he mumbled 'My father – forgive me. Bad blood.' She closed her eyes again and lay as though in a dream while he poured out all the details of his childhood and of his life since then.

His mother had committed suicide when he was two, he told her, and various other women had lived briefly with his father until one more depraved than the rest had stayed with him. Clive talked of what had happened to him at their hands but fortunately for Mary she kept drifting off into unconsciousness and so missed hearing of most of these incidents.

During one of her conscious spells she heard him speak of Toronto as a staid place, but too hot to hold him. Too hot, she thought muzzily before drifting off again, and when she became fully conscious Clive was telling her that his uncle's death had come just in time to save him. He had come to England determined to make a fresh start and live a decent life. 'I want respect, Mary,' he wept. 'I want people to look up to me.'

She who had shrunk away from him in revulsion ever since their wedding night found herself feebly lifting her hand to stroke his cheek and comfort him. She was still unable to speak and when Clive had fallen into an exhausted sleep she lay wondering with terror if she would ever speak again.

He woke when the morning coffee arrived. Mary tried to drink but her tongue seemed to fill her mouth and her throat to have closed up. There was no question of her being able to rise. She lay back weakly upon the pillows.

Clive was quiet and subdued. He bathed and dressed, then gently sponged Mary's face and brushed her hair. Afterwards he dressed her in a nightdress and peignoir. When the chambermaid came he told her that Madame was unwell, and lifted Mary into an armchair while the woman changed the bed.

Mary looked on dreamily as Clive talked in a low voice to the Frenchwoman and money changed hands. The chambermaid swiftly tidied the room and left, and Clive bent over Mary and lifted her back to bed. 'She's going to bring something to ease your throat and help you to sleep. Can you speak at all?'

She opened her mouth but no sound came. She stared up at him, her eyes wide with fear. 'It's all right,' he soothed her. 'You'll be better shortly.' Fortunately the chambermaid returned at that moment holding a feeding cup with steam rising from it, and an ice pack.

She raised Mary's head and dribbled some of the liquid through the spout of the feeding cup into her mouth. In dumb show, the maid urged her to swallow. The effort brought tears to Mary's eyes but at last she managed to swallow the liquid and the woman patiently fed the rest of the drink into her mouth, and then applied the ice pack to her throat.

Both women ignored Clive who hung about the bed for a while then went into the drawing room of the suite. The chambermaid wrapped a towel about the ice pack, and Mary patted her hand in gratitude. The woman made consoling murmurs and gently stroked her hair back from her forehead.

She was still there when Mary drifted off into sleep, and throughout the day came back as often as her duties allowed to bring soothing drinks and try to make Mary comfortable.

Clive spent most of the day either in the bedroom or the drawing room of the suite, but towards evening Mary managed to croak 'Go – dinner. I'll sleep.' She closed her eyes and when she opened them again Clive had dressed for dinner and was standing beside the bed. 'Are you sure you'll be all right?' he said. 'Ring if you need anything.'

Mary nodded and he left. A little later the chambermaid returned. This time she had brought thin creamy soup in the feeding cup, and now Mary found it easier to swallow. She had established a system of sign language with the chambermaid now, and when the woman pointed to Mary's wedding ring she realised that she wished to know if they were really married. She pointed to the drawer and the woman lifted out the certificate that lay there. She was unable to read the words but clearly understood what it was. She shrugged and flung out her hands palms uppermost, looking pityingly at Mary. She tried to ask for the photograph which also lay in the drawer and at last the woman understood and brought it to her.

It had been taken some years earlier when her father had decided to use his overtime pay on a studio photograph of the family – partly, Mary suspected, to help the young photographer who was struggling to establish himself.

The photograph showed Lawrie in his Sunday suit, sitting on a chair with Sally standing beside him with her hand on his shoulder, and Mary and Cathy sitting at their feet. They had all stared sternly at the camera, Mary remembered, until her father had looked up at her mother and said, 'It's not a hanging matter, Sal.'

They had all laughed until the photographer had said chidingly: 'Compose yourselves, please. Keep perfectly still.' They had obeyed but traces of a smile showed on her father's face and Cathy's dimples were still in evidence.

Now Mary's tears flowed as she remembered the occasion and looked at the simple goodness in her parents' faces. The chambermaid passed Mary a handkerchief then pointed to Sally and Lawrie, saying, 'Papa?' Maman?' Mary nodded and the woman said something which Mary was unable to understand. She tried to smile, and a little later the chambermaid left.

Mary felt that her mind was functioning normally for the first time since her wedding night. She made herself look back and try to make sense of all that had happened since she met Clive.

Her memories of the previous night were hazy, but she remembered enough of his revelations to know that the image of a perfect gentleman he had presented in England was very different to the man he had been in Canada. In Paris the mask had slipped.

Clive seemed to have come to England determined to make a fresh start and to live as the respectable members of his family had lived, but Mary could only guess at what his life in Canada had been. He had evidently been ill used as a child, particularly by his father, and seemed to fear that he had inherited his father's bad blood.

Was that why he had reacted so violently when she had called him a pervert? Mary wondered. Had someone else used that name to him and did he fear that it was the truth? And I'm married to him, she thought with horror, tied to him for life.

She wept for a while then tried to compose herself and think clearly. Why had Clive married her? She had been so sure that he was attracted to her in Liverpool and he had treated her so well that she believed that he loved her, but how could he have abused and degraded her if he loved her?

Her head ached and when the chambermaid appeared with another soothing concoction she drank it gratefully and almost immediately fell into a deep sleep. When she woke the following morning she felt much better and was able to make her way very shakily to the bathroom.

She carried her hand mirror back to bed with her and examined herself. Her face was less swollen but there were still swellings under each eye and her throat was extensively bruised. Her lips too were cracked and swollen and it was obvious that she was unfit to appear in public even if she felt well enough. When Clive woke he was quiet and nervous, looking away from her damaged face as he asked how she felt.

Mary replied that she felt better, and suddenly realised that she was, not only physically but almost free of the revulsion and loathing she had felt for Clive. She had always had the ability to pull down a shutter over anything she wished to forget, and now she made a determined effort to shut out from her mind all that had happened in that room.

The fright will have cured him, she told herself optimistically. Seeing him looking and behaving like the man of their courtship days made it easier for her to convince herself.

When the chambermaid appeared he had another low-voiced conversation with her before leaving the room. Then the woman helped Mary to wash herself and change her nightdress, before going for her breakfast tray.

While she was away Mary made her way to the dressing table. Every night Clive emptied the contents of his pockets on the end of the dressing table, and while he slept Mary had quietly filched some of the money. When he had been gambling there had always been sovereigns and half sovereigns there as well as French money, and although Mary had started by taking only one half sovereign, she had grown more daring when she realised that he only swept the money back into his pocket each morning without looking at it.

Now she had about twenty pounds wrapped in a handkerchief in the drawer and she took out two sovereigns for the maid. The woman refused it, pointing at Clive's side of the bed, then at herself, then stroking her palm to indicate that he had paid her.

Mary thankfully returned the money to its hiding place, and the maid drew out a photograph from under the bib of her apron. It was of a small boy in a white suit holding a prayer book. Mary thought he looked remarkably ugly with his dark hair growing low on his forehead, and his ears standing out like jug handles, but she made admiring noises and gestures and the woman smiled proudly.

Mary stayed in the suite for the rest of the time they remained in Paris, but before they left Clive brought her some postcards with views of Notre Dame to send home. She wrote to her mother, apologising for not writing sooner and saying that she had been ill.

'It was probably the French cooking,' she wrote. 'Everything is covered in strange sauces, and you can't even drink the water from the taps. I long for your scouse, Mam.'

She signed the letter and sat thinking of home, her throat tight with tears. Suddenly she dipped the pen in the ink again.

'I love you and miss you all very much. Fondest love, Mary,' scrawled at the bottom of the letter.

At least her mother would be prepared to see her looking thin and pale, she thought. The maid had continued to bring her food that could be easily swallowed and the drinks that made her sleep at night, and Mary asked Clive if she could make her a gift to show her gratitude.

'Sure, honey,' he said. 'Whatever you give her I'll buy you another. I've given her money.' Mary finally decided to give her a fox fur she had admired when she was unpacking.

Mary owed the woman more than she realised. In all that had befallen her the loss of her self-esteem had been the factor which nearly destroyed her. All her life she had been accustomed to admiration and affection.

She had always had a good opinion of herself, reinforced by the many men who had admired her and by Sam's constant, unquestioning devotion. Her mother might warn that 'Pride goes before a fall', but Mary knew that her mother, father, and Cathy were all proud of her beauty and elegance, and believed that only the best was good enough for her.

Mary believed it too. Even her experiences at Bella's party and with the coarse young man had not altered her mental image of herself, but only convinced her that she was a sophisticated young woman who knew how to deal with the sleazy side of life.

Confident of her power to charm, she had accepted her conquest of Clive and ignored any warning signs that he was not all he seemed.

It had been a tremendous shock to her to see herself as a silly ignorant girl who knew nothing of real life or real evil. A creature to be used contemptuously by a sadistic man and have her own feelings ignored, with no power to change the situation.

She had reached the lowest depths of misery and self-contempt when the maid's kindness, her cries of admiration as she brushed Mary's hair and her obvious belief that she was a great lady had restored her pride and belief in herself.

There was a subtle change too in her relationship with Clive. With the memory of his distress on the night that he had almost killed her, and of his concern for her since, Mary was gradually able to convince herself that he truly loved her, and that he was simply a victim of his circumstances and nature.

While she slowly recovered he showered her with gifts of fruit and sweets, and brought her flowers: once a bunch of violets encircled with an amethyst bracelet, and another time orchids with a diamond brooch pinned to them.

With her return to health her buoyant spirits also returned and she was able to shut out of her mind some of her unpleasant experiences and regard the future with cautious optimism.

Chapter Twenty-Nine

It was a beautiful day when they left Paris, and the sun was shining as they arrived at the house in Neston. They were warmly welcomed by the caretaker's wife, who was now acting as housekeeper and anxious to retain that position.

Clive had brought lavish gifts for Mary to give her family and she was impatient to visit them. It was arranged that they should go on the following day, but when they reached Liverpool Clive changed his mind. 'I'll put you in a cab,' he said. 'I've got business in Liverpool, honey.'

She was not sorry. She wanted to give her mother a carefully edited version of her honeymoon, and she knew she would find it easier if Clive was not there.

She spent a happy day. The family were delighted with the gifts she brought and impressed by her new fur coat and her jewellery, and Mary's confidence flowered. They were all shocked to see how thin she had become, but accepted her explanation that it was because of the French food. Her mother urged her to eat.

'Did you hear much talk of war?' her father asked.

'Not really,' Mary said. 'Of course, I couldn't understand the language anyway.'

'You'd have heard it in this kitchen,' her mother said, banging the teapot down on the stand. 'Your father and Greg talk of nothing else.'

'Do you think there'll be war then?' Mary asked, but her father shook his head. 'No, love. There's been war talk for years, but they're all just bluffing each other.'

Although Mary enjoyed her day she felt that she was looking at her home with new eyes. How small and crowded the kitchen seemed, how thick the cups and how comfortless the chairs and sofa. It was hard to believe that she had only been away for a month.

Even the family looked different. Her mother looked smaller and older with streaks of grey in her brown hair and shoulders rounded from hours spent at the sewing machine.

Her father's hair was almost completely grey now although still thick, and Mary noticed how calloused and work-worn his hands looked as he filled his pipe. This couldn't have happened in a month, Mary thought. It must have been happening gradually and she had been unaware of it.

Cathy seemed different too, more mature and confident, taking the teapot from her mother and urging her to sit down. Sally noticed Mary's glance and said with a smile, 'She's getting proper bossy, this one, since you went, Mary. Always telling me to rest.'

'You don't take any notice though,' Cathy said. 'Of me *or* Dad.' She turned to Mary. 'Mam tries to do as much sewing and keep the house the same although she's in Southport three days a week. She'll make herself ill.'

'But I don't want anyone put out because I'm out so often,' Sally said.

'Nobody's put out, Mam,' Cathy protested. 'The important thing is visiting Aunt Emily.'

'That's right,' Lawrie said. 'It does Emily good, and eases your mind, love. And the rest – well, people can wait for their sewing.'

'But you and Cathy. The house and the meals—' Sally began.

Lawrie interrupted her. 'The house isn't getting dirty while we're all out,' he said. 'And food – I'd eat a horse between blankets, you know that, and our Cathy doesn't know whether she's eating or not while she's thinking of Greg.'

They laughed and Mary said quickly, 'How is Aunt Emily?'

Her mother sighed. 'The mild winter helped her,' she said. 'And now, with the good weather, I'm hoping she'll pick up. She's happy in that nursing home anyway.'

Mary looked round the kitchen. 'I feel as though I've been away for years,' she said. 'Anything else happened?'

'Mr Finestone died in his sleep two weeks ago. I'm glad it happened like that. He was such a good old man.'

'What happens now with the business?' Mary said.

'The eldest son, Hymie, has taken over. He's all right but nothing like his father,' Cathy said.

'And how is Tinkerbell?' Mary asked.

Cathy smiled ruefully. 'I've managed not to strangle her so far,' she said, 'but any day now.'

Then, as her mother looked up in surprise, she said quickly, 'Only a joke, Mam, about Mrs Redmond.'

It was Greg's late night at the shop but he arrived a little later and Mary felt a familiar pang as she looked at him, intensified by the knowledge that she was tied for life to Clive. She gave no sign though, and when she left felt that they were all convinced that she was perfectly happy.

For the first few days in her new home she watched Clive carefully, hoping that the part of a cultured gentleman he was playing would rule out any further attacks, but it was not to be.

His next assault on her was as sadistic and degrading as anything that she had endured in Paris, and the following morning she crawled from bed and huddled over the fire in the bedroom.

'Tell the housekeeper I'm not well,' she mumbled, keeping her face turned away from him. 'You'll have to cancel the dinner party at the Bagshaws'.'

'I don't intend to do that,' he said. 'I don't want to ruffle Bagshaw's feathers. Get yourself ready for this evening.'

Mary looked up in surprise then looked away again, saying nothing. At six o'clock in the evening she was preparing for the dinner party.

All her evening dresses were low-cut and would expose the marks on her neck and breasts, and her eyes were swollen with crying, but she draped a lacy shawl about her shoulders.

'I'll keep the shawl on,' she told her hostess when her coat was taken. 'I've got such a dreadful cold. Perhaps we shouldn't have come but we wanted so much to see you.'

Clive gave her a nod of approval but she turned away from him with her head in the air, wondering why he needed to be on good terms with his solicitor. There were many occasions during the next few months when Mary found it necessary to conceal the evidence of his brutality, but while she had new clothes and jewellery to flaunt she felt that none of her acquaintances suspected the truth.

She was less sure of her parents' views about her marriage. Her mother often looked anxiously at her but she only spoke about Mary's thinness and urged her to eat when she visited home.

They were all secretly worried about her although none of them admitted it. Clive had not been to Egremont Street since their marriage, but Lawrie had twice seen him in Liverpool without her. The first time, as he drove past on his wagon, Clive was turning into a doorway with a young man holding his elbow.

The second time Lawrie was on foot, taking a short cut through Lime Street Station, and saw Clive on the platform of the London train with a smartly dressed woman. They boarded the train before he could obtain a platform ticket and go through to accost Clive, but he was determined to challenge him about it at the first opportunity. Meanwhile, he worried constantly about Mary.

Cathy also worried about her. She had noticed Mary's hectic gaiety in company, and her sad expression when she thought she was unobserved, and grieved to think that all was not well with her sister. Cathy missed her, particularly at night, and still found it strange to wake and not hear Mary's soft breathing or see her head on the pillow.

She missed being able to talk about Mrs Redmond to Mary and to listen to her confidences. It was not a happy time for Cathy in other ways.

Finestone's workroom, where there had always been harmony in the old man's time, was now a place of discord as Hymie introduced new methods of payment and systems of working. 'Anything to squeeze another farthing,' one of the men grumbled to Cathy. 'More work and less pay for all of us.' She could only agree.

Every day there was someone in tears or someone walking out in disgust, until she began to dread going in to work. When she came home things were not much better. Her mother visited Southport three times a week, but Emily's health was failing rapidly and Cathy found it hard to comfort her mother.

If she went next door there was trouble there too. Jimmie Burns and his eldest son were at loggerheads, and Peggy was worried not only about that but about the girl that Robbie was courting, and Mabel's boy friend. Most of all she worried about seven-year-old Michael, and Cathy could say little to cheer her when she looked at the pale, thin child lying listlessly on the sofa.

Norah's father had been told that she had been seen with Jack Carmody and had come home and beaten her up.

'I wouldn't care if it was true,' Norah said to Cathy. 'At least we'd have had the pleasure of meeting, but Jack's afraid to meet me in case it gets back to his mother, the crying cow! She's like one of them snakes that crush men to death.'

Cathy walked home thinking of Norah's words and feeling that she could say the same about Mrs Redmond. She seemed to be tightening her grip on Greg all the time, but he had become so defensive whenever they spoke of his mother that Cathy felt that the subject was taboo.

It was impossible for them to make wedding plans as these depended on Greg making enough money to set his mother up in her own house, but she was spending money faster than he was able to save it, and Greg seemed powerless to stop her.

Cathy had spoken so bitterly about Mrs Redmond when Greg complained of her extravagance that now he said nothing about it, but Cathy knew that his mother was still travelling about spending money on cures for her imaginary ailments, and her own feelings were even more bitter because she had to hide them.

She could have talked to Mary and comforted herself by poking fun at Mrs Redmond, but without her there was only her mother or Norah. She was unwilling to worry her mother and felt that Norah blamed Greg. 'If he was half a man he'd stand up to his mother,' she'd said once, and Cathy was hurt.

'It's not as simple as that,' she said stiffly. 'Greg feels responsible for his mother. Anyway, Mam says a good son makes a good husband, so I should be all right.'

Cathy said little more to Norah about Mrs Redmond, but she often thought of her words, and wondered with shame at her disloyalty if perhaps they were true. Why did Greg not simply refuse to let his mother spend money that he could not afford? He was too intelligent to be fooled by the excuses she gave for her expensive holidays.

Cathy saw her less frequently now but whenever they met Mrs Redmond criticised the Suffragettes. She ignored Cathy's explanation that she was a Suffragist and disliked violence and continued to talk about the Suffragettes, managing to slide an insult to Cathy into the conversation.

Even though it was now twelve months since the Suffragette Emily Davison had flung herself at the King's horse at the 1913 Derby and been killed, Mrs Redmond still harped on it.

'I hope no one will copy that woman's behaviour this year, Catherine,' she said. 'What a way to go to meet your Maker, and what a shock for the dear King.'

'There are plenty of people who should be afraid to meet their Maker,' Cathy said, 'because of their spitefulness and selfishness.' But Mrs Redmond went on unheeding, in her sweet piping voice, 'Ladies who damage property and then complain about being sent to jail should be ashamed of themselves.'

'What about the Cat and Mouse Act?' Cathy said hotly. 'Ill treating women in jail until they're broken, then sending them home to recover, only to drag them back and start again.'

'All their own fault,' Mrs Redmond said. 'And such a bad example to show to the lower classes, especially to girls who have never known a Christian home.'

Cathy glanced at Greg who had stood by looking embarrassed but saying nothing. She knew that it was useless to argue with Mrs Redmond about her spite because she would always protest that she had been misunderstood, but she felt that Greg should have tried, even at the risk of making matters worse.

When they were alone neither of them spoke about it, but the barrier between them grew. Altogether it was an unhappy summer for Cathy in spite of the glorious weather, but in later years she looked back with regret and wished that she had ignored the pinpricks and enjoyed the last summer before war changed all their lives.

It was a strange summer for Sally, too, as she divided her time between her sick sister in Southport and her home in Liverpool.

'Your husband must be an easy man,' the Matron remarked to Sally on one of her frequent visits, and when she met Lawrie she was charmed by him. Lawrie, Cathy and Greg visited Emily but they were only free on Sundays and Albert paid his duty visit on Sunday afternoon so they had to scheme to avoid him. Lawrie had never seen Albert again since the interview about Bronwen, and had no wish to, he told Sally.

The visits to Emily were useful as face-saving excuses to Sally's neighbours for the rarity of Mary's visits home, and the lack of invitations to visit her and Clive. The family had only been twice to Neston.

The first time Clive met them at the ferry in his Maxwell motor car, and drove them to the house at such a reckless speed that Sally was terrified. Always nervous in motor cars, she had clung to Lawrie's arm and the side of the car, and been relieved when Clive disappeared after tea, and they could return to the ferry by bus. On their next visit Clive was away from home, 'on business' Mary told them, and they enjoyed their trip far more.

'I'm glad he's looking after the business, whatever it is,' Sally said to Lawrie later. 'They seem to spend money like water.'

Mary told her parents of the many invitations they received from families who had entertained Clive in his bachelor days, but said nothing about the way he abandoned her at these gatherings and flirted with other women. Nor did she tell them how often Clive disappeared for days at a time on his mysterious 'business trips'.

Shortly after they had returned from Paris he had taken her on shopping trips to London and Chester, but these had not been repeated. Mary preferred the business trips, as they meant that she could be sure of several nights free of him, and he always left money for her and brought her lavish gifts.

She wondered about the trips sometimes, especially when an effeminate young man appeared in the garden one day and greeted Clive aggressively. Her husband hurried him down the garden, obviously trying to soothe him. She could still hear the young man's voice raised in peevish anger, but later they reappeared, smiling, and drove off in Clive's motor car.

He offered no explanation when he reappeared, but a few weeks later Mary wandered down the garden and surprised Clive with the new young gardener. They were sitting with their faces close together and Clive's hand lay on the boy's thigh. They jumped guiltily to their feet when she arrived.

'Oh, Clive,' she said appearing to notice nothing. 'Do you mind if I invite Elizabeth Fairburn on Sunday?'

'No. Do as you like,' he said gruffly, turning away from her. Mary walked back to the house with her mind in a whirl. He *couldn't* be! Not a man who could behave as he did with her. Surely a man must be one thing or the other? But when Elizabeth came to visit, she was able to enlighten her friend.

Mary talked about her new neighbours and acquaintances, and slipped in a tale of one man who seemed like a 'nancy boy', yet his wife had whispered that he was a perfect lover.

Elizabeth had many friends at the College of Art where she hoped to enrol in September, some of them with very advanced ideas and Mary knew that she had learned a great deal from them.

Now she told Mary with a worldly wise air that such a situation was quite possible. 'A man can love both men and women with different sides of his nature. One of the girls has a book by Freud called *The Interpretation of Dreams*. It would really surprise you, Mary.'

'I doubt it,' she murmured. She felt that she was past being surprised by anything. But even more now, the prospect of a lifetime tied to Clive filled her with terror and revulsion.

She made excuses to avoid visiting Egremont Street, feeling that no matter how beautifully dressed or prosperous she appeared to be, her mother knew her too well not to guess that she was unhappy.

There was another reason too. When she saw Cathy and Greg together she was filled with bitterness. Why should things always go right for her sister? She thought of the days when she might have charmed Greg away from Cathy and told herself that she had been a fool not to, conveniently forgetting that she had tried and failed.

During the happy days of her engagement Mary had managed to crush down her feelings for Greg, but when she met him again after her return from Paris she was dismayed by the tide of love and longing for him that swept over her.

He had given her a brotherly kiss in greeting and she had pressed her lips hungrily against his. But he appeared to notice nothing and treated her with quiet friendliness.

Mary kept stealing glances at him and comparing him with Clive, as she had once compared Greg with the weedy Sam Glover. She looked at his thin, sensitive features, his pleasant smile and air of quiet strength, and thought with distaste of Clive's showy good looks and bulky figure. Particularly she compared Clive's full moist lips with Greg's firm mouth, and felt she could scream with pain.

Cathy seemed to be staring at her, she thought, and wondered whether she had betrayed her feelings. It would be better to keep away from her old home, she decided.

Cathy's glance had nothing to do with suspicion. She was only thinking that her sister had changed, and wondering if Mary had noticed that she and Greg said nothing about their wedding plans.

It was true that Mary had changed. She had lost the air of happy confidence which, combined with her beauty, had charmed all who knew her. Now the strain of her life showed in her tightened lips and the anxious expression in her blue eyes. Uncertainty over Clive's behaviour, the fear of his brutal assaults and the nights when she lay sleepless in bed hoping that he was away for the night, almost destroyed her.

Before her marriage she had felt slightly nervous about taking her place in Wirral society, although she felt her experience in the homes of Isabel and Elizabeth, and the time spent with her Aunt Emily, would be helpful.

Now it was not etiquette that worried her, but explaining Clive's absences when they were invited out or his behaviour when he accompanied her. Once he even disappeared and left her to be taken home by her host.

The unmarried Mary, quick-witted and plausible, would have carried off many situations which now left her distressed and embarrassed, and caused raised eyebrows and pitying looks among her new neighbours and friends.

Often Mary longed to ask Clive if he thought that this was the way to win the respect he had told her he wanted, but she was too afraid of him to ask.

Mary had noticed nothing of the constraint between her sister and Greg, but Cathy wondered how long she could bear to go on avoiding all mention of Greg's mother, or of plans for the future.

She rarely visited Mrs Redmond now but knew that Greg's mother was determined to do all she could to delay or prevent their marriage. Any discussion of his mother seemed to lead to a row between them or to tears from Cathy and an angry silence on Greg's part, and she felt that she was beginning to hate his mother. It was worse because she had to bottle up her feelings out of loyalty to Greg, and a reluctance to worry her own mother.

On the day after Mary's visit Cathy had stayed up late with Sally, helping to finish a sewing order which was wanted in a hurry.

'You're a great help to me, Cath,' she remarked. 'I don't know what I'll do when you're married.'

'Aye, *when*!' Cathy said bitterly before she could stop herself, and suddenly she found herself telling her mother all her worries. 'Greg is too soft with her, I know,' she said, 'but I can understand. Sometimes I feel I hate her, but I feel sorry for her too in a way. It must be awful to be a widow, and even if her ailments are imaginary I suppose that's an illness really and maybe she can't help her nature.'

As usual, Sally went right to the heart of the problem.

'You think Greg should put his foot down and be harder, but if he was tough and hard he wouldn't be Greg, Cath. If he was more like his mother he'd be better able to deal with her, but would you want him to be like that, love?'

'No. Indeed I wouldn't,' she exclaimed.

'There you are then. Greg probably takes after his father and those sort of gentle, soft-hearted men are no match for harpies like Mrs Redmond. She's struck lucky, of course, because you're just the same.'

'*I* am?' Cathy exclaimed.

'Of course you are. Our Mary would have waded in to that woman long ago. Made the wedding plans and told her to like it or lump it – and made Greg unhappy at the same time.'

Cathy looked up in surprise and her mother smiled at her.

'As God made you he matched you, as Mrs Mal would say, so don't let that faggot come between you, Cath.'

Sally prided herself on never interfering in other people's lives, but she felt that something should be done to spoil Mrs Redmond's tactics and a few days later Fate played into her hands.

She was walking up from the station after staying late at Southport when she met Greg on his way to see Cathy. They spoke about Emily and Mary, then Sally said casually, 'Mary was asking about your wedding plans but I said you and Cathy are thinking of a long engagement.'

Greg's face grew red. 'No longer than we can help, Mrs Ward,' he said. 'But I'd – er – I'll have to fix something up for my mother. Cathy and I would rather be on our own.'

'I think you're right, Greg. No matter how little you have to start with, you're better on your own.' Sally said.

'It's difficult though, Mrs Ward. You see Mother would need a house in a good neighbourhood, and fairly large because of her furniture, so I'll need to save a lot and it's a slow business. There are so many expenses.'

'Why doesn't your mother stay over the shop where she's settled with her own furniture, and you and Cathy get a little house? Anything would do you for the time being as long as it was near the shop, wouldn't it?'

Greg stopped dead, and she walked on a few steps then turned back, smiling.

'I must be daft!' he exclaimed. 'Why didn't I think of that? It would solve everything.'

'Cathy didn't think of it either, did she? Sometimes, someone outside can see things a bit clearer.'

'Mother didn't think of it either,' Greg said. 'She *does* want us to marry, Mrs Ward. It's just that things seemed so difficult.'

'Yes, I'm sure,' Sally said. She hesitated then added quietly, 'Whatever you decide, Greg, I wouldn't discuss it with your mother until you get things sorted out. No need to worry her too soon.'

He agreed and they smiled at each other with understanding before going into the house. Greg was out again within minutes with Cathy, eager to tell her of her mother's suggestion.

Sally's ambiguous phrase about 'not worrying Mrs Redmond too soon' was useful in making it easy for them to discuss Greg's mother, and the restraint of the past few weeks vanished as they excitedly made plans.

With all these preoccupations none of them paid much attention to outside. Greg and Lawrie discussed the rumours of imminent war, but Lawrie dismissed them. He thought there would be civil war in Ireland but that war with Germany was unlikely.

'They sailed as close to the wind as they're likely to with that business in Agadir,' he told Greg. 'That's when we would have gone to war if we were going to.'

'What was that, Dad?' asked Cathy. 'I don't remember it.'

'It was just before the 1911 strike, love, so we had more on our minds at the time,' Lawrie said. 'The Germans sent a gunboat to Morocco, but Lloyd George gave a speech at the Mansion House about it and they backed off.'

Even when Germany declared war on Russia on August 1st then entered Luxembourg the next day and presented a twelve-hour ultimatum to Belgium, Lawrie believed that they were bluffing and would still draw back from war with Britain.

Chapter Thirty

August Bank Holiday was a beautiful, sunny day and Cathy and Greg rode to Thurstaton on their bicycles. They preferred to go out together now instead of with the group, and rode down secluded lanes to their favourite spot. It was a sloping stretch of turf, dotted with wild flowers and aromatic plants, shielded on one side by a low wall and on the other by gorse bushes.

There they lay in each other's arms, breathing the scented air and listening to the birdsong and the bees humming in the heather. Cathy gave a sigh of happiness. It had been almost worth having that barrier between herself and Greg, she thought, to feel such relief and happiness now that it was gone and they were close again.

'Penny for them,' Greg said. 'That was a big sigh.'

'I'm just happy,' she said. He kissed her and held her closer. 'So am I,' he said. 'I just wish it was June.'

They had planned their wedding for June 1915 when Cathy would be nineteen. Now she laughed. 'It's funny – when we thought we'd have a long engagement we weren't as impatient as now, when we've fixed a date.'

'Speak for yourself,' Greg said, kissing her nose and tickling her face with a grass stalk. Then, suddenly serious, he said quietly, 'It's not what I wanted for you, Cath, a two up and two down, but I'll do better soon, I promise.'

'Greg, I don't care where we are, as long as we're together,' she exclaimed. 'I was never like Mary, wanting a posh house.' She drew back a little from his arms, looking thoughtful. 'Do you think she's all right? She seems unhappy.'

'She doesn't look well,' he said. 'I think she might have been quite ill in Paris, but she's got a lovely home and plenty of money. All she ever wanted, really, hasn't she?'

Cathy said nothing and they rode on in silence for a while. What's wrong with me? she was thinking. Always at happy times I get a queer feeling to spoil things. She remembered the way she had shivered the day that she met Clive, and today another cloud seemed to have fallen over her happiness.

By the time they had reached the ferry she had managed to throw it off and was able to laugh and joke with the other cyclists as they wheeled their bicycles on board.

When they reached Liverpool they were surprised to see crowds gathered round a paper pinned to the door of the Town Hall. Greg asked a man what it was.

'Mobilisation,' the man said. 'Germany's invaded France, and Belgium rejected the ultimatum from Germany. So this is it,' he added with a beaming smile.

Cathy soon found that the man was right. Germany asked Britain not to intervene but the newspapers reported speeches in Parliament announcing that Germany had invaded Belgium and that Britain, to honour her treaties, would give Germany an ultimatum expiring at midnight on August 4th.

Excited groups gathered in the streets and Norah told Cathy that her brothers Sam and Willie, who were Reservists, had been called up.

After that everything was confusion and excitement. Charlie and George Benson had been on their annual Territorial camp for a fortnight, but instead of returning home were sent to Hampshire for training.

Soon Cathy heard that Norah's twin brothers, Teddy and Luke, were in France, and remarked to her friend that her family seemed more affected by the war than most.

'Only because my brothers joined up to get away from my father,' Norah said frankly. 'Charlie and George just like the idea of the camp. That's why they joined the Terriers.'

They were passing a recruiting centre with young men standing outside it in an untidy queue. Norah jerked her thumb at them. 'Makes me laugh to hear some old fellers going on about lads joining to fight for King and Country. Half of them lot are joining to get away from home.'

'A bit of both, Norah,' Cathy protested. 'People *are* worried about brave little Belgium.'

They were nearly home when Norah revealed the reason for her bitterness. Jack Carmody had joined the Eighth Irish and had already departed for training camp. 'If he gets killed, I'll know who to blame,' Norah said, and Cathy could only squeeze her arm in wordless sympathy.

She thought of Norah's words when Peggy Burns came in to tell them that her Robbie had joined up. 'They're all making out they're made up when their sons join up or go to sea, saying they're proud of them, but I tell you straight, Sally, that's not what I feel,' she wept.

'It's Jimmy picking on him, and that weaselly little bitch pestering him to get married what's caused this.'

'Never mind,' Sally consoled her. 'They say it will all be over by Christmas, so Robbie'll be home again in no time.'

'Let's hope so,' Peggy said, brightening. 'Thank God you've got none to go anyway, Sal, only Greg and Clive.'

Cathy's main thought was Greg, and how the war would affect their plans. Warlike speeches and sermons were being made exhorting all young men to join up. 'Your King and Country Need You' was the slogan, but the boys Cathy knew seemed to be going from one recruiting centre to the other, being refused by the regiments they wanted to join and going to others where often only their names were taken and they were sent home to await orders.

It was impossible for Greg to join up without first arranging for the business to be carried on in his absence. He had extended into the shop next door a few months earlier and now had to arrange for Mr Braithwaite to supervise the two shops, and to replace two of the assistants who had already left.

'I hope it's not too much for old Braithwaite,' he said to Cathy. 'He should really be doing less now, rather than more.'

Greg had another worry which he confided to Cathy one night as they sat in the parlour which was almost in darkness, lit only by the glow of a small fire.

'I don't think I could kill a man, Cath,' he said suddenly. 'Especially not with a bayonet.' They had been talking about a customer who had told Greg that he was home on leave and had been training on Salisbury Plain. He had described the bayonet training and how they plunged bayonets into sandbags and twisted them.

'You mean the actual killing or having it on your conscience?' she asked.

'Both,' he said ruefully. 'I want to do my bit, Cath, but I don't think I could kill another man, even if he was a German.'

'Perhaps you won't need to go,' Cathy consoled him. 'If the war's over by Christmas. It said in the paper that our troops did so well at Le Cateau, and so many Germans were killed, that it's bound to be over soon.'

'I want to go, Cath, and do my bit for England but I just can't see myself killing another man. I can't believe that it's right.'

'Is it because of what Dad says?' Cathy asked. His idol, Keir Hardie, was a pacifist and Lawrie declared that he agreed with him that war was wrong. He also said that reports of German atrocities sounded suspiciously like the things the Boers were supposed to have done in South Africa, and that maybe the German papers carried the same tales about the British soldiers.

Greg shook his head. 'I respect your dad's views but I don't always agree with him,' he said. 'It might be because I wanted to be a doctor and save life. I don't know, Cath. Sometimes I don't know what to think.'

'Neither do I,' she said. She had been amazed by the swift change of attitude among the leaders of the Suffragettes. The women's suffrage cause had been abandoned at the outbreak of hostilities, and Christabel and Emmeline Pankhurst were as vociferous in the cause of war as they had been for the Suffragettes. Other changes amazed Cathy but she was soon to find that what had seemed odd and inexplicable quickly became normal.

Few people seemed to think as deeply as Greg and her father and the general mood for the rest of 1914 was of cheerfulness and optimism, with bitterness towards Germany stirred up by newspaper tales of German atrocities.

It was soon evident that the war would not be over very quickly but rumours were rife. People seemed unable to stay at home but had to be out on the streets, listening to the latest stories and adding to them before passing them on. There were tales of Russians being landed in England, of stores being completely cleared of food by people driving from shop to shop in motor cars, and of Germans signalling with lanterns from tall buildings and deserted seashores.

The newspapers whipped up anti-German feeling with tales of atrocities committed by their troops in Belgium. Lawrie came home one night with his head cut and his clothes torn. 'I saw a poor old German waiter from the Grenville being chased up Brownlow Hill by a gang of toughs. Poor old beggar couldn't get along on his flat feet, and was terrified. I tried to tackle them but there were too many.'

He expected Sally to reproach him for risking his life but she said immediately, 'I'm glad you tried. I only wish there'd been someone to help Solly.' She shed angry tears as she told him that old Solly from the pawnbroker's, a German Jew who had lived in England for fifty years, had been attacked by a mob.

'He's nearly eighty,' she said. 'And when I think how good he was to us when you were out of work and we were desperate, I could break my heart.'

'Is he all right?' Lawrie asked. 'I mean, is he badly hurt?'

'A broken arm and his head cut open, but it was the shock and the fright at his age,' she said. 'They ransacked his shop too, and stole his watch and the money in his pocket.'

'That was probably the idea,' Lawrie said grimly.

Norah's brother Teddy was injured in the British action near Mons, and when he had been transferred to a hospital near Warrington Cathy went with her friend to see him. He was lying with his left shoulder and arm swathed in bandages and his leg suspended in the air, but Cathy was surprised to find that he was not bitter towards the Germans.

He told them that the trenches were being dug 'all over the place', and one day he had been with a small party making their way along a trench when they had turned a corner and come face to face with some German soldiers.

'Did you kill them?' Norah asked, and he smiled.

'No. They were lost same as we was, and they were lads like us. The nearest one got such a shock he said "Goot Morgen", and our Luke said "Good morning" and we all just turned round and went away from each other. We didn't tell the officers, though.'

When they left Teddy, Norah said that he might get into trouble if anyone knew what he had said, but Cathy felt that she must tell her father and Greg.

Casualty lists began to appear in the *Echo* and *Express* every night, but the first one in Egremont Street was Frank Mellor. By a cruel chance the telegram about his death arrived in the morning and Mrs Mellor's screams had scarcely died away and her family gathered to comfort her, when another telegram arrived.

Two more of the Mellors' sons were now at sea, and the telegram informed them that Bert's ship had gone down with all hands while homeward bound. His wife was a favourite daughter-in-law of Mrs Mellor's, a motherless girl who was expecting her first baby. Comforting her helped Mrs Mellor to bear her own double loss.

Mary had not been to Egremont Street for several weeks and the family had not been invited to Neston. She had replied so briefly to letters from her mother and Cathy that each of them had decided to wait for a letter from her before writing again. 'She's jumping out of her latitude, as my da would say,' Sally said to Lawrie. 'But she needn't think she can snub her own mother because she's got new friends.'

Cathy had been hurt too, but now she decided to write to tell Mary about Frank Mellor. No one suspected the real reason why she stayed away.

Clive's behaviour had become so outrageous that Mary was ill with worry. His attacks on her continued but often he disappeared for a couple of days and nights, and now he had started to bring young men home to stay. On the night that he ordered Mary to sleep in a spare bedroom and retired into theirs with a young boy, she had stayed in the spare room all the next day until the housekeeper, Mrs Stewart, came knocking on the door in the early evening.

'Can I get you something, Madam?' she called, when Mary ignored the knocking.

'Come in,' Mary called, and when the woman appeared she said faintly, 'I feel ill, Mrs Stewart, but I'd like tea and dry toast.'

'Very well, Madam,' the housekeeper said stiffly. She went out and Mary lay wondering whether Clive was still in the house and whether the housekeeper was surprised to find her in the spare room. She hoped that the woman would think she was sleeping alone because she was ill, but felt too ill and upset really to care. I can't take much more, she thought.

Later she went along to her own bedroom and found that Clive's travelling case had gone, which meant he would be away for a few days at least, she hoped.

The invitations to dine with neighbours had almost ceased since the night when Mary had been brought home by her host, and she declined the few which arrived, pleading illness. She longed to be comforted by her mother but she was too proud to admit the reality of her life with Clive and fearful that her parents would guess it, so she stayed away from Egremont Street and lived the life almost of a recluse.

Clive seemed to have forgotten his ambition to shine in local society and to be intent only on his own pleasures. The uncertainty of Mary's life continued, with his sudden appearances or disappearances. When he was at home, they rarely spoke.

After the night when Mary had slept in the spare room, Clive stayed away for several days. For the sake of appearances in front of the servants, she had moved back to her own bedroom and lay in bed most of the day or got up and drifted about in a wrapper, in a stupor of misery. Sometimes she lay on the sofa weeping as she thought of her mother and father and how upset they would be if they knew all that had happened to her. Thoughts of Cathy and Greg were more than she could bear and she closed her mind to them, but sometimes she allowed herself to remember happier days.

She told the housekeeper to refuse all callers and to say that she was ill, but one day young Mrs Bagshaw called and insisted on seeing her. She came into the drawing room, talking as she came.

'Now I know you don't want to see anyone but I insisted. You *must* join our Home Nursing Class or Comforts for the Troops, Mrs Walden. Much better for you than moping at home.'

Mary was lying on the sofa with the blinds half drawn and it was only when Mrs Bagshaw was quite close that she saw her clearly. 'My *dear*,' she exclaimed. 'Oh, you *are* ill.' She took Mary's hot, dry hand and bent over her. 'Have you seen a doctor?' she asked, and when Mary shook her head said decisively, 'Then you must do so immediately. I thought you were just fretting because your husband had gone to join up but you are *ill*, my dear. Do your parents know?'

Mary sat up with a sudden access of energy. 'No, and please don't say anything to your father, Mrs Bagshaw. I don't want my family to be worried.'

'But are you sure? You seem quite feverish.'

'Quite sure,' Mary said firmly, opening her eyes wide in a way that her mother would have recognised. 'You know I suffer from colds and I've just been very silly as you say, moping at home.' She rang for tea and began to ask about the Home Nursing and Comforts for the Troops, and Mrs Bagshaw launched into an account of all that the ladies of the area were doing to help the war effort.

Mary's mind was racing as she sat pretending to listen and skil-fully parried questions about Clive. The outbreak of war had gone almost unnoticed by her, shut away from society as she had been for these early weeks of August. The cook had been upset because her nephew had been recalled to the Royal Navy, but Mary had not realised that civilians were enlisting.

Now she listened eagerly to all that Mrs Bagshaw told her of the various young men who had joined up. When she had gone, after Mary had assured her that she felt much better and would join one of the groups of ladies soon, Mary rang and asked for a newspaper.

She was surprised to see the extent of the mobilisation and of the fighting in France, and delighted to see that all young men were expected to fight for King and Country according to the speeches reported in the newspapers. Surely that must include Clive even though he was a Canadian. He had been born in England.

She was too excited to sit still and, her earlier weakness forgotten, went up to her bedroom to change her clothes to go out. She was shocked when she looked in the mirror.

No wonder Mrs Bagshaw had been surprised! For the first time for weeks Mary examined her reflection carefully. Her eyes looked unnaturally large in her thin face, with a yellow tinge to the whites and dark shadows beneath them. Even her skin, once so clear, looked dry and mottled, and when she drew her hairbrush through her hair a large amount came away on the brush.

Mary looked at it with horror and ran her fingers through her hair. How thin and dry it was! I'll be bald soon, she thought, then a slow anger began to burn in her. Why had she let that monster do this to her?

She thought of him travelling about, entering hotels and being treated with respect and deference, while she hid herself away as though she was the one who should be ashamed.

Not any more, she thought fiercely. Whether he went to the war or not things would be different from now on. She wished that Clive would come home while she was in the first heat of anger, but however long it was before he came she would never allow herself to be cowed again.

She dressed carefully and an hour later was being ushered into the surgery of a doctor in Wallasey. She had given her name as Mrs Jones and chosen an unknown doctor, but he assured her that there was no sinister reason for her condition.

'Have you received a shock recently?' he asked.

'A series of them,' Mary said grimly.

He shook his head. 'Sad times, sad times,' he murmured. He prescribed an ointment to be rubbed into the scalp and a bottle of tonic to improve her general health, and patted her shoulder in a fatherly way as she waited for his dispenser to make them up.

'Try not to worry, my dear. Sad times, but at least we are winning. Twenty-five thousand Germans killed and scarcely any of our brave troops, so our boys should soon be home again.'

He had recommended a diet of milk, butter and eggs so Mary ordered an omelette and a glass of milk when she returned home and took a dose of the medicine.

She was in the garden when the Maxwell roared up the drive and she began to tremble but walked to meet Clive with her head high. He was alone and greeted her pleasantly. The usual feeling of unreality swept over her. Which was the real man? she wondered. He seemed to have as many facets as a diamond.

She had been determined to demand an explanation for his absences and to tell him that his treatment of her must change, but when she saw him she was seized with the familiar trembling. They went into the house and she went to sit by the window, clasping her hands in her lap.

Clive poured himself a whisky and soda and remarked that the garden looked well. Now or never, Mary thought, gripping her hands together even more tightly.

'*I'm* not well, Clive,' she said. 'Mrs Bagshaw was shocked to see me when she called, and she thought I should see a doctor.'

'Indeed,' he said. 'And just how does that concern Mrs Bagshaw?'

'She called to talk about sewing parties and Home Nursing. The doctor said I'd had a shock and I must have rest and calm,' Mary gabbled, beginning to cry. 'My hair is falling out, Clive.'

He turned to refill his glass and his glance fell on the letters on his desk. Immediately he lost interest in her and picked up the letters, sorting through them rapidly. Most of them seemed to be bills and he simply glanced at these and flung them into the fire but one envelope he slit quickly and eagerly read the contents.

Mary watched him nervously as he pulled out his watch and snapped it open, then strode to the bell pull and tugged it.

'Get me something to eat,' he ordered the maid. 'Cold meat, anything, but be quick. And get my bag from my motor.'

'Yessir,' she said, scuttling away, after a glimpse of his frowning face.

He came to the window biting his thumbnail and looking out into the garden, seeming oblivious to Mary although he was near enough to touch her. She sat still and silent, until suddenly he noticed her.

'Get a Bradshaw from the desk and come upstairs with me,' he said, then strode out of the room, shouting to the maid to get out his suitcase.

Mary took the timetable from the desk and nervously followed him upstairs to the bedroom where the maid was lifting a leather case on to the bed and opening it. The Gladstone bag from the motor had been carried upstairs and Clive was pulling out his brushes and his dressing case.

The maid went and Clive put his small cases into the suitcase and began to take out shirts and underwear from the drawers and pack them in the case.

'Lookup the trains to London,' he ordered Mary.

'But you've just come from there,' she said.

'I've come from Nottingham,' he said. 'Lookup the London trains.' Mary obeyed meekly, and as he came back to the chest of drawers he paused beside her, and tilted her face up to him. 'You've grown mighty thin, honey,' he said. Mary wanted to scream at him the reason for her thinness but the kindness in his voice weakened her.

She gave a sob. 'My hair's falling out,' she said, her eyes filling with tears. He smoothed his hand over her head.

'It'll grow again, honey,' he said, bending to kiss her gently. At that moment the gong boomed through the house and he said with a laugh, 'I guess that's the cold meat.'

He took the Bradshaw from her and swiftly ran his finger down the page, murmuring to himself, then he flung the book down and took Mary's hand. 'Come and eat with me,' he said. 'That should put some flesh on your bones.'

The housekeeper was standing in the dining room, swelling with indignation. She said with an injured air, 'Cook has done her best, sir, but—'

Clive interrupted her. 'Yes, all right. Lay a place for Mrs Walden.' A tureen of soup was on the table, and he lifted the cover of a plate on the sideboard. It was filled with cold meat and small savoury pancakes.

'Mrs Walden will have the same,' he said firmly.

The housekeeper flounced out and Mary smiled at him as she served the soup. Her smile faded as she wondered why moments like this could never last. If only Clive could always be like this. A few months ago she might have thought that this was a sign that he was turning over a new leaf, but too often moments of tenderness had been followed by vicious attacks on her.

Even now she found it hard to believe what lay behind that smiling façade, and wondered whether even if he changed she could ever be happy with him. Ever learn to trust and lose her fear of him. She knew that her disillusionment and shock had been too great for her to forget her sufferings.

Clive was eating rapidly and he pulled out his watch and checked the time several times. When the maid came with Mary's meal he told her to send the boy for a taxicab, and after the meal he completed his packing very quickly.

Mary had gone up to the bedroom with him. As he fastened the straps he said, 'I'll be away for about a week, I guess. There's someone I want to see, but keep that Bagshaw witch away from here, honey. She's only scouting for the old man.'

'But I thought he was your friend,' Mary exclaimed.

'Not him. He's been croaking at me like a raven, so keep her away and don't tell her where I am.'

Mary longed to ask why he was going to London but already he had told her far more than he had ever done about his plans, and she was afraid to press him. Instead she said, 'I haven't been out. I haven't seen Mrs Bagshaw until she came to ask me to join things. She seemed to think I was moping at home because you'd joined up.'

He threw back his head and laughed, and was still chuckling to himself when the maid came panting upstairs for his case because the taxicab had arrived. He took Mary's arm as they walked down and at the foot of the stairs turned to face her. 'What would you say,' he said, tapping the end of her nose playfully, 'if I was to tell you that I've applied for a commission in the Sherwood Foresters?'

'Why the Sherwood Foresters?' she gasped.

He laughed. 'I guess I just like the name, honey. It's not through yet so keep it to yourself, huh?' He kissed her, still laughing at her stunned expression, and went off, saying airily, 'See you in about a week.'

She sat down on the stairs, feeling as though her legs had turned to jelly. A phrase of her father's flashed into her mind. 'What a conundrum of a man,' her father had said, and now she echoed the expression which perfectly described Clive.

Her father had been speaking about a devious workmate, but how simple the man seemed now, compared to Clive. Surely no one but he would have told his wife in that way and at that time that he was joining the Army.

Mary stood up as the young maid came down the hall. 'I'm going to bed, Milly,' she said. 'I'd like a pot of tea and some thin bread and butter brought up in half an hour.'

She turned and walked sedately up the stairs, resisting the temptation to run up them singing, then took a leisurely bath and put on her prettiest nightdress. As she lay in bed later, drinking tea, she let her mind drift back over the day.

What a day! To think how weak and ill she'd felt only a few short hours ago, and now she was confident she could climb a mountain. How different Clive had been too. For a few moments she thought of him almost with tenderness, but the bedroom held too many unhappy memories for her to retain that feeling for long.

She stretched luxuriously in the bed, thinking of Clive speeding to London and revelling in the certainty of seven days and nights of peace. And soon he would be going away for a longer spell and his movements would be dictated by the Army, so there would be none of the sudden, horrifying arrivals when she had thought herself safe.

Mary's natural optimism returned as she lay thinking and planning. She felt better already and with plenty of good food and peace she would soon put on weight and her hair would grow. I've always been lucky, she thought, and now things are going my way again.

Even this war had come just in time for her. She remembered Mrs Malloy saying to her, 'If you fell down a well, you'd come up with a gold chain around your neck,' and her mother telling her she was born under a lucky star when the job in Denby's dress department was offered to her.

Then meeting Elizabeth whose uncle happened to bring home the bales of silks from China just at the time that she needed new clothes to go out with Clive, and even the marriage which had seemed such a disaster might turn out well for her.

I've got this house, the servants, all my lovely clothes and jewels and plenty of money, she thought, and Clive safely in the Army. For a moment the thought of Greg flashed into her mind but she thrust it away, and fell asleep planning her clothes for the next day when she meant to visit her family.

Chapter Thirty-One

Cathy's letter about Frank and Bert Mellor arrived the following morning and Mary's first thought was that it was providential, although this was followed by a feeling of guilt that she could think that about such a tragedy. It meant though that she had an excuse to visit Egremont Street after the long weeks of silence.

She had slept well and rose early for her bath. The bathroom was over the kitchen at the back of the house and as Mary opened the window to allow the steam to escape, voices floated up to her.

'At least he came home on his own last night,' the housekeeper said. 'None of his nancy boys. Taking that one into his bed, and her conniving at it sleeping in the spare room, no less! I tell you, Cook, if it happens again I'll walk out. Men have been locked up for less.'

Mary stood as though frozen with her hand on the window latch, then she heard the cook say, 'I'm thinking of looking round myself for another place. I'm a respectable woman and I'm not getting mixed up with these goings on. Enough to make the old gentleman turn in his grave.'

Mary had wondered whether the servants guessed about Clive but it was a shock to hear them speak in such a way and she went back to her bedroom seething with rage. The cheek of them, she thought, to make empty threats about walking out! None of them were likely to leave such an easy berth. She knew that she was too inexperienced and Clive too open-handed to check on the housekeeping, and the servants had taken advantage of them.

Later as Mary walked downstairs the cook came through from the kitchens and stood at the back of the hall with her arms folded. 'Beg pardon, mum,' she said loudly, 'was the meal to the master's liking last night?'

Mary could see the housekeeper lurking in the dining room and listening with a sneer on her face, and her temper rose. 'It was – adequate, Cook,' she said coolly.

'Well, if I was to know where I was,' the cook blustered, 'not knowing one day to the next who's going to be brought in and who's out. It's not what I'm used to.'

'I don't see the difficulty,' Mary said. 'I *know* there are ample supplies of food delivered to this house, but if you need a day's notice to provide a meal, Cook, you are free to find another place.'

That's wiped the smile off your faces, she thought triumphantly as the cook hurriedly vanished and the housekeeper said obsequiously, 'Can I get you anything, Madam?'

'No, thank you,' Mary said, looking at her unsmilingly. 'You may tell Cook that I will be out all day. Tomorrow I'll see the housekeeping books, if you please, and discuss certain other matters with you.'

A quarrel always invigorated Mary and she walked down the drive with her head held high, but weakness soon overcame her, and she was thankful to step on to the bus which would take her to the ferry.

Cathy's letter had been brief, simply telling Mary that the Mellor sons had been killed and that their own family was well. She had said nothing about Greg and throughout the journey to Liverpool, Mary wove fantasies that Cathy and he had parted and that someday Greg might take Clive's place.

Sally had become steadily more angry with Mary, more on Lawrie's behalf than her own as she knew how much Mary meant to him, how proud of her he was, and how much he was hurt by the way she had treated them.

Sally too was hurt that Mary could so quickly forget her family in favour of her new friends, and at such a time. She was always a hard, selfish faggot, Sally thought, and there's Cathy too soft for her own good and taking everything to heart. Why can't they strike the middle course?

Cathy had been upset for days about the long queues of ragged women and crying hungry children outside the office in Commutation Row where Miss Rathbone had been appointed by her cousin, the Lord Mayor, to sort out problems and organise relief funds.

The women were destitute because their husbands had gone to serve in the Army or Navy and as the service pay was paid monthly in arrears, they had been completely without money for three weeks. Most of them lived a hand to mouth existence anyway as their husbands could only get casual work on the docks, so when the last few shillings the men had earned were gone the families were left without food or money and with nothing to pawn to tide them over.

To add to the distress, official bungling and the men's inability to fill out the allotment form properly meant that even after the three weeks the women failed to receive the allotment or the men their pay. Cathy was harrowed by the sight of the women and children and every night she shyly slipped whatever money she had to the mothers and took food and sweets for the children.

Sally willingly gave Cathy food for the children but she told her that if it upset her so much she should come home a different way. 'But I'd still know they were there, Mam,' she protested.

'You're your father all over again,' Sally sighed.

'And what's wrong with that?' Cathy flashed back, but it was unusual for her and her mother to disagree.

Sally had reduced her visits to Southport to two days a week, partly because Emily's health had improved slightly, but chiefly because she felt that she was being unfair to Cathy.

While she was spending three days a week with Emily, it had been necessary for Cathy to help her several evenings a week with sewing orders. Although she did it willingly Sally knew how precious her time was now, while she and Greg were preparing for their marriage and he for joining up.

Greg was still trying to simplify the paperwork of the business to make it easy for Mr Braithwaite to supervise both shops, but the old man seemed nervous about the responsibility. Greg and Cathy decided that it would be a good idea if she acquired some basic knowledge of the shop so that Mr Braithwaite could refer to her if Greg was unavailable, and this seemed to reassure the elderly man.

It meant that they needed to spend several evenings each week going through the books, but they were happy working together and Greg felt that they grew even closer as he shared some of his difficulties with Cathy. They were both surprised at the ease with which she understood the details of ordering, invoicing and insurance.

They were house hunting too although the date of their wedding had not yet been fixed. Greg felt that he had taken a giant step forward towards it when he persuaded Miss Nugent to come to live with his mother, and his mother to agree to it.

Miss Nugent, as the only unmarried daughter of a large family, had been at the beck and call of her married brothers and sisters since her mother's death, and she was eager to move to the rooms above the shop for her 'keep' and pocket money.

Mrs Redmond at first viewed the plan with disfavour, but when Greg appeared ready to drop the idea she became enthusiastic about it.

'If you are quite determined to volunteer, Gregory, I can't be left alone here obviously. I would have thought that your first duty was to your mother, but of course you have never considered my wishes.'

Greg and Cathy had decided to say nothing about their wedding plans to Mrs Redmond until they had fixed the date, but Greg now felt that this was a suitable time to tell her.

'I would be leaving here in any case very soon, Mother,' he said calmly. 'Cathy and I will be married before I go in the Army.'

His mother wept and protested as he expected, but the outburst was not as prolonged as he had feared. Mrs Redmond had begun to realise the advantages of the arrangement. It would improve her standing with the Duvals and other friends if she could say that her son was fighting for his country, and he had arranged for a paid companion to ease her loneliness so she could order Miss Nugent about as much as she wished.

Suddenly it seemed that everything was falling into place for Cathy and Greg. A friend in the Red Cross had solved his worries about killing by suggesting that he joined up as a stretcher bearer. He was accepted but told that his call-up would be deferred until he had put his business affairs in order.

Houses to rent were plentiful now, and Cathy and Greg had found a small but solidly built redbrick house in Anton Street, off Kensington.

At the time that Mary was being told by Clive of his enlistment, Cathy and Greg were excitedly making plans for their wedding and fixing on the last Saturday in October as the date.

Mary had dressed very carefully for her visit to her family and puffed out her hair to disguise its scantiness as much as possible, but when her mother opened the door to her, her eyes widened in shock.

'Mary,' she gasped. 'Good God, girl, what's happened to you?' When she removed her hat her mother was even more shocked, and Mary found herself in her mother's arms crying as though her heart would break.

Her mother wept with her. 'I'd no idea you were so ill, love. Why didn't you tell us? We thought we weren't posh enough for you.'

Mary sat up and wiped her eyes. 'I didn't want to worry you, Mam. That's why I stayed away.'

'But what happened to you at all to make you like this?' Sally said. 'There isn't a pick on you.'

'It was the fever I had in Paris, Mam,' Mary said glibly. 'I couldn't throw it off, and couldn't eat.'

'And what does Clive say about it?'

'He made me see a doctor, and he's given me ointment for my hair, and medicine. He said I should eat butter and cream and eggs, and you know how open-handed Clive is. There's always lashings of food in the house but I just haven't been able to eat it.'

'I'm glad he got a doctor for you but he should have told us, love.'

'I told him not to,' Mary said. 'Young Mrs Bagshaw insisted on coming in to see me and I was afraid she'd tell her father-in-law and he'd tell Dad. That's why I came. I was sorry to hear about the Mellor lads too,' she added hastily as she remembered that that was the pretext for her visit.

'Ah, yes, God help them,' Sally said. 'Poor Mrs Mellor's never been sober since she heard but, still, if it helps her it doesn't matter. The only thing is, Bert's wife is drinking with her, and I'm afraid she'll harm the baby she's carrying, while she's falling drunk.'

'Cathy didn't say anything else in her letter,' Mary said. 'Is Dad all right?'

'Yes, and we're made up about the news we had last night,' Sally said. 'Cathy and Greg have got a house in Kensington Fields and they've fixed the wedding day.' She beamed with delight. 'The last Saturday in October so we'll have to get our sleeves rolled up to be ready.'

She suddenly realised that Mary was leaning back in the chair, her face as white as a sheet, and she bent over her in concern.

'Are you all right, love?' she said rubbing her hands, but Mary lay with her eyes closed, and Sally dashed into the parlour and came back with brandy in a glass. She held it to her lips and as the fiery liquid touched her throat, Mary sat up and blinked her eyes.

She tried to smile. 'I'm all right, Mam,' she said. 'It's just the weakness that comes over me.'

'Dear God, child, you frightened the life out of me,' Sally said. 'I don't know what kind of fever that must have been. Is Clive coming here?'

Mary opened her eyes wide and smiled at her mother. 'No. He's applied for a commission in the Sherwood Foresters and he's gone to London to try to hurry it up.'

Sally shook her head. 'I know the lads feel they've got to go, but it's hard on the girls left at home. Greg's going as a stretcher bearer and our Cathy'll be heartbroken when he goes, I know.'

Mary felt as though a hand gripped her heart and squeezed it, but now she was more prepared she showed no sign, only asking her mother for more details about Greg and Cathy, and how Mrs Redmond had behaved when she heard the news.

'Greg's arranged for someone to live with her when he's married,' Sally said, 'Well, at least it was supposed to be because he was going in the Army. Greg's going to tell her the date of the wedding today.'

'I don't envy him,' Mary said with a smile. 'I can just imagine how she'll carry on. Is she still as catty with Cathy?'

'Yes. I think it was causing trouble between them too, but they've learned sense now and they don't let her bother them. I don't know how she'll be at the wedding but we'll cross that bridge when we come to it.'

Sally had kept glancing at Mary, horrified by what she saw. It was not only her emaciated body and claw-like hands that upset her, but also the traces of suffering on Mary's face.

How could this have happened in a few short months? she thought. It was only six months since the wedding and Mary looked years older than the beautiful bride who had left this house. To think that they had been condemning her for snobbery, and all the time she had been suffering like this!

The usual tea and cake had been produced soon after Mary had arrived but now Sally went into the back kitchen and returned with a glassful of dark liquid.

'Drink this,' she said to Mary. 'It's beetroot wine that I've been making for the Mangan girls, but I've made plenty. Those Mangan girls have got poor blood, not a bit of colour even in their lips, but this has done them the world of good.'

'What's in it?' Mary asked, eyeing it with distaste.

'Beetroots and brown sugar, standing for three days, then the juice is mixed with stout. It's very strengthening,' Sally said. 'It should cure what ails you.'

If it only could, Mary thought, but to please her mother she drained the glass, then Sally cooked herrings dipped in oatmeal for their lunch. Mary enjoyed the fish and ate several slices of her mother's home-made bread, liberally spread with butter.

'No bread like yours, Mam,' she said. 'The cook would have a fit if she heard me, but that's the best meal I've had since I left home.'

They talked all afternoon. Mary gave her version of her lifestyle and friends, and Sally told her about the improvement in Emily's health and all that had been happening among neighbours and friends since the outbreak of war.

'Your father's against it, of course,' she said tartly. 'You know he always has to be out of step with everyone else except Keir Hardie and that crowd.'

Mary laughed. 'He often turns out to be right though, doesn't he?' she said. 'What about Cathy and her Suffragettes?'

'*Suffragists*, Mary,' Sally said in a parody of Cathy's indignant voice as she had often corrected them. They laughed and Sally said, 'It seems they're all shouting for the war now. Cathy's been getting all worked up about women being left without money when the men go away but it seems Miss Rathbone is looking after them, and Sylvia Pankhurst is doing the same thing in Bow in London.'

'Does Cathy still think the sun shines out of Eleanor Rathbone?' Mary asked.

'Yes, but mind you, Mary, she's a good woman and she gets things done. Cathy's been going on about it being a disgrace, the families left hungry when the men are fighting for the country.'

'You'd think her mind would just be on Greg,' Mary said, but she saw her mother looking at her with a strange expression and said hastily, 'What time is Dad in?'

'He won't be long now,' Sally said, but she still looked thoughtful, and Mary decided that she would have to be more careful when she spoke of Greg.

'Cathy might be a bit late,' Sally went on, 'Greg was meeting her after work to say how he got on with telling his mother the wedding date.'

A few minutes later Lawrie came down the lobby and stopped at the kitchen door in surprise when he saw Mary. She had expected an exuberant welcome from him, but although she smiled confidently at him, he said coolly: 'Hello. You're a bit of a stranger, aren't you?'

'She's been ill, Lawrie, and kept away in case she worried us,' Sally said swiftly. He glanced at her but still stood in the doorway and said in the same hard voice, 'Your mam's been very upset, Mary.'

Her eyes filled with tears and she stood up and said in a small voice, 'I know.' Lawrie came forward and for the first time saw his daughter properly. 'Good God,' he exclaimed. 'What – whatever—?' The next moment Mary was in his arms, sobbing, 'Oh Dada, Dada.'

Lawrie held her close, making soothing noises and rubbing his right hand rhythmically round and round her back.

'What are you trying to do?' Sally asked him after a few minutes. 'Bring her wind up?' They all laughed and the tension was relieved as she'd intended.

'I used to do that when you were a baby,' Lawrie told Mary, 'but you won't remember that.'

'Wash yourself, Lawrie, and I'll put the dinner out,' Sally said briskly, and he lowered Mary into the chair and patted her head before going into the back kitchen.

Sally lifted a hotpot from the oven and Lawrie came back, rolling down the sleeves of his shirt. 'Are we waiting for Cathy?' he asked.

'No. You know what those two are like when they get together,' Sally said. 'Time means nothing to them. I'll put the hotpot back in the oven so it won't matter.'

Sally had talked to Lawrie in a low voice while he washed before she came to the oven, and now he turned to Mary.

'Your Mam tells me you've had some of her jollop, love. You should be able to eat after that, if only to take the taste out of your mouth.'

'It'll do her the world of good,' Sally said indignantly. 'It's done wonders for the Mangans.'

Mary sat letting the talk flow round her, feeling that coming home was like sinking into a soft feather bed which enclosed her and kept her safe, but she was jolted out of her reverie when she heard the front door opening.

Cathy and Greg came down the lobby laughing, and Cathy stopped in surprise at the sight of her sister. 'Mary!' she exclaimed.

'I got your letter,' she said hurriedly, and at the same time Sally explained: 'Mary's been ill, and she didn't want to worry us.'

Cathy had impulsively hugged and kissed Mary, and Sally had opened the oven door. 'Should I put this out right away?' she asked. As Cathy turned to her, Greg bent over Mary and kissed her. She slipped her hand round the back of his neck and held him so that his lips pressed firmly on hers. He gently drew away and she said quickly, 'I heard your news. Congratulations.'

Cathy turned to her, her eyes dancing with excitement. '*Did* you?' she said. 'About our wedding and our house. Mam's coming on Saturday to look at the house in daylight.'

She looked at Mary's gaunt face and seemed about to say something but her father gave a warning shake of his head and Cathy only smiled, then she and Greg sat down at the table.

Sally told them about Clive's applying for a commission and they talked about their plans and said that Greg's mother had accepted the wedding date and the news about their house.

Mary sat taking no part in the conversation, but leaning her head on her hand and feasting her eyes on Greg sitting opposite to her. She was filled with a great weariness and wondered how she would summon the strength to go home, but suddenly she realised that her mother was suggesting that she stayed the night.

She was about to agree when suddenly she remembered the scars on her body, and hurriedly refused. 'No. I didn't tell the servants and the housekeeper's such a fusser. She'd have search parties out for me.'

She consented to sit in her father's chair with her feet on a stool and to drink another glass of beetroot wine, and after a little felt rested and stronger.

Before she left she asked them all to visit her on Sunday. Her father escorted her to the ferry.

'Never leave it like that again, love,' he said. 'Your mam and I didn't know what to think when you didn't come or even answer letters properly. Whatever happens we'd rather know, love, and that way we'd worry less than if we're kept in the dark.'

She promised and at last was alone, sitting in the corner of the lounge on the boat and free to close her eyes and think of Greg, of his thin sensitive face and grey eyes, and the feeling of his lips pressing on hers. What could she do about the wedding? she wondered. Could she make an excuse to be away? She felt that she would be unable to bear to watch Greg and Cathy become man and wife.

A note came from Cathy before the weekend, apologising for the fact that she and Greg would not be able to visit Mary on Sunday as they had so little time to prepare their house before the wedding.

Mary was not sure whether she was glad or sorry. She longed to see him again, but felt that her mother had become suspicious and that she would have needed to be on her guard all the time on Sunday in case she betrayed how she felt.

Sally and Lawrie were impressed by the evidence of wealth everywhere in Mary's house, and by the lavish meal which was provided for them. She had not yet carried out her threat to examine the household books, but had alarmed the cook and the housekeeper enough to make them very anxious to please.

After the meal Mary took them to her bedroom and showed them her cupboards full of expensive clothes and her masses of jewellery, and they left the house convinced that Clive was a doting husband, and the change in her due solely to illness.

Mary hoped that Clive would go straight into the Army, that she would be left alone to recover from what had happened to her and service life would effect a change in him.

She followed the doctor's orders and was already beginning to put on weight and to look better when ten days after he had left for London, Clive arrived home in Army uniform. Not the bulky ill-fitting khaki that Mary had seen on many young men in the streets, but a well-tailored officer's uniform with a gleaming Sam Browne belt.

Mary had been lying on the sofa with her eyes closed when he walked in. Her horrified glance flew at once to the belt, but Clive seemed in high good humour.

One of the neighbours was holding an 'At Home' and he immediately agreed to go with Mary. He was much admired by all the ladies, and when he and Mary returned home still seemed in good humour, but restless. Later he suddenly decided to look up friends at his Liverpool Club, and to Mary's relief stayed overnight there.

The next morning he returned and spent some hours at his desk, burning many papers and returning others to the pigeon holes in the desk, without explaining any of his actions to Mary.

'I'm going to Liverpool this afternoon,' he told her. 'I'll take you and we'll do some shopping, and I may look in on Bagshaw.'

They went in the motor car and he sang as they drove along, but as the Maxwell rolled off the luggage boat at Liverpool he changed his mind about visiting Bagshaw.

Instead they went to Bold Street and he bought Mary a magnificent sable coat, and a velvet toque with a feather in an aigrette at the side.

'Could we call into Denby's, Clive?' Mary asked eagerly and he agreed, smiling indulgently at her.

They went into Denby's and the girls clustered round Mary, exclaiming enviously at her new coat and hat, and gazing admiringly at Clive. When they left there he filled Mary's cup of happiness by saying, 'How would y'like to visit with your mother, Mary?'

She looked about her eagerly when they reached Egremont Street and stepped slowly out of the car so that as many people as possible would see them. Lawrie and Sally were both at home and were delighted to see Mary and Clive, apparently happy together.

After a short visit they returned to Neston and Clive changed into knickerbockers and a Norfolk jacket after their meal, and drove the Maxwell into a shed behind the house.

A man went in with him and they spent some time there. When Clive came in later his good humour seemed to have vanished and when Mary timidly asked about the black marks on his clothes he told her that they had been putting the car 'on ice'. Mary was puzzled but was afraid to ask any further questions.

Clive prowled restlessly about the room and Mary hoped that he would decide to go to Liverpool again, but her worst fears were realised when he said abruptly, 'C'mon. Bedtime.'

Afterwards she could never decide whether that night was really the worst she had endured or whether she suffered more because she had unconsciously relaxed, feeling that she was safe from attack for some time to come. It might even have seemed worse because of the happy day which had preceded it.

Clive rose early and dressed in his uniform. Mary forced herself to get up and dress, and to sit at the breakfast table with him, to keep up appearances.

He ate a hearty breakfast and chatted about the weather as though nothing had happened. She drank coffee and watched him silently. He's mad, she decided. Mad or bad, or both.

He left shortly after breakfast, saying carelessly, 'Old Bagshaw will attend to everything, Mary. You've got some left of your allowance, haven't you?'

'Yes, thank you,' Mary murmured. She had more than Clive knew as she had been prudently feathering her nest ever since their marriage from the money he left carelessly around, but she said nothing of that.

He stepped into the taxicab and was driven away and Mary watched with heartfelt relief, hoping that it would be a long time before she saw him again.

Chapter Thirty-Two

Mary visited her old home several times before the wedding of Cathy and Greg, but was annoyed to find that she was not the centre of attention. Even her visit with Clive seemed to have aroused little interest among the neighbours.

'People have got a lot on their minds,' Sally had said apologetically when Mary asked her about it.

All the attention seemed to be on preparing for Cathy's wedding and furnishing her house. Mary refused to be matron of honour, saying that Cathy should have a single girl as her bridesmaid, so Cathy had asked Norah.

It was to be a simple ceremony in keeping with the times and Sally had made a cream flannel costume for Cathy, and one in stone colour for Norah. They were to wear matching hats and Cathy would carry cream and orange roses, and Norah bronze chrysanthemums.

Mary's hunger for Greg seemed to grow stronger every time she saw him, and the thought of him and Cathy married was unbearable to her. There was nothing Mary could do to prevent the marriage and no miracle was going to occur to part Cathy and Greg, but she felt that to watch them being married was more than she could bear.

A few days before the wedding she announced that she had to travel to visit Clive in camp. She declared that she was heartbroken but her first duty was to her husband, who might soon go overseas.

Mrs Redmond retired to her bed two days before the wedding with what Cathy laughingly described to her mother as a 'diplomatic' illness.

'You don't mind, love?' Sally said anxiously.

'Not a bit,' Cathy assured her. 'I'm glad she won't be there, and Greg didn't even pretend to believe her, but he doesn't mind either so it's all right.'

'I don't think there's much that would upset either of you at this minute,' Sally said, smiling indulgently at her. It was true that Cathy and Greg seemed to be alight with happiness. They had decided that they would put the prospect of parting firmly out of their minds until it happened and live for the day, and the optimistic newspaper reports of German defeats made them confident that the war would soon be over.

'It's a pity about Mary,' Sally said, 'but it's the way things are now.'

'I don't mind,' Cathy said and when her mother looked surprised she added hastily, 'It's just the war as you say.'

Cathy had been surprised herself to realise how little she cared about Mary's absence. She had been shocked to see her so ill and changed in appearance, on her first visit home, but subsequent visits had convinced Cathy that the hard, sophisticated woman had little in common with the sister she had known and loved.

Only in one respect was Mary unchanged, she thought: in the furtive greedy glances at Greg when she thought she was unobserved, and in the way she schemed to sit close to him or to touch him.

Cathy suspected nothing of Mary's unwilling passion for Greg but thought only that she resented any man caring for anyone but herself, and that flirting came as naturally as breathing to her. Greg had paid no attention to her anyway.

Cathy thought that Mary's excuse for not attending her wedding might be as 'diplomatic' as Mrs Redmond's and the true reason might also be snobbery but she was unconcerned.

It was a happy day with a simple ceremony in a small chapel in Goronwy Street, followed by a cheerful wedding breakfast and a party in Cathy's home.

The October morning had been still and grey but a fugitive beam of sunlight shone on Cathy and Greg just as they were pronounced man and wife.

'Happy is the bride the sun shines on,' Sally whispered to Lawrie, but he pressed her hand and smiled. 'They don't need sunshine, love,' he whispered. 'They carry it round with them.' Sally could only agree as she looked at the radiant smiles on their faces as they gazed at each other, seeming oblivious to everything and everyone except each other.

Events seemed to move so rapidly afterwards that Cathy often thought of a kaleidoscope that her father had bought her years ago. When the tube was shaken the coloured fragments which lay at the bottom swirled about and settled into a completely different pattern.

In just the same way all their lives were whirled about to settle into a different pattern, only to be disturbed again and again.

Every day someone they knew seemed to vanish only to reappear in uniform some time later. She was walking to the shop one day with Greg when a large group of recruits still in civilian clothes were marched down London Road. They wore dark suits and cloth caps or bowlers and as they passed Cathy saw Sam Glover, wearing a bowler, at the outside of the column of men.

Crowds had gathered on the pavements to cheer them, and Cathy and Greg stood to watch the long procession, so they saw that as the men turned into Lime Street one man's bowler hat was blown from his head.

'I bet that's Sam's,' Greg exclaimed involuntarily.

A woman standing in front of them turned round. 'The fellers is very near fighting to join up,' she said aggressively. 'Three of mine have joined the King's, and nobody better skit them.'

Greg said nothing although he coloured slightly, and Cathy was about to challenge her when they were separated by the movement of the crowd.

'Why didn't you tell her you've joined?' Cathy said indignantly. 'I suppose her sons joined up to get away from *her*.'

'She might think I'd joined to get away from my wife,' Greg said, and they went into the shop laughing although the sight of the marching men had unsettled both of them.

Greg was called up at the beginning of December, but those few blissful weeks in their little home gave Cathy a memory to treasure all her life. Even with all that was happening around them, and the shadow of parting hanging over them, they moved through the days and nights in a golden haze of happiness.

They went together to tell Greg's mother that he was about to go away, and predictably she threw a fit of hysterics and had to be revived with smelling salts by Miss Nugent.

Greg wondered whether he should privately give Miss Nugent 'Ma's' recipe for curing hysterics but decided against it.

Miss Nugent seemed happy to minister to his mother and to be needed, and he felt that he had fulfilled his promise to his father by leaving her in good hands.

Sally wept quietly and held him close when he said goodbye to her. 'I lost a son, a stillborn son, years ago, Greg, but you've made up for him. You've been more than a son to me. Take care, lad.'

Greg was unable to speak but he hugged Sally and kissed her again. He knew how sincere her words were, and how much they meant when spoken by someone as reserved as she.

Lawrie shook his hand and promised to look after Cathy, and as they left the house Greg said to her, 'I've been damned lucky, Cath. Not just meeting you and getting married, but with your mam and dad. They're the salt of the earth.'

'I know,' she said. She was about to share her worry about her father but she decided not to. Nothing must spoil these last hours.

Greg had made all the necessary financial arrangements before he went away, and he and Cathy had been to see Mr Braithwaite at the shop.

The elderly man who had at first seemed to welcome the thought that he could refer problems to Cathy, had now changed his mind.

'You can leave everything in my hands, Mr Gregory,' he said huffily. 'I heard a speech by Lord Derby and he said those of us who are unable to fight can do our bit by releasing a young man to fight. I'm proud to release you for Kitchener's Army.' Greg could do nothing but look at Cathy and agree.

'I'll call in the shop to give him news of you,' Cathy consoled Greg, 'I'm sure he'll tell me then if there are any problems.'

Greg was also frustrated in his attempt to explain the financial arrangements to Cathy. 'But you need to know, Cath,' he protested when she brushed the explanation aside. 'In case anything crops up while I'm away, or in case – anything happens to me.'

Cathy put her finger over his lips. 'I don't want to talk about money,' she said. 'And nothing's going to happen to you, I just *know*.'

Greg could only hope that she was right, and leave a clearly written explanation with the papers. 'I like to have everything in order,' he said to Cathy and she laughed.

'Yes, I know.'

Even in their few weeks in their own home it had become clear that Greg was as neat and orderly as Cathy was untidy, and she now realised why her mother had complained so often about the state of her bedroom.

When the time of parting arrived Cathy and Greg both tried to appear cheerful, telling each other that they would write often and that the war would soon be over. Greg asked Cathy to go to her mother's when he had gone and to stay there for the night.

To ease his mind Cathy said that she would, but when he was gone she went back to her own house where she could discard her air of false cheerfulness and weep bitterly and long. However, the pain of parting was soon dulled for her by the exhaustion she felt after each day's work.

Hymie Finestone had taken over a large building at the end of Hall Lane and started producing Army uniforms there. Cathy and a few of the other tailoresses had been moved there to supervise the extra girls he had taken on and the work was hard and exhausting.

Hymie was a bully who was never satisfied with the amount of work done, and Cathy felt that he picked on her more than anyone.

The girls she was supervising were untrained and he constantly raged about the quality of the work. 'Look at that,' he screamed at Cathy one day, thrusting a pair of khaki trousers at her. 'It's a bloody disgrace. D'ya want your feller to get trousers that drop to pieces on him?'

There was loud laughter and comments that made Cathy's cheeks burn, from the rough girls at the machines. She snatched the trousers from him. 'They're doing their best,' she said. 'They're not trained, and you want the work too quickly.'

'Any bloody excuse,' he snarled. 'You'd better shift yourself or you're out.'

She would have liked to walk out then but the job was convenient, so near her new home, and she needed the money. She had made up her mind not to take anything from the shop while Greg was away. His army allotment of twelve shillings and her own wages would be sufficient for her, and the shop money could accumulate until his return.

Greg wrote cheerfully from his training camp in Kent and Cathy wrote to him every night. Often she was too tired to do more than write the letter, have a snack and fall into bed, although she tried to see her parents as often as possible.

Cathy was worried about her father. He had changed his mind about the war after talking to some of the Belgian refugees who were flooding into the country after the fall of Antwerp, but Cathy felt that that was not the reason he had become so quiet and subdued.

She spoke to her mother about it, but she only said that he 'had things on his mind'. Sally too had grown even quieter than usual, but Cathy hoped soon to have news which would cheer them both.

When her period failed to arrive in December she blamed it on the shock of parting from Greg, but January came and went without any sign of it and by February Cathy was sure she was pregnant.

She was about to write to Greg with the news when she heard that he was coming home on leave and decided to keep the news until his return.

She planned a special meal in a romantic setting of flowers and candlelight, after which she would tell Greg that he was about to become a father.

Instead as soon as he stepped off the train she flung her arms round his neck and exclaimed. 'Greg, I'm going to have a baby.' But his delighted response was all she could have wanted.

They walked home arm in arm, talking and planning, and later they went to see her parents. Sally and Lawrie were delighted too and Cathy followed her mother into the back kitchen while Greg talked to her father. 'Are you surprised, Mam?' she asked.

Sally smiled. 'No, love. I thought your nose was looking a bit pinched.'

'Pinched?' Cathy exclaimed indignantly.

'Yes, you've got the look, that's the only way I can describe it. But you've lost weight altogether, Cath. You'll have to watch yourself or you'll be as bad as our Mary.'

'It's just the work,' Cathy said. 'Have you heard from her?'

'Not a line,' Sally said shortly.

'Perhaps they're not sending the letters on,' Cathy said. 'I've written three times and heard nothing.'

'Perhaps,' Sally said. 'Have you been sick in the mornings?'

Cathy recognised the hint to drop the subject of Mary but as they walked home she told Greg. 'I wonder if that's why they've gone so quiet,' she said.

'Don't worry about it, Cath,' Greg said. 'Don't worry about anything. Promise me.'

'I won't,' she said. 'No harm's going to come to our son.'

'What if it's our daughter?' Greg teased her.

'Just as welcome,' she said. 'Then we'll have a son next time.'

Greg's leave flew past. The day before he left he told Cathy that it was embarkation leave and that he would shortly be leaving for France.

'But you've only been away such a short time,' she said. 'Clive's been away all this time and he's still in England. Mary's still with him, too,' she added wistfully.

'It varies,' Greg said. 'Depends what you're in.'

'You won't be in any danger as a stretcher bearer, will you?' Cathy said. 'You take the wounded men to hospital after the battles are over, don't you?'

Greg wondered where Cathy had heard this story, but he agreed, thankful to leave her with such illusions.

Cathy wanted to tell Mary her news but she felt that her letters were just dropping into a void. She was also beginning to wonder if her parents were keeping something from her about her sister. She decided to test her theory.

'I think I'll go over and see that woman in her house,' she said to her mother. 'See what's been happening to my letters and if she can give me Mary's address.'

Her mother had been at the oven and now she sat down as though her legs had given way, twisting the oven cloth between her fingers. 'It's no use, love,' she said. 'There's no one there.'

'No one?' Cathy echoed blankly.

'No. The house has been sold,' Sally said. 'Oh, I didn't want to upset you about it, love, especially now. Greg will have my life.'

'I want to know, Mam. It'd upset me not to know what's happening,' Cathy said. 'Anyway, I forced your hand.'

Quietly and wearily her mother told her the little they knew about Mary's activities. 'You know when she went away just before your wedding?' she said. 'You know she was away for a few weeks.'

'Yes, but she wrote to me,' Cathy said. 'Only once, but I showed you the letter.'

'She wrote to us as well, just saying she didn't know when she'd be home,' Sally said.

She sat looking into the fire, her face sad. 'We just thought she was somewhere with Clive and she didn't have time to write, but your dad met Elizabeth Fairburn and she told him that Mary was at home.'

'When was this?' Cathy exclaimed.

'Just when Greg was going away at the beginning of December so we didn't say anything to you. It was a Sunday and he came dashing home, all worked up. I was laying out poor Mr Scott who'd just died, but you know your dad. He was off like a shot over to Neston. He got the idea in his head, you see, that Mary'd come home because she was ill and she wasn't going to tell us.' She stopped again. A dozen questions rose in Cathy's mind but she only said gently, 'And *was* she ill, Mam?'

Sally shook her head and began to cry but gradually she told Cathy the story. Lawrie had walked up the drive and Mary must have seen him from the window, because she flew out of the house like a fury and pulled him round the side of the house.

'She didn't want her friends to see him, Cath,' Sally said. 'He told her he'd only gone to see if she was all right. But she said something about having people there and he should have told her he was coming. But what upset your dad most, she said it wasn't the slums where you just walked in and out of the houses.'

'The cheeky bitch!' Cathy exclaimed. 'To say that to Dad. What did he say to her?'

'I don't know, Cathy. It was weeks before he told me that much but he was properly upset when he came home that day. He hasn't got over it yet, and what he's heard since has upset him more.'

'You shouldn't let it upset you, Mam,' Cathy said. 'It's all just gone to her head.'

'But she's disappeared, Cath. Mr Bagshaw asked Dad for her address and he couldn't give him one and said Bagshaw got in a real twist. You know how close-mouthed he is usually but he told Dad that they had gone through all the money and the house had been taken. I don't understand it but he said Clive had raised money on it.'

'But I thought there was a pile of money left by the uncle,' Cathy said.

'I know but it's all gone. Mr Bagshaw was going mad because he couldn't reach either of them for instructions, he said.'

'But where's Clive? Isn't Mary with him?' Cathy said.

'No. He's in France. That's all Mr Bagshaw could find out from the War Office, he said. Clive transferred to a Canadian Regiment and he's in France.'

Sally stood up and went to the dresser. 'This is all we've heard,' she said, taking a card from the drawer and handing it to Cathy.

It was a plain postcard with a few words scrawled in green ink. 'Don't worry. I can look after myself. Will write soon. Love, Mary.'

Sally had begun to cry again, quietly and hopelessly, and Cathy put her arm around her mother's neck. 'Don't get upset, Mam,' she said. 'It's true. Mary can look after herself. She's quick-witted, and you know what we always say: "Nothing daunts Mary". She'll turn up when you least expect her.'

Sally dried her eyes. 'You're right, love,' she said. 'Now I hope you're not going to worry about her either.'

'I won't, Mam, but I'm glad she sent that card. It shows she cares about you and doesn't want you to worry.'

'Aye,' Sally said rather doubtfully. 'I think she got a bit spoiled, you know. Everything always fell her way. Don't make that mistake with yours, Cathy.'

Cathy laughed, sure that *her* child would never cause her any worry.

'I wonder what it will be, Mam?' she said. 'A girl or a boy?'

'Well, it'll be one or the other anyhow,' Sally said dryly, and Cathy gave her a quick kiss, glad to see her mother back to normal.

Chapter Thirty-Three

Mary needed her quick wits now. Clive had not left an address when he went away, but told her that he would write when he knew exactly where he would be sent.

No letters arrived, and when Cathy's wedding drew near Mary decided to pretend to join him to avoid having to attend.

She felt that Fate played into her hands when she chanced to meet someone she had known in Isabel's set. Dora Roberts was then a meek young wife but her husband had been an early war casualty, and Dora had blossomed into a self-confident young widow, intent on having a good time.

She and Mary soon arranged to spend some time in London together. Mary took the money she had accumulated and some of her smartest clothes, and soon the two girls were wining and dining and visiting dances and theatres with young officers on leave.

Although Mary was enjoying herself there was always the worry in her mind that Clive might return and find her missing.

'What would you do?' Dora asked.

'Tell him I'd come here to look for him, because he didn't write,' she said. 'I've told the housekeeper to send letters on.'

'So he knows where you are,' Dora said. Mary's uneasiness grew and after a couple of weeks she decided to go home.

'But not to stay,' she told Dora. 'As soon as I know where he is or if he's to be posted overseas, I'll be back.'

'Make it soon,' Dora told her. 'And if he comes home, don't forget what I told you.'

'I'll remember,' Mary said. 'I should have thought of it myself.'

Dora told Mary that her husband had been a 'beast', insatiable in his demands for sex, but she had 'taken steps'. She had picked up the spirit kettle to refill the teapot and managed to drop it in her husband's lap.

'He was scalded in just the right place,' she laughed, lighting one cigarette with the stub of the other. 'He knew I'd meant it, too. Everybody else was impressed because I was such a devoted little wife and so sorry for what happened, but *he* knew.'

The weeks with Dora hastened the change in Mary which her marriage had begun, and the events of the next few weeks made her even harder.

When she arrived home there was still nothing from Clive but a large number of bills had arrived and some letters addressed to her.

All the letters were similar in form, asking if she would kindly furnish Mr Clive Walden's address at her earliest convenience. She decided to open the bills next. The amount and variety of the debts appalled her. Had he paid for nothing? What had he done with his money?

The tone of the demands frightened her and she bundled them up and thrust them into the desk. I can't do anything, she thought. They're nothing to do with me. She remembered Clive saying that Mr Bagshaw would attend to things and she decided to send them to him.

The next day, however, she had a visit from the solicitor. His manner was cold and formal. 'I usually conduct such business only in my office, Mrs Walden,' he said. 'But the circumstances are unusual. Can you give me your husband's address?'

'I'm afraid I can't, Mr Bagshaw.'

'But I understand from Mrs Stewart that you have been visiting your husband,' he said.

So that's how he knows I'm home, Mary thought. 'I don't discuss my business with the housekeeper, Mr Bagshaw,' she said haughtily.

His stringy neck grew red. 'It is most important that I reach your husband, Mrs Walden, in your interest. He made several appointments with me but failed to keep them, and now it is imperative that I communicate with him.'

'He's fighting for his country,' Mary said.

'Quite so, but it is – ah – usual to put one's house in order before going. I am considering your interests, Mrs Walden, although I respect your loyalty.'

He doesn't believe me, Mary thought. She allowed her eyes to fill with tears, and looked pathetically at Mr Bagshaw.

'I didn't want anyone to know,' she said. 'He went away without leaving his address because he said he would write when he was settled, but I've heard nothing.'

Mr Bagshaw's manner changed. 'Dear me, dear me,' he said. 'Don't distress yourself.'

'I went to London to try to find him,' Mary said. 'I have a friend and her husband is a staff officer. I thought she might be able to help me.' She stood up and went to the desk. 'I found all these when I came home,' she said, handing him the bundle of bills and letters.

He looked through them and then sat pulling at his lip. 'I find myself in a dilemma,' he said. 'But you've given me an idea. Perhaps I can trace him through the War Office. I must have instructions.'

'But why, Mr Bagshaw? Why do you need to see Clive?' Mary said. 'I know he's careless about money, but couldn't you just tell these people that he'll pay them, or perhaps you could pay them out of his money.'

He rubbed his chin. 'There's a – a difficulty – a problem. Could you come to my office with your father, Mrs Walden, and I can explain.'

'Can't you explain now?' she said. 'Do you think that something's happened to him?'

'No, no, not at all. Purely a financial problem, but I'm concerned about you, Mrs Walden,' he said. Finally he told Mary that Clive had raised a loan using the house as security, and that he had raised another loan on the contents of the house. 'He took the deeds of the house to study them as a matter of interest, but failed to return them,' Mr Bagshaw said, his anger showing in the red colour on his neck and cheeks.

'But why? He had plenty of money and was always so generous with me.'

Eventually he told her that there was a lot that she was unaware of but that he would do his best for her. He took the bills, telling her to refer anyone who approached her to him, and before he left he took her hand and said kindly, 'I have the greatest respect for your father, my dear, and I'm sure that whatever happens he will always look after you, so don't worry. A loving family is a great asset.'

Mary was more bewildered than worried by his visit, but the more she thought it over, the more she realised that Mr Bagshaw suspected Clive of deliberately covering his tracks.

She rapidly realised that he was right when, shortly after he left, three of the tradesmen to whom Clive owed money arrived in swift succession. They had each decided independently that as their letters were ignored, they would call in person.

One alone Mary might have been able to placate but the three together were very angry men, and when they realised that there was little hope of their money they became very abusive.

The row was at its height when Mary glanced out of the window and saw her father walking up the drive. Her first idea was to conceal her position from him, and she flew out of the house and pulled him round the side.

'What are you doing here? Why didn't you tell me you were coming?' she hissed at him.

Lawrie looked at her with surprise and anger. 'Why? Do I have to make an appointment to see my own daughter?'

'I've got people here,' she cried, too flustered to realise how much she was hurting him. 'This isn't the slums where you walk in and out of each other's houses.'

Lawrie pulled his arm away. 'I came to see how you were,' he said with dignity. 'Elizabeth saw you at Lime Street and thought you looked ill, but never mind. You'll wait a hell of a long time for another unannounced visit, *Madam*.'

He turned and walked away, and Mary went back and hustled the men out of the house, telling them to speak to Mr Bagshaw. Then she wept angry tears. How dare Clive leave her in this state? To think of what she had suffered for the sake of the lifestyle he could provide.

That had been the only compensation for the dreadful nights, she thought, the fact that by day she was surrounded by luxury and envied by so many people. Now it seemed that even this house would go but she told herself that she didn't care.

I can tell people it was because of the war, she decided, but then another thought struck her. Which people? Who cared about her now, and who did she care about for that matter? Not the people from Denby's she had wanted to impress, not the so-called friends she had made since her marriage. Not even her family, especially her father after today.

She couldn't bear them to know how she had been brought down, and they wouldn't care either. All they cared about were Cathy and Greg. Mary shed a few tears of self pity, and told herself that she was glad she had made Bagshaw promise to say nothing to her father. I can look after myself, she thought, wiping her eyes.

That declaration was put to the test sooner than she expected. Soon after dark two men appeared in the drawing room although Mary had heard no sound of a knock or bell and they had not been announced.

'What do you want?' she said, as one shut the door and leaned against it, and the other one walked over to stand close to her.

'We want a lot of things,' he said, 'but chiefly we want your dear husband.'

'He's not here,' Mary said in a trembling voice.

'We know that, but you're going to tell us where we can find him,' the man said. 'Aren't you?'

'But I don't know,' Mary said. 'He didn't leave an address. He said he'd write but he hasn't.'

'Aw, come on. You can do better than that,' the man said, and the other by the door laughed.

Mary looked from one to the other. 'It's the truth. I've been to London to try to find him. Mr Bagshaw is dealing with everything.'

'And who's Mr Bagshaw?'

'The family solicitor,' Mary said, and the man by the door laughed again.

'We don't mix with solicitors,' the first man said. 'We're what you'd call more direct.'

The thought of Mr Bagshaw had given Mary a surge of courage and she started towards the bell pull, but the man nearest to her said calmly, 'I wouldn't.' He took a cut-throat razor from his pocket and opened it, then began to clean his nails.

Mary watched in terror and when he asked again for Clive's address she hastily improvised. 'I only know what I found out in London,' she said. 'I wrote to him there, and came home to see if he'd replied.'

'And had he?'

'Not yet,' she said. She had met an officer from the Sherwood Foresters in London and he had told her that he was stationed at Lowestoft. She had asked if he knew Clive but he said he had not met him. Now she said that Clive was stationed there and gave them a fictitious address she said she had written to. Her hand shook as she wrote it down and handed it to the man, then collapsed into a chair.

'It had better be right,' he said. 'Or we'll be back.' He bent over her and she shrank back in the chair. 'People who can't pay shouldn't gamble,' he said softly. 'I'll take this on account.'

Before she realised what he was doing he had sliced through the material of her dress to take the diamond brooch from it, then picked up her hand. She wore only her wedding ring with a keeper ring to stop it from falling off. All her other rings had been bought before her hands had grown too thin to keep them on.

The man by the door walked over to a side table and picked up a porcelain figure from it. He examined the base of it then slipped it in his pocket and took a silver cigarette box for his other pocket.

'Don't forget. We'll check this tomorrow and it'd better be right,' they threatened. Mary had no need to simulate terror as she huddled in the chair, shaking with fright. The men smiled at each other with satisfaction as they left.

Mary lay trembling for a few moments before fright was succeeded by anger. Gambling debts! So that was why Clive had run away, the rat, leaving her to face the music. Well, two can play at that game, she thought grimly. The men's actions had given her an idea and she swiftly collected the most expensive items in the room that were small enough to carry.

She took them upstairs then rang for the maid. 'Get the boot boy,' she said. 'And bring down my husband's trunk and his Gladstone bag.' She knew that the housekeeper and her husband the gardener were out for the evening and swiftly packed the trunk with her furs and most expensive clothes.

Mary had never examined the drawers and cupboards where Clive's clothes were kept, but now she needed to find the keys of the trunk. She found them almost immediately but in the same drawer there was a box containing three sets of gold cufflinks, several gold studs, and pearl and diamond tiepins.

Mary put them with her own jewellery and the items from the drawing room and decided to explore further. She found one gold and two silver cigarette cases, silver and leather hip flasks, unused silver-backed hairbrushes and a gold card case, and put them with the growing pile on the bed.

Best of all she found several sovereigns and half sovereigns and some silver coins in the top drawer. She still had some money left and was sure that she could raise money on the items on the bed but anything else was welcome. I don't think I'll get much cash from old Bagshaw, she thought ruefully.

She put the brushes and the hip flasks among her clothes in the trunk then locked and strapped it, and rang again for the maid.

'I'll need my hat box and my suitcase too,' she said to the girl, 'Then send the boot boy to me.' To the boot boy she gave some silver and told him to go to the man who ran a carrier's service and bring him back.

'Now?' the boy said. 'He might 'a put the horses up, Mum.'

'Tell him I'll make it worth his while,' Mary said. 'Tell him it's because of the war.' The lad scurried away and she rapidly packed her hats and more of her clothes and shoes, distributing the jewellery and the items from the drawing room among them.

When it was done she went through Clive's belongings again to search for anything else that was saleable. At the back of a shelf in the wardrobe, she literally struck gold. It was a canvas bag containing gold coins and although she was afraid to count them in case she was disturbed, there seemed to be about three hundred pounds there.

Mary felt stunned. Why had he kept so much money there, and even more to the point why had he not taken it with him? Could he have forgotten it, or had he left it there to retrieve in case of emergency?

This is *my* emergency, she thought, putting the canvas bag safely into the Gladstone bag. She was trembling with impatience to get away, but felt weak and realised that she had eaten nothing for hours. She felt that she would need her strength so she rang again for the maid.

'Where's Cook, Milly?' she asked.

'She went to lay down, Mum. Her feet were killing her.'

'Don't disturb her then. Can you bring me a glass of milk and something to eat, and tell me as soon as Charlie comes back.' She took half a sovereign from her purse and gave it to the girl. 'You've been a good help to me, Milly, and I'll tell you something but I don't want it talked about. Mr Clive is going to France and I'm going down to see him first.'

Milly's hand flew to her mouth. 'Me brother's in France, Ma'am, and me other two brothers are at sea. Me mam's near demented with worrying about them.'

'Never mind, it'll all be over soon,' Mary said. 'Now get me that tray, Milly.'

She forced herself to eat the food and soon heard the wheels of the carrier's cart.

She felt exhausted but triumphant when at last she was on the London train with her precious luggage and her trunk safely stowed in the guard's van.

Dora welcomed her exuberantly, and approved of all that Mary had done. She suggested that they should move out of the hotel and take an apartment together, and soon they were established in a flat near the centre of London. Mary sent her new address to the War Office and the two girls settled down to enjoy themselves.

With their good looks and high spirits they were never short of escorts, and Mary firmly closed her mind to the past and threw herself into the hectic social scene of the war years.

When she was notified of Clive's death in action on April 22nd 1915, her first feeling was of relief, although in bed that night she remembered how kind and generous to her he had been at times and wept a little for him.

The news of the capture of Hill 60, shortly followed by news of the German use of gas against the French, filled the newspapers and the British victory was overshadowed by the indignation aroused by the gas attack. There was a small item in the newspapers praising the heroism of the Canadians who 'held the line', and Mary felt proudly that Clive was probably one of them.

'I'm glad he died of wounds and not of the gas,' she said to Dora. 'Gassing must be dreadful.'

'The main thing is he's dead,' Dora said cynically. 'Now you've got nothing to worry about.'

Mary agreed with her but for several nights she dreamed continuously about Greg.

She dreamt of him blown up by shells or blinded, or falling clutching his throat after a gas attack as she had seen in a photograph of a Zouave in a newspaper.

The longing to know what was happening to him and to her family grew unbearable and finally she wrote a short letter to her mother, telling her of Clive's death and asking for news of the family. She gave a box number for the reply, saying that she was moving around on war work.

'I don't want any visits from anyone,' she told Dora. 'And I'm not sure how I stand about that stuff I brought away with me.'

Her mother's reply said that she was sorry to hear of Clive's death, although they were pleased to hear that Mary was all right. Cathy was expecting a baby in September and Greg was now in France. Aunty Emily had taken a turn for the worse again and one of Norah Benson's brothers and a cousin had been killed. Mary's father was well apart from a cough.

It was a stiff letter and she was annoyed by it, although she had to concede that the family had good reason to be hurt. At least Greg was all right, but Cathy was expecting a baby… Mary flung the letter in the fire and decided not to write again.

Chapter Thirty-Four

It was a relief to Mary's family to know that she was alive and well, but they were shocked by the offhand way in which she told them of Clive's death.

'She doesn't seem very upset,' Sally said. 'I know he was a bit dishonourable about money, but he was good to Mary. I thought she'd have shown more grief.'

'Not her,' Lawrie said shortly. His belief that she was perfect had been shattered on the day he was turned away from her house.

As he hurried down the drive, deeply mortified, he had glanced back and caught sight of a man in the window of the drawing room. So that's it, he thought grimly. It's not snobbery. She's carrying on behind Clive's back.

He knew nothing of Mary's sufferings at Clive's hands and he thought she was treating a good husband badly, being unfaithful to him and ruining him by her extravagance. Even Mr Bagshaw's cautious disclosures about Clive's shady dealings only convinced Lawrie that his daughter and Clive were equally unscrupulous about money.

A few days later all thought of Mary was driven from their minds. The *Lusitania* had been the pride of Liverpool since her maiden voyage from there in September 1907, and most of her crew were local men. When the news reached Liverpool that she had been torpedoed without warning while homeward bound from New York, on May 7th 1915, the people of the city were stunned with shock and grief.

Crowds besieged the Cunard offices in Water Street, hoping for news. Most of the 'black gang' of stokers and firemen came from Scotland Road, and their families had hurried into town.

Crowds of distraught women carrying babies in their black shawls, and with small children clinging to their skirts, roamed round the offices and the waterfront asking everyone they met for news.

Lists of survivors were published in the newspapers, but still hoping against hope, many of the women went to Woodside Station on the other side of the river on Sunday. They had heard that the last of the survivors would arrive at five-fifteen. When none of the few people who stepped from the train had been able to give them any news of their husbands or sons, a Cunard official told them that there would be no more survivors. 'It's better for you to know the truth,' he said, and the women went sadly away.

Despair soon turned to anger and crowds gathered to wreak vengeance on the Germans who lived in the city. Many of them had been naturalised and had relatives fighting for the British but that meant nothing to the crowds of wreckers.

It was the first time a passenger ship had been attacked, and some of the crowd were genuinely full of anger and indignation because of this, but others were only intent on destruction and looting.

Old Solly's sons lived on the outskirts of Liverpool now, and his grandsons were serving in the British Army, but the old man still lived among his junk in the shop near Egremont Street. Sally had been out trying to console a neighbour whose son had gone down on the 'Lusy' and was coming home when she heard the sound of breaking glass and saw the crowds outside the pork butcher's. They were moving off and she hurried to Solly's shop to warn him.

Within minutes the crowd had arrived and begun to attack. 'Wharrabout yer bloody Mad Mullah now?' one woman was screaming. 'Yer bloody Kaiser saying God's on his side.'

The window had been broken and the crowd were pushing into the shop behind the woman when Sally stepped in front of the old man. 'Leave him alone. He's Polish,' she shouted, but the crowd were too wild to heed her.

'I hope they all rot in Hell, the Kaiser and every last one of them,' the woman was still screaming. 'The likes of youse too that sticks up for them.' She swung the piece of wood she carried at Sally, and a few stones flew, but most of the crowd were busy helping themselves to Solly's stock.

Sally put her arm round the old man and almost carried him from the shop and down to her house. It was only when they were inside and she had helped him into a chair that she realised that her right arm was hanging at a strange angle.

The riots were soon over, and Solly's sons arrived to take him to live with one of them. They had been trying to persuade him for a long time, they told Sally, but he wanted to stay among his old neighbours.

'Neighbours,' the son said bitterly. 'A lifetime he lives here, and where were his neighbours today? Except you, Mrs Ward,' he added hastily.

'I just happened to be handy,' she said. 'I was glad to help. Your father was always good to me.' She bent over the old man. 'You remember when you bought my furniture when Lawrie was out of work, Mr Solomon? You pretended you were storing it so I wouldn't be shamed in front of the neighbours. And the good prices you gave me when I sold things.'

'Oy, hard times,' old Solly muttered. 'But better times than these. Better they came back.'

'This madness will pass,' Sally comforted him. 'We don't want those hard times back. Let's hope things will be better for everyone after the war's over. No more "popping" candlesticks to buy food, eh?'

'And vot of Solly if nobody pops, hey?' the old man said, but he was smiling and Sally was pleased to see the tender concern the sons showed as they took him away.

Sally's arm had been put in a splint and she was trying awkwardly to cook and cut bread using her left.

'I never realised how much I used my right hand until now,' she told Peggy Burns who had come in to help.

Her accident brought to a head what they had all been thinking for some weeks. Cathy's pregnancy was going smoothly, but she was spending less and less time in her own home. After an exhausting day at the factory she was too tired to do more than make a snack, and Sally often insisted that she came by for her evening meal.

She often stayed the night and it seemed to make sense for her to give up her home and stay with her parents until the war was over. Greg wrote in favour when she mentioned this in a letter, saying that he would worry less about her and they could easily start again after the war.

Although Cathy had mentioned the idea to Greg she had said nothing to her parents, fearing that they might feel obliged to agree if she did, and the idea might not suit them. Sally and Lawrie were silent for the same reason, that they might force Cathy and Greg against their will.

Sally's accident gave them the excuse they needed to talk about it, and soon Cathy's furniture was added to the parlour and her bed replaced the bed she had shared with Mary. Sally's idea was that Cathy should regard the parlour and the back bedroom as her own rooms, to furnish as she wished, and that she and Greg would have privacy there when he came on leave.

They all settled back together happily. Cathy left the factory and took over the household chores while Sally was incapacitated, and she did some of her mother's sewing orders under her supervision.

Greg hoped to be given leave when the baby was due in September, but all leave was cancelled for the 'Big Push' that was planned.

On September 8th Cathy's son was born with very little trouble. In their frequent letters Cathy and Greg had discussed the baby's name at some length. Cathy wished to include Gregory in his name, but Greg thought the baby should have the names of his two grandfathers, and she agreed to call him John Lawrence.

He was like a tiny replica of Greg, and a source of endless delight to Cathy, and Lawrie and Sally. As soon as possible Cathy took him to show to his other grandmother.

Sally had kept Mrs Redmond fully informed of the progress of Cathy's labour and had expected a visit from her soon after the birth, but she only sent a note and some grapes which Sally suspected were provided by Miss Nugent. She seemed more interested than Mrs Redmond when Cathy took the baby to them.

'All she did was talk about how disappointed she was when Greg couldn't come home,' Cathy told her mother indignantly. 'And it wasn't because she wanted to see him either, it was just because she said there were things she needed him to do for her. She hardly looked at the baby.'

'It's her loss,' Sally said soothingly. She took the baby and cuddled him. 'You're going to bring a lot of joy to this grandma anyway, John love.'

'I went into the shop too and they're as bad,' Cathy said. 'I wanted to know how things were going so I could tell Greg, but old Braithwaite is so touchy you can't ask him anything and I don't like that first assistant either. He's a proper Uriah Heap.'

'Who's he?' Sally asked, as she took off the baby's outdoor clothes.

'A character in *David Copperfield* who was always saying he was a "very 'umble person" and tricking them out of the business,' Cathy said.

Sally looked alarmed. 'You don't think that's happening, do you?' she said.

'No, Mam. I just don't like his manner. Greg showed me about the paperwork but I couldn't look at anything. They made me feel as though I was poking my nose in and I was too stupid to understand anyway. I wish I had more push, Mam.'

'You can't change your nature, love,' Sally said calmly. 'The shop looks as though it's being run well anyway, doesn't it?'

'Yes, it does. I suppose I'm as touchy as old Braithwaite really.' Cathy laughed. 'I just didn't like being brushed off.'

Sally held the baby close. 'Never mind, love,' she said to Cathy. 'John is all that matters now. He'll be a joy and comfort to us anyway, and he won't need that selfish old faggot.'

Sally soon needed to be comforted by the baby. Although Emily had been frail and delicate for so many years she clung tenaciously to life, and often had periods of remission from her illness. Her health had improved in Southport.

As Sally had told Mary in her letter, however, Emily was seriously ill in the Spring of 1915, but had rallied again and though she seemed even weaker there was little further change during the summer months.

She was looking forward eagerly to the birth of Cathy's baby and Sally sent her a telegram as soon as John was born. While Cathy was in bed after the birth Peggy Burns came in to sit with her several times so that Sally could go to see her sister, and Emily listened eagerly to all that Sally could tell her about the baby.

On a grey, wet day in late October Sally set off to travel to Southport feeling low in spirits. Everywhere newspaper placards screamed outrage at the German execution of Nurse Edith Cavell, for helping British and Belgian soldiers to escape.

In Lime Street she met Gertie who had been one of her first sewing customers and learned that two of Gertie's sons had been killed in the same action.

'It's a terrible thing to be a mother,' Gertie sobbed, clutching at Sally. 'It's true what they say. If you've got none to make you laugh, you've got none to make you cry, either.'

Sally tried to comfort her, but as she sat on the train travelling to Southport she thought of Gertie's words and was inclined to agree with her.

Thoughts of Mary were never far from Sally's mind. No matter how angry she was with her eldest daughter, nothing could stop Sally from loving and worrying about her. The knowledge that Lawrie was suffering in the same way only made her grief worse.

They had been terrified to read of the Zeppelin attacks on London and to learn that forty people had been killed. There was no way they could find out if Mary was safe except by writing to the box number and waiting anxiously for a reply.

The usual scrawled postcard had eventually arrived. 'Quite safe. Hope all are well. Mary.'

'Not even love or a word about the baby and I wrote to her about it,' Sally said angrily to Lawrie. But he said soothingly: 'She might not have got it, love, the way things are now.'

Now Sally wondered sadly how she had gone wrong in Mary's upbringing, that she had turned out so cold and selfish. As the train pulled into Southport station she decided that she must put these sad thoughts behind her, and be more cheerful when she called on Emily. But a shock awaited her at the nursing home.

The Matron appeared in the hall as Sally entered, and drew her into a side parlour. 'You must be prepared for a change in your sister, Mrs Ward,' she said gently.

'Has she had another haemorrhage?' Sally exclaimed.

'No. She's been growing weaker for some time, but now – I'm afraid she's sinking fast, Mrs Ward. I've sent a telegram to her husband, but it's you she really wants.'

Sally followed the woman as though in a dream, hoping against hope that she was wrong. Emily was lying propped up on her pillows and at first glance seemed no more frail, but there was an indefinable change in her. Sally could see death in her sister's face.

She went to Emily and took her in her arms. Over her sister's head she looked at the Matron, and the woman looked back at her sorrowfully. There was nothing to be said. It was clear that all hope was gone.

The Matron slipped away, and Emily lifted her hand to Sally's face, saying thankfully, 'Sal. You've come.' She sat holding Emily in her arms, stroking back her hair and struggling to conceal her own tears.

After a while she gently laid Emily back on her pillow and gave her a drink from a feeding cup, then sat holding her hand until a nurse looked in and said, 'Your husband's here, Mrs Deakin.'

Sally stood up but Emily clutched her hand. 'Don't leave me, Sal,' she whispered weakly.

'I'm just going outside for a while, love,' she said. 'Albert's here but I'll come back soon.' She nodded to her brother-in-law as she passed him and went to sit in a side room. The Matron came to her, carrying a cup of tea and offering food, but Sally could eat nothing.

'Your visits have meant such a lot to Mrs Deakin,' the Matron said. 'She thinks the world of you, and your husband and family. She has a good husband too. Very generous. He has never missed his Sunday visit, and he'll pay for any extra little comforts for her.'

Sally said nothing and the Matron went on, 'Mrs Deakin's happy while you're here. She told me you'd been mother and sister both to her. How long can you stay, Mrs Ward?'

'As long as she needs me.'

'Good. Would you like me to send a telegram to your husband in case he worries if you stay overnight?'

'Oh no. My daughter – her husband's in France,' Sally said. 'A telegram, she'd think—'

'Of course. If you'd like to write a postcard for the one o'clock post he'd get it for seven o'clock,' the Matron said, and Sally wrote briefly to Lawrie.

Albert soon left, and Sally went back to sit holding Emily's hand and talking to her of the days she loved to hear about, when she was a tiny child and Sally brought her up after their mother's death.

The shadows gathered as the afternoon wore on and Emily lay smiling happily as she held Sally's hand and heard of the days when as a baby she'd been the apple of her sister's eye, before she was adopted by her aunt, before their young brothers died, and when their father was loving and cheerful, instead of the bitter man he became later.

As she talked of those days and recalled Mrs Malloy bustling in and out of the house, the happy outings with Emily, the fun one Duck Apple Night when the baby Emily had suddenly climbed into the bath to seize an apple while fully dressed, Sally was happy too.

It was a shock when the nurse came in with a lamp and Sally and Emily had to return to the sad reality of the present.

Sally came out and the maid brought her tea and cake, and after a few minutes she was able to go back to Emily. She lay on fresh pillows, wearing a white nightdress threaded with blue ribbons, and with her hair neatly braided.

'You'll feel better, love, after being freshened up,' Sally said, and Emily smiled weakly.

'I feel better now you're here, Sal. I couldn't go without seeing you.'

Sally took Emily's thin hand and kissed it, and for a while they sat in companionable silence, until Albert came again. Sally left him alone with his wife and went to the small side room where the Matron joined her. 'I've offered Mr Deakin a bed here,' she said. 'I think he should stay.'

Sally glanced at her. 'You think—?' she said, unable to put her thought into words, and the Matron nodded.

Later Albert retired to bed, but Sally sat up talking to Emily and crooning some of the songs she had sung to her as a baby. The house was quiet and peaceful. From time to time the night nurse peeped in but went away again quietly.

'I've been very lucky, Sal,' Emily said suddenly. 'I had that happy time when I was little, and even on the farm. It was only later – but then Albert married me, and he's been a good kind husband, Sal.

He's done all he could for me. Poor Albert. I haven't been much of a wife to him.'

Sally pressed her hand. 'I've told you before, love, Albert has been happier with you even with all the illness than he would be with anyone else. You've brought him happiness.'

More than he deserves, Sally thought grimly, but Emily was smiling with relief.

She lay quietly for a while, and when she spoke again her voice was weaker. Sally had to bend close to her to hear. 'You've been the one, Sal. You've loved me,' she murmured. 'Made me happy. You and Lawrie and the girls. I've been lucky – you – my sister.'

She was gasping for breath and Sally said urgently: 'Don't tire yourself, love. Don't talk.'

She sat holding Emily's hand, tears running down her face, and her sister seemed to drift off to sleep again. Just after two o'clock in the morning she stirred and began to cough. Blood trickled from her mouth and the next moment, as though by instinct, the nurse arrived in the room. She wiped Emily's mouth and rearranged the bedclothes, and she must have raised the alarm for within minutes the Matron and Albert arrived.

Sally moved away to allow him to the bedside but Emily made a weak sound of protest, and without a word Albert moved to the other side of the bed. Emily looked beseechingly at Sally, and she took her sister in her arms again. Emily lay with her head on Sally's shoulder and held out her hand to Albert.

He took it, and sank suddenly to his knees, kissing Emily's hand with tears pouring down his face.

The nurse had been hovering in the background but when Emily gave a small sigh she came and took her wrist, then signed to Sally to lay her back on the pillows. 'She's gone,' she said. 'Thank goodness it was peaceful at the end.'

Albert and Sally stood for a moment, looking at Emily's thin face, peaceful in death, before they left the room. The Matron was waiting for them. 'My condolences,' she said.

'Thank you,' Albert mumbled. He looked old and bewildered and the Matron said kindly, 'Now if you'll take my advice, Mr Deakin, you'll go right back to bed. There's nothing you can do here.'

'Thank you,' he said again, then he held out his hand to Sally. They said nothing as they gripped each other's hand then she patted his arm and he turned and went upstairs.

Sally stood as though in a trance until the Matron took her into a back room. She gave her a glass of something bitter and stood with her while she drank it, then she said briskly, 'I haven't had a bed made up for you, Mrs Ward, but I'm sure you'll be all right on this sofa.'

Sally allowed herself to be settled on the sofa and covered with a blanket, and within minutes sank into merciful oblivion.

Chapter Thirty-Five

Sally woke when the maid brought her a cup of tea, and lay for the moment wondering where she was. Remembrance swept over her, but a tall figure rose from a chair in the corner and bent over her.

'Lawrie,' she gasped as he bent and kissed her. Then he sat beside her on the sofa, and put his arms round her. She clung to him and wept, and he said quietly, 'The nurse said she had a peaceful end, love, in your arms. She died happy anyway, Sal.'

After a few minutes she sat up and dried her eyes. 'How did you know? When did you come, Lol?'

'First thing. I've changed shifts with Jimmy Burns,' he said. 'I just came to see how things were in case you needed me, love.'

Tears welled up again in her eyes. 'I do, Lol, I do need you,' she said as he put his arms round her again. 'I can't believe it. My poor Emily.'

'We'll go home now, Sal,' Lawrie said. 'I think Albert's gone already.' Sally went to wash her face and tidy herself then Matron came to her. 'Mr Deakin has left, Mrs Ward,' she said. 'He said he would get in touch with you about the arrangements.'

'Thank you, Matron,' Sally said quietly. 'And thank you for all your kindness to my sister and to me.' Her voice trembled, and the Matron patted her arm.

'We'll all miss her,' she said. 'She was a wonderful patient, so brave and uncomplaining. We were all very fond of her.'

'She suffered for so long,' Sally said, 'but I never heard her complain once.'

'I'm glad you were with her at the end, Mrs Ward. She only ever wanted you with her. She loved you and your family so much.'

'And we all loved her,' Lawrie said, as Sally stood, trying to control her tears. She looked appealingly at Lawrie and he understood and said to the Matron, 'May we?'

'Of course,' she said, and they went in to where Emily lay, dignified and peaceful, her thin hands crossed on her breast.

Lawrie bent and kissed her forehead, then whispered to Sally, 'I'll wait outside, love.'

When Sally had said her last goodbye to her sister, she joined him and they left for the station, walking arm in arm through the crisp October morning, both busy with their own thoughts.

As they stepped on to the train Sally suddenly thought of all the times she had travelled to see her sister, and that now she would make the journey no more. Lawrie seemed to sense her distress and said quickly, 'I wonder how Cathy got on with the baby. He was yelling his head off when I left.'

'Why? What was wrong?'

'I don't know. Cathy was trying him with gripe water. There's nothing wrong with his lungs, Sal. We'll be having complaints from the neighbours.'

'Let them dare,' she said indignantly, 'after what we've put up with in our time.' Her thoughts had been successfully diverted, but as the train drew into Liverpool, sadness swept over her again.

So many places brought back memories of Emily, and as they walked from the station her eyes brimmed with tears again. As soon as Cathy saw her face she said, 'Oh, Mam,' and put her arms around her mother to weep with her. Lawrie took Sally's coat and Cathy went immediately to the cradle and lifted the baby into her mother's arms.

'She never saw him,' Sally wept, but when the baby cried she walked up and down nursing him, comforting the child and being comforted by the feeling of the little body in her arms.

Sally often wondered how she could have borne the months after Emily's death without the baby to comfort her. Cathy was generous with him, letting her mother nurse him and do many of the things for him that she longed to do for him herself.

There were few people at Emily's simple funeral. The death of a quiet invalid woman seemed to mean little when young men were being mown down in thousands and tragedy and suffering had become a way of life, but Sally and her family mourned Emily deeply.

'Her time had come, love,' Lawrie gently comforted Sally after the funeral. 'She'd suffered enough.'

'That's true,' she said with a sigh. 'Albert looked very old, didn't he?'

'Yes, he seems to have taken it hard,' Lawrie said.

'Emily reckoned he was a good husband to her, and the Matron said he was very generous, paying for extra comforts. Perhaps we've misjudged him, Lawrie.'

'There's good and bad in all of us, I suppose,' he said.

As weeks then months passed with no prospect of home leave for Greg, some of Cathy's pleasure in her son was spoiled by the fact that his father was missing these stages of his progress. John's first tooth, the day he said Da Da, and his first shaky steps were minutely described in Cathy's letters to Greg but she knew that they were a poor substitute for his actually seeing John.

When the baby was three months old Cathy took him to have a photograph taken to send to Greg. The baby's dress and bonnet were triumphs of fine stitching and embroidery by Sally and he lay on a lacy shawl which Cathy had made, but she asked the photographer not to bother about the clothes but to concentrate on John's face.

'It's to send to his father in France,' she explained.

At just the right moment the baby smiled and Cathy turned to Sally. 'Now you can't say *that's* wind,' she exclaimed triumphantly.

They were delighted with the photograph, and on the card beneath it Cathy carefully printed a verse she had seen in a newspaper.

> Only a baby small, never at rest
> Small but how dear to us, God knoweth best.

Greg's letter, written when he received the photograph, revealed more than he had ever done. Usually his letters were formal and Cathy teased him when she wrote about always being business-like.

He had always written cheerfully, praising the other soldiers and the fortitude of the wounded men, but saying little about himself.

Now he wrote from his heart.

> My darling Cathy,
>
> I can't tell you what your letter and the baby's photograph meant to me. I have never felt so low in spirit as I did last night. The thought of another Christmas come and gone and we seem no nearer the end, and the death and destruction all around us. Mud and dead bodies and the continuous noise of the guns and the screams of wounded men. I felt as though I was in hell. We carried a brave young lad nearly a mile, horribly wounded but no complaints even when we stumbled in shell holes, then as we got to the Clearing Station he died.
>
> I came back feeling as low as I'll ever feel, then when we got back the letters had come up. When I opened your letter, Cath, and saw the baby's picture – well, I

can't explain how I felt. If I say I went from hell to heaven it sounds a bit ornate but it's the truth. You know how much I love you, Cath, but I felt as though I've never loved you enough. And now our son. I've looked and looked at his picture until his little face is imprinted on my mind, and the verse you wrote is repeating in my head all the time.

I showed it to one of the other bearers, John Savage, one of the best and wisest men I've ever known, and he said, 'That's what we're fighting for, Greg, for a better world for him. Makes it all worth while, doesn't it?'

I feel a different man to the miserable creature who crawled in here a few hours ago. The other lads are asleep but I'm too happy to sleep, Cath. You've given me fresh courage, love. All my fondest love to you and John, sweetheart.

Your loving husband,
Greg.

Greg's letter became one of Cathy's dearest possessions, read and re-read until it almost fell apart. For a while his letters became more infrequent and sometimes only field postcards arrived, but even these were welcome proof that he was still alive.

The casualty lists in the *Echo* and the *Express* grew longer every night, and Cathy read them, dreading to see names of friends and brothers of friends.

Some families seemed to suffer one tragedy after another. In many cases brothers served on the same ship or had joined up together so there were double tragedies when a ship was sunk or during a battle, and two more of the Mellor sons were drowned when the ship they served on was sunk.

Norah's brother Teddy recovered from his wounds and returned to the Front, but shortly afterwards was killed by a shell. Within two weeks his twin brother Luke was wounded and died of his wounds before reaching England. Sam Benson lost an arm and the sight of one eye, and George and Charlie Benson, Norah's cousins, died at Ypres.

Cathy often thought of the nights at the Roller Rink with Charlie and George, and grieved for them and for their families. Mixed with her sorrow was terror that Greg might be next but she always wrote cheerfully to him, telling him that she was confident that he would be all right.

She had long since lost her illusion that stretcher bearers were in no danger. Bill Hasty from the corner house had received a

'Blighty' wound which meant that he would remain in England and he considered himself the neighbourhood authority on the war. He told Cathy tales of stretcher bearers going out to bring in the wounded under fire from both sides.

'I don't believe that,' Cathy exclaimed. 'Our fellows wouldn't fire on their own.'

'Not deliberate, like, but when one side starts the other side fires back,' Bill said. 'An' if the stretcher bearers are in No Man's Land, they've gorra take their chance like.'

Cathy would have disbelieved him, but another officious neighbour showed her a picture in *War Illustrated* of stretcher bearers carrying wounded across devastated ground with only a few bare stumps of trees among the shell holes and bodies, and earth being flung into the air as a shell exploded close to the stretcher party.

The picture was often in Cathy's mind but she resolutely pushed it away, and told herself that she *knew* that Greg would come home safely.

One night when she was walking down from Kensington she met Norah at the corner of Mount Vernon who told her that she had been to the convent for instruction to become a Catholic.

'It'll make me feel closer to Jack,' she said. 'Sharing his beliefs.'

'Does your father know?' asked Cathy.

'I don't care whether he does or not,' Norah said. 'When you look back, Cath, we were fools, weren't we? Mind you, we were different people before the war. Nobody'd push me around now.'

Cathy agreed rather doubtfully. She felt that she could be pushed around just as much as ever, but she could see that Norah was different.

She was a conductress on a tram now and so was Josie Mellor. They had thought of being munitions workers but the Bennet girls worked in the Ordnance factory and the sight of their yellow faces and hands changed Norah's and Josie's minds.

'Me mam thinks I should because the money's good but I don't care. I don't want to be as yellow as a guinea when Walter comes home from sea,' Josie said.

He was a merchant seaman and now that shipping losses were so heavy, Josie told Cathy that she was afraid to open the newspaper.

'A woman in Gildart Street read it in the paper about her husband's ship going down before she got the telegram,' she told Cathy. 'I wish we'd got married before he went. I might have had a baby like you by now.'

Robbie Burns and two of the Ashcroft boys were in the 57th West Lancashire Division which were detailed for Home Service so for a while Peggy's fears for her son were lulled, although she dreaded to hear that they had been ordered abroad.

'Let's hope they go to Mesopotamia or Egypt when they go,' she said one day. 'That one from thirty-six is bragging about another parcel off her son. Brass lizards and some leather things. Sending stuff home when other people are scratching round trying to get stuff together to send to their fellows.'

'Those Cookes would always live where anyone else would starve,' Sally said. 'They're all storemen, aren't they?'

Peggy nodded at a neat pile on the dresser of items which Cathy was collecting to send to Greg.

There were some of his favourite Black Cat cigarettes, a large fruit cake, sweets and candles and a tin of throat lozenges.

'Does his mam send him anything?' Peggy asked.

'Only crying letters as far as I can make out,' Sally said crisply. 'Honest to God, Peg, I don't know how she ever had a son like Greg.'

'Takes after his dad, I suppose,' Peggy said. She turned to where Baby John was playing in the corner of the kitchen, safely penned in by a chair lying on its side. 'Like this little feller,' she said. 'He's the model of Greg, isn't he?'

'Yes, and the same pleasant nature,' Sally said. 'If only Greg could get home to see him, even if he had to go back. Our Cathy tries to put a good face on it, but I hear her crying in bed sometimes.'

'Things seem to have gone a bit quieter now anyway since May came in,' Peggy said, 'I haven't heard of as many deaths. Let's hope it lasts.'

One evening in early June Cathy went to see Rosie who had now become Mrs Hackett, but still lived at home with her mother and sister and sister-in-law. Cathy rarely went out visiting since John's birth but had felt restless and uneasy all day, and decided to visit Rosie whom she had not seen for some time. Her brother and her husband were serving on the Western Front and Cathy took her latest letter from Greg with her to exchange any news with Rosie.

They had scarcely settled down to talk when a commotion outside drew them to the window and then out of the door as newsboys raced down the road, yelling at the tops of their voices.

'What are they sayin'?' Rosie's mother said peevishly. 'I can't make it out.'

But Rosie had run up to one of the boys and thrust a ha'penny at him as she grabbed a paper.

'Oh, *no!*' she screamed. 'Oh, Mam, Kitchener's dead.'

'*Kitchener?*' Cathy cried, snatching at Rosie's paper.

In minutes the street was full of wailing women as the news spread. Kitchener, whose face above his pointing finger and the legend 'Your country needs You', was as familiar to them as that of their neighbours or family.

They were struck with a sense of personal loss, and more than that. Rosie's mother expressed what everyone felt as she sank down on her doorstep, covering her face with her apron and moaning, 'What'll we do? What'll we do? We're finished now.'

Cathy hurried home through the streets filled with people mourning the great man, but soon she saw even greater grief. The 8th Irish had been in action and as she came through Soho Street in the area where many of the men lived, women who had received the dreaded telegrams from the War Office mingled their lamentations with those who wept for Kitchener.

All the front doors in Egremont Street stood open as everyone gathered in the street, stunned by the news. Sally was there with John in her arms, and as Cathy came to her she said miserably, 'Cathy, I can't believe it. Lord Kitchener of all men. Those Germans have a lot to answer for.'

'And *drowned*,' Peggy Burns broke in. 'Instead of with his army.'

Lawrie was standing at the house door and Cathy took the baby from her mother and went in, followed by her father.

'You wouldn't think Kitchener had roused their sons and husbands to go and fight and maybe be killed, would you?' he said.

Cathy looked at him in surprise. 'But the fellows were proud to join Kitchener's Army,' she said. 'We'll be lost without him, won't we?'

Lawrie laughed at her puzzled face. 'Aye, no doubt, love. Take no notice of me. It was just a thought.'

'No wonder Mam says you're always out of step, Dad,' Cathy laughed.

'Maybe I step to a different tune,' he said. Cathy often thought of those words in later years when the child in her arms 'stepped to a different tune', and wondered whether it was the direct influence of his grandfather, or whether he had inherited the urge.

Soon rumours began to circulate of another big battle coming, and rumours that Kitchener had not really been drowned but was in Russia and would suddenly reappear with a plan that would finish the war within weeks.

Sally was inclined to believe these rumours about Kitchener but Lawrie dismissed them. 'It's only because people are afraid to be without him, Sal,' he said. 'They are just trying to bolster up their courage with those yarns.'

The rumours of a great battle were soon proved to be true and Cathy felt that she went through the days and nights frozen with terror that Greg would be killed, as the papers carried vivid accounts, often untrue, of the British offensive on the Somme, and the lists of casualties grew longer than ever.

Cathy was reassured by a letter from Greg in which he said that things were quiet in his sector so there was no need to worry. He often mentioned John Savage in his letters and now he wrote that they were in a rest sector for three days.

> I like John more the more I know of him. I've never met any man whose mind was so much in tune with my own. His situation is much like mine, with a young wife and a young baby just a few months older than ours. He was fortunate enough to see his little daughter just after she was born, but he told me that it was very hard to leave his wife and child after two weeks.
>
> It's strange to see how these French people go about their business disregarding the war although some buildings in the village have been destroyed. Every house almost is a shop or café. We have been able to buy fresh bread and fruit and the souvenirs which I enclose.

The souvenirs were postcards embroidered with flags and mottoes in bright silks, and a model of Rheims Cathedral backed by red transparent paper. When it was held to the light the red paper behind the empty window spaces made it seem that the Cathedral was on fire again.

The baby never tired of seeing this and whenever Cathy showed it to him she also showed him a photograph of Greg, taken on his last leave, and said, 'Dada, John. Dada.'

It was not a good likeness of Greg and it had been crudely coloured which made it worse, but Cathy was determined that the child would learn to know his father. No matter how often she corrected him, he still said 'Dada' more often than 'Grandad' to Lawrie.

Cathy still took John to visit his other grandmother although Greg's mother showed little interest in the baby. She had become a complete invalid, leaving all responsibility to Miss Nugent, and expecting to be waited on hand and foot.

'I'm sorry, Miss Nugent,' Cathy whispered after one visit. 'You didn't expect to have to do all this, did you?'

'Don't worry, Mrs Redmond,' Miss Nugent said, 'I'm quite happy. I keep up with all my church activities, you know.'

'Mrs Redmond doesn't try to prevent – she's not ill when you wish to go out?' Cathy asked diffidently.

'No. I made it quite clear that I had other duties, and she understands my position,' Miss Nugent said firmly. Cathy looked at her with respect, feeling that Mrs Redmond seemed at last to have met her match.

The shop seemed to be flourishing, but although Cathy was always fulsomely welcomed by Albert Kettle, the first assistant, Mr Braithwaite still seemed suspicious and unfriendly. Cathy thought the old man looked ill and shaky but she was afraid to ask how he was.

Before he went away Greg had taken Cathy to register her signature at the bank so that she could draw money from the shop account, but she had never done so.

One of Mrs Redmond's comments made out of Greg's hearing when she realised that he and Cathy were serious about each other, was that the girl was interested in the business, not the man.

Cathy had not told Greg about it, but it had rankled with her for years, and she was determined that the vicious accusation would be proved wrong.

After Cathy left Finestone's she had only her Army allotment of fifteen shillings for herself and the baby to live on, and although her parents told her they needed nothing from her, she felt that it was unjust to them not to make a fair contribution.

Sally had been unable to do much sewing since her arm had been broken, but she enjoyed looking after the baby, and when John was nine months old Cathy went back to work. Women were employed now in the Maypole and the Home and Colonial grocery stores to replace the male assistants who were in the Services, and Cathy took a job in a family grocer's in Brunswick Road.

It was convenient for home, and Cathy liked the work, although she soon began to dislike the owner of the shop. The son whom she had replaced when he was liable for conscription was a model of all the virtues, according to his father, but he had nothing but scorn for the son who remained.

Edward had tried to join up in August 1914, he told Cathy, but had been rejected on medical grounds.

'My brother thought I was trying to show him up for not volunteering,' he said. 'And he and my father have given me a dog's life ever since. We got on all right before.'

Another result of this damned war, Cathy thought, but she was sorry for Edward and refused to agree when his father belittled him to her.

One of the advantages of working in the shop, Cathy found, was that a sort of freemasonry existed among shop workers, and they 'looked after' each other with goods that were in short supply.

Sugar, potatoes, milk and butter were in short supply and Cathy had spent many weary hours standing in queues, but soon after she started work in the shop Edward gave her a small parcel to take to the greengrocer's next door.

'Go in the back way,' he said, and when Cathy handed over the parcel she was surprised to receive two newspaper-wrapped parcels in return. 'One for you and one for them,' the woman explained. 'Just a few spuds, love.'

Cathy learned that the parcel Edward had given her had contained bacon bones, and he produced a similar parcel for Cathy.

'Me dad boned that side,' he whispered. 'But I'll do the next one. Leave a bit of meat on the bones, like.'

True to his word, when Edward boned a side of bacon, he always managed to leave extra meat on the bones he gave Cathy, but even without that she found rich rewards in her job, in addition to her wages.

Mr Wilson was not mean, and he often gave her a couple of eggs 'for the baby', or a tin of treacle or some dried fruit from the meagre supplies he received. He turned a blind eye to the trading that went on between the shops although he was willing to eat the result, as Edward told Cathy.

He was ever ready to provide bacon bones, ends of cheese, some flour or jam for the other shop workers, and in return he and Cathy reaped a harvest of potatoes or fruit, liver from the butcher's, or black puddings from the pork butcher's, who had reopened after being wrecked by the mob after the sinking of the 'Lusy', as she was always known.

Sally was delighted with the food Cathy brought home. She shared the largesse with Peggy who was finding it difficult to feed her large family, and they often wondered how they would have managed without it.

'No wonder John's growing so sturdy,' Sally said when Cathy had brought home a marrow bone from the butcher's and potherbs from the greengrocer. 'We fell on our feet when you went there, Cath.'

'I nearly had a row with Mr Wilson today though,' Cathy confessed.

Sally looked alarmed. 'Dear God, watch your tongue, Cathy,' she urged. 'What about?'

'The way he treats Edward for one thing, and then he was moaning because just when people have got money to spend he can't get the stuff.'

'But that's true. There's money about, Cath, and jobs for anyone who wants one. I don't begrudge it to the Bennets but the money that's going in that house, with Mr Bennet back on light work and the two girls in Munitions! Even Mrs Bennet's working in Huntley's.'

'I know, Mam, and as you say you don't begrudge it, but he does. He was carrying on about a woman that came in for butter. Saying she'd never had two ha'pennies to knock together before the war, never knew the taste of butter, and now she was coming in demanding it, large as life. She didn't demand it, she only asked.'

'And I suppose you told him that?' Sally said with a sigh.

'I told him it was a pity we had to have a war before people got their share of what was going,' Cathy retorted.

'I wish you'd learn to keep a still tongue in your head.'

Cathy longed to ask if it was for the sake of the food, but she managed to restrain herself and went into the scullery to get washed, banging about to relieve her feelings.

She sat and cuddled the baby as her mother served up the meal, feeling that she would go mad if the war didn't end soon. How old would John be before he saw his father or his father saw him? How much longer would she have to stay here instead of in her own home with her own husband and baby?

Her mother seemed to forget that she was a married woman with a baby and would scold her as though she was a child. I've made a rod for my own back with this food too, she thought. Now I daren't leave the shop yet I hate it more every day.

She began to play with the baby, running her finger round the palm of his hand and chanting, 'Round and round the garden'. When she came to 'tickle him under there' the baby screamed with delight as she tickled under his arm, and Sally said sharply, 'Don't get him so excited just before his bedtime. Put him down and come and eat this while it's hot.'

Cathy put the baby down without a word, but her face was set in angry lines. A few moments later her father came in and bent over John. 'Dada, Dada,' the little boy shouted and Lawrie replied, laughing, 'John, John.'

'You might at least tell him you're not his dada,' Cathy said angrily. 'Greg's entitled to that surely.'

'Aye, aye,' Lawrie said, 'Give us a chance. What's up with you?'

'I'm fed up, that's what's up with me!' Cathy shouted.

She jumped up from the table and dashed through the back kitchen down to the lavatory. Lawrie looked blankly at Sally. 'What's up with her? What brought that on?'

'She came in in a paddy,' Sally said shortly. 'Been having a row in the shop, but I'm not having this.'

'Ah, well, she's worried about Greg, I suppose,' he said. 'It's hard for these young ones.'

'It's not easy for anyone nowadays,' Sally said, 'but she needn't take it out on us. She had a face on her because I told her not to get John excited just before his bedtime.'

Lawrie gave her a quick glance and although he said nothing, Sally felt uneasy. They heard Cathy come into the back kitchen and run the water, and both knew that she had been crying and was trying to remove the traces.

Cathy touched her father's arm as she passed him and murmured, 'Sorry.'

He patted her hand. 'Steady as a rock now, isn't he?' he said, nodding at the baby who had pulled himself to his feet by the chair leg.

Sally took Cathy's plate from the oven and put it on the table. 'I put it in the oven to keep warm,' was all she said, but for the rest of the evening there was the old pleasant atmosphere between them.

Chapter Thirty-Six

As the weary months of 1917 dragged on, Cathy felt that Greg's letters and Baby John were the only things that made her life bearable, yet the baby was often the cause of friction between herself and her mother.

'She seems to forget John is *my* baby,' she said angrily to her father one day. 'Everything I do for him is wrong according to Mam, but I think a lot of her ideas are too old-fashioned.'

'Well, between the two of you, John's thriving, that's the main thing,' Lawrie said soothingly. 'Greg's going to be made up with him when he comes home.'

'I don't know how old he's going to be by then,' Cathy said.

'It won't be long now, love,' Lawrie said. 'Always darkest before the dawn, as they say. Your mam's fretting for Aunt Emily you know, love, as well as about our Mary, but she told me the other day it brings back the happy days she had when Emily was a baby, when she's doing things for John.'

Cathy smiled at him.

'Always the peacemaker, Dad,' she said. 'I don't begrudge Mam taking over with John – I'm thankful she's willing to look after him – but I want *some* say with him, and I want him to know I'm his mam.'

'He knows that. You have him to yourself all night, Cath,' Lawrie said, and she kissed him lightly.

'Pity you're not on the War Cabinet or whatever they call it,' she said. 'You'd have them sorted out in no time.'

Lawrie also had a diplomatic word with Sally, and matters improved between her and her daughter, but outside the home Cathy felt that everyone was reaching the limit of what they could stand.

German submarines were taking a terrible toll of shipping and causing not only shortages of food and other necessities but, in Liverpool particularly, sorrow to the families of the many men whose ships were sunk.

The daily search for food and the petty restrictions imposed, added to the constant see-saw of hope and despair brought by the newspaper reports, made everyone nervy and bad-tempered and quarrels were frequent.

In the shop it was not only the arguments with customers which tried Cathy, sometimes she felt beyond bearing, but the tension between Edward and his father. Mr Wilson was starting to include Cathy in his attacks, saying that she was siding with his son against him, and she felt that everything she said or did was used as ammunition by one of them against the other.

She had another cause for worry too. From the beginning she had been sorry for Edward and tried to protect him from his father's anger. Now he showed every sign of being in love with her.

If she appeared to take his father's part he looked at her like a whipped dog, yet if she seemed to favour him he seemed to take it as proof of her affection for him.

She told Norah about it when she took John down to go for a walk with her friend on her Sunday off. 'I can't say anything to Mam about it, and if I even say they drag me into their quarrels, Mam tells me I open my mouth too wide and I should tell them it's between them and nothing to do with me.'

'That seems good advice,' Norah said.

'I wish it was as easy as that,' Cathy said with a sigh.

She bent over the baby and slipped a piece of chocolate in his mouth, carefully tucking a handkerchief under his chin. 'I'll have to make sure there's no trace of that or I'll get a telling off from Mam,' she said. 'Honest to God, Norah, all the instructions I got before she'd let me bring him out today. My own child!'

'She means well,' Norah said. 'But why can't you tell the Wilsons to fight it out themselves?'

'They can't agree on anything and if they ask me a question, whatever I say is different to what one of them has said. If I say I don't know, the old man starts about the son in the Army, the wonder boy who knew everything, and then the next thing he's saying nasty things about Edward. Saying he's a reject, and a pathetic specimen, and no woman would have him. You wouldn't believe, Norah.'

'Doesn't seem very pleasant,' she said. 'Why don't you try for the trams, Cath?'

'I know it seems a queer reason,' Cathy said, 'but I get the extra bits of food and it's saves Mam some of the queuing. It's not much now, mostly bones and things like that, but it all helps. And give old Wilson his due, he'll often hand me extra bits for John. Enough of my moaning anyway. How are things with you?'

'Much the same,' Norah said. Her father had suffered a stroke and now lay in bed unable to speak or to use his right side, but Norah had told Cathy that she would feel a hypocrite if she pretended to be sorry.

'My dad's no different,' she said now. 'Not that I see much of him or my mam either with working shifts.'

'Does he know yet about you taking instruction to become a Catholic?' Cathy asked.

Norah shrugged. 'I don't know. Mam writes on a slate for him and he writes back but I don't think she's told him yet. She hasn't said anything to me about it. Jack hasn't told his family either. It's just between the two of us.'

'Oh, Norah, *when* are they going to come home again?' Cathy exclaimed. 'I feel as though all our young life's going while we're waiting.'

Within the week one of Cathy's problems had been solved. A row had broken out in the storeroom behind the shop between Mr Wilson and a delivery man. It ranged over the shipping losses, public house closing hours, the shortage of beer, Lloyd George, the trouble in Ireland the previous year, and the Russian Revolution.

'Anything else?' Cathy said wearily to the woman she was serving, feeling that she could as easily have said it to the two men shouting each other down in the back room.

The second man on the wagon was a discharged soldier suffering from shell shock, and he had run into the shop and was cowering down behind the counter as Mr Wilson banged a scoop on the flour bin to emphasise his arguments and the driver kicked the metal bin to retaliate.

Edward dashed from behind the bacon sheer and into the back room. 'Stop that bloody din!' he shouted. 'Look at your mate.' The driver went immediately to the shell-shocked man but his father turned on Edward. 'Don't you give me yer orders, you bloody upstart! That feller there's a better man than you'll ever be for all his carry on now. At least his country *wanted* him,' he jeered.

Edward tore off his white apron and snatched up his coat and cap, before rushing out of the shop. It was nearly closing time when he returned and announced triumphantly, 'I'm in. I've had another medical and I've passed.'

His father looked at him blankly, 'But – but you'll be going then? What'll I do? How will I manage?' he stammered.

'You'll have to ask for your precious Sidney to come home, won't you?' Edward said boisterously. His face was wreathed in smiles and he looked a different person to the harried, resentful youth of the morning.

Men! I'll never understand them, Cathy thought, marvelling at the change in Edward. Everyone knew by now the horrors of the Western Front, the sea of mud, the dead bodies in the ground over which the armies fought, the rats, and the steady killing and wounding of young men, day after day. Yet here was Edward, bright-eyed and smiling because he might be sent there.

She said as much to her father that evening, and he said that he understood Edward. 'Bad enough to be rejected, love, but to have it rubbed into him day after day by his own father – no wonder it got him down.'

'But people didn't know what it was going to be like, at first,' Cathy protested. 'Now, with all these things in the newspapers, you'd think he'd be glad to stay at home. I feel different now to the way I did at first about the war.'

'Don't be dwelling on all that newspaper talk, Cath,' her father said. 'Greg seems be able to stand things out there, apart from being away from you and John, doesn't he?'

'He's always cheerful in his letters,' Cathy said. 'But I suppose he doesn't want to worry me. This'll make a difference in the shop anyway.'

Cathy found that Mr Wilson was easier to work with when Edward had gone, although she had to work much harder. A simple-minded boy, son of one of the customers, was employed to help with the lifting and carrying, and he managed very well with Cathy's patient help and tuition. She was surprised to find how much the lad, who had never been considered bright enough for school, could understand and remember.

Peggy Burns had an unwelcome addition to her family in 1916 when Mabel married the young man her mother had always detested.

'He only did it to save himself getting called up,' Peggy told Sally. 'Thinks being a married man will save him, but I hope it doesn't.' He had moved in with the Burns family, and Ben and Ritchie Burns were sleeping in Sally's third bedroom.

Peggy refused to be parted from Michael even for a night. He was still thin and delicate and any little titbit that Peggy could get went to him, but it seemed to make little difference.

Peggy soon had fresh cause to worry as Robbie's Regiment, the 57th West Lancashires, was ordered to France.

The people of Liverpool had been saddened in August 1917 to learn of the death of one of the heroes of the city. Captain Noel

Chavasse was the son of the Bishop of Liverpool and a medical officer with the Liverpool Scottish Regiment.

He had been awarded an MC then a VC in October 1916, and with a mixture of pride and fear Cathy had read the citation of his bravery. It said that he had taken a stretcher bearer with him and rescued a wounded man under heavy fire. So stretcher bearers *were* in danger, even more than she had thought, but she comforted herself with Greg's latest letter.

'John and I seem to bear a charmed life,' he wrote, 'and we both feel confident that we will soon be at home with our families again.'

Captain Chavasse lost his life while courageously caring for the wounded, although wounded himself, in July 1917, and for this was awarded a second Victoria Cross.

Peggy brought the newspaper to show Sally and Cathy the account. 'And our Robbie's out there now,' she said with a sigh. 'Eh, the cream of the crop are going.'

Sally looked expressively at Cathy and when Peggy had gone she said: 'I don't know what's come over Peggy lately. Does she think their Robbie's going to win a VC?'

'Could happen, I suppose,' Cathy said. 'Look at Sam.' They had seen a small item in the *Express* some time previously which stated that Lieutenant S. Hurst Glover had been awarded a Military Cross for bravery and devotion to duty. When all his superior officers had been killed, he had taken a small party of men and destroyed a machine gun which was holding up the British advance.

Cathy sent the cutting to Mary but it was never acknowledged. She very rarely wrote to her sister, but when John was two years old she had his photograph taken and sent a copy of it to Mary for Christmas 1917.

Cathy had decided that John should be 'breeched' when he was two, so his baby frocks were discarded and he wore his first pair of trousers. Sally had been opposed to the idea, saying that John was far too young, but when she saw him dressed in the trousers she was enchanted with him.

'He looks a real little man,' she exclaimed, 'and the absolute model of Greg.' Cathy thought so too, and she was proud to send a copy to her sister, and hurt when it was ignored.

It had been a shock to Mary to open the envelope and see the picture of the little boy, so like a miniature copy of Greg, looking up at her.

She had tired of the charade of the box number some time earlier and given her mother her address, telling her that she was sharing accommodation with another girl who was also on war work.

Dora had hooted with laughter at this description of their nightly expeditions to the West End.

'I don't know why you bother to keep up with them, quite frankly,' she said.

'I have my reasons,' Mary said vaguely. Family feeling was not part of the sophisticated image she now projected, and even to herself she was not willing to admit that she cared about them. Still less could she admit the need to know what was happening to Greg, which made her eagerly read the letters from her mother.

She sent only brief postcards in reply, saying that she was well but giving no other information about herself. Life was too hectic for letter writing, she had decided.

Mary was enjoying every moment now. She had been surprised by the amount of money she had been able to obtain for the jewellery, and together with the contents of the canvas bag she now had a comfortingly large bank account.

'You certainly made Clive pay for his antics,' Dora laughed. 'I wonder whether he found enough boyfriends to satisfy him before he popped off. I think my latest would suit him very well. *Such* a pretty boy.'

'I don't want to talk about him,' Mary said. 'I don't even want to think about him.'

'Then don't, darling,' Dora cried. 'Have a glass of bubbly instead.'

Mary found Dora an ideal companion at this time. Wild and reckless, she attracted a crowd of kindred spirits around her, many of them Society girls who would not have accepted Mary or Dora before the war.

Now the class barriers were down and the only aim in life was to have a good time. Young officers on leave, anxious to squeeze the last ounce of enjoyment before returning to the Front, were happy to join the set, and Mary turned down several proposals from men she could only have dreamed of marrying in former days.

She was happy to spend the evenings with these young officers at the dance clubs, the theatre or music hall or wherever the mood of the set took them, but she made it clear from the outset that she would provide companionship and comfort but nothing else.

Never again, she thought with a shudder. For her that side of life was *out* completely.

The young men accepted her ruling and assured her that they respected her too much, they would never suggest, they just wanted to worship at her feet. Mary accepted their protestations with a cynical smile, but she was never short of escorts, and soon all the young men seemed to merge into each other, and she could never remember them as individuals.

Only once did she come near to breaking her vow, but at the last moment she drew back, afraid. A slightly older man had joined their party and Mary felt at ease with him right away. He seemed so familiar that she wondered whether she had known him before the war, but his name was unknown to her and he said nothing of having met her previously.

They were sitting near each other when, as the crowd became wilder, a young Scotsman jumped on a table and began to dance a hornpipe, spraying everyone near him with champagne from the bottle he held.

Two of the girls pounced on the man near Mary. 'Tommy! Tommy Ross,' they were screaming. 'Come on. You must dance too.' But he pulled away. 'I'm not a Scotsman,' he said, and the girls went to someone else.

'I always heard that Scotsmen were dour,' Tommy Ross said to Mary, laughing as the young man on the table began to give loud war whoops.

'Nothing dour about him,' Mary said. Tommy moved closer and they began to talk. He told her that he had had been a staff officer in London since 1915 but soon he was going out to the Front. 'We're all being dug out,' he said. 'Winkled out of corners.' As the wild party surged all round them, Mary stayed with him, feeling relaxed and at ease.

'I know you're not a Scotsman,' she said later. 'But where *do* you come from?'

'If I said I was a Dicky Sam, you'd be no wiser, would you?' he said with a lazy laugh.

'But yes, I would,' Mary said. 'I'd know you were born on Mann Island near Liverpool Pier Head.'

'Good God,' he said, sitting up straight. 'How do you know that?'

'Because I was born in Everton,' she said. They withdrew from the noisy crowd and compared notes about their homes in Liverpool. For once Mary told the truth about her home and family, only briefly mentioning her aunt and uncle in Aigburth when Tommy told her that his father had been a gardener at a large house in Grassendale.

The owner of the house, a wealthy single lady, had taken an interest in him after his father's death and arranged for him to be educated at a minor public school.

They went back to Mary's flat and sat together on the sofa, drinking and talking, then as he put his arms round her and began to kiss her, Mary felt herself being borne along by his passion and kissed him back. As he became more urgent she responded, but suddenly she pulled away from him and burst into tears.

'Darling, darling, what is it? What's wrong?' he asked, trying to pull her hands away from her face, but she only wept more bitterly. He left her and went to the bathroom, and when he returned Mary was calmer. He sat down beside her and spoke to her quietly and gently and she told him that she had endured a dreadful experience and could never go with a man again.

Even to the unshockable Dora, Mary had never been able to talk in detail about her degradation by Clive, and had erected a mental barrier against sex in any form. Now she felt that it could never be breached, and with a sudden change of mood she jumped to her feet.

'Pour the drinkies, darling,' she cried gaily. 'I'll repair the damage then we'll join the others at the Black Cat.' She plunged back into the hectic round and closed her mind to all memories.

Cathy was hurt and annoyed when Mary said nothing about the photograph on her next postcard, but Greg's response to his copy was ecstatic.

> I feel as though he is looking straight at me and we can almost speak to each other. I feel so proud of my manly little son and of you, Cath, for bringing him up so well. John Savage and I have wondered sometimes how it will be after the war and whether we will be like strangers to our children, but I feel that I know our son through the photographs and the details you send me. John Savage's wife does the same so we feel we are very lucky men.

Cathy read the letter aloud to John when they were in bed that night and to her great delight the baby shouted 'Dada, Dada'. The baby slept in the big bed with her and she was so tired these days that often she went to bed at the same time as he did and lay cuddling him until they both fell asleep.

She had been weeping bitterly in bed one night after a customer in the shop had insisted on giving her details about the German advance on the Front, and the British losses, and her mother had come in to comfort her.

'Take no notice of people like that,' she said. 'She's like one of those women who used to frighten the life out of young women having their first babies by telling them about everything that could go wrong. Your dad says the war'll be over soon.'

'But people seem to think it'll still go on a long time,' Cathy said. They looked at each other and laughed.

'Trust your dad to be different,' Sally said. 'But he gave me all sorts of reasons and they seemed good. I can't remember all of them but one was that the German people are in a worse state than us, and the other was that the Americans are coming.'

'Mrs Dunn said she saw some in town,' Cathy said. 'She said they looked big and clean and healthy.'

'Anyway, you just stop worrying,' Sally said. 'Remember what Greg says. He lives a "charmed life".'

All trace of friction between Cathy and her mother seemed to vanish after that and they were united in adoring John. They thought he was the handsomest and cleverest child ever born and Cathy's only regret about him being so advanced for his age was that Greg was missing even more of his babyhood.

He was a great favourite with the Burns family, where there had not been a baby since Ritchie was born. His had been a breech birth and very difficult for Peggy but she told Sally that she thought it had done her a good turn.

'Whatever happened to me then, I've never been "caught" again,' she said. She was nursing John while Sally made bread, and held him close. 'I miss having a baby on my knee, Sally, but these are the best kind. The ones you can hand back.'

'I hope he won't be the only one for Cathy,' Sally said. 'It's hard for only children for one thing, and I know she'd like more, but it would mean Greg was safe home too.'

'I see Josie Mellor's expecting,' Peggy said. 'And Walter's ship was only in port two nights. Mind you, I can't talk. It never took Jimmie Burns two nights.'

Sally smiled. 'It'll be a comfort for Mrs Mellor. She's had her share of troubles with this war. I see Mary Mellor's husband was lost at sea.'

'*That* wasn't a trouble to Mrs Mellor,' Peggy said forthrightly. 'She wouldn't say it to you in case she shocked you, but she said to me it was the best thing the Germans ever done.'

Liverpool people had always been used to seeing seamen of many nationalities in the town, and French and Belgian troops had been numerous since the war, but quite suddenly the town seemed full of Americans. A YMCA opened in Church Street and crowds of American soldiers and sailors thronged round it.

To the war-weary Liverpudlians they were like a breath of fresh air and Cathy could see what her customer had meant by saying that they were big and clean and healthy. They were also very friendly and one day when Cathy was walking down Church Street with John, a big American soldier suddenly crouched down in front of the child.

He pulled out a bar of chocolate from his pocket. 'Hey, sonny, do you like candy?' he said.

'Say thank you, John,' Cathy said, and the soldier was delighted. 'His name's John, Ma'am? That's the name of my boy, Wilbur John.' He pulled out a folder and proudly showed her photographs of his wife and child.

Cathy wondered afterwards if she should have asked him to come to the house for a meal and some family life, but at the time she was overcome with shyness. She called in to see Norah on her way home and told her about it. 'I wonder would Greg do that in America?' she said.

'He might,' Norah said. 'But I think the Americans are just naturally friendly. And very confident,' she added.

'They all seemed very cheerful,' Cathy said.

'Yes. They're sure the war will be over tomorrow, now that they're here.' Norah laughed but then her face clouded. 'Let's hope they're right. I've got a funny feeling about Jack.'

'Oh, Norah, don't say that,' Cathy begged, but the next day Norah rushed in to the shop to show her a note from Jack's sister which told her that he had been wounded and was in hospital in London.

Cathy knew that the sister who was nearest to Jack in age and outlook, had promised him that she would let Norah know if a telegram arrived. When Norah told her friend that she intended to travel to London, Cathy hoped that she could go with Jack's sister, but Norah said it was impossible.

'There's three of them going, and she'd daren't let the other sisters or her mother know she's told me.'

'Oh, Norah, at a time like this,' Cathy exclaimed. 'Did she give any details?'

'They don't know any,' Norah said. 'We can only hope.'

She rushed away, and a few days later a letter came from her. She had found Jack in good spirits although in a lot of pain. He had been wounded in the left arm and thigh, and there was shrapnel in his neck.

'At least he has not been blinded which I was worrying about all the way down in the train. I can't tell you what it was like to see him again, Cath, even like this. We just hung on to each other. His sisters came back and stood there with faces like wet Mondays, but we didn't care.'

Later she wrote that she was staying down there and had taken a cleaning job in the hospital. 'Jack thinks it will soon be over anyway,' Norah wrote, and Cathy could only hope and pray that he was right.

Chapter Thirty-Seven

John was three years old in September 1918 and Cathy took him to see his other grandmother, although she rarely visited Mrs Redmond now. Greg's mother showed no interest in the baby, although he was so like Greg, and her hostility towards Cathy was undiminished.

'I suppose she doesn't care for John because he's *my* child,' Cathy said resentfully to Miss Nugent.

'Don't worry about it, dear,' Miss Nugent said. 'Just ignore her little moods, as I do.'

'I don't know how you stand her,' Cathy said, but Miss Nugent smiled. 'I'm very well suited here, dear,' she said. 'Mrs Redmond and I understand each other, and she relies on me. I have much more independence than I had with my family and I'm quite happy.' So Cathy could write reassuringly to Greg about his mother.

Mr Braithwaite still jealously guarded his authority in shop matters, but twice since Greg had been away he had written to Cathy to ask her to arrange to increase his mother's allowance, so Cathy knew he must have received complaining letters.

She was very nervous about entering the bank. The expanse of glass and mahogany, the silence and the formal dress and manner of the clerks intimidated her, and she walked up and down several times, peeping through the revolving doors, before she could summon up enough courage to go in.

Cathy had chosen a bad day. The bank manager, who was a young-looking forty-year-old man, was forbidden by Government order to leave his job, which was classed as a 'necessary occupation'.

The male clerks were gradually being replaced by ladies but the manager's requests to be allowed to join up were always refused. On the morning of Cathy's visit he had been handed a white feather on his way to work, and was in a foul mood.

Cathy would have liked to ask him about the amount of the money which she was leaving to accumulate for Greg's return but his manner was so frigid and disagreeable that she was glad simply to sign the papers and escape.

On her second visit he was less disagreeable but his manner was so weary and remote that Cathy, never very confident, felt that it would be presumptuous to ask any questions.

The shop seemed to be flourishing, although the two male assistants had been replaced by girls and Mr Braithwaite now was in a pitiable state, with his head and hands constantly shaking. He still came in to the shop every day, and Albert Kettle, whose curved spine excused him from service, was very tactful with the old man.

'I can manage very well, Mrs Redmond,' he assured Cathy on one of her rare visits. 'The girls are very good, and I understand Mr Braithwaite's little ways.'

Mr Braithwaite and Mrs Redmond made a good pair, Cathy thought as she left, but they had both been lucky enough to have found people who would put up with them.

Quite suddenly all the news seemed good. 'I knew we'd do well once our Robbie got out there,' Peggy Burns said.

'That was half joke, whole earnest,' Sally said to Lawrie. 'She really thinks he's winning the war on his own.'

'The 57th *are* doing well,' Lawrie said. 'They're with the lads who've broken the Hindenburg Line. The tide's turned all right now, Sal.'

'Yes, but Peggy seems to think they're the only ones out there,' Sally said. 'D'you know what she said to me yesterday – that she always reminds Robbie to keep his tin hat on, when she writes, because she thinks the Germans might pick him out with his red hair.'

'You must admit he'd stand out with his copper nob,' Lawrie laughed. 'Jimmie told me Peggy's blaming him because he passed on his red hair to the kids.'

On Bonfire Night the newsboys ran the streets, shouting exultantly: 'Lille taken. Ours troop enter Lille.' Cathy said to her father, 'Oh, Dad, is this really the end? I'm afraid to hope, we've been disappointed so often.'

'This is it, Cath,' he said. 'It's not only the way our lads are pushing ahead but the Germans have had enough at home. Look at the mutiny at Kiel too. No, this is peace, Cath, I'm sure.'

'If it isn't, I don't know how I'll go on,' she said with a sigh.

'It should have come in '16,' Lawrie said. 'It would have done too if the politicians and the dug-in generals were at the Front. They'd have been glad to take the German offer.'

'But it was the same on their side, wasn't it? I remember a soldier in the shop talking to Mr Wilson about it.'

'Aye, Cath, there's too many people who don't want the war to end because they're doing well out of it, and I'm not talking about people like the Bennets either.'

They were interrupted by Sally who had been assisting at the birth of a neighbour's child. 'A little girl,' she said. 'And what do you think they're calling it? Susan Lille.'

'She'll never be able to lie about her age, anyway,' Lawrie said with a laugh.

Cathy felt as though she was almost holding her breath for the next few days then suddenly the Armistice was signed, and 'peace broke out', as one of the papers put it.

On November 11th a gun was fired and church bells and ships' hooters filled the air with joyful sound. People poured out of their houses and Josie, with Mabel and Chrissie Burns and Jinny Ashcroft, called to Cathy to ask her to come into town.

'It's great there. Everyone dancing and singing,' Josie shouted.

'Go on, Cathy,' Sally urged. 'We'll mind John.'

The girls linked arms and danced down the hill to join the crowds in Lime Street and round the fountain. Liverpudlians of every age and type mixed with soldiers and sailors of every nationality to form a swaying, dancing, singing crowd, delirious with happiness and relief.

'I'm afraid your feather eez broken, mademoiselle,' a French soldier said to Cathy, retrieving her hat which had been knocked from her head.

'I don't care. I don't care about anything,' she cried, flinging her arms round his neck and kissing him.

'All right, Cathy, I'll tell,' Josie shouted, laughing, but the next moment she was being kissed by a big American. The crowds were singing 'Mademoiselle from Armentieres' and 'It's a long way to Tipperary', but someone shouted 'Enough of that', and they sang 'Hold your hand out, you naughty boy' and 'Ta ra ra boom de ay'. Bottles were being passed from hand to hand, but most of the crowd was drunk with happiness.

Suddenly Cathy felt that she wanted to be at home with her baby and her mother and father, to think about Greg and savour the thought that he was safe and would soon be home.

Josie joined her as she broke away from the crowd and they walked home together. 'God, Cathy, I can't believe it, that it's all over. Before the war – it seems like another life, doesn't it? Remember the Roller Rink?'

Cathy smiled and nodded and they walked on in silence for a while. The thought of the Roller Rink made Cathy think of Mary and wonder what she was doing. Was she celebrating like this in London?

As though she could read Cathy's mind, Josie said dreamily, 'I wonder what all the people we know are doing. Not just Walter and Greg and the fellows, but all the girls who were with us. Wonder what Norah's doing now, and your Mary. Will she come home again now, Cath?'

'I don't know. I think my mam thinks she will but I don't know.' Unbidden the thought flashed into her mind that Mary might come back to see Greg, but she thrust it away. Her behaviour with Greg was only the way she was with any man. 'She'll make up to anything in trousers,' a spiteful neighbour had once said to Sally, and Cathy thought it must be true and the reason for Mary's interest in Greg.

Young John was asleep in bed but her parents were still downstairs, and Cathy sat with them for the rest of the night, talking and planning for after the war.

Cathy would have been alarmed to know how Mary's thoughts turned immediately to Greg when peace was declared, but soon she was celebrating with her usual noisy crowd.

One of them had commandeered a horse and wagon and someone else had acquired some streamers and balloons. They piled on to the wagon and drove in a noisy, shrieking crowd to Piccadilly, flinging streamers at the crowds and blowing up balloons before releasing them. A barrel organ had been pushed into the crowd but the tinkling tunes were almost drowned by the noise of rattles and trumpets and a stolen police whistle, until suddenly Mary heard the barrel organ playing a song from *The Merry Widow*. 'Now or never, and forever I'll love you', it played, and suddenly Mary was back in the parlour at Egremont Street, handing a drink to Greg and looking deeply into his eyes.

It was a New Year's Eve, she remembered, and Dick Ashcroft who had a pleasant tenor voice had been singing while Cathy played the piano.

Mary remembered too how her fingers had touched Greg's as he took the drink and then she had squeezed into a small space beside him on the sofa, so that their bodies were pressed close together. It had been bliss until Norah Benson had called, 'Time you had a break, Cathy. I'll play.'

Greg had stood up immediately to stand with Cathy near the door, and Norah had given Mary a sneering look as she went to the piano stool.

The tune had finished and the barrel organ was now playing something else, but Mary still stood motionless, her thoughts far away, until someone blew a toy bugle close to her ear. 'Wake up, darling!' he yelled, and Mary threw off her mood and plunged into the revelry again.

Cathy had hoped that Greg would be home for Christmas, but he was not demobilised until early in January. He had not been able to give her an exact time of arrival but Cathy and Sally had scoured the house, and flags were in readiness to hang out to welcome him home.

Cathy had new outfits ready for herself and John, and the child had been rehearsed in a welcome-home speech by Lawrie.

'Welcome home, Dada!' the little boy shouted over and over again as he rushed about the house, fired by the general excitement.

'He's already said it to the postman and the milkman,' Sally said. 'I'll bet he'll forget it when Greg comes, though.'

Cathy had to go in to the shop still as there was no one to take her place, but her mother promised to send for her as soon as the telegram from Greg arrived.

When it finally did, it announced that Greg would be home 'on the 22nd or 23rd' and would see Cathy at home.

'They can't be too exact with the way the trains are, and having to get discharged,' Sally said. 'I'm glad Greg put that about seeing you at home, because you couldn't sit on the station all that time.'

'I feel nervous now, Mam,' Cathy confessed, but her mother assured her that she would feel all right as soon as she saw him.

In London Mary and her set were still following their hectic round of enjoyment, and some of the men had begun to arrive back in civilian life. The latest craze among the young ladies was serving tea at railway stations to returning servicemen.

Various women's organizations had provided tea to trainloads of wounded men or to crowded troop trains throughout the war, sometimes while London was suffering Zeppelin raids or bombing attacks. Now the work had suddenly become fashionable and crowds of socialites descended on the station, to the dismay of the regular helpers.

'Such *worthy* women, darling,' Arabella Seton drawled to Mary. 'And wonderful work, but not for little me. No, darling, welcoming home the heroes is my forte.'

A train had pulled into the station and Mary turned away from her, smiling. Soldiers spilled from the carriages and as they surged towards the tea stall Mary heard the familiar Liverpool accents. The next moment there was a cry of: 'Mary! Mary Ward.'

A young man who had worked at Denby's was pushing through the crowd and Mary neatly slipped away from her friends to draw him out of earshot. 'Billy Dunn, isn't it?' she said.

'Yes. What a' you doin' down 'ere, Mary?'

'I live here,' she said coolly. 'I'm a widow now.' Her gaze went past him to a slightly built man standing a little apart from the crowd. He was smaller than Greg but he had the same thin, sensitive features and Mary gazed at him wistfully.

The next moment the man beside him turned round and Mary's eyes widened in disbelief and her hand flew to her throat.

'Greg, Greg,' she tried to say, but could make no sound. But Greg had seen her, and with a shout of 'Mary!' he was thrusting through the crowd towards her.

The next moment she was in his arms, clinging to him, unable to believe that it was really Greg and that she had not conjured him up by her imagination, while she looked at the man who was like him.

He was speaking to her but she heard nothing and could only hold him tight, murmuring his name over and over again.

Billy Dunn had disappeared into the crowd, and Greg's friend had been to the stall and now came back with two cups of tea. Greg released himself from Mary, and took the tea with a smile of thanks. 'Mary, this is my friend, John Savage,' he said. 'John, my sister-in-law, Mary.'

Mary shook hands with John and tried to recover her poise. 'Where are you going?' she asked. 'Back to Liverpool?'

'Yes. Back home,' Greg said with a beaming grin. 'We've been demobilised.' He and John smiled at each other then Greg turned back to Mary. 'When are you going home, Mary?' he said. 'There's nothing to keep you here now this show's over, is there?' She shrugged but said nothing. The train's hooter sounded and the men began to go back aboard but Greg hesitated. 'Will you come for a cup of tea and have a talk, Mary?' he said, and she agreed eagerly.

'You don't mind, John?' Greg asked. The other man shook his head and Greg said quickly, 'Wait here for me, Mary, while I get my kitbag.'

He walked to the train with his friend, explaining that he wanted to persuade Mary to go home. 'Her mam and dad are fretting about her, I know, and I'd be made up if I could get her to go home. They've been so good to me. Cathy's worried about her, too.'

'But why is she down here?' John asked. 'Was her husband a Londoner?'

'No, a Canadian, but he was killed early on in the war. She came down here – told her mother she was on war work. They don't know what she's been up to. She just sends cards saying she's well, as far as I can make out, but reading between the lines—'

They had reached the train and John helped Greg to get his kitbag off. 'It's been a hard time for women, too, Greg,' he said quietly. 'But she'd be better at home with her family. Good luck. I'll see you soon.'

The train moved away and Greg went back to Mary. 'Who are you with?' he asked.

'That crowd,' she said indifferently, waving her hand at the gaily dressed throng near the tea stall. 'But they won't miss me.' She linked her arm through his and looked up at him, her eyes sparkling with delight. He wants to be with me, she thought exultantly. He doesn't want to go rushing back to her.

Outside the station she hailed a taxicab, and as she stepped in gave the address of her flat to the driver.

'What have you told him?' Greg said, puzzled.

'I've given him the address of the flat I share,' she said gaily. 'You can't go anywhere decent with that thing.'

'I should have dumped it at Left Luggage,' he said, looking ruefully at the kitbag at his feet, 'but it hardly seemed worth while.'

Darkness had fallen when they reached the flat, and fog had begun to fill the air.

Dora was away for a few days but Mary said nothing of that to Greg. She took his greatcoat and poured a whisky and soda for him, and a glass of sherry for herself, then drew him down to sit beside her on the sofa.

Greg was looking uneasy. 'I can't stay long, Mary,' he said. 'I didn't intend to come so far from the station. I thought I'd get the next train.'

'Good heavens, Greg, you've had years of having to obey rules. Surely you can please yourself now,' she said, pouting. 'Anyway, *you* suggested missing your train to talk to me.'

He smiled at her and she felt again the sensation of her bones turning to water, but as she swayed towards him the look of alarm on his face made her draw back. Greg swallowed his drink in one agitated gulp, but Mary sipped her sherry then as she put the glass down moved from the sofa to sit on a small embroidered stool.

The flat was lit by electric lamps, shaded in pink silk, and Mary knew that she looked very beautiful in the soft light as she smiled up into Greg's face.

'Go on then, Greg,' she said softly. 'Talk to me.'

He seemed uncertain how to begin. 'Er – the other girl in this flat – she's from Liverpool, isn't she?'

'Yes. A friend of Isabel Willard's. She's a war widow like myself,' Mary said, opening her eyes wide and looking up at him pathetically.

'I was sorry to hear about Clive,' Greg said. 'I should have said that sooner, Mary.'

'That's all right. It seems a long time ago now,' she said.

Greg nodded. 'I know,' he said. 'But is there anyone else, Mary? Have you met anyone down here that you care about?'

Only you, Greg, she longed to say, but felt that she would need to tread carefully. She was sure that he cared for her, but was afraid to admit it even to himself. He felt the pull of her attraction but he was resisting it out of a sense of duty. But *I* know, Mary thought joyfully. I know he's only making excuses to be with me by asking me to go home.

She smiled at him and shook her head. 'No, no one, Greg,' she said. 'I dine with people or go to the theatre but usually they're men on leave. I'm just trying to cheer them up. They mean nothing to me.'

'Then why don't you go home, Mary?' he said eagerly. 'It would mean so much to your mam and dad, and to Cathy of course. She says your mam's worn out worrying about you, and about your dad overworking and his cough. It's only the baby that keeps her going, Cathy says.'

'She doesn't need me, if she's got Cathy and the child,' Mary said sharply. A large lump of coal smouldered in the centre of the fire, and she picked up the poker and hit it viciously, shattering it and sending yellow and blue flames spurting.

Greg bit his lip and stayed silent, nervous of saying the wrong thing, but presently he ran his finger round his collar. 'Hot in here, isn't it?' he said. 'I don't know whether it's the fire or the whisky.'

'Take your tunic off,' Mary said. 'You don't have to stand on ceremony with me, Greg.'

Thankfully he pulled off his tunic and unfastened the top button of his khaki flannel shirt, 'Phew, that's better,' he said, smiling at her.

'I don't want to interfere, Mary,' he said, leaning forward. 'I just thought it would be such a tonic for them if you went home, even if it was only for a visit. And you've nothing to keep you in London now, have you?'

Mary's good humour seemed to be restored as she took Greg's glass to the sideboard and poured whisky then added soda from a siphon, smiling to herself. He wants me in Liverpool, she thought happily.

She handed the glass to him then sat down again on the sofa, gazing into his eyes. 'Do *you* want me to come to Liverpool?' she asked softly.

He drank some whisky. 'Yes, of course,' he said. 'It'd be great to have everyone back home again like before the war.'

'I wish we could turn the clock back, Greg,' she murmured.

He shifted a little further away from her on the sofa. 'Speaking of clocks,' he said, 'is that one right?' Mary nodded. 'What time will your friend be home?' he asked.

She had taken a quick glance through the window before pouring the whisky and seen that the fog had thickened, so now she said gaily, 'Dora won't be home tonight. The fog's too thick.'

Greg strode to the window and lifted the curtain. 'Good God!' he exclaimed. 'I've never seen anything like that.'

Mary had joined him at the window, and said airily, 'Yes. It's a real pea souper, isn't it?'

'But – will I be able to get a cab?' he said. 'Or are the buses running? I'll have to get to the station.' He was fastening the button on his shirt but Mary put her hand on his arm. 'It's no use, Greg. You can't go in this. Everyone understands that fog like this stops everything running.'

'I'll have a look out,' he said, going to the front door and pulling it open. Fog came swirling into the hall. There was an uncanny silence in the street outside, and no matter how Greg strained to peer through the thick yellow fog, he could see nothing moving.

Mary shivered. 'Shut the door,' she said. 'There's nothing to be done. You'll have to stay the night.'

'I'll walk,' he said stubbornly.

'Carrying that thing?' she said, pointing at the kitbag.

'I've carried worse than that,' Greg said grimly. He thought of the wounded men he had carried. The sixteen-year-old boy who had lied about his age to enlist, and cried for his mother as they tried to get him to a dressing station before he bled to death. The grey-haired man at the other end of the age scale who told them he'd had four horses shot from under him in the Boer War, and two in this. Talking desperately while he held his shattered insides in place with his hands and they tried not to jolt him.

Greg wrenched his mind away from these memories and back to his present predicament. It had seemed such a good idea when he saw Mary to persuade her to come home, then get the next train back to Liverpool.

How had he ever managed to get in this pickle, with Cathy waiting for and him stuck here with Mary?

She slid her hand through his arm. 'You can't walk, Greg. You'd never find the station. Come to the kitchen with me and light the gas. There's no electricity out there but I'll find us something to eat if you light up for me.'

'I can't take your food,' he protested. 'There's a shortage, isn't there?'

'Not in this house.' She laughed. 'Dora has useful friends.'

War profiteers, I suppose, Greg thought grimly. Poor Mary! She's in with a rum crowd all right, judging by this and the people at the station. I'll have to do my best to get her to come home, for the sake of the family.

'You can go and sit by the fire,' she told him as she tied an apron about her waist. 'I'll call you when it's ready.'

Greg went back to the room with the fire, but only to walk about restlessly. If only Mary would be sensible, he thought. She was behaving like a silly girl instead of a woman who had been widowed and had left her youth far behind her.

He thought of the way she had snuggled up to him on the sofa, gazing into his eyes, and suddenly remembered similar occasions, it seemed like in another life, before the war. Then he had been a callow boy, upset and troubled by it; now he was a man with a wife and child he loved. The problem now was to make this clear to Mary without hurting her, but then with a sudden change of mood he felt a wave of self-disgust.

Where did I get these big ideas? I'm just kidding myself, he thought. This flirting is the way that crowd behaves, and here I am, reading all this into it! That crowd at the station, some them over thirty, all behaved like flappers.

Mary called him and he went out to the kitchen.

'The fire isn't lit in the dining room, Greg. We'll eat here,' she said, putting plates of egg and bacon and a pot of coffee on the table. Fog had seeped in and hung about the corners of the kitchen, so they ate the meal quickly and returned to the fire.

Greg had looked out of the door again but the fog seemed even thicker, so that it was impossible to see more than a few yards.

Mary had come to stand beside him and said gaily, 'We might as well be on a desert island.'

'I hope a desert island would be warmer,' Greg said, closing the door and following her into the room. He was determined to keep the conversation light, and it seemed that Mary also had decided to be more circumspect.

She curled up in the corner of the sofa, not touching Greg, and he said casually, 'How long have you lived here, Mary?'

'Since just after the war started,' she said. 'I met Dora again when she was widowed, and we came here and lived in a hotel at first. Then we thought we might as well have our own place.'

'It's very nice,' he said. 'But if Dora's a Liverpool girl, won't she want to come back to her family and friends now?'

'She hates her family,' Mary said, laughing. She took a cigarette from a box on the table, and when Greg leaned forward to light it for her, laid her fingers over his and looked up into his eyes.

He sat back and took a folder from the pocket of his tunic. 'Have you seen any photographs of our son?' he said, taking out several. Mary barely glanced at them, but looked again at the first photograph and the verse which Cathy had printed beneath it. Her lip curled.

'Still hopelessly sentimental, isn't she?' she said. Then, as Greg made a quick gesture of protest, she said, 'Dear Cathy. Never changes, does she? She sent me copies of them.'

'Did you get this one?' Greg asked, taking another photograph from the folder. It was a family group, with the baby on Cathy's knee and her mother and father on either side of her, all smiling down fondly.

Mary moved closer to him. 'Very cosy, isn't it?' she said. 'You'll be an intruder there when you go back, Greg.' She allowed her eyes to fill with tears and leaned her head on his shoulder. 'We're both outsiders now,' she wept.

Instinctively he put his arm round her to comfort her. 'That's not true, Mary. Your family loves you. They all worry about you, and they'd love to see you again.'

Mary sobbed convincingly and held him close. 'Oh, Greg, Greg,' she cried.

'Don't cry, Mary, don't cry,' he urged her. 'I didn't mean to upset you.' But she only cried more bitterly.

He held her and offered her a handkerchief, then as she grew a little quieter, he said, 'Come on, love. Dry your eyes.'

She dabbed at them, and he said, 'You see, Mary, you do care about them, just as they care about you. Dora and the crowd sound hard, Mary, but you're not like that. Why don't you come home, if only for a visit?'

He tried to withdraw his arm but she pressed closer to him. 'No, you're wrong, Greg,' she said. 'I can tell by the letters. Just the three of them and the baby in a tight little circle. There's no room for intruders like us.'

'And I think you're wrong. In fact, I'm sure of it,' he said. He withdrew his arm on the pretext of gathering up the photographs and putting them back in the folder.

'It's a good thing I didn't give Cathy a definite time,' he said. 'We have fogs in Liverpool as you know, but I've never seen anything like this. It's more like a smoke screen or a gas attack.'

Mary had dried her eyes and rearranged herself on the sofa, satisfied that she had at least planted an idea in his mind.

'Tell me about the war, Greg,' she commanded, but a shutter seemed to come down over his face.

'It's over,' he said shortly, 'and best forgotten. At least there'll never be another. This was the war to end war. Tell me what you've been doing, Mary.'

'This and that,' she said airily. 'I've had quite a good time really, consoling war heroes.' She looked challengingly at him. 'But don't make any mistake, Greg. I gave them my company during their leaves for social occasions only – nothing else. I demanded respect and got it, and I turned down several proposals.'

'I'm glad,' he said simply. 'Your mam and dad will be glad too.'

'Why? What do they think? They seem to have told you more than they told me.'

'I'm sorry. I put that badly,' he said. 'I just mean that they worried about the dangers to a young girl alone in London. But that's all finished now, Mary, so it would be a good time to come home.'

'Home!' she said scornfully. 'Think about it, Greg. I couldn't live in Egremont Street, and if I took a house what society could I expect? The Bagshaws and that crowd? The Willards? When I think of them, believing they were doing me a favour by accepting me! Why, they'd go on their knees for just *one* of the invitations I get now.'

'But what about Elizabeth Fairburn?' Greg said stubbornly. 'You'd soon build up a circle of friends again.'

'Oh, Elizabeth's gone all *worthy*,' Mary said. 'She's a VAD. Mam sent on a letter from her all about some gruesome experience she had in France. I don't know why she told *me*.'

Mary seemed to have forgotten her bout of weeping as she lit another cigarette and smiled at the expression on Greg's face. 'I'm afraid we're a very lighthearted crowd,' she said. 'It's the only way to be.'

'Who are they – your crowd?' he asked.

'You'd be surprised. All the class barriers are down now. One of my greatest friends is the daughter of a lord. At least the war did that.'

Greg shrugged. 'Let's hope it lasts,' he said.

He made up the fire and went again to look out of the door but the fog was as thick as ever. He felt that he had done as much as he could to persuade Mary and that it was unlikely that she would come home to Liverpool to live. He would have one last try to persuade her to come home for a visit, then let the matter rest and leave himself as soon as he possibly could.

At intervals he went to check on the fog, but it showed no sign of thinning, and he and Mary sat chatting about the days before the war. At one stage he asked her if she had intended to go out, but she told him that it was out of the question anyway.

'Dora'll have to put up somewhere,' she said. She yawned. 'You might as well have her bed, Greg,' she said. 'This isn't going to lift before morning.'

'I'll sleep on the sofa,' he said quickly. 'But you go to bed when you're ready, Mary. I'll be fine here.'

'Nonsense,' she said. 'The sofa's far too small.'

'Then I'll sleep on the floor,' he said, but she persuaded him at least to stretch out on top of Dora's bed.

She took him across the hall and showed him into the room, then kissed him goodnight and went to her own room.

Chapter Thirty-Eight

Greg felt unutterably weary. As he took off his boots and trousers and lay down under the quilt, he cursed the impulse which had led to his being stranded here instead of at home with Cathy.

Cathy. His face softened as he thought about her, and he hoped that she had not expected him home earlier. Lucky that he hadn't been able to give her an exact time, but even if he failed to get Mary to come home, just for a visit, Cathy would understand that he had to take the opportunity to try when he saw her.

He stretched out on the soft bed and within minutes was asleep. He was used to sleeping lightly in the trenches so as soon as the door opened he was wide awake. At first he thought that it was Dora, come to claim her bed, but the next moment Mary slipped in beside him.

'Mary!' he exclaimed, but before he could say any more her arms were about his neck and her lips pressed hard upon his. Even when she broke away momentarily he was too stunned to speak and Mary began to weep. 'Oh, Greg, I'm so unhappy,' she murmured. 'All those memories. You've really upset me.' She pressed her wet cheek to his and clung to him tightly.

'I'm—I'm sorry,' he stammered.

'I love you, Greg. You should have married me. It was all a mistake,' she wept.

'Mary, don't! Don't say it. You're just upset. You've been dreaming,' Greg gabbled, feeling this was a nightmare from which he would soon awake.

Mary's body was real, though, clad in a filmy nightdress and pressing close against his. He tried to release himself from her embrace but she only clung more tightly. 'You don't know, Greg,' she sobbed. 'Clive was a beast, an animal. I wanted to die.'

'Mary, Mary,' he pleaded. 'Don't!' But she swept on: 'I was *glad* when he was killed, but now I can't bear a man to touch me. Only you, Greg. Help me. I want *you*. I *need* you, Greg. Love me.'

'Mary, *don't*,' he said. He gripped her hands and pulled them away from his neck. 'Be sensible. You've just got upset talking about home, and you're dreaming. You think I'm someone else.'

'I don't, I don't,' she cried, wrenching her hands away and clasping them behind his head. 'I love you, Greg, and you love me. You know you do. You were only sorry for Cathy but I need you now.' She pressed her body and lips even more closely to his, but with a superhuman effort Greg pulled away from her and slid out of the bed.

Mary burst into wild hysterical weeping and he bent over the bed, pulling the quilt up over her writhing body.

'Mary, you've had a bad dream,' he said urgently. 'You've been sleepwalking. I'll go now.'

'No, no!' she screamed, grabbing his hand and kissing it. 'Love me, Greg. Love me.'

'I can't, Mary. You know I can't. Oh, God.' Sweat poured down his face and he was shaking. He dragged his hand away. 'Mary, I can't leave you like this. What can I do?' he said wildly. 'Shall I make you some tea?'

She began to scream with hysterical laughter and he snatched up his boots and trousers and fled from the room. He could still hear her screams as he pulled on his trousers and boots with shaking hands, then grabbed his tunic and kitbag and left the house.

Outside the fog was thinning. He pulled on his tunic, picked up his kitbag and strode away, still feeling dazed with shock.

He had walked for ten minutes before he calmed down and realised that he had left his cap and greatcoat in the flat. I don't care, he thought, I'm not going back. I'd sooner face a firing squad.

It was still very early but a wind had sprung up to clear the fog. Greg had no idea where he was but at some stage he passed some shops. A swarthy man was standing in the doorway of one of them.

There was a barber's pole outside it, and the man said to Greg, 'Shave, Tommy. Bath?' He stepped back invitingly. Greg felt his chin, then followed the man into the shop, still feeling as though he was in a daze.

He sank into a chair and the man shaved him, then gestured for Greg to follow him into a back cellar which had been divided into cubicles containing baths. The barber offered to steam his uniform. 'Get rid of the little hoppers, eh?' he smirked.

Greg silently emptied his pockets and handed the uniform to the man before stepping into the bath. Half an hour later he came out feeling better, and took a cab to the station.

The Liverpool train was in the station and Greg was soon in a carriage with a crowd of other soldiers. 'Lost your cap and coat, mate?' one of them asked. 'Or had it snitched?'

'Left it somewhere,' he said. 'But I don't care.'

'No, we don't care about nothing now, do we?' the man said. 'Never no more worries like, mate.'

The men were all cheerful and excited and one of them produced a mouth organ and began to play, but Greg closed his eyes and pretended to sleep. He felt that he had to think and try to make sense of what had happened, and also decide what to do.

He felt ashamed that he had fled, leaving Mary in that state, but he wondered what else he could have done. He was only making matters worse by being there.

Whatever had come over her? He thought uneasily of the signs she had given of caring for him in the past, but he had always believed that he was one of many. Or perhaps it was a challenge to Mary that he loved Cathy. Certainly he'd been quite unprepared for that scene in the bedroom. Even now he could hardly believe it had happened.

I should have left earlier, he thought, even to walk round in circles in the fog. But how could he have guessed what would happen? Mary had seemed so normal and friendly when she left him to go to her own room. I wonder, is she on drugs? he thought suddenly. I've heard of Society girls taking cocaine.

Why, oh why, did I ever have that barmy idea of getting her to come home? I thought it would mean just having a cup of tea somewhere while I tried to talk her into coming, then I could get the next train. I never bargained for going back to her flat and then that carry-on.

His thoughts were still chaotic as the train neared Liverpool, then another thought struck him. Cathy! What should he tell her? It wasn't a question now of explaining to her how he had tried to persuade Mary to come home, then got caught up in the fog.

I don't think I'd better mention Mary, he decided. I'd give myself away if I tried to mention her casually, yet what if Cathy's seen some of the lads who were on the train with me? And I owe it to Mr and Mrs Ward to tell them I've seen Mary and she's all right. The thought of her writhing on the bed passed through his mind but he dismissed it quickly. She was all right really, that was just a sort of brainstorm.

He opened his eyes and looked round the carriage as the men began to pull kitbags from the luggage racks. Most of them were grimy and unshaven after their long journey, and that gave Greg an idea.

I'll tell Cathy that I stopped to clean up before coming home. I don't suppose she'll know I should have been home yesterday anyway, he thought. It's only my guilty conscience.

On the previous day Cathy had watched the door of the shop all day, hoping to see a messenger from her mother, but there was no message and Greg had not arrived by midnight.

'We might as well go to bed,' her mother said. 'He won't come now.'

They had gone to bed but Cathy was too excited to sleep.

A few weeks earlier Sally had suggested that John should be moved into the small bedroom where the two Burns boys had slept until recently, so that he could get used to sleeping apart from his mother before his father came home. Cathy had agreed that it was a good idea but now she was tempted to take him back with her for a cuddle. She resisted, knowing the wisdom of her mother's plan.

She had told Mr Wilson not to expect her at the shop so she got up early and cleaned up, then changed into her fresh clothes to be ready for Greg. John was playing in the backyard with strict instructions to keep his clothes clean, and Sally had gone to the corner shop, leaving the door ajar, when Greg walked down the street.

Cathy heard the noise at the door and his call of 'Cathy', but she stood in the kitchen suddenly feeling too nervous to run to meet him. He came down the lobby and when he saw her he flung his kitbag down and reached her in one stride, to fling his arms around her.

'Cathy, Cathy, Cathy,' he said, squeezing her until her ribs almost cracked and showering her with kisses.

She was unable to speak at first, then could only say 'Thank God, thank God,' as she clung to him, stroking his face.

Suddenly they were interrupted as a small figure dashed in and flung himself between them. 'My mama, my mama!' John said, throwing his arms round Cathy's knees and glaring up at Greg.

'John, it's your dada,' Cathy exclaimed, and Greg bent his knees until he was on a level with the little boy.

'Hello, son,' he said trying to take the child in his arms, but John pulled away from him and clung to Cathy's skirt.

'It's my mama,' he said. 'Go 'way.'

'John, it's your dada,' Cathy said again. 'What were you going to say to him?' But John only glowered at Greg.

There was a noise in the lobby and Sally walked in. 'Greg!' she said in delighted surprise. He went to her and kissed her, and Cathy bent over John and told him firmly to say, 'Welcome home, Dada.' But he thrust out his lower lip mutinously and said nothing.

Cathy stood up again, her face flushed, and said to Sally, 'John's being very silly, Grandma.'

'He can come and help me,' she said, taking the child's hand. She drew him into the back kitchen, saying to Greg, 'I'll make you a cup of tea, son,' before closing the door firmly behind her.

'Now I know I'm home,' he said to Cathy. 'Your mam making me a cup of tea.'

'Her cure for all evils,' Cathy said, then they looked at each other and burst out laughing, although Greg fleetingly remembered offering tea to Mary, and her response.

He put his arms around Cathy again and said softly, 'You could have put that better, but I know what you mean. God, Cath, I can't believe this. I've thought of it so often.'

'So have I,' she murmured. 'I thought I'd go off like a rocket yesterday.'

Greg's arms stiffened for a moment, then he said quietly, 'I stopped to get cleaned up, Cath.' Blast Mary! he thought, starting me off with a lie to Cathy. Even spoiling the homecoming cup of tea.

'I'm glad you did,' she was saying, stroking his smooth chin. 'Robbie Burns came home muddy and unshaven and *lousy*.'

They were still standing with their arms about each other in wordless happiness when Sally called, 'Open the door for me, Cath.' Greg pulled open the door to the back kitchen and Sally came through, carrying the teapot and milk jug. 'John's bringing the spoons,' she said as the child followed her.

'Have you had any breakfast?' she asked, and Greg confessed that he had forgotten all about it. Cathy eagerly rushed to cook black puddings for him, and Greg tried to make friends with his son but the child still hung back watching him warily.

It was only when Greg went to his kitbag and brought out some carved wooden animals, and a wooden tower with a flag on top which revolved when a handle was turned, that John gradually drew closer until he was sitting on Greg's knee and turning the handle. He still looked from Cathy to Greg occasionally with a puzzled air.

After a while Sally tactfully decided to take John to show his toys to Peggy Burns. 'Why don't you go in the parlour?' she said. 'The fire's burning up nice now and John's all right with me for as long as you like.'

She went out with him and Cathy and Greg went into the parlour which was now furnished with their belongings.

'But this is ours,' Greg exclaimed, looking round.

'Yes. Remember Mam said we could have the parlour and the back bedroom when we gave up Anton Street? We don't often light the fire in here though, because we're in with Mam.'

'Remember us buying this sofa,' Greg said. 'It seems a lifetime since then.'

Cathy sat down on the sofa and he sat beside her and took her in his arms. 'We've got a lot of time to make up, Cath,' he whispered. He kissed her hungrily and she responded fiercely, but soon they heard the front door open.

'Cathy,' Sally called. 'I'm going down to Peggy's mam's. I'm taking John and we won't be back till four o'clock. Lock the back door, love, and shut this one, and don't take any notice of any knocks. I'll be back at four.'

The door banged as she went away and Cathy looked at Greg. 'Mam's a case, isn't she?' she said, blushing.

'She's one in a million,' Greg said huskily. 'I'll lock the back door while you go up, Cath.'

She blushed again but went upstairs and soon Greg followed her. They made love with passionate tenderness, then Greg smoothed Cathy's hair back from her forehead and lay looking at her face.

'I've missed you so much, love,' he whispered. 'I don't know how I've borne being away from you for so long.'

'I feel as though I've been dead and now I've come to life again,' Cathy said softly.

They lay in each other's arms talking for a while, then they made love again and afterwards Cathy quite suddenly fell asleep. Greg raised his head and looked again at her beloved face.

It was thinner than when he saw her last, and the bloom of health had gone from it, but in sleep the anxious lines he had noticed when he came home were smoothed away.

Greg stroked her cheek. I'll look after her now, he vowed to himself. She'll never have to worry again.

They went downstairs and Cathy began to prepare the evening meal, then Sally came back with John and a little later Lawrie came home.

'Glad to see you back, lad,' he said, gripping Greg's hand. 'Good times ahead now, eh?'

'Thanks for all you've both done,' Greg said, looking from Lawrie to Sally, 'looking after Cathy and young John.'

'A pleasure, lad,' Lawrie assured him. 'We were only sorry for the reason. It's been the other way round anyway. Cathy's looked after us, and so has this young shaver, haven't you, John?'

John brought Lawrie's slippers to him and he ruffled the child's hair. 'You'll have to start doing that for your dada now,' he said, but John gave Greg a glance of dislike and said, 'No,' loudly.

The adults ignored his outburst and soon Cathy took him up to bed and told him about the good times that they would have now that his father was home. John only buried his head in her shoulder and said stubbornly, '*My* mama.'

Downstairs Greg took the opportunity to say to Sally and Lawrie, 'I saw Mary. When I was on the train in London she was on the platform handing out tea with a lot of Society women. She looked very smart.' I haven't told any lie, he thought, and was glad that he had spoken about Mary when he saw the relief and pleasure on her parents' faces.

They were still exclaiming about it when Cathy came downstairs and he told his tale again, word for word, finding it easier the second time.

'That must be her war work,' Cathy exclaimed, and Sally said tartly: 'Well, I didn't think she'd be scrubbing floors.'

Later in bed Cathy felt glad that she and Greg had been able to make love earlier when the house was empty. Now she felt tense and worried about every sound they made, knowing that her parents lay on the other side of the thin wall.

Before long, fortunately when she and Greg were only lying talking, the door opened and John scrambled on to the bed.

'Mama, make that man go away,' he said, clinging round her neck and kicking out at Greg.

'It's your dada, John,' she said, trying to release herself, but he only yelled and kicked even more fiercely.

'I'll take him back,' Greg said. 'It's bound to be strange for him. He'll soon get used to me.'

He lifted John up, but when he went out on the landing Sally looked out of her bedroom door. 'Let him come in here, Greg,' she said. 'Just for tonight.' Greg put the struggling child down and he ran to Sally, yelling, 'Grandma, make the naughty man go away.'

'It's all right, son,' she soothed him. 'Come and rub Grandad's back and make him better.'

She drew him into her bedroom and Greg went back to bed, thinking ruefully that he was fated with bedroom doors.

'He's usually so good,' Cathy said when he drew her into his arms again.

'Bound to take time,' he said, stroking her soft arm and kissing her neck.

'I thought it would with me. I was nervous of meeting you again, Greg,' she whispered.

'You didn't show it.'

'I didn't feel it once I saw you. I felt as though you'd never been away.'

A little later she said suddenly, 'Greg, your mother! You should have gone to see her.'

'I'll go tomorrow,' he said. He felt that he was in no hurry to see his mother. He knew that Cathy visited her, because she always told him in her letters that things were working out well with Miss Nugent, but his mother's letters never mentioned either Cathy or John.

She never talked of anything but herself and her complaints, Greg thought grimly, or else reproached him for not finding her a 'suitable house' before he left. He would pay a duty visit but any complaints from her would get short shrift, he decided.

'How is old Braithwaite?' he said aloud.

'He's failed a lot,' Cathy said. 'Very shaky but just as stubborn, but Albert Kettle's very patient with him.'

Cathy had looked forward to telling Greg that she had drawn nothing from the shop profits, so that a nest egg had been building up for them while he was away, but his only response was, 'I hope you didn't leave yourself short, Cath.'

'No. I had my money from you and the money from Wilson's,' she said. 'I thought this would be useful if you wanted to expand the shop or anything like that.'

He said nothing for a while, only held her close and stroked her cheek. Then he said suddenly, 'I don't want to go back to the shop, Cath.'

'But I thought you enjoyed it,' she said. 'Building it up and all that.'

'Only because it brought our wedding nearer,' he said. 'I didn't really think about things then, but now – it seems such a futile way to spend your life, Cath. Worrying about selling bits of jewellery. I want to do something with my life.'

'It's a shame you can't be a doctor, Greg,' she said softly. 'Is there no way—?'

'No, Cath. I wish there was. I think I'd have made a good doctor. I was told I would, too, by one of the doctors at the field dressing station.'

'Then what can you do?' Cathy asked.

'The chaplain suggested that I might get a job as a laboratory assistant where they're doing research. An assistant only does the most menial jobs though it would be very interesting. But what I'd really like to do, Cath, is to take a smallholding, grow our own food and keep a few hens and maybe a pig. What do you think?'

'I'd love it,' she said. 'But what would you do about the shop?'

'I'd sell it. Make a condition that the new people kept Albert on. Mr Braithwaite will be glad to retire, and the other lads – I'm very sorry they won't be coming back, but I won't have to consider their jobs.'

'I'm annoyed that your mother wrote to tell you when Harry Osborne and Cecil Jones were killed. I thought it was time enough to tell you when you came home,' Cathy said.

Both of the shop assistants had been killed on the Western Front, Harry in 1916, and Cecil only in September 1918.

'Oh, well, that's my mama,' Greg said drily. 'These are just dreams of mine, Cath, but of course I wouldn't do anything unless you agreed to it. There's something else too.' He lay in silence for a while and Cathy said nothing, then he said quietly, 'I'd like to be received into the Catholic Church. Would you mind, love?'

She was too stunned to reply for a moment. This is the night for surprises, was her first thought, but then she said gently, 'No. If that's what you want, Greg, go ahead.'

He told her then that he had been impressed by the way John Savage's religion had guided his life. 'It wasn't just a matter for church parade on Sundays – he lived his beliefs, Cath. Do you know he was chosen as the most exemplary Catholic to represent the Regiment at Lourdes? It was a well-deserved honour too.'

'Strange that both your best friends have been Catholics, isn't it?' Cathy said. 'And both named John.'

'I suppose that's influenced me,' he said, 'but it goes deeper than that. We'd better not talk any more now. It'll be morning before we get any sleep.' They kissed goodnight and soon Cathy, in spite of her astonishment, was asleep, quickly followed by Greg.

They set off to visit his mother shortly after breakfast the next morning, with John walking between them. Some of the shutters were still up when they reached the shop and one of the women assistants ran out when she saw Cathy.

'Mrs Redmond,' she said then burst into tears, and ran back into the shop. They followed her to find a scene of confusion and Mr Braithwaite slumped on a chair, being supported by the other assistant.

The old man's face was paper white, but his lips were blue and his head shook uncontrollably. Greg went to him and loosened his collar and took his wrist. 'Better get a doctor,' he said quietly to Cathy who had followed him, then he bent over the old man and said soothingly. 'You'll be all right, Mr Braithwaite. We'll soon have you home in bed.'

Mr Braithwaite tried to speak but his words made no sense and his agitation seemed to increase. One of the girls grabbed Greg's arm. 'It's the shock,' she said. 'That Kettle, the swine!' Cathy's eyes widened when the girl, usually so quiet and ladylike, went on: 'He's scarpered, and taken the stock!' Both women sobbed hysterically.

The shop boy came back and said the doctor was coming, and Cathy said firmly: 'Wait outside for him, and you two, come in the back.' She bundled the two women into the back room and took John with them, then shut the door into the shop leaving Greg to calm the old man.

Gabbling incoherently and interrupting each other frequently, the two women told Cathy what had happened. The previous day a customer had told them that Greg had arrived in Liverpool, and shortly afterwards Kettle had gone out and remained away for most of the day.

When he came back he told them that they could leave early and told the boy to put the shutters up as he wanted to get the shop ready for Greg's inspection.

They had suspected nothing but when they came to work at the usual time, the shop was still locked and Kettle had not appeared. They had waited outside until Mr Braithwaite came, then they all came in to find the safe wide open.

In the shop the doctor had arrived and the shop boy had taken down the rest of the shutters to discover that even the items that had been left in the window overnight had been taken. The boy rushed into the shop with the news but Greg told him to be quiet, and told the doctor that he would take Mr Braithwaite home in a cab.

In the midst of the confusion Miss Nugent came in and nervously told Cathy that Mrs Redmond was insisting that her son should visit her immediately.

'Does she know what's happened?' Cathy asked. Miss Nugent nodded. 'Yes. We heard the commotion and she sent me down. I couldn't stay to help. Mrs Redmond was so upset.'

'Greg has to take Mr Braithwaite home. He's the only one who can tell the old man he doesn't blame him for this. I'll come up to her.'

She left John with the shop girls, knowing that there would be a scene with Greg's mother, but it was even worse than she expected. Mrs Redmond was lying on the sofa drumming her heels, her face purple. As soon as she saw Cathy, she started to scream at her.

'Where is he? Where's my son? Going to you instead of coming to his mother? Where is he?'

'He's taken Mr Braithwaite home,' Cathy said quietly. 'He's very ill. He may be dying.'

'What does that matter?' Mrs Redmond shrieked. 'I'm his *mother*.'

Cathy was disgusted. The old man had served her well for more than forty years, she thought, looking at her mother-in-law with contempt.

When Mrs Redmond's tantrum reached new heights Cathy had no hesitation in getting a cup of water from the kitchen and throwing it over her. Miss Nugent looked on in dismay, but Mrs Redmond was silenced. 'The best cure for hysterics, I believe,' Cathy said, turning on her heel and walking away.

When Greg returned Cathy told him what had happened and he went up alone to see his mother. 'Was she all right?' Cathy asked, but Greg only said briefly, 'I wish you'd thrown a jugful.'

He sent the assistants home, telling them that the shop would remain closed for the rest of the week while he sorted matters out, but paying their wages and asking them to return on Monday.

He and Cathy quickly tidied up the shop and Greg parcelled up all the papers he could find to study them at home. They locked up and on the way home they called in to a police station to report the theft.

The sergeant shook his head dolefully. 'We'll do our best to catch him, sir,' he said. 'But at a time like this it's easy for a wrong 'un to disappear.'

Greg was whistling lightheartedly as they walked home, and Cathy said cheerfully, 'The nest egg will come in useful now, anyway.'

'How much is it?' Greg asked, and she confessed that she didn't know. 'I didn't like to ask,' she said, 'but it's been building up for nearly four years. You know, Greg, I feel guilty about the shop. I should have watched things more closely, after you explaining everything to me before you went away, too.'

'Don't be daft, Cath,' he said. 'I only explained things so that you could help old Braithwaite because he seemed nervous about being in charge. We weren't to know he was going to turn out so stubborn or that Kettle would turn out to be a rogue. Don't worry about it.'

Chapter Thirty-Nine

Even when a visit to the bank revealed that the nest egg was almost non-existent, Greg was not worried. Albert Kettle, it seemed, had been siphoning off the profits of the shop since almost immediately after Greg had gone, but he remained cheerful.

'We'll have to postpone the smallholding, Cath,' he said, 'but I'll manage it eventually.'

'I'm glad you're not upset,' she said. 'It's a blow, just after coming home.'

'It doesn't matter,' Greg said. 'The way I see it, we've come through, we're young and healthy, and we've got a healthy little son. We're damned lucky, Cath. Nothing else matters.'

'That's true,' she said. 'That's what I think. We'll soon get on our feet.'

'Mind you, if I ever find that rogue Kettle, I'll make him sorry he was ever born. Particularly on old Braithwaite's account,' Greg said.

Mr Braithwaite had lived for only three weeks after his collapse and although Greg did all he could to assure the old man that he had not been to blame, his distress hastened his death, Greg thought.

It was soon clear to him that the business had been dealt a mortal blow by Albert Kettle's depredations, and he decided that the only course was to close the shops.

'I can just about clear the debts,' he told Cathy. 'Luckily the shops are owned, not rented, so I should make something on them.'

One of the assistants planned to marry when her boyfriend's ship docked, and the other girl found another job, so Greg had no worries about them.

His mother was a trial to him, constantly sending for him to be reassured that her living standard would not be affected by the shops' closure. Every time he saw her she had some fresh pain or illness to complain of, so he was not concerned when yet another message arrived that she was not well and wished to see him.

Cathy never went with him, and when he seemed a long time away she was worried because his dinner was drying up but was quite unprepared for the news that he brought. His mother was dead, a victim of the influenza epidemic which was sweeping the world.

Cathy was in the parlour when he arrived home, clearly upset. She sat on the arm of his chair, saying nothing but holding him close to her.

'I kept thinking, Cath,' he said, 'about when I was a kid and she'd come to say goodnight to me, before she went out. She was so beautiful. Like a fairy princess, I used to think, with her jewels and often a sort of lacy scarf around her head, and her lovely scent.'

'Yes. I can imagine,' was all that Cathy could bring herself to say. Even death could not change the implacable dislike she felt for the selfish old woman, who had never cared for anyone but herself. She had been like a leech, Cathy thought, fastening first on his father and then on Greg, and denying him the chance to fulfil his ambition of becoming a doctor.

Even after his father's death his uncle would have paid for his training, if his mother had not quarrelled with him and demanded that Greg should leave school to live with her, and look after her.

After a while Greg decided to go out for a walk to think. Cathy agreed, only insisting that he drank a cup of cocoa first. Later in bed Greg talked about how his mother's death would affect his plans.

'It seems callous to say this now,' he said, 'but I've had an offer for the shops only they wanted the rooms above too so I couldn't close with them. I wouldn't ask Miss Nugent to leave but she told me tonight that she'd been very undecided for a few weeks. Some friends had asked her to go in with them for a café in New Brighton and she wanted to do it, but didn't like to leave Mother in the lurch.'

'It was good of her to stay,' Cathy said. 'Her life couldn't have been easy.'

'Far from it,' Greg said. 'But she told me that she was glad that she'd stayed, otherwise she might have blamed herself for Mother's death.'

'I'm a bit worried,' Cathy confessed. 'You don't think she might have caught cold when I threw that water over her, do you?'

'Cathy, that was weeks ago,' Greg exclaimed. 'No, the doctor looked exhausted. He said people are dying like flies with this 'flu. A mother and five children in one house.'

After the funeral Greg gave some of his mother's furniture and her jewellery to Miss Nugent, and a sum of money in thanks for her help, and promised to bring Cathy and John to the café in New Brighton when it opened.

'I'd be a hypocrite if I said I was sorry Greg's mother's died,' Cathy told her own. 'She'd always have been a millstone round his neck, and so would that shop. We can enjoy ourselves now without worrying about anything.'

'And so you should,' Sally said. 'God knows, you young people have earned a good time.'

Elsewhere in the country young people were filled with an almost hysterical gaiety, dancing all through the night, joy riding, doing all the things that they felt they would have done during the youth that had been stolen from them by the bitter experience of war, but for Greg and Cathy there was a quieter happiness.

Yet they felt the same feeling of reprieve, of having to come to terms with their memories and of starting a new life. Cathy told Greg of the time when she had been standing on a corner, waiting to cross the road, when a group of American soldiers had marched past on their way to camp in Knotty Ash.

'I'd been feeling miserable because the war news was bad, and I thought everyone looked so shabby and hungry-looking but they looked like men from another world. So confident and untouched-looking. One of them said to me, "Cheer up, babe. Today's the first day of the rest of your life." They moved off again but I've never forgotten that slogan.'

'"The first day of the rest of your life." Yes, it's good that, Cath,' Greg said. Cathy felt that she had only two small worries at this time. One was the tension when she and Greg were in bed, and she was conscious of her parents on the other side of the wall.

She always thought of her mother rapping on the wall when she and Mary were giggling in bed, and telling them to go to sleep. She half expected to hear the knock on the wall if she and Greg made a sound.

Her other small worry was John's naughtiness, and his resentment of his father. 'He's never been like this before,' she told Greg. 'He's just showing off in front of you.'

She felt that she could cope with the child better if her own parents were not there to see his behaviour and sometimes to laugh at it.

John had always been quick to learn nursery rhymes and soon after Greg came home, Cathy stood the boy on the rug and told him to recite for his father. 'Say Twinkle twinkle, John,' she encouraged him. But John said in a loud voice, 'Bow to the Queen, Fight for the King, and kick the Kaiser up the bum.'

Lawrie gave a shout of laughter and Cathy said in a scandalised voice, 'Don't laugh at him, Dad. That's through playing with Bella Mellor's children.'

'The kids say worse than that about the Kaiser,' Lawrie said, while John stood looking about him and smiling proudly.

Both these problems were solved, Cathy felt, when she got the tenancy of a four-roomed house in Norris Street, near the Necropolis in Everton Road. It was soon furnished with some of Greg's mother's furniture and their own from Egremont Street, and Lawrie and Greg decorated it throughout before they moved the furniture in.

One of the main advantages of the house was that it was within ten minutes' walk of Egremont Street.

'I wouldn't like to go far away from Mam,' Cathy told Greg. 'She looked after John all the time I was working so she's bound to miss him.'

'I wouldn't like to be far away from them anyway,' Greg said. 'I enjoy a talk with your dad. He's a very interesting man.'

'It's funny, you know,' Cathy said. 'Mam always was against anything to do with trade unions or politics if Dad talked about them, but now she's really taking an interest. She reads the papers and you should hear her talking about Wilson's Fourteen Points and about the miners and the coal owners.'

'She was always an intelligent woman but she just didn't have the time before,' Greg said. 'With the house to look after and her sewing.'

Cathy shook her head. 'No, it's not that. I think it was just some little niggle between herself and Dad. Mrs Mal told me once that Dad lost his job because of the union and that made Mam bitter about them, but now – I think she can't bear to be at odds with him about anything.'

'Because she's worried about him?' Greg said. 'I didn't think either of them looked well when I came home, and that's a bad cough your dad's got; but they both look better now.'

'It's just that food's been short but it's easier now,' she said. 'And Dad's cough will be better in the warm weather. No, I think it's because they've both been so worried about Mary, and they've been doing all they can to console each other. That's what I think, anyhow. I'd like to knock her block off, for worrying them like this.'

Greg changed the subject as soon as possible. Already Lawrie and Sally had each separately questioned him about his glimpse of Mary and about her friends, and he had suffered agonies of embarrassment. He was sure that sooner or later he would make a mistake. Already he had betrayed the fact that he knew that Elizabeth Fairburn had been a VAD and had had to pretend that Cathy had told him in a letter.

He had another worry now. Although Mary had given an address so that her mother had been able to write to her, she had only sent postcards in reply saying that she was well. Now the postcards had stopped and Sally's last letter had been returned marked 'Gone away'.

Greg felt that he was to blame and reproached himself bitterly. Useless to tell himself that he had acted with good intentions. The end result was that her parents' grief about Mary was increased.

Cathy told him that her parents were hurt as well as worried when Mary went away. 'You know how Dad idolised her,' Cathy said. 'He went over to see her because she hadn't been here. She'd been away, but Elizabeth saw her in Liverpool and said she looked ill. Dad went dashing over to see her but something happened. He took a real turn against her, but now he thinks it was Clive's fault.'

Greg felt as though he was holding his breath as Cathy talked, afraid of what he would hear, but now he said cautiously, 'In what way, love?'

'He got into debt. He spent all that money and gambled and everything. Mam and Dad were upset that Mary went to London instead of coming home when she found out about the debts.'

'But how did she find out about them?' Greg asked, trying to keep the conversation about the past.

'I think Mr Bagshaw told her. There was something about her not having an address and trying to find Clive, but I've only heard odd bits about it from Mam and Dad. My mother always says Mary's as deep as a drawn well. I remember Mam saying to her when we were children, "I'd rather have a thief than a liar. I'd know where I was with a thief." And it's true, Greg. Mary's an awful liar.'

That's not all she is, Greg thought grimly, but he began to talk about their house. Soon they were delighted to find that Cathy was expecting another baby, due in November.

Greg had applied for several jobs in laboratories without success and he began to realise that any sort of job was going to be hard to find. He was thankful to obtain a position as a clerk in a firm of fruit importers but it was only temporary until the pre-war man returned home from Egypt. Nevertheless he was glad to find it, and felt that it would give him a breathing space to look around.

There had been several deaths from influenza among Sally's neighbours but the one that affected her most was that of Mabel Burns. Mabel's husband, the shifty Sidney, had been called up but had spent some time in the 'glasshouse' then, after shooting himself in the foot, had been discharged.

Peggy had refused to have him back to live in her house, and the young couple had been living in a basement kitchen and bedroom in Fitzclarence Street.

Mabel had a little daughter and she was expecting another baby when her husband died suddenly of the influenza. Two days later Mabel gave birth to twins but within a week she and both of the babies had died. Sally had been with Peggy at the birth of the twins, and with all the sad duties connected with the deaths, but when Lawrie came home from work ill, she devoted herself to him.

'I'll never forgive myself if I've brought the 'flu home to him,' she told Cathy and Greg, but they reassured her.

'This isn't the 'flu,' Greg said. 'It's an ordinary cold that's gone to the weak spot on his chest.'

'He's got no strength to fight it though,' Sally said fearfully.

'He's got a good spirit, Mam, and that's very important,' Cathy consoled her.

Lawrie had some very bad nights, racked by his cough and finding it difficult to breathe, but with Sally's devoted nursing and his own determination, he eventually managed to recover.

He was left very thin and weak and it was six weeks before Sally reluctantly allowed him to return to work. She was delighted when he arrived home with a beaming smile on his face and with some news for her. He had always been popular at the yard because of his cheerful manner and his readiness to help a mate, either in covering for him when he was off by doing an extra shift or by putting a grievance to the boss.

Now the men had heard of a checker's job becoming vacant while Lawrie was off work, and a deputation had gone to ask for the job for him.

'Wasn't it good of the lads, Sal?' he said with delight. 'I was called in to the office this morning and the long and the short of it is, I've got the job.'

'Thank God,' she exclaimed. 'I was worried to death at the thought of you out in all weathers, the way you are.'

'It'll be a bit less money. No overtime,' he said. 'But we'll manage, won't we?'

'Of course we will. On half the money if it meant you worked under cover.'

Nevertheless, they found that the lack of overtime money made a difference and Sally had to budget very carefully to make ends meet. She had developed arthritis in the right arm which had been broken some years previously, so was now unable to earn money by sewing.

A solution to their shortage of money soon presented itself. An elderly widower worked in the office with Lawrie, and he had been told that the rooms he rented were needed for the widowed daughter of his landlady. He was finding it impossible to get anywhere else to live and Lawrie suggested to Sally that they could let him their parlour and back bedroom.

He suggested it chiefly because he was sorry for the man, but his rent was very useful, and the plan had unexpected results.

The arrangement was that the man, Josh Adamson, should provide and cook his own meals as he had done in his previous accommodation, and Sally provided him with a gas ring to supplement the fire and a cupboard for his dishes. His previous landlady had imposed strict rules on him, and Sally found him a quiet, self-effacing man, anxious not to give trouble.

Before long he had been invited to have meals in the kitchen with Sally and Lawrie on most evenings.

'I couldn't let him come in perished and start cooking a couple of sausages on the gas ring when I had a pan of scouse or a hotpot here with plenty for three,' Sally excused herself to Cathy.

'Are you doing his washing yet?' Cathy asked mischievously.

'Oh, no,' Sally said seriously. 'He sends it out.' Then she looked at Cathy and began to laugh.

'You're getting as bad as Greg,' she said. 'Pulling my leg and keeping your face straight.'

Cathy still spent a lot of time in her mother's house, and John was always good when with his grandparents. Josie Mellor, now married to Walter and the mother of a little girl, still lived with her mother across the road from the Wards' house, and she and Cathy were closer than ever. The loss of her four brothers, and her fears for Walter, as well as having to console her mother, had changed Josie from the scatterbrained girl she had been to a quiet and sensible woman, seeming much older than her age.

She had not entirely lost her sense of fun and she and Cathy often spent happy hours in the Park with their children. Cathy valued her friendship. Sometimes she thought that they were like survivors clinging together, because so many of their friends had gone, some never to return.

It was not only that the boys they had known had been lost at sea or killed in battle, but the fact that their girlfriends had been scattered. Rosie Johnson had married a man from the Liverpool

Scottish Regiment and they had gone to live in his father's birthplace near Aberdeen.

Jinny Ashton had secured a job as a stewardess on a Cunard liner and shared a flat with another girl when she was ashore.

Norah and Jack Carmody were now living in Middlesex. Jack had found a job locally when he was released from hospital and he and Norah had been married very quietly. Jack's sisters had travelled down from Liverpool for the wedding but Norah's mother and family had returned their invitations cut into small pieces.

'I knew they'd be annoyed with me,' Norah wrote to Cathy, 'but I thought my mother at least would have come to my wedding. As Jack says, we'll just have to hope the next generation will have more sense.' Cathy missed Norah but they corresponded regularly.

Greg's friend John Savage had returned to his home in Bootle on the outskirts of Liverpool, and to his job in the local Maypole grocer's. He and his wife and daughter had visited Cathy and Greg, and they had been invited to the Savages' small house near the docks.

Cathy liked John's wife but she also was expecting another child, the distance between their houses was too great and the women were too busy for the friendship to develop.

John quite frequently came to see Greg on Wednesday evenings, his early closing day, and Greg sometimes went to Bootle on a Saturday evening. They had long discussions and Cathy sometimes left their supper ready and went to her mother's house with John, leaving the men to talk in peace.

'Do they talk about the war?' her mother asked one night.

'Never,' Cathy replied. 'It was Original Sin when I left.'

The two women laughed then Sally said seriously, 'Has Greg said any more about joining the Catholic Church?'

'It's still in his mind, but I think he's bothered about the bitterness in Liverpool on both sides. I think he wants to talk about it a bit more.'

Later, before they went to sleep, Greg spoke to Cathy on the subject. He told her that it had all seemed clear-cut to him when he was in France. 'The chaplains were good friends,' he said. 'There was none of this bitterness like there is here. There was an Anglican, a Catholic and a Quaker padre and they all respected each other. The Anglican and the Catholic used the same quotation to me: "In My Father's house there are many mansions".'

'And are you still muddled?' Cathy asked.

'No,' Greg said. 'I've never really had any religion. My mother paid lip service to her church but it was a social thing really. I was never confirmed, Cath. Would you mind if I joined the Catholic Church?'

'No. It's up to you, Greg, if that's what you want.'

'I feel I need something, some certainty to make sense of things. I think I'll find it in the Catholic religion but I don't want to influence you, Cath. It's just my own personal feeling.'

'We've never attended church but Dad always says we were brought up with Christian principles, me and Mary,' Cathy said. 'I think it's true about "many mansions". Even with different faiths, people seem to have the same sort of framework to their lives if their religion means a lot to them.'

'Yes, I noticed it in France,' Greg said eagerly.

'Mr Finestone was an Orthodox Jew and I know when his son died he mourned in ashes for three days and it sort of comforted him, yet when he was happy he went to the synagogue to celebrate. Miss Nugent now, she was a devout Anglican and it meant a lot to her, kind of gave her strength. It was the same for Mrs Mal yet she was a Catholic.'

'I knew you'd understand, Cath,' he said, hugging her.

'I think I'll join with you, Greg,' she said. 'I can't understand all the things you and John Savage talk about, but when I went to Mass with Mrs Malloy I always felt very peaceful, and I'd like to be like she was, just trusting. I think it would be better for our children too, if they grew up to believe in something definite.'

'I don't know why you say you don't understand things, Cath,' Greg said lovingly. 'That's the best summing up I've heard.'

Cathy's daughter was born on November 4th. It was an easy birth, and the baby, fair-haired and blue-eyed, was very like Sally, most people thought.

Everyone was delighted with her, especially Greg, who never tired of nursing her, and John who hung over her cradle saying, 'Likkle hands, likkle nose.' Cathy feared that the baby would be spoiled but she felt that she could say nothing to restrain Greg, knowing that he had missed all the delights of John's babyhood.

They had decided on the names Sarah Emily if the baby was a girl, and Sally was quietly delighted about them. Lawrie was pleased too, and was charmed by the baby, but there was always a special bond between him and John.

The baby was christened in St Francis Xavier's, with John Savage and his wife as godparents, and afterwards there was a small party at Sally's house. While everyone was enjoying the food that she had provided, Cathy suddenly realised that her mother was missing and went in search of her.

She found her sitting on her bed, weeping quietly.

'Mam, what's wrong?' Cathy exclaimed.

'It's just brought it back to me, seeing the baby,' she said, dabbing at her eyes. 'About when you and Mary were little. She should have been here to stand for the baby.'

'I know, Mam,' Cathy said, sitting down beside her mother and putting her arm round her shoulders. 'But you know what our Mary's like. She'll turn up when you least expect her.'

'I can't make out why she's just cut herself off, Cath. At least she used to send those postcards and she knew what was happening here. What if something had happened to your Dad?'

Cathy could think of nothing to say to comfort her mother so she just hugged her, saying nothing. Lately she had begun to have a quite irrational feeling that Greg could say more about Mary if he wished.

It was something about the way he changed the subject if she was mentioned, and the way his account of seeing her on the station platform was always given in exactly the same words like a well-rehearsed speech. All Cathy's mistrust of Mary had returned and she felt that anything that her parents learned of what she was doing would only bring them more grief.

She persuaded her mother to come downstairs, and Sally was soon busily looking after her guests. She said no more about Mary, but a few days later Lawrie spoke of her to Cathy.

He was nursing Sarah. Looking down at her, he said, 'Do you think she has a look of our Mary?'

'*No*,' Cathy said vehemently. 'I think she's the model of Mam. I hope she grows up like Mam, too.'

'She couldn't do better,' Lawrie agreed. He sighed. 'The trouble is, Cath, sometimes things just go wrong. We did our best for you and Mary, but it's just circumstances. I wish to God I'd never introduced her to that fellow Clive.'

'You can't blame yourself, Dad,' Cathy said. 'She just happened to walk down while you were talking to him, but after that it was up to them.'

'Yes, but if Mary hadn't met him, she'd have married one of the lads who were always hanging round her and settled down here.'

'Sam?' Cathy said sceptically.

Lawrie laughed. 'Maybe not Sam, but there were plenty of others. Anybody but that so and so! I know he's dead now and I shouldn't speak ill of the dead, but he left Mary a lot of trouble, Cath. She'd never have gone away, only she was too proud to let us know about it.'

Cathy said nothing and he went on, 'It worries me to see your mam fretting about her, and to feel it's my fault.'

'Of course it's not your fault, Dad. Put that out of your head,' Cathy said. She took the baby from him and settled her in the baby carriage, then called John in from the yard. 'Now just stop worrying, Dad,' she said, before leaving him.

As she pushed the carriage home she thought angrily about Mary. The selfish bitch! Mam worrying about her, and worrying because Dad's fretting about her, and him worrying about what's happened to her and blaming himself for her troubles. He's worried about Mam worrying and God knows I'm worried about both of them! And Mary, I suppose, not giving a tinker's damn about any of us.

She probably never gives us a thought. Too busy enjoying herself with her posh friends. I wonder what she's doing at this minute...

Chapter Forty

When Greg left the flat Mary screamed until her throat was sore and she was exhausted. She lay for a while feeling drained and sick, then got up and tidied Dora's bed and went back to her own.

She picked up a novel and tried to read, but soon she threw it down and let her mind go back to Greg. What had he done when he left the flat? she wondered. Probably rushed back to Liverpool as fast as his legs or the train would carry him.

She heard the woman who 'did' for them arrive and bang about lighting the fire, then a little later the daily came up with a cup of tea. 'There's a sodyer's 'at and coat on the 'allstand,' she said suspiciously.

Mary's mind worked rapidly. So he'd left his coat and cap. Would he come back for them? She laughed lightly. 'I pinched them for a bit of a rag last night,' she said. 'Kept me warm on the way home anyway.'

'So you was out in that fog then?' the charlady said. 'Chronic, wasn't it?'

'I came home when it started to thicken. Mrs Roberts must have been caught in it,' Mary said.

'Her bed's not been slep' in,' the woman agreed.

That's what you think, Mary was tempted to say, but she only remarked that it was the worst fog she had seen for ages.

She got up and dressed, feeling too restless to stay in bed, and discovered that Greg's tunic and kitbag had gone although his greatcoat and cap hung in the hall. Before Dora returned she had moved them to her own clothes cupboard.

By the noon post several invitations had arrived for Mary, and a letter from Tommy Ross. He had been wounded two weeks before the Armistice and was now in a London hospital. Mary had written to him and sent fruit but she had never visited him.

Now she felt too restless and unhappy to sit still, and on a sudden impulse slipped on her sealskin coat and pulled on her latest hat. It was a close-fitting brown velour with a turned-up brim with a feather in it, pulled low over her eyebrows. She felt confident that she looked smart as she set off to visit Tommy.

She told the taxi driver to stop while she bought a sheaf of bronze chrysanthemums and a bunch of grapes. Tommy greeted her with delight.

'What a vision of loveliness on such a grey day,' he said. There were other flowers beside the bed but no fruit, and Mary opened the tissue paper in which the grapes were wrapped.

'Would you like one?' she asked. He gave a short, bitter laugh, and waved his hand at the numerous tubes which emerged from under the bedclothes.

'I'm afraid the answer is no,' he said. 'You see, my dear, Fritz hit me literally below the belt.'

'I didn't know where you were wounded,' she said. 'So you can't eat yet?'

'I can't eat,' he said bitterly, 'and even more importantly I'm likely to be of little use to a nubile young female like yourself – but of course that's how you prefer your men, isn't it?'

A flood of angry colour rushed over Mary's face and she jumped to her feet, but he reached out and gripped her arm.

'Mary, don't go. Forgive me,' he said. 'I'm just so—'

She sat down again. 'I suppose you are,' she said in a muffled voice. 'I know. That's how I feel – as though I want to scream and kick and hurt someone.'

Tommy was in a private room and the sounds of the hospital were muted and far away. Suddenly Mary found herself weeping bitterly and telling him all that had happened with Greg.

'I always believed that he loved me,' she said wretchedly. 'I thought it was all a mistake, that he'd got involved with Cathy because he was sorry for her and she threw herself at him, but he doesn't care about me at all.'

He said nothing, only stroked her arm as she talked. When she finished he said quietly, 'Forget him, Mary. Forget he ever existed – in fact, shut off your life before today.'

'I wish I could.'

'You can and you must,' he said with certainty. 'You're in the same boat as the rest of us who've come back. We've got to forget. We couldn't go on otherwise.'

'Forget the war, you mean?' Mary said, looking into a mirror she had taken from her bag.

'Yes. The war. The men we killed, the bodies, the rats, the wire.' He shuddered. 'We had to be there, but we don't have to remember. We can close our minds and you can do the same, my dear, on your trouble. Forget it.'

'It wasn't your fault that you killed people,' she said. 'You had to do your bit.'

She spoke at random, her mind still more on her own troubles than on Tommy's words, but he said bitterly, 'My bit! Oh, I did that all right, but then I did a bit more, didn't I?'

'What do you mean?' Mary said indifferently.

Tommy turned his head restlessly upon the pillow. 'I was a very clever boy, wasn't I? I discovered how to make a gun that once killed four men, kill ten. I've been lying here thinking about the clever fellow who discovered how to do this to me. Does his government pour the shekels out to him? Poetic justice this, wouldn't you say?'

His voice had risen and Mary was just saying, 'Tommy—' when a Sister rustled into the room.

'You've excited my patient,' she said angrily to Mary. 'You'd better go.'

She took Tommy's wrist but as Mary retreated from the Sister's angry glare, he called to her, 'Do as I say. And come tomorrow.'

'I will,' she said, defiantly blowing him a kiss.

She had arranged to dine out then go to a dance, and drove into town to shop and fill in the hours until it was time to dress. She found that she was looking at every soldier who passed, still hoping against hope that Greg was in London. Eventually she hailed a cab and flung herself back against the seat angrily.

It's got to stop, she told herself. Surely last night should have cured her. Tommy's idea was the right one. How suddenly he had got excited though, and the way that Sister had glared at her when he asked her to visit tomorrow! I'll go, just to spite her, Mary decided.

Her escort for the evening exactly suited her mood. He was a young man recently demobilised who had been training to be a barrister before the war. Now he had inherited money from his grandmother and declared that he intended to enjoy life until the money was finished.

'And what then?' someone asked.

David laughed heartily. '*Then* I'll think what to do,' he said. 'Anyway, who knows? I might have inherited from someone else by then.'

They went with a crowd to the dance, all wild and reckless, and Mary was the wildest of them. She drank cocktail after cocktail and had only a hazy memory of returning home as the milkmen were delivering.

She slept late the next morning and was sitting up in bed fitting a cigarette into a holder when Dora slouched into the bedroom. 'How's the head?' she asked, throwing herself into a chair.

'Awful. Like a hammer beating my skull,' Mary said with a grimace. 'No more cocktails for me.'

'Till when?' Dora said flippantly. 'Where did you go yesterday? I missed you completely.'

'I dined with David Bligh and we went to Muriel Huntley's thing,' Mary said. 'In the afternoon I went to see Tommy Ross.'

'Sick visiting? My *dear*,' Dora said.

Mary shrugged. 'I had a letter from him and I was bored,' she said. 'What about you?'

'My American, of course,' Dora said. 'Who else?'

'Getting quite serious,' Mary laughed. Dora only nodded.

Tommy Ross was repentant when Mary arrived at the hospital.

'Sorry about my performance yesterday,' he said. 'Quite a loss to the stage, aren't I? I'm glad I didn't frighten you off.'

She laughed. 'You didn't, and neither did that dragon of a Sister. I thought I'd walk past her today with my nose in the air, but she's not about.'

'So you came to see Sister, not me?' he said, and Mary told him he was quite right.

Neither of them spoke of the confidences of the previous day, but although the conversation was light-hearted the time passed pleasantly. When Mary rose to go, he said quietly, 'You look rather tired today. Didn't stay awake weeping, did you?'

'No, I was too drunk,' Mary said truthfully, and he laughed aloud before his face contorted with pain.

'Tommy, should I call someone?' Mary said, but before she could ring the bell the nurse came into the room. 'Come tomorrow,' he gasped and Mary nodded before hurrying away.

After that she visited him most afternoons until the day came when he could return to his house in Mayfair, and his batman moved in to look after him. The tubes had been removed and his wounds had healed superficially but he could still only take liquid food and was very weak.

'I suppose you'll desert me now,' he said to Mary. 'Is this a farewell visit?'

'Why should it be?' she said crisply. 'Unless it's what you want?'

'You know it isn't. But it's one thing visiting an invalid in hospital, another visiting half a man in his own house.'

'If you're going to start feeling sorry for yourself, I won't come,' she said. 'But that'll be the reason.'

Tommy looked ruefully at his batman who had come in with a feeding cup. 'My ministering angel, this young lady, Duggan,' he said. 'Very sentimental, and afraid of hurting my feelings.'

'So I see, Sir,' the man said. 'Just what you need, I'd say.'

Mary winked at the man, and Tommy said laughingly: 'I saw that. None of your Everton tricks here, Mary.'

Her face darkened and Tommy waved his batman away and reached out his hand to her.

'I'm sorry, Mary,' Tommy said softly. 'That was clumsy of me. I was the one who told you to pull down the shutter on it, on that life, too. Have you done it?'

'I've tried,' she murmured.

'Are you still in touch?' Tommy asked.

Mary shrugged. 'I still get letters occasionally from my family,' she said.

'And they mention this chap, and his wife and child?'

'Nothing else,' Mary said bitterly.

'Then make a clean break. It's the only way. You've moved on, and you don't want to drag old luggage with you,' Tommy said. 'They might want it too. They've never visited you, have they?'

She sat with her head bent, thinking. A clean break. It might be the only way: to put all that life behind her and start afresh.

Perhaps Tommy was right. Perhaps her family would be glad to forget her too. Even for Mary this was hard to believe and for a moment she saw her mother's face, then she remembered her father's fury as she sent him away from the house at Neston.

He took offence very quickly, she thought, and they were only concerned about Cathy and her wedding. They don't really care for me. It's all Cathy, Cathy, and now her brats. Greg, too, and I don't want to know about him. I want to forget. She bit her lip as she recalled the scene in the bedroom, but then she pushed the thought away. I'll forget it all, she decided, make a clean break and pull down the shutter on that life. I've tried to do it with Clive, and perhaps I'll be able to get over that if I make a completely fresh start.

As though he read her mind, Tommy said quietly, 'That other baggage you've carried with you – the swine who abused you. He was connected in your mind with Liverpool, so forget him too. Tell yourself you were born when you stepped off the train at Euston Station.'

For the next few weeks Mary visited Tommy regularly although she continued her round of frantic pleasure at night. She tried hard to close her mind completely to her old life, and for most of the time succeeded. She had always been able to thrust away unwelcome thoughts, but a complete break with her family was rather more difficult, she found.

A letter came from her mother and she longed to open it, but steeled herself to ask Dora to return it marked 'Gone away'.

For a while she half hoped, half feared, that her father would come to London to search for her, but no one came and she decided that Tommy was right. Her family wanted the break too.

She was unaware how often Lawrie had thought of travelling to see her, and how the thought of the day at Neston made him hesitate. He still believed that the men he saw there were her admirers, and wondered what he would find if he came to see her in London.

He would be unwelcome, he felt. Either because of what Mary was up to in London, or because she would be ashamed of him before her posh friends. The brief messages on the postcards made it clear she wanted to keep them at arm's length.

Lawrie loved Mary, but he was a proud and stubborn man, reluctant to push himself where he was unwelcome.

Dora approved of Mary's decision and willingly marked the letter. 'You might be marking mine like this soon,' she remarked. 'Hank wants us to marry and go back together to America.'

'And will you?' Mary said.

'I think so. It's the best offer I'll get,' Dora said cynically. 'There's only one condition: I have to call him Henry when we're with his family.'

'That's not too hard,' Mary said with a laugh.

'I'll be sorry to leave you,' Dora said. 'It worked out very well, didn't it? Never a cross word, as the saying goes.'

'Yes. For two war widows doing our war work, we've managed to have a good time, haven't we?'

'We have indeed,' Dora said. 'What will you do? Get someone else in or look for something smaller?'

'I'll think about it,' she said vaguely.

Tommy Ross had improved in health and they had been out several times for drives, but today they intended to go to a tea dance for the first time.

'Not that I can either take tea or dance,' he said, 'but I'll grace the room with my presence.' The outing was a success. Tommy was warmly welcomed by the people who had known him before, and by several newcomers who were attracted by his dry wit. Mary danced several times but he always had company while she was away, though he welcomed her back after every dance and told her that she looked superb.

She knew him well enough now to realise when he was tiring although he said nothing, and she asked for a cab to be called and quietly withdrew him from the noisy crowd.

They went to several tea dances after that, and when Tommy grew stronger he accompanied her to evening dances. There were always unattached men to dance with Mary and take her in to supper, and old friends or flirtatious young ladies to keep Tommy company.

Mary was still undecided about the flat. Dora was almost due to leave and Mary knew that she must soon make up her mind. The flat had been possible for them with both their pensions, because most of their food and all their entertainment had been paid for by their escorts, but for Mary alone it was impossible.

Could she find anyone she could share with who was as compatible as Dora? Mary wondered. Could she indeed find anyone to share on the same terms as Dora? One of their friends had been very anxious to move in, but Dora had laughed when Mary spoke of it.

'You're still an innocent, Mary,' she had said. 'Hilda wants to share your bed, darling, not just the flat.'

Mary decided that she would have to be very careful, and wondered whether it would be better just to take a room. Even then she might have to work, because her capital was almost exhausted.

She was still racked with indecision when she was in Tommy Ross's house one afternoon, playing cards with him. She told him about her problem, and about Hilda.

'You could always have a male flatmate, darling,' he said idly.

Mary sat up and slammed her cards down indignantly. 'On what terms?' she said. 'There are two sides to that sort of bargain and I couldn't keep mine. Anyway, I've too much respect for myself to be a kept woman,' she added virtuously.

Tommy began to chuckle. 'Mary, what would I do without you?' he said. 'I can never guess what you'll say next and that's your greatest charm. No, don't fly into a temper,' as she turned away huffily.

He took her hand and stroked it 'Don't say it, kitten. Sheath those little claws and listen to me.'

Mary had long ago found out the explanation of Tommy's remarks about his invention on the first day she visited him. He had devised an adaptation to a gun which brought him massive royalty payments, so she understood him when he went on.

'I have all these ill-gotten gains, darling, and the way I see it, there are three possible solutions to your problem. One, we go on as we are and I pay the rent of your flat. Two, I move in to your flat. No, no, let me finish. Three, you move in here.'

Mary's mind was racing, trying to decide how she should react, but Tommy said quickly, 'Now don't feel you have to parade your virtue, kitten. We know all about that. I'm talking about marriage, you know.'

Her eyes widened, and she stared at him, too confused to speak. Tommy said quietly, 'I'd say we're uniquely suited to each other, Mary. We're both casualties, me physically and you emotionally, and neither of us is likely to recover. I can comfort you with my shekels and you can comfort me with your undemanding company.'

His words were mocking but his tone and his expression were sincere so she answered him sincerely. 'I think that's true, Tommy. I'd be a poor bargain for anyone else, but you understand.' She leaned forward and kissed him briefly. 'I'll be glad to marry you, Tommy, and not just to solve my problem.'

'Thank you, darling,' he said, lifting her hand and kissing it. 'So – shall we live here? It would be better, I think, but you must say.'

'I think so too.'

Tommy laughed. 'I hope all our problems are as easily settled,' he said. He rang, and when the batman appeared, said, 'Duggan, congratulations are called for. Mrs Walden is about to become Mrs Ross.'

For a moment a look of surprise flickered across the man's face, then he said quickly, 'Congratulations, Sir, and to you, Madam. I hope you'll both be very happy.'

'Thank you. This calls for a drink, I think,' Tommy said. 'Bring three glasses, Duggan.'

Mary and Tommy had planned to go to an evening dance, but they decided to cut it and stay at home. They sat together talking over their plans, and the only reference to the past was made by Mary. 'I feel safe with you, Tom,' she said. 'And happy. That was good advice you gave me about never looking back. I'll never get over those months with Clive, but at least I don't think of them often now. It's finished me with men though in that way, so don't think I'll ever be cured and go gallivanting.'

Tommy laughed. 'It's a long time since I heard that word,' he said. 'No, I've no fears on that score, Mary. I know you'll play straight with me, and to be truthful, my dear, I don't think you'll be cured. Your Liverpool swain was your last hope in that direction, I think.'

'You can forget about him,' Mary said. 'I'm cured of *that* anyway.' Tommy looked surprised and she shrugged her shoulders. 'Remember that show we went to with all the "Tommies" marching on the stage? One of them was like Greg in build and everything, and I looked at him and felt *nothing*. It was like being cured of an illness.'

'You said nothing about it.'

'I felt foolish about the fuss I'd made,' Mary confessed. 'I realised that it had just been a silly girl's "pash" and I'd outgrown it. I compared him with the men I knew, and I could see how stupid and unsophisticated he was. I'd have tired of him in weeks, Tom.'

'Probably,' he agreed, concealing a smile. By now he knew Mary's capacity for self delusion, but if this was the version of events that suited her, what did it matter?

He suddenly felt weary and Mary, always sensitive to his feelings, noticed immediately. 'I'm going now, Tom,' she said. 'We'll talk more tomorrow. I think you should go to bed, and I'll go home and do the same. Duggan will call a cab for me.'

'I won't argue,' he said, attempting a smile. 'Goodnight, my dear, and thank you.'

She kissed him lightly and went into the hall. Duggan was outside whistling for a cab, but he came back and held Mary's coat for her.

'I've told him he should go to bed, Duggan,' she said. 'He seems tired.'

'Quite right, Miss,' the man said. He hesitated then said gruffly, 'He's one of the best, Miss, and straight as a die. I think everyone – should be straight with him too.'

Mary looked him in the eye. 'So do I,' she said. 'I agree with you absolutely.'

The cab arrived and Duggan escorted her to it, slipping the fare to the taxi driver. 'He'll be all right, Miss, don't you worry,' he said. 'It might have been the drink upset him but I'll look after him.'

Mary lay back in the cab, thinking over the events of the night. Strange, she thought, that she had never considered Tommy when she was mulling over her problem. Not as a husband anyway, though she had considered asking for a loan or something.

She let her mind wander over the pleasant thought that she would never have to worry about money again. She would be the wife of a rich man, and Tommy would always look after her and keep her safe. Perhaps at last my luck has changed, she thought.

Mary was still awake when Dora arrived home, and she called her in to tell her her news. Dora congratulated her, but said doubtfully. 'Won't there be problems though? I heard the Hun had damaged him rather vitally, enough to put marriage out of bounds anyway.'

'Don't believe all you hear,' Mary said lightly. 'He can't take solid food, but I don't think that rules him out for marriage.'

'Is that it? How *do* these rumours start?' Dora said, but Mary was sure that she would pass the word around.

There was a hitch in Dora's arrangements which meant that she was still in England when Mary and Tommy were married. It was a quiet wedding at a Register Office with George Duggan and Dora Roberts as witnesses. Tommy had insisted that Mary's dress should come from a fashion house. He had sat with her while models had paraded before them, and she had marvelled at the change in her fortunes since her days at Denby's.

They had finally chosen a dress in chiffon and marocain in a shade of green so pale that it was almost white. 'Sea Spray' was the name on the card that the model carried. With it Mary wore a wide-brimmed hat in the same shade, and carried lilies-of-the-valley.

She had always been a beautiful woman, even if she had never again achieved the breathtaking loveliness of the days before her marriage to Clive. Yet today she bloomed again.

Tommy felt both proud and happy, not only because his bride was so beautiful, but because he felt that the bloom of happiness upon her meant that she knew she had made the right decision and promised well for their future.

The promise was fulfilled and for the next two years they were both very happy. A sunny room at the back of the house was furnished as a sitting room for Mary, and the room above it was her bedroom.

Duggan continued to run the house and a maid was engaged for Mary, but Tommy told her she must feel free to spend her time as she pleased. That she chose to spend most of it with him was very gratifying to him, and made her a firm favourite with Duggan.

Mary rarely went out alone, partly because she found that it made her feel restless to be with some of the wilder spirits of the set and hear about police raids on nightclubs, groups crowding into cars to drive to the East End for breakfast at cabmen's pull-ups, or moonlight bathing parties.

She concealed these feelings from Tommy just as she concealed the overtures made to her by some of the unattached men. 'What did you expect, darling?' one of the women said. 'Married women are fair game. They won't risk getting entangled with widows or single girls, those sort of men, in case marriage is expected. Married women are safe.'

Tommy's health had improved so they often went to tea dances and Bridge parties, and occasionally to the races. In January they went to Cannes to enjoy the sunshine, and met many of their

London set there, too, but Mary enjoyed their quiet evenings at home best.

She also enjoyed having unlimited money to spend on clothes and anything else she fancied, and being known as the wife of a wealthy man. Shortly after their marriage Tommy explained to her the terms of his will.

'If you're a rich widow, the vultures will soon gather round you, darling,' he said. 'I want to guard you against that.'

'I might die first,' she said.

'No problem then! While I'm alive I'll look after you, kitten, but if I'm not here, I'll have to have made the best possible arrangements for you.'

Mary kissed him impulsively, but he insisted that she should sit down and listen carefully. He was leaving the bulk of his fortune to her after provision for Duggan and some other bequests, for her lifetime or until she remarried. Then it was to be divided between the welfare fund of his Regiment and the London Hospital where he had been cared for.

'It's the best way of keeping you safe,' he said earnestly, 'I thought of leaving a sort of dress allowance for you after remarriage in case you marry a poor man, but even that would carry a risk, Mary. For a man in desperate straits, even a small sum might be tempting.'

'Thanks very much,' Mary said indignantly. 'You don't think anyone might want to marry me for myself.'

He smiled. 'Of course I do, but I'm thinking of your problem, darling. If you marry it must be a man who understands and who is ready to marry on those terms, not a fortune hunter. What you need really, kitten, is another crock like myself.'

Mary jumped to her feet. 'I don't know why we're talking like this,' she said. 'For one thing, I might die before you, and even if I don't I'll never marry again, you can be sure of that.'

'I want you to come with me to see my lawyer tomorrow, Mary, and after that we'll forget all about it. I just wanted you to know my reasons for leaving the money under these provisions, that's all.'

Later that evening Mary told Tommy something that she had never confided to anyone, not even Dora. After the last night she spent with Clive she had passed blood for several weeks and feared that he had damaged her physically as well as emotionally.

'You didn't go to see a doctor?' Tommy asked, and she recoiled in horror.

'That's the very *last* thing I'd do,' she exclaimed. 'No, I'm telling you this so you'll know that I would never remarry.'

'I'd be glad if you could find the right man to look after you,' Tommy told her. 'I'm just making sure I fend off the other kind.'

'Let's hope it will be a long time before we need to think of such things,' Mary said, but it was not to be.

They had another holiday in the South of France, and soon after they returned home had a quiet evening over cards and playing records on the gramophone Tommy had recently bought.

Shortly after ten o'clock he said that he felt tired and would have an early night. Mary had just called Duggan when suddenly Tommy slumped down in the chair and within minutes was dead.

Chapter Forty-One

Cathy and Greg were very happy in the little house in Norris Street. It was not as solidly built as the house in Anton Street, which had had a vestibule and an inner door with coloured glass panels, but although the front door opened straight into the living room in Norris Street, Greg built bookshelves at right angles to the door to give more privacy.

He also built a lean-to wooden shed where Cathy could keep the pram, and fitted it with shelves to store pans and dishes to give more room in the tiny kitchen.

At first Cathy felt an intruder in the street as nearly all her neighbours were related, and the matriarch of the tribe, always known as 'Me Mam', lived opposite to her.

Usually when a house became empty, 'Me Mam' spoke to the landlord to reserve it for one of her family, but she had been fully occupied with a daughter who had given birth to triplets when Cathy innocently applied for the house and was given the tenancy.

Cathy felt some hostility at first, but soon after they moved in John ran across to where Mrs Parker, 'Me Mam', sat in state on a kitchen chair outside her front door. He said nothing but stood in front of her, staring at the braids of jet black hair which were wound round and round her head.

'Yer'll know me again when yer see me,' Mrs Parker said with asperity.

John disregarded the comment. 'I like your hair,' he said. 'Can I touch it?'

'Oo, Mam, yer've clicked,' one of the attendant daughters giggled, but Cathy had run across the street and grabbed her son.

'I'm sorry,' she said, her face pink. 'John, say you're sorry.'

'I'm sorry,' he said cheerfully. He had inherited Greg's charming smile, and all the women smiled at him as Cathy hauled him away.

'There's a lad that's gettin' well reared,' Mrs Parker announced, and from then on Cathy was accepted by her neighbours.

John was often involved in fights with the Parker grandchildren, and this could have caused trouble for Cathy, but 'Me Mam' pronounced loudly for the benefit of the other mothers that kids should be left to fight it out, and that it was no use falling out over them.

'They'd get yer hung,' she announced, 'and while the mams are falling out over them the kids have made it up.' She told John that he was 'a little divil', but he was a firm favourite with her.

Because his job was not permanent Greg tried hard to find something else, but dozens of men were applying for every post. It was a great relief when he heard that the man whose job he held had decided to go into partnership in a garage instead of returning, so Greg's appointment was made permanent.

'We can't go wrong,' he told Cathy exultantly, and it certainly seemed that Fortune smiled on them.

Cathy kept her house shining and her children were always clean and well dressed, but she found it hard to be tidy, and even harder to budget her week's housekeeping as her mother had always done.

Her tidiness soon improved, partly because the small house made it a necessity and partly because of good advice from Mrs Parker. 'Don't put things down outa yer 'and,' she told Cathy. 'Put them away right off.' Cathy found it good advice.

She even wrote a slogan, 'Don't put it down, put it away,' and entered it in a competition in the weekly magazine she took.

It won a prize of ten shillings and Cathy decided that she would spend a shilling on a special meal for the family, and put nine shillings in a jar to save as her mother had always done in the handleless teapot.

She put the nine shillings away, but from her next week's housekeeping bought a bag of pear drops for her mother and an ounce of tobacco for her father as a treat, and half an ounce of thick twist for Josh in case he felt left out.

Consequently she had to borrow from the jar to get through the week, then during the following few weeks, if fish or meat was a little more than she had budgeted for, she always thought, I can borrow from the jar. Within a few weeks the money had all gone and with it Cathy's dream of saving.

'Why worry?' Greg said. 'We're doing all right compared with most people, and things might get even better for us later on.'

It was true that they were lucky by comparison with others. The joy of the first few months of peace had quickly turned to disillusionment, and to hardship when the men's 'pay offs' were spent.

The 'homes fit for heroes' often turned out to be a damp basement or a share in an already overcrowded house with relations.

Men returned to the frantic scramble for casual work and women to a hand to mouth existence and furtive trips to the pawnshop, where the windows were soon filled with pawned medals.

Unemployment was like a rising tide, reaching sixty thousand in Liverpool, and when the twenty-six weeks of unemployment pay was finished, families had to apply to the Board of Guardians for relief, with all the degradation and humiliation that involved.

Cathy felt the familiar feelings of helpless rage when she saw the ragged, barefoot, hungry children in the streets.

'If only I could *do* something,' she raged to Greg.

'Never mind, love,' he said. 'People are trying to get things done. Miss Rathbone's fighting hard for children's allowances and that would make a difference, wouldn't it? And don't forget, you did your bit before the war. You got the vote.'

'Only for women over thirty,' she said. 'I've got five years to wait!'

In September 1921 she was on a tramcar with John and the baby when in Lord Street it was held up by a crowd of marching unemployed men. There were thousands of them, walking silently arm-in-arm, filling the road and the pavement and stopping all the traffic. Most of them wore war medals or the pawn tickets for them pinned to their ragged jackets.

'God love us,' a stout woman said to Cathy. 'Makes yer wonder what we was fighting for, doesn't it?'

The conductor was standing inside the tram and he pointed at Cathy's children. 'That's what we was fighting for, Missis,' he said. 'So them kids'll never have to go through what we did.'

'Aye, an' to stop the Huns from taking over the country,' a little man in a bowler declared.

Good job Dad's not here, Cathy thought. He'd ask him if we'd be any worse off, and start a riot. She was glad when the tram could move, because she felt weak and bilious. She was almost certain that she was pregnant again.

After another week she was quite sure and estimated that the baby was due in June. Her mother had been to see her and Cathy had told her the news. 'You always wanted a big family, didn't you?' Sally said calmly. 'It'll just be nice, too, with John nearly seven and Sarah two and a half.'

The next time Cathy went to her mother's house, Peggy Burns was in the kitchen with her granddaughter, Maggie. The child flung herself at John with cries of joy and he tried to lift her into the air.

'John, be careful,' Cathy shouted, but Peggy only laughed.

'She wouldn't care if her neck was broken as long as it was John that broke it,' she said. 'Maybe they'll make a match of it.'

'He'll have to get in the queue when she's a bit older,' Sally said. 'She's going to be a real heart-breaker.'

Maggie had escaped the Burns ginger hair, and was very blonde with light blue eyes and delicate features.

Cathy heard her mother's soft sigh and knew that she was thinking of another pretty child who had grown up in the house.

The same thought seemed to strike Peggy and her eyes went to the photograph of Mary which stood on the dresser. Before either could speak, Cathy said swiftly, 'Did Mam tell you my news, Mrs Burns?'

'Yes, she did,' Peggy said. 'Are you pleased?'

'Of course, and so is Greg.'

'No of course about it, the way things are now,' Peggy said. 'But Greg's job is safe, isn't it? He's done well settling down there after being his own boss.'

'It's not all jam being your own boss,' Cathy said with a laugh. 'When that jeweller's in London Road was looted during the Police Strike, Greg said he was glad to be free of the worry of the shop.'

'Did you tell him to come for his tea?' Sally said. She turned to Peggy. 'No sense in Cathy rushing home to cook when I'll have a pan of scouse here that'll do all of us.'

'It's hard to get used to cooking small meals,' Peggy said diplomatically, but Cathy smiled at her mother.

'Especially on Thursdays, eh, Mam?' she said. She knew that it was her mother's way of helping her to get through the week by inviting them to tea on the day before pay day, and pretending that she had cooked too much.

Lawrie worked regular days now and he and Josh Adamson arrived together, shortly followed by Greg. John had been given his meal earlier but Lawrie drew the child to him and asked about school, and John announced proudly: 'I'm the cleverest in the class.'

'And the one with the biggest head,' Cathy said reprovingly. 'It's wrong to boast, John.'

'He's got to tell the truth, haven't you, son,' Lawrie said, and Sally and Cathy looked at each other expressively.

'Go and play in the yard, John,' Cathy ordered and when the adults sat down to their meal they could hear the regular thud of his football against the back door.

Greg jumped to his feet. 'Mind Grandad's plants,' he called, knocking on the kitchen window.

'Not much to damage this time of the year, Greg,' Lawrie said.

'That puts me in mind,' Josh said, as Greg returned to the table. 'I was talking to a fellow in Maybury's last night, about the sage and mint and stuff you grow out there. He's got an allotment near the end of West Derby Road somewhere and he says there's one coming vacant. He says nobody knows about it yet, but the fellow told him, just on the quiet like, he can't keep it up. He says if you want it, he'll speak up to the committee for you.'

'An allotment!' Lawrie exclaimed.

Sally said quickly, 'But the digging, Lawrie. Your chest.'

'It'd have to be in Greg's name, like,' Josh said. 'Being as he's an ex-serviceman and they get preference.'

'You could share it,' Cathy said eagerly. 'Greg could do all the hard work, the digging and that, and Dad could plant things.'

Lawrie looked at Greg and laughed. 'It's a talent they have, Greg, picking out the jobs – all the hard work for you.'

'I wouldn't mind that. You're the one with the green fingers,' Greg said. 'What would we have to do, Josh?'

'Write a letter, and I'll take it to Maybury's tonight,' he said. 'Say about your Army service and how you've got a small house, no garden, and two children.'

'And another one expected,' Sally put in. Cathy blushed but Josh went on calmly, 'All the better. Say your father-in-law grows herbs in the back yard and he'd help you.'

'I don't see what the Army's got to do with it,' Greg said. He intended to make Lawrie feel better about needing his Army service to get the allotment, but Lawrie said quickly, 'Why not, lad? You fought for the country. You're entitled to own a bit of it, apart from the six feet we'll all have at the end.'

John had come in and was leaning against Lawrie's knee. Now he piped up, 'Six feet, Grandad? What's got six feet? A cat's got four.'

Sally clicked her tongue and shook her head at Lawrie, but he lifted John on to his knee and said easily, 'Yes, and a dog's got four feet, but d'you know there's an insect that's got a hundred feet. It's called a centipede.'

'It's not safe to open your mouth in front of him,' Cathy murmured to her mother. They were all excited at the prospect of having an allotment and as soon as the meal was finished and the cloth cleared away, Sally got out the pen and ink and notepaper and Greg wrote the letter.

'Don't let Josh forget to take it,' Cathy whispered to her mother as she and Greg prepared to take the children home. 'I don't suppose he'd go any earlier?'

'I doubt it,' her mother said. 'We'll just have to hope we strike lucky.'

Josh Adamson had a chiming clock in his room and every night as nine o'clock struck, he stood up, took his bowler hat from the hallstand and brushed it, then placed it squarely on his head and walked up to Maybury's public house in Everton Road. If the weather was cold he wore a dark overcoat, but winter and summer he left the house just after nine o'clock and returned a few minutes after ten.

He followed his usual pattern that night and Lawrie waited impatiently for him to return, but Josh could only say that the man thought they had a good chance of the allotment.

Within a few weeks Greg heard that he had been allocated the allotment, and it was the start of many happy hours for all of them. Greg built a small wooden shed on the plot and on fine Sundays the whole family spent the day there.

They had a primus stove there, and a teapot and crockery, and Sally and Cathy contrived tasty meals. Lawrie and Greg went there on Saturday afternoons and for the light evenings and soon a regular supply of salad stuff, vegetables and flowers flowed to both houses.

Josh only went once. He preferred to follow his regular pattern of a substantial breakfast followed by morning service, a meal left ready by Sally and a nap in the afternoon, but he enjoyed the fresh vegetables and salads and congratulated Lawrie on his green fingers.

Cathy could do little to help as she was very big and unwieldy with the coming baby and wondered sometimes if she was going to have twins, but on June 18th her second son was born. As usual it was an easy birth, and the large fair child was a very placid baby.

He was christened Michael Matthew but speedily became Mick to everyone. 'Nothing bothers Mick,' was the general cry as he fell downstairs, shut himself in the lavatory, got smacked for taking the alarm clock to pieces, and smiled imperturbably through it all.

Greg was still worried about his job, although so far it was safe. He worked for the family firm of John Powell and Sons, but both sons had been killed on the Western Front, one in 1915 and the other a few months before war ended, and the father struggled on without much heart to keep the business going.

John Savage had lost his job and was taking any kind of casual work to keep his family. He had served his time in the grocery trade, and was first hand in the Maypole when he joined the army, but women had taken the men's places behind the counter during the war for lower wages.

The men's jobs were guaranteed for their return, but as soon as possible they were again replaced by women assistants.

In July 1924 Greg and Cathy took their three children to see King George V and Queen Mary drive past to the Consecration of the new Anglican Cathedral. Ice cream sellers and hoky coke men were busy among the crowds lining the route, and Cathy and Greg were shocked to see John Savage pushing a small handcart and selling ice cream.

Greg hailed him and bought ice cream cornets for the children, and John said with dignity, 'I feel a bit self-conscious doing this, but I'm not ashamed. There's nothing degrading in honest work.'

'Of course there isn't, I admire you for it,' Greg said. 'I'll feel the same if my job goes west, believe me.'

'Look at the kids,' Cathy said. 'John's made up. Bragging to all the other kids, "That's my dad's friend."' They smiled at each other and John moved on along the crowd but afterwards Greg said to Cathy, 'It's true what John said. There's nothing for him to be ashamed of in doing that, but I know how he must feel. It makes my blood boil to see a chap like him – when I think of what he is and what he's done, and what he could do, come to that. The damn world's upside down, Cath.'

'Something might turn up for him, Greg,' she consoled him, and they were delighted when they heard a few weeks later that John had found a job in a cobbler's shop.

They had a sadder experience with another old friend. They were walking along Shaw Street one Saturday with Mick and Sarah in the pram and John walking beside it when, as they passed a large house which had become a common lodging house, Sydney walked down the steps.

His left sleeve was empty and he looked gaunt and shabby, and ill at ease when they spoke to him. He was reluctant to come to their house but eventually they persuaded him, and in the house the children helped him to feel at home.

John asked questions about his empty sleeve but his direct matter-of-fact approach never gave offence and Sydney readily answered him.

Sarah brought the doll she had been given for her fifth birthday and laid it on Sydney's knee. Cathy said laughingly, 'You're highly honoured, Syd. We're not allowed to touch Lucy.'

Cathy quickly prepared a meal while the two men smoked and talked, with Sarah standing beside Sydney's knee. He told them that he had married a girl in Southampton during the war but she had gone when he returned home. His job in Liverpool had 'sunk without trace', he said bitterly, and he had been tramping the country looking for work.

He had come to Liverpool on an impulse, not expecting to meet anyone he knew. And not wanting to, Cathy thought silently.

When the children were in bed and she sat with the men to talk, she felt that Sydney was anxious to go.

There were too many ghosts in the room, of the lads who had sung lightheartedly as they rode through country lanes or skated at the Roller Rink. Now they lay in foreign fields or beneath the sea, and Sydney revealed the depths of his bitterness when he said at one point, 'They were the lucky ones.'

He left early, promising to return, but they all knew that they would never meet again. Cathy wept bitterly when he had gone and she compared the haggard, twitching man with Sydney as he had been only a few short years before, bustling about, confidently organising everything.

The following day she wept again as she told her mother about him. 'I'm sorry I ever laughed at him for being fussy, Mam,' she said. 'When I think of those days and the way he is now.'

Sally was sympathetic but had her own news to impart. 'Do you know who I met this morning?' she said. 'That nurse who looked after Emily – who went away with her. And do you know what she told me? That money Albert spent on Emily and we thought he'd changed his ways – it was her own!'

'Her own – but where from?' Cathy asked.

'From Walter. He left it to her,' Sally announced, smiling at Cathy's astounded face.

'It's a wonder Aunt Emily didn't tell you,' Cathy said.

'She didn't know. The nurse said Albert brought papers for Emily to sign and she witnessed them, but Emily was very ill at the time.'

'And how did the nurse know?' said Cathy.

'There wasn't much she didn't know about what went on there, by all accounts,' Sally said. 'She kept saying, "I just happened to see" or "I just happened to hear".'

'The crafty blighter! Albert, I mean,' Cathy exclaimed. 'Letting Emily think he was so good to her and all the time it was her own money.'

'Yes, and Emily mightn't have wanted to take it from Walter,' Sally said. 'Fancy him having money to leave anyway. I know he'd discharged his bankruptcy or whatever they call it, but fancy him making more money.'

'Will Albert get the socks this Christmas?' Cathy teased her mother. Since Emily's death Sally had sent two pairs of hand-knitted socks and a bunloaf to Albert every Christmas, although they had no other contact with him.

'No, he won't,' Sally said. 'Or a bunloaf either. I only sent them for Emily's sake because I thought he'd been good to her.'

When Lawrie came in and Cathy had gone, Sally told the tale again. 'If that – woman knew so much, did she know about Bronwen?' Lawrie said.

'I think she did. She dropped a hint but I didn't encourage her.'

'Albert's lasting all the same,' Lawrie said. 'He must be eighty.'

'He'll live till a dead horse kicks him, that fellow,' Sally said wrathfully. 'The way he looks after himself. And my poor Emily, being tricked like that.'

'Never mind, love. It was a good thing she didn't know,' Lawrie said. 'She was happy thinking he was good to her.'

Sally talked about it for several days until the subject was swept aside by the preparations for Christmas and New Year. The children's excitement and joy made Christmas happy for the adults in the family, but they wondered what 1926 would bring.

The outlook was grim. Falling profits followed by savage wage cuts, particularly in the mining industry, meant that there was strife and unrest throughout the country, Lawrie, now treasurer of his union, looked grim and anxious.

Cathy was again expecting a baby, due in March, but she was not as well as during her previous pregnancies. Greg told John and Sarah that 'Mama wasn't well and they must try to help', and both children tried to restrain Mick and help generally.

John had been frightened by Greg's words, because a woman from the street had recently died of consumption, leaving three small children. He stayed by Cathy's side as much as possible, watching her anxiously, until Greg snapped at him.

'Go out and play, for God's sake. Don't be hanging round your mam all the time like a sissy.'

John rushed out and Cathy turned angrily on Greg. 'It's your fault,' she said. 'Frightening him, saying I'm ill.'

'Of course, it would have to be my fault!' Greg said. 'It couldn't be your darling John at fault.'

'I treat all the kids the same,' Cathy said. 'You're the one who makes the difference between them. John can't do anything right as far as you're concerned.' Her hands were trembling as she mixed dough for bread, but she was determined not to cry.

'The others don't give me cause. It's the way he behaves that causes trouble,' Greg said angrily.

'And of course *you* were here to bring them up. The clever fellow,' Cathy taunted him. 'You're just getting at me about John because I brought him up on my own till he was nearly four.'

'That's ridiculous,' Greg shouted, and in spite of her efforts Cathy's tears overflowed. In a moment he was beside her, holding her close and saying that he was sorry.

'You are mistaken though, Cath,' he said. 'I don't pick on John. It just seems like that because he's older. You know I'm very proud of him, the way he's doing at school.'

Cathy was not convinced but she said no more, only did her best to reassure John and to keep the peace between him and his father. Greg was irritable because he was worried about his job, she knew, and worried about her persistent sickness.

In January one problem was solved when Josh Adamson told them that he had heard of a vacancy for a railway clerk and had asked for an interview for Greg. The interview went well and he got the job, so they were all very grateful to Josh.

'The railway money's poor,' Sally said, 'but it's a job for life and a pension at the end of it.' Cathy agreed that now they felt secure.

In March her fourth child was born, a tiny dark-haired girl, after two days of labour.

'Not much to show for all that,' the midwife said robustly, but Cathy smiled down at the child. 'I'm glad to have her,' she said softly.

She had been slightly dismayed when she found that she was pregnant again while Greg's job was still uncertain, but had stifled the feeling immediately. Even to herself she would never admit that a child was unwelcome, feeling that from conception it would know if it was not wanted and loved. Also if anything went wrong, she would feel guilty if the child had been unwanted in the first place.

The baby was a tiny replica of her and Greg was adamant that she should be called Catherine, but Cathy was doubtful. Her parents were with her when Beattie, still wearing black for Billy who had died of war wounds, arrived to see the baby.

'She's the model of you and your dad, Cathy,' she exclaimed. 'What are you calling her?'

'Greg wants to call her Catherine, but I think it's better to have different names.'

'I think he's right,' Beattie declared. 'She looks a Catherine. What about Catherine Mary?'

She spoke quite innocently because she had only been told that Mary was living in London, but having to move about and change her address frequently.

There was silence for a moment then Lawrie said, 'That's worth thinking about. What did you call your youngest, Beattie?'

The conversation moved on, but after Beattie had gone no one mentioned her suggestion. Lawrie and Sally never spoke about

Mary, each hoping that the other was managing to forget their worry and grief for her, and both angry with their eldest for distressing the other.

Cathy was more angry with her sister than either of them. She knew what they did not, that Greg had asked Mary to come home even for just a visit and she had refused.

Her suspicions about Greg's account of seeing Mary from the train had grown until in the end he had told her that he had actually spoken to her. He said he had urged her to come home if only for a visit, but she had refused and he felt that he had done more harm than good, because she had cut herself off after that.

The explanation satisfied Cathy but increased her bitterness towards Mary. If I ever meet her, she told herself, I'll walk past her as though she doesn't exist. I'll never speak to her again as long as I live.

She was determined that her baby would not be given Mary's name, but Greg was still pressing for her to be named for her mother. 'We don't want two Cathys,' she protested. 'It only causes confusion.'

'Christen her Catherine and call her Kate, then,' Lawrie suggested, and the baby was named Catherine Laura, shortened to Kate.

Chapter Forty-Two

After Tommy's funeral, Duggan told Mary that he intended to marry and open a boarding house in Torquay.

'I wouldn't have left the captain while he needed me, Madam,' he said, 'but I've been friendly for a long time with the widow of a friend of mine. He was killed at Neuve Chapelle and she's had a hard time of it since.'

'I'm very glad,' Mary said. 'You did a lot for the captain and you deserve to be happy. If there's anything I can do—'

'That's all right, thank you, Madam,' he said. 'Mamie's had her eye on a certain boarding house and with the money from Captain Ross, I can do it. I'll see you settled before I go though.'

Mary had decided not to keep the house but to move to one of the luxury flats which were being built, and with Duggan's help the move was soon made.

Mary was surprised at how much she missed Tommy, but as a rich widow her life was easy and comfortable, and she was soon involved again in the raffish set, and free now to enjoy the wild times she had hankered for.

She told the terms of Tommy's will to one of the gossips in the set, and added that she had no intention of marrying again, knowing it would deter the men who hoped to replace Tommy as her husband.

She was not prepared for the men who offered a proposition instead of a proposal, and seemed to think that they would be doing her a favour if they moved in to console her, and incidentally to spend her fortune.

Dora would tell me I'm an innocent, Mary thought grimly, but she was far away in America. Tommy had not foreseen that men would chase her without marriage in mind. Maybe these were post-war types, but whatever they were, Mary enjoyed telling them that they were wasting their time.

There were other men though who were ready to flirt with her on her own terms, simply to pass the time, and she was never without an escort or a group of friends for her constant round of pleasure.

The fun grew fast and furious sometimes and often some of the set appeared in court either because of a police raid on clubs where they drank outside licensing hours, or because of a prank which had gone too far. They felt no shame at this but regarded it as a great lark and relied on Mary to find the money for their fines. She was always generous with her funds and very popular as a result.

By 1925 she had decided that she was thoroughly bored with life. She was lying on the chaise-longue in her flat eating chocolates while her maid changed the records and wound up the gramophone, when the telephone bell rang.

The maid handed the telephone to her and a shrill voice announced, 'It's Esme here, darling. How are you?'

'I'm bored, bored, bored,' Mary said petulantly.

'Listen, darling, I've thought of something,' Esme shrilled. 'Actually it was the man we met at The Green Cockatoo who gave me the idea. What do you think of a cruise? They're great fun.'

Mary sat up. 'Do you know, I like the idea most awfully,' she said.

'The only thing is, they're fearfully expensive, darling,' Esme shrieked, and Mary smiled cynically. 'Don't worry, darling. I'll take care of it. Come round and talk,' she said.

For the following months Mary spent very little time in England. A cruise to Norway was followed by one to the Mediterranean, then one from Plymouth to the West Indies, calling at Trinidad, Santa Marta, Cartagena and Livingston. By this time Mary was becoming bored by shipboard life, but she and Esme sailed from Southampton to Montreal, and spent a festive Christmas on board.

They spent a short holiday in Montreal and Quebec, then went to New York for shopping and sightseeing. Nothing interested Mary for long, and she soon booked passages on a ship sailing from New York to Liverpool.

Many of the passengers who embarked were businessmen, determined to mix work with pleasure and join in the activities aboard ship.

There was dancing every night. Normally Mary loved dancing, but even that was beginning to pall on her. Esme had already gone to the ballroom when Mary drifted along there one night and stood at the side of the room, smoking a cigarette in a long holder and disdainfully watching the couples dancing a foxtrot to the sound of 'Horsey, keep your tail up'.

Mary was a striking figure in a lilac chiffon dress falling in points just above her knees, with diamonds and amethysts round her neck and in her ears. Her thick red-gold hair had been bobbed and was like a shining cap on her head around which she wore a band, low on her brow, with a feather standing up at the side.

She was alone but not for long. Esme was dancing with a broad-shouldered man in well-cut evening dress, but other people soon joined Mary.

Like bees round a honey pot, she thought cynically. She knew that it was her reputation for free spending that drew acquaintances to her, to enjoy drinking and dining at her expense and the excellent service her lavish tipping always ensured.

The foxtrot had changed to a waltz and Mary was claimed by one of the young men. The band played and a singer sang dreamily, 'What'll I do when you are far away, and I am blue, what'll I do?'

The sadness of the song seemed to increase Mary's feeling of depression, and she said abruptly, 'I've had enough. I'm going for a breath of air.'

'No, don't come with me,' she said as the young man attempted to accompany her. She snatched up her cloak and walked out on to the deck.

The night was clear and calm and the deck deserted as she stood at the rail deep in thought. Why do I go on? she wondered. What's it all for? Trying to fill the days and nights, to amuse myself, but everything palls so quickly. I wish I was out of it all.

She stood looking into the smooth water far below. If I slipped under that water, who would care? The crowd in there would miss my money but after a few days they'd forget I ever existed.

Her cloak had slipped unnoticed from her shoulders and she shivered and gave a dry sob.

The next moment it was placed about her shoulders again and a quiet voice said, 'Hello, Mary.'

Mary swung round and looked up at the man who had been dancing with Esme.

'What? How do you know my name?' she stammered, shaken from her usual poise.

He moved closer. 'I've known it for a long time,' he said. 'Remember me?'

'Sam Glover,' she gasped.

'The same. I knew you right away, Mary. You're as beautiful as ever.'

She gazed at him with disbelief and he took her arm and drew her away from the rail. 'You're cold,' he said. 'Come round here.' He led her to a seat in a sheltered corner of the deck and they sat down.

'But, Sam, you're not American,' Mary said.

He laughed. 'No, but I've worked there since the war. I'm going over to England on business, but never mind that,' he said masterfully. 'Tell me about yourself. What's been happening to you?'

'Oh, Sam, I'm so unhappy,' she wailed, and the next moment she was in his arms with her head on his broad shoulder as she poured out the story of her life in recent years.

'But your mam thought you were happily married to Clive,' Sam said. 'I went to see her before I went in the Army.'

'When was that?' Mary asked.

'August 1914,' he said grimly. 'I couldn't wait to get away.'

Mary only outlined the events in her life to Sam that night, saying that Clive's debts had caused her first marriage to be unhappy, but she told him more as the days passed.

Finally, as they sat on their secluded seat on the deck a week later, she told him more about Clive's brutal treatment of her, and that she felt that it had damaged her emotionally and physically, making her unfit for marriage.

As usual she was in his arms and he had tucked a rug around her. As she wept bitterly and whispered her fears, he held her close and kissed her gently. When she stopped talking, he said firmly, 'Nonsense! Put that out of your head, Mary. I'm no doctor but my commonsense tells me that if you were damaged physically you'd have known about it by now. You've got no symptoms of any trouble, have you?'

'Not since those first few weeks,' Mary said, 'but my mind's damaged, Sam. I know it is.'

'We'll soon sort that out,' he said confidently. 'Don't worry about it.'

'Everything's always gone wrong for me, Sam.'

'You had a bad deal with Clive, but you've been lucky in other ways. Tommy Ross sounds a good man. You were lucky to meet him.'

'Yes, but then he died and there was nobody else who cared about me.'

'What about your mam and dad and Cathy?' he said. 'They care about you, Mary.'

'No they don't,' she cried. 'They only care about Cathy. Dad didn't even come to London to look for me.'

'How would he know where to look if you'd stopped writing to them?' he said. 'How do you know he didn't try, anyhow?'

'You're hard, Sam Glover,' she cried, turning away from him.

He waited calmly until she turned back. 'They don't care about me, Sam, I know they don't,' she said piteously.

Sam took her hands. 'Now face facts, love,' he said kindly but firmly. 'You know that's not true. You've probably broken their hearts by staying away from them, and it doesn't look as though *you* care very much about *them*, cutting yourself off like that. Do you even know if they're still alive?'

Mary's eyes opened wide with shock. 'Sam,' she gasped, 'they must be.' She thought for a moment. 'They were all right in 1919 anyway. I saw Greg Redmond going home and he asked me to go and see them.'

'But you didn't?'

'No, I didn't think they wanted to see me,' she said sullenly. Not even to Sam would she say anything about what had happened with Greg.

'Greg Redmond, Cathy's husband!' Sam exclaimed. 'He came through the war then? I'm glad about that. Cathy deserved to be happy – she was a good little girl.'

'There you are,' Mary burst out. 'Even you! It's always Cathy, Cathy.'

'Don't be silly,' he said. 'You know I thought you were the sun, moon and stars in one, always. But Cathy was kind. She waylaid me to tell me that you were marrying Clive so that I wouldn't hear it more brutally from someone else.'

Mary sat with bent head. 'You don't think much of me now, Sam, do you?' she murmured. 'You're disgusted with me because of the way I've behaved with Mam and Dad.'

'I think you were wrongly advised by someone who didn't know what your parents were really like,' he said. 'But it's not too late to make things right, love.'

A few days later he told her that he had made some enquiries and her parents were still alive and living in the same house in Egremont Street.

They went on deck as usual after dinner and to the seat they now regarded as their own. The wind was cool and Sam tucked a rug round Mary, but she opened it out and spread it round both of them. 'This is cosy,' he said. 'It reminds me of a "den" I had when I was a lad.' He kissed her gently. 'Are you happy, love?' he said.

'Yes. Are you?' she whispered.

'Yes. This is a dream come true for me, Mary,' he said. He stroked her cheek and tilted her face up to him and kissed her. 'Will you marry me, Mary love?'

'I can't, Sam. I told you about Clive,' she said. 'It wouldn't be fair to you.'

'Don't worry about that. You'll soon forget it when we're married.'

'You're very sure of yourself, Sam Glover,' she exclaimed. 'How do you know I will?'

'Because I'll see that you do. Trust me, love.'

'Oh, Sam,' she murmured. It was very dark and quiet in their secluded corner, lit only by the stars twinkling overhead. Sam held Mary in his arms and kissed her ever more passionately until she was responding to his kisses. She felt safe and happy in his arms, and gently and tenderly he coaxed her passion to meet his own.

Quite suddenly, it seemed to Mary, all her fears and bitter memories were swept away in the tide that engulfed her, and Sam was murmuring huskily 'You see, love, it was easy wasn't it?'

'I can't understand why I was worried for all those years,' she said wonderingly.

'It was because you were waiting for me,' he said. 'I'll make you happy, Mary, I promise. I love you.' He kissed her passionately again and she whispered, 'I love you too, Sam.'

'This is a dream come true for me,' he said again, quietly. 'I've thought about you so much. When I was young in Liverpool, and all through the war and since – there hasn't been a day when I haven't thought about you, and loved you. I could never have married anyone else, you know, love. Even if I'd never seen you again, I'd have loved you till the day I died.'

With unusual humility, Mary whispered, 'Sam, I'm not good enough for you. Not to be loved like that.'

But he put his finger against her lips, 'Just let me love you, Mary, and I'll be happy.'

Later they sat cuddled together under the rug and talked of the days before the war. 'By God, you put me through hoops!' Sam said. 'A dog's life, you gave me, but I'll get my own back when we're married. I'll really boss you around.'

'I hope it keeps fine for you,' Mary flashed, and Sam laughed aloud. 'You sounded just like your mother,' he said.

'I hope you meant that as a compliment.'

'Of course I did, and the more like your mam you grow, the happier I'll be.'

'I wish we could stay here forever,' Mary said, 'but the voyage is nearly over, isn't it?'

'Yes, we'll be drawing near Liverpool soon,' Sam said, 'but we're still on the high seas so the Captain can marry us.'

'I've got no wedding dress,' she objected.

'Wear that purple thing you wore on the first night,' he said masterfully.

'You've changed, Sam Glover,' Mary said. 'If you'd been like this years ago I would have married you and saved myself a lot of trouble.'

'I'd have saved a bit for myself, too,' he pointed out. 'But never mind. All is well that ends well, as the saying goes.'

'I told you the terms of Tommy's will, didn't I?' she said a few minutes later. 'If I remarry all the money goes to the hospital and the welfare fund. Tommy was trying to protect me from fortune hunters.'

'Good idea,' Sam said. 'I've got all we'll need and the charities will be glad of the money.'

The Captain readily agreed to marry them, and Mary wore her lilac dress. Esme was her bridesmaid and one of Sam's business friends was his best man. A reception for all the passengers was arranged, and Mary and Sam moved through it all in a blissful haze of happiness.

Soon the ship was being escorted up the Mersey by tugs and Mary and Sam stood hand in hand, watching the Liverpool skyline come into view. They were both too full of emotion to speak and could only smile at each other, but later she said sadly, 'I feel so ashamed, Sam, when I think of Mam and Dad. I seemed to become a different person when I married Clive.'

She looked hopefully at Sam, expecting him to reassure her and tell her it was all Clive's fault, but although he smiled tenderly at her, he said firmly, 'You behaved very badly towards them, Mary, but I'm sure they'll forgive you if they know you're sorry for hurting them.'

She pouted and said nothing, but in her heart she acknowledged the truth of Sam's remarks. He won't let me get away with things like other people do, she thought, but she respected him more for his honesty.

They went ashore on May 12th. When they booked into The Adelphi, the clerk told them they had just missed the General Strike.

'The TUC have ended it,' he said, 'but the miners are still on strike. It's been a bad time – shortages, and troops here working on food supplies, and battleships in the river. You've arrived just in time to miss it.'

'Aye, but it's left bitterness and hatred all round,' said a man who was collecting mail from the desk. 'Cast a long shadow, will this.'

'That won't affect this gentleman,' the clerk said smoothly. 'New York is your home town, I think, sir.'

'Liverpool is my home town,' Sam said pleasantly. 'New York is where I live. Where can I hire a car?'

Sam had originally planned to spend a week in Liverpool on business then a week in London before returning to Liverpool to sail back to New York. They decided to keep to the plan except that he would do only the most essential business in both cities.

'If everything goes well, we'll be able to spend some time with your mam and dad here, and in London we'll be able to clear up your affairs.'

Now that she was so close to facing her family, Mary found various reasons why the visit should be postponed until another time, but after a few weeks with Sam she was not really surprised to find herself being driven along Egremont Street in a hired motor car.

Sam stopped the car outside number forty. 'Now go and knock on the door, Mary,' he said. 'If you're not welcome, come back to the car and we'll drive away and forget it.'

'Come with me, Sam,' she begged.

'No, it's important that you go to them, love. Alone, not under escort. Go on. It'll be all right.'

Mary stepped out of the motor and walked nervously up to the door. She raised her hand and knocked on the door.

Chapter Forty-Three

Kate was eight weeks old when the General Strike began on May 4th 1926. Miners had been told that their wages were to be cut and had come out on strike and asked other workers to support them.

Cathy was in her mother's house when her father and Greg arrived home to tell them that the railwaymen were on strike. She thought how much her mother had changed when she saw her put her hand on her husband's shoulder and say quietly, 'You did right, lad. You've got to stand together.'

Cathy knew that now her father and mother discussed politics and union matters quite amicably, and her mother's hostility towards her father's involvement with the union had vanished. It was as though their grief for Mary drew them together in everything else.

Her cares for her family and the worry of making ends meet left Cathy too harassed to give any thought to wider issues. Her main worry now was how long the strike would last.

It seemed that the country might be brought to a standstill but the Government, led by Stanley Baldwin, had been kept well informed of the union plans and were well prepared. They quickly recruited special constables and used volunteer labour in various industries, and for printing emergency news sheets.

In London it was considered a lark by the Bright Young Things, as they were dubbed, to drive tramcars and wagons, accompanied by crowds of friends, shrieking with delight.

Lawrie was disgusted when he was told of this.

'Just a game to them, Sal,' he said bitterly. 'And there could be one of me own flesh and blood as one of them.'

'Now don't go jumping to conclusions,' she said. 'There's thousands of girls in London, and we don't even know if she's still there, anyway.'

'Yet Mary came into my mind right away when I heard of it. It's the kind of thoughtless thing she'd do, treating something serious as a game.'

'Different people see things different ways,' Sally soothed him.

Lawrie said bitterly, 'Aye, the coal owners see the coal as black gold, and the miners see it as facing death or maiming for a pittance – and now even that being cut.'

Sally was pleased to see young John running up the yard, knowing that he could always cheer his grandfather. There was still a strong bond between them, and John was never happier than when he sat by Lawrie's knee and listened to his grandfather's stories. He often called in to see them on his way home from school.

Soon rumours were circulating that the strike was to be called off. On May 12th Cathy felt weary and dispirited as she wheeled the pram down to her mother's house, with Mick walking beside her.

She had almost quarrelled with Greg before he left the house that morning to go to a meeting. He had been searching for a clean handkerchief and had exclaimed irritably, 'Can you tell me why there's a top and whip and the baby's dummy mixed up with the clean washing?'

'I can't but the children might,' Cathy said.

'Now a paste jar and a spoon,' Greg cried as he delved further. 'Good God, Cathy, you're better at writing slogans than acting on them.'

A dozen angry retorts rose to her lips but she said nothing. She knew that Greg was worried and on edge over the conflict between his responsibility to his family and the principle of solidarity with his colleagues.

Cathy wheeled the pram into the backyard at Egremont Street and warned Mick that he was to behave himself when they went into the house. Sally greeted them with a smile and the ever ready cup of tea, then went to look at the sleeping baby.

She came back carrying Kate. 'She was stirring,' she excused herself. Cathy smiled, knowing that it was an excuse for her mother to nurse the baby.

'Dad's at the meeting, I suppose?' she said.

'Yes, I'm worried to death about him.'

'I'm worried about Greg,' Cathy said. 'He's like a bear with a sore head. We could fall out every five minutes if I didn't hold my tongue.'

'It's the only way, love,' her mother said. 'A bit of give and take. I'm sure Greg's often kept quiet when you've been ratty about something.'

Cathy laughed ruefully. 'I'm sure he has. We don't often fall out as you know, Mam, and I suppose that's why. It seems to have worked with you and Dad, anyhow.'

'Aye, give and take,' Sally said, rocking the baby in her arms. 'Keeping back the cross word when you know Greg's upset and him doing the same with you. Mind you, Mrs Mal had a different idea about give and take.'

'Something wise, I'll bet.'

'She used to say people were either givers or takers and some people went through life thinking only about themselves and others put others first.'

Sally sighed. 'She said some took all the time and others gave. She had you down as a giver and our Mary as a taker, and I think she was right.'

'I think everyone's a bit of both,' Cathy said. 'I'd better get down to Great Homer Street while there's anything left, Mam. Should I leave the baby?'

'Yes. Leave her with me but take Mick with you,' Sally said.

Cathy laughed. 'I wouldn't inflict him on you, Mam. I'd come back to find the house wrecked. I wonder what he's doing now?'

She went out to the backyard and came back a little later with Mick. 'He'd filled the lavatory pan with newspaper,' she said. 'But I've got it out and put it in the midden.'

'Well, you'd never be dull where he is,' Sally said, and Cathy left the house feeling more cheerful than when she arrived.

When she had finished her shopping she walked up Langsdale Street and turned into St Francis Xavier's church. Mrs Malloy was very much in her mind since her conversation with her mother, and she always felt very close to her old friend when she was in church.

A few huddled figures were dotted about the church and a shabby man was moving along the aisles, pausing at each of the Stations of the Cross, but the church was quiet and peaceful and Cathy knelt for a while, letting the peace flow into her worried mind.

She said a prayer for Mrs Malloy and suddenly remembered what the old lady had once said.

Mrs Malloy had been worried about her increasing infirmity but she had said to Cathy, 'If I'm troubled at all, girlie, I say a prayer and leave my worries to God, then I feel easy. Sure, isn't He better able to deal with them than I am meself?'

A smile touched Cathy's lips as she remembered and she knelt for a few moments longer, then gathered up her shopping and went to find Mick.

For once he was quiet, standing as though fascinated before the statue of Our Lady of Sorrows. Cathy stood with him and looked at the names on the Roll of Honour above the statue, of men who had given their lives for their country in the Great War.

There were so many of them, a great number of the names familiar to Cathy. She thought of the boys she had known, and now that she was a mother herself, she thought of the mothers of the boys who had died, and wondered how they could bear their sorrow.

Mick was tugging at her hand. They left and hurried back to Egremont Street. Sally had fried onions and bread for a snack for them and Cathy stayed with her mother, knowing that Greg would walk back with her father from the meeting.

Before long they came in together, both looking weary and dispirited. Lawrie sank down in his chair, like an old man.

'It's over,' he said. 'We've pulled out on the miners.'

'What about the wage cuts?' Sally asked.

'Going ahead,' he said briefly. 'The miners are staying out.'

'It was no use,' Greg said. 'The owners and the Government were too well prepared. They'd had plenty of information.'

'Aye, more than one Judas, I think, Greg,' Lawrie said bitterly. 'I'm ashamed of letting the miners down.'

'Never mind, lad, you did your best. You can't do any more,' Sally said gently.

Cathy had quickly made a pot of tea and she handed a mug to her father. 'Never mind, Dad,' she said. 'Remember Mrs Mal – "It's always darkest before the dawn".'

Lawrie smiled ruefully. 'Aye, Mrs Mal. She had a saying for everything, and she never let anything get her down. I wish you'd known her, Greg.'

'I feel as though I do,' he said. 'I've heard so much about her from Cathy.' She poured him a cup of tea and he sat down by the table and took Mick on his knee.

There was a knock at the front door and Cathy said, 'All right. I'll go.' She walked down the lobby.

When she opened the door she looked blankly for a moment at the fashionably dressed woman on the step, then cried: 'Mary!' The next moment the sisters were in each other's arms.

Five minutes earlier if anyone had asked Cathy how she felt about Mary she would have said that she hated her, but the moment she saw her sister all her love for her welled up again, and she hugged Mary as though she would never let her go.

They clung together, laughing and crying, then they went down the lobby and Cathy stepped back to let Mary go first into the kitchen. She was never to forget her first sight of the well-remembered room, after her long absence. Greg sat by the table with a child on his knee, and her mother stood near the fireplace, with a cloth in her hand.

Her father was rising from his chair and turning towards her, and for a moment they all stood transfixed. Then Mary flung herself at her parents and hugged them, weeping, saying: 'I'm sorry, I'm sorry,' over and over again. Cathy had rushed to Greg and was sobbing as he held her. Then an indignant small voice said, 'Why is everybody whingeing?'

It was Mick, standing looking up at them in amazement, but it broke the spell and everyone began to wipe their eyes and calm down. 'Meet Mick,' Lawrie said. 'Mick the Menace.'

Under cover of the slightly hysterical laughter, Greg held out his hand and said, 'Welcome home, Mary.'

'A few years late,' she said shakily. Mick had run out to play in the street. Just as Sally was saying, 'Put the kettle on, Cath,' he returned.

'There's a man in a motor out there,' he announced.

'Oh, heavens!' Mary said, mopping her eyes. 'It's my husband. We were married on the ship coming from America.'

'America,' her mother echoed, and Lawrie said, 'I'll call him in.'

'I'll call him, Dad,' Mary said. She went to the door and beckoned to Sam who came towards her, smiling broadly. He followed her into the kitchen, and for a moment no one recognised him. Then Sally said, 'Sam Glover!' There were exclamations of surprise and disbelief as they tried to see in the burly confident man the weedy youth they had known. Sam took Sally's hand and kissed her.

She turned to Mary. 'Thank God you've learned sense at last, girl,' she said.

Everybody talked at once and in the confusion Greg said quietly to Mary, 'I told Cathy I spoke to you on the station, but your mam and dad think I only saw you from the train.'

'I told Sam the same, that I spoke to you on the station,' she said, looking down self-consciously. Once again Mick saved the day. 'Now *Kate's* whingeing,' he said disgustedly.

'The baby,' Sally and Cathy exclaimed, and both dashed out to the pram in the yard. Sally came back carrying her while Cathy returned to her tea making, then her mother soothed Kate and handed her to Mary.

She cradled the child in her arms and said to Cathy, 'She's the image of you, Cath, and of Dad. So you've got two children?'

'We've got four,' Cathy said. 'The two older ones are at school.'

Mary sighed. 'Of course,' she said. 'I didn't realise how the years had passed.' For a moment there was an uncomfortable silence, then she glanced up and saw her photograph on the dresser. Suddenly she turned and laid her head on her father's shoulder. 'Oh, Dada,' she wept. 'You still kept that when – when—' Greg took the baby and Mary drew her mother close too and cried bitterly, 'Oh, why did I stay away so long? I thought you didn't want to see me, but I should have come.'

'I don't know where you got that idea from,' Sally said.

Sam said quietly, 'The truth is, Mary had a very bad time with that Clive fellow and she didn't want you to know. Then, when she met her second husband, she told him about Clive and he thought it would be better if she put the past behind her completely. Isn't that right, Mary?'

She nodded and Sam went on, 'He didn't mean any harm. He didn't understand about you, and Mary had got herself in such a state she thought you didn't want any more to do with her.'

'So it was your husband put you off writing to us?' Sally said.

'He thought it was for the best, Mam. He was a good man, but I told him you had Cathy and the baby and I'd only brought you trouble,' she said, beginning to cry again.

'It was all a misunderstanding. He was a good chap but he gave Mary bad advice,' Sam said firmly. 'I had the benefit of knowing you and I knew you'd forgive Mary. The longer it went on, you see, the harder it was for her to come home.'

'I think Clive was the root of the trouble,' Lawrie said. 'I wish to God I'd never introduced you to him, girl.'

'Well, it's all water under the bridge now,' Sally said practically. 'We can't turn the clock back but we can start afresh.'

'Amen to that,' Sam said. 'You're a pearl, Mrs Ward.'

'Yes, and I often think I'm cast before swine,' she said drily, but she was smiling, well pleased.

'I've been telling Mary she's growing like you,' Sam said. 'And the more like you she grows, the better I'll be pleased.'

John and Sarah came home from school and were introduced and Mary found that she could look at the boy, so like Greg, without feeling a pang. I'm completely cured, she thought. Then, looking over to where Greg and Cathy were saying something and smiling fondly at each other, she thought with a touch of her mother's dry humour: Just as well, too.

'I was glad to hear you'd stayed in this house,' she said. 'I was afraid you might have moved away.'

'No, I think we'll go out of here feet first, eh, Sal?' Lawrie said. 'Mind you, I was just telling Greg today about the big ideas I once had. Remember, Sal, twenty years ago I sat in this chair just after your da died and talked about my plans.'

She smiled. 'Yes, I remember.'

'We were looking back over the twenty years since Sally had lost her mam, and I thought that after another twenty years we'd have heaven on earth. The things I wasn't going to do for my children in the wonderful world we'd be living in! What a hope,' he said bitterly.

'Never mind, it'll all come true for your grandchildren,' Sally said calmly.

'The war wrecked things for our generation,' Greg said. 'But it'll all be plain sailing for them.'

'I was going to have a pair of horses in the stable for you, Sal, remember? A pair of matched greys.'

'I'm very happy with what I've got. And what I've had, come to that.'

'So am I,' Cathy said, smiling at Greg, and Sam took Mary's hand.

Sarah had been sitting quietly on her little stool by the dresser. She evidently thought that Lawrie was upset and came to stand by him and look up into his face.

'I'm happy, Grandad,' she said timidly.

Lawrie drew the child to him and kissed her. 'Lord love you, pet,' he said. 'Let's hope you always will be. Let's hope we'll all be happy, always.'